MW01137065

EXTINCTION CYCLE: DARK AGE 1

EXTINCTION SHADOW

AN EXTINCTION CYCLE *STORY*

NEW YORK TIMES BESTSELLING AUTHOR
NICHOLAS SANSBURY SMITH
AND ANTHONY J. MELCHIORRI

Extinction Cycle: Dark Age
Book 1: Extinction Shadow
By Nicholas Sansbury Smith and Anthony J. Melchiorri

Cover Design by Deranged Doctor Design
Edited by AJ Sikes

Copyright © January 1ˢᵗ, 2019
All Rights Reserved

GREAT WAVE INK
PUBLISHING

Thank you for purchasing this book. Sign up for Nicholas's *spam-free* newsletter to learn more about future releases, how to claim a book patch, special offers, and bonus content. Subscribers will also receive access to exclusive giveaways.

eepurl.com/bggNg9

You can also sign up for Anthony's newsletter to receive info on his latest releases and free short stories exclusive to subscribers.

http://bit.ly/ajmlist

For my co-author and good friend
Dr. Anthony J. Melchiorri.

Your scientific input helped bring the Extinction Cycle
saga to life, and I'm thrilled to work with you again
in bringing readers the next chapter.

The boundaries which divide life from death
are at best shadowy and vague.
Who shall say where the one ends, and where the other begins?

— *Edgar Allan Poe*

Introduction to the Extinction Cycle
and Historical Recap:

From Extinction Cycle creator Nicholas Sansbury Smith

Dear Reader,

For those of you that are new to the Extinction Cycle storyline, you are about to embark on a completely new saga based on the original award winning, Amazon top-rated, and half a million copy best-selling seven book series. Critics have called the Extinction Cycle, "World War Z and The Walking Dead meets the Hot Zone." *Publisher's Weekly* added, "Smith has realized that the way to rekindle interest in zombie apocalypse fiction is to make it louder, longer, and bloodier … Smith intensifies the disaster efficiently as the pages flip by, and readers who enjoy juicy blood-and-guts action will find a lot of it here."

Extinction Cycle: Dark Age is the continuation of the original story, taking place eight years after the events of book seven, *Extinction War.* Before you dive in, please read this for a brief history of the series, and what to expect for new and old readers.

In creating the *Extinction Cycle*, my goal was to use authentic military action and real science to take the zombie and post-apocalyptic genres in an exciting new direction. Forget everything you know about zombies. In this story, they aren't created by black magic or other supernatural means. The infected are a result of a military bio-weapon called VX-99, first used in Vietnam in a government program to design a super soldier. Chemicals from VX-99 activate proteins encoded by dormant genes that separate humans from wild animals—a real process known as epigenetic changes. In other words, these weapons turned men into monsters.

Known as Variants, these creatures become the perfect predator as they evolve from epigenetic changes. The result in the Extinction Cycle is catastrophic, and the infection spreads worldwide. Governments and militaries fall and civilization is destroyed in a matter of months. Scrambling to find a cure and defeat the monsters, humanity is brought to the brink of extinction. By the end of book 7, the human race hangs on by a thread.

Now, eight years later, the survivors in the United States (now called the Allied States) have migrated and settled into approximately one hundred outposts. Most of these walled off cities are in the Midwest and the East Coast, with the West Coast largely abandoned due to the severity of the damage from the war. President Jan Ringgold and her administration have worked tirelessly to rebuild, bringing back basic infrastructure, the agricultural industry, manufacturing, and the energy grid.

A few other key players helped humanity survive the Great War of Extinction and continue to drive progress in the aftermath. Team Ghost, an Army Delta Force team, played a vital role in winning the war and pushing back the Variant scourge. They are still in action under the leadership of Master Sergeant Joe "Fitz" Fitzpatrick. For eight years they have run missions into enemy territory to hunt Variants and rescue human prisoners.

Other heroes from the era include Captain Reed Beckham and Doctor Kate Lovato. They are now married and live in Outpost Portland, Maine with their son, Javier

Riley; Master Sergeant Parker Horn; and his daughters.

With President Jan Ringgold's term coming to an end, a new election looms on the horizon, an election candidate and current Vice President Dan Lemke should win easily due to the tremendous progress their administration has made. The country is recovering, and aside from random Variant and raider attacks, the outposts are safe.

The surviving Variants and the human collaborators remain in the shadows, starving and dying off. At least, that's what the military thinks... In *Extinction Cycle Dark Age*, they are about to find out how wrong they are.

Strap in, you're about to re-enter the world of Variants and the heroes that stand in their way, in the next chapter of the Extinction Cycle. Welcome back to all of the old readers. I'm so glad you encouraged me to return to this storyline. I promise, you're in for a ride with some of your favorite characters and new twists.

To new readers, we invite you to embark on this post-apocalyptic adventure and hope you enjoy the science, action, and characters in this expanding universe.

Thank you to all for reading. Please feel free to reach out to me or Tony if you have questions or comments. Our contact info is provided in the back of the book.

Best wishes,

Nicholas Sansbury Smith, New York Times Bestselling Author of *Hell Divers* and the *Extinction Cycle*.

Anthony J. Melchiorri, Bestselling Author of *The Tide*.

Foreword from DJ Molles,
NYT Bestselling Author of *The Remaining*

Trust.

If you were to go out into the wilderness, and you had to pick a guide, you'd want one you felt you could trust. You'd want to know that he'll accurately read the weather, choose the right trails, and get you from point A to point B, all the while keeping you from being washed down some rapids, eaten by wolves, or using that poison ivy leaf as toilet paper.

Picking up a new book is kind of like that. You have to trust the author, just like you trust a guide. You want to know that the author can deliver on their promises, pull your mind into a crazy world of their creation, and get you from point A to point B, all the while keeping you engaged and throwing in a few twists and turns to keep things spicy.

Nicholas Sansbury Smith is the grizzled old pro guide. The wilderness that you are about to head into? The universe of Extinction Cycle. Your traveling companions? Team Ghost. The paths that you're going to take? Ha ha! There are no paths out here, buttercup. We're bushwhacking into unknown terrain this time.

Extinction Shadow is an all-new continuation of the bestselling Extinction Cycle series, and though Smith is going to take you into some uncharted territory, you can rest assured that he knows what he's doing. The journey might be hair-raising, but he'll get you there in one piece (mostly).

If you're picking up Extinction Shadow after already being a fan of the original series, then hold onto your favorite characters--maybe utter a prayer for them and remember all the good times you had following their adventures in the other series. This one is going to thrust them straight into the thick of it, where no quarter is given, and the chances for survival are slim.

If you're brand new to the Extinction Cycle Universe, don't worry! You don't have to be an expert in the original universe. Just trust your seasoned guide. Through a combination of fast-paced action, military realism, and credible science (which makes the whole thing just a hair freakier), Smith delivers the goods to old readers and new ones alike.

So trust your grizzled old guide, and head out into the wilderness of Extinction Shadow. But keep your head on a swivel. And keep sniffing the air for the smell of rotting fruit...

Good luck out there,

D.J. Molles,
NYT Bestselling author of *The Remaining* series.

— 1 —

The crackle of a bonfire was a familiar sound at Outpost Turkey River, and would be even more common now that autumn had set in. The smoke was supposed to keep bugs away, but it didn't always work.

Retired Master Sergeant Cedric Long swatted a mosquito away from the cavity where his left eye had once been, smearing the damn insect across his cheek. It was already swollen with blood. The little vampires reminded him of the monsters beyond the walls. The same type that took his eye during the war.

Variants.

The result of a chemical weapon gone wrong. Former humans that had turned into the perfect predators would do far worse than a swarm of bloodthirsty mosquitoes if they got into the outpost.

But that wasn't going to happen.

Not on this eve, and not on any other day that Cedric held watch.

Outpost Turkey River was one of the most secure townships in what was now called the Allied States because of the men that served here before Cedric arrived, and it was even stronger now that he was here.

That's what Commander Justin Bell had told him, and Commander Bell was no liar. Now in his late thirties, Bell was just a young man during the Great War of Extinction that ended eight years ago. But he was no stranger to the monsters that lurked deep in what had once been the United States of America.

The commander had fought and bled to keep this outpost secure and safe.

Cedric squinted into the darkness. There hadn't been an attack for over three months. He knew the Variants still dwelled in the shadows, but it was mostly humans they had to worry about now.

Bandits. Raiders. Collaborators.

Whatever people wanted to call them, they would always rather take something that didn't belong to them instead of working to get it themselves, and the most evil among them worked with the Variants.

Many outposts weren't lucky like Turkey River with a plentiful supply of fresh food and clear water provided by the fertile land. Supplies were abundant here, which made them a target, not to mention a political hotspot.

President Jan Ringgold had stopped by a week earlier with Vice President Dan Lemke. Now that their two terms were almost up, Lemke was running to succeed her. Retired General Mark Cornelius, Lemke's opponent and leader of the Freedom Party, was slated to stop by in another week.

Cedric sat at a picnic table in the center of the communal area, enjoying a late supper of mashed potatoes, corn, bread, and water from the neighboring river their community was named for.

Two trucks were parked across the street, their beds nearly overfilling with harvested corn from the surrounding fields. The food within their walls was more than enough to support the three hundred people that lived in the compound. Most of the grain, corn, and beans they produced were shipped by rail to the nearly hundred other outposts in the Allied States.

He thought of the mass migration from the Western states to places like Turkey River over eight years ago, when the government focused on consolidating, protecting, and rebuilding the agricultural industry in the Midwest and manufacturing factories on the East Coast.

Now most of the population lived in places like Turkey River. Families of those who had made that migration ate quietly at the other tables around him.

He sat alone and enjoyed his meal. He didn't mind the solitude, but it wasn't always that way. In his former life he had once looked forward to meals with his wife and sons.

But they were gone now, and he was here. Besides, most of the kids were scared of him, whispering behind his back about the 'pirate' with a patch over his eye.

He didn't mind that either. He was a kid once and remembered how his own boys would have reacted. They might have thought he was a monster with his scarred skin and missing eye. But the truth was they had died knowing there were far worse monsters than a deformed old man.

Most of the kids under eight at Outpost Turkey River were lucky to have never even seen the creatures Cedric fought. They no doubt heard the gunshots and the lone cries of a dying Variant, but they had never come face to face with one of the scab-covered, fanged creatures.

Not like his sons.

Cedric pushed aside the painful memories. His job was no longer to be a father and a husband. He was just a simple soldier protecting the people that lived here, and the food they harvested. At least it gave him purpose.

A bell dinged as the moon rose higher in the autumn

sky. Cedric wolfed down the rest of his supper. He took a flask from his ballistic vest and washed the food down with a shot of whiskey.

The liquor warmed his gut. He stood, well-fed and relaxed. Grabbing his M4A1 carbine, he set off for a patrol with the other half-dozen men on night perimeter duty. The team was just one cog helping spin the security wheel at the outpost.

Two soldiers manned the M240 fighting position outside town hall. Guards walked on flat rooftops, their weapons cradled, looking out over the sleeping outpost. Everywhere Cedric looked the soldiers seemed relaxed.

There wasn't much to be stressed about out here.

Most of the men hadn't seen action for years besides skirmishes with raiders.

Hell, this was the best gig of Cedric's career. And he'd had a ton of assignments since the Hemorrhage Virus first raced across the world, from a cruise ship sailing in the Atlantic during the first year of the outbreak to security duty in the relocated White House at the Greenbrier.

Cedric had even guarded Captain Reed Beckham; his wife, Doctor Kate Lovato Beckham; and their son, Javier Riley, back when the boy was just a toddler. After Cedric hit retirement age, they transferred him here.

"Turkey River is a modern-day retirement community, my friend," Beckham had said, patting Cedric on the shoulder with his prosthetic hand. "Plenty of food, good neighbors, and peaceful enough you can actually enjoy a well-earned nap in the afternoon."

President Ringgold had even thanked Cedric for his service, and the next week he boarded a train to northern Iowa.

Field of Dreams didn't seem so far from the truth.

Cedric considered pulling his flask out and taking another slug of whiskey, but he was old enough and smart enough to know evil never slept. The Variants might not have attacked recently, but beyond the wall, guard towers, razor wire fences, sensors, and mine fields, they were still out there.

Waiting…

He continued the trek through town square and past the houses and businesses. Like most outposts this one had everything from a general store to a post office with solar panels mounted on most of the roofs. He walked by both buildings and moved to the sidewalk to let a pickup truck down the narrow road.

The circular community was surrounded by a twenty-foot steel wall. He exited through a gate that opened to a bridge over a creek. On the other side six soldiers waited. Two German Shepherds sat on their hind legs, anxious for their noses to be put to work.

"Evenin' Sarge," said a private named Malcom.

"Evenin'," Cedric replied.

They set off. All of them knew the drill. Alpha Team went to the right, and Bravo went left, each team taking a dog. Cedric was an exception. Commander Bell had given him his own route to walk, operating as a lone ranger of sorts. He walked toward the next line of defense, multiple razor wire fences.

On the other side, moonlight captured a sea of corn and soybeans planted in the rich topsoil beyond the minefields.

The gate at the road was closed now that the harvesting for the day was over. No one was allowed outside after dark unless Commander Bell gave the order.

Guard towers rose above the fences, and Cedric raised a hand to the men in Tower Four. Both of the soldiers there were about the same age he had been when he first enlisted, over forty years ago. But these kids were too young to have fought in the war against the monsters.

Chances were good neither of them had ever come close to meeting a Variant face to face. Cedric, on the other hand, had scars to show off his battles, including his empty eye socket.

He smiled when he recalled how he had killed the beast that had done it. Who would have thought a flare would do so much damage if you stuck it in the right place?

"Got anything on infrared?" Cedric called up to the guards.

"Negative, Sarge, just deer."

"Well shit, maybe we should go hunting," Cedric replied. It had been a long time since they had even seen a deer. Like humans, the animals had almost been wiped out by the Variants.

He continued his walk along the perimeter, scanning the dirt on the other side of the fences for any flash of movement and sniffing the air for the rotten fruit odor of the beasts.

The Variants had rapid evolution and adaption on their side. Epigenetic changes had turned the abominations into the perfect predators that could camouflage their skin and see in the dark. Some had morphed into terrifying creatures ranging from gigantic beetles to monstrous flesh-eating worms in Europe.

Most of those beasts were nothing more than dust now. Only the first generation of Variants had survived the bullets and the bioweapons the government designed to kill them.

America was on her way back. Some European countries were starting to recover as well. He didn't know much about South America, Africa, or Asia, but the little bits of news that made their way to Turkey River gave him hope the human species would recover fully in time.

Cedric walked for an hour before his joints started hurting and the chill of the evening finally got under his layers. He let his rifle sag on its sling as he rubbed his gloves together.

Then he pressed on, ignoring the pain of his lower back, and the persistent arthritis in his fingers. He didn't mind that his retirement was being spent doing what he did best, but he did wonder how many more years he had left before Commander Bell assigned him to some boring guard tower.

Not happening anytime soon.

As the whiskey wore off, the cold crept into his feet. His toes started to numb. He found a seat on a swing hanging from the solid limb of an oak tree, a favorite of the children that lived here.

He sat and wiggled his toes to get the blood moving. Pulling out his radio, he contacted Alpha and Bravo teams. No contacts sighted by any of them. He asked for reports from the guard towers next.

All clear, came the responses.

Another quiet night at Outpost Turkey River.

Cedric stood and walked toward his next stop. The barns were always his favorite part of the rounds.

A farmer named Will slept in a chair outside the barn door, his head slumped against a shoulder. Cedric cleared his throat, waking the man.

Will shot up and raised a hand in defense. "What... What's wrong?"

"Relax," Cedric said. "I'm just checking on things."

Will looked around and then seemed to relax and sat back down.

"Does your wife know you're out here?" Cedric asked.

A sly grin spread across Will's face. "She's the *reason* I'm out here."

Cedric chuckled. "You're in the dog house again?"

"Better than the barn, right?" Will stood and stretched.

Cedric held back a laugh.

In a town this small, everyone knew everyone's business, and everyone knew that Will and his wife had been on the outs for months.

Commotion from the animal pens distracted Cedric, and Will joined him on the path to the livestock. The beasts were all crowded in the corner of their pens.

Will spat a glob of tobacco on the dirt.

"What the hell has them riled up?" he asked.

Cedric pulled out his radio. "Alpha, Bravo, you got anything?"

"Negative."

"Negative."

The guard towers all reported the same thing. Nothing on infrared, and nothing moving in the night vision. Cedric knew the Variants could sometimes avoid detection, but they couldn't avoid the mines or the fences, and they couldn't dodge bullets either.

Cedric aimed his rifle at the cornfields beyond the animal pens and jerked his chin for Will to return to the safety of the walled-off compound.

"Go home to your wife and lock the doors," he said.

Will backpedaled away from the barn, nearly tripping,

then he turned and ran. Most men would have done the same thing, but Cedric clenched his jaw and scanned the fields for the monsters.

Moonlight illuminated the white blades of two massive wind turbines churning in the distance, providing energy for the outpost by harnessing the wind.

His radio crackled on his vest as he searched for hostiles.

"Master Sergeant, what's going on out there?" came the gruff voice of Commander Bell.

"Not sure, sir, something's got the animals spooked."

"Meet me on the bridge," Bell replied.

Cedric cursed.

So much for a quiet night.

He jogged back toward the bridge, the gate opening and disgorging ten more men and three dogs. From the east side of the outpost came the guttural barking of the other German Shepherds with Alpha and Bravo. A flare shot up into the sky, bursting into a red glow over the cornfields.

"Everyone that's not in a guard tower fall back to the bridge," Bell ordered over the radio.

Search lights flipped on in the towers, the beams raking over the cornfields beneath where the flare had burst. The stalks rustled in the breeze.

Bell, a good foot taller than almost every man on the bridge, stepped out in front of the pack. All five of the dogs growled, their fur standing like needles.

Cedric straightened his stiff body.

"Show yourself, you diseased son of a bitch," Bell grumbled.

The spotlight from tower four roved over the field, Cedric's only eye moving with the light. The guard brought it to a sudden stop over a patch of corn. Alpha and Bravo soon returned with their dogs.

"Commander, I've got a heat signature northwest, close to the area I spotted a deer earlier," came the voice of Isaac in tower four. "Not sure what it is."

"Can you get a shot?" Bell replied.

"Sir… It's pretty far out."

Bell turned back to the men on the bridge. "Get ready, I want a team to go out there with dogs and take a look once it's dead," he said. "If it's a Variant, leave it there. We'll try and find where it came from in the morning."

"And if it's a deer?" Cedric asked.

"Then we're going to have a nice venison steak," Bell said.

The other men seemed to lighten up at that.

"Take the shot, T4," Bell said over the comm.

A crack pierced the night.

Crows took flight around the compound. For an eerie moment, the cawing was the only sound.

"Target down," Isaac reported over the radio.

"Nice shot, T4," Bell replied. He looked again at the soldiers standing around him. "Who's going out there to check it out?"

Cedric's hand shot up. "I'll go, sir."

"Who else?" Bell asked.

The men all avoided his gaze, looking at the ground in shame. Cedric didn't blame them. Even one Variant was enough to kill a team of greenhorns, and they were likely worried there were more beasts out there.

"Malcom, Agan, Kelly, you go with Cedric, take two dogs. The rest of you fall back inside the compound," Bell said.

Cedric led the other three soldiers over the bridge, the

dogs pulling on their leashes down the road to the main gate. They stopped when they reached the guard tower that looked over the minefield beyond the gate.

"You sure you got it?" Cedric called up.

Isaac emerged from the tower. "It ain't movin', Sarge."

Cedric looked down the road cutting through the cornfields. A shudder tore through his flesh. He blamed it on the cold, but worried it was from fear.

"Go on, Cedric," Bell said. "Take your team out there and see what's going on."

"Yes, sir," Cedric said.

They unlatched the main gate and swung it open.

Cedric led the team outside, listening to the gate click shut behind him.

"T4, tell me if that heat signature moves," he ordered over the comm.

"Copy that," Isaac replied.

"Combat intervals, keep sharp," Cedric said. He started out onto the road with the dogs on each flank. They sniffed the ground and air, their muzzles searching for the rotting lemon scent of the diseased beasts.

Cedric scanned for movement but saw nothing besides the shifting corn stalks. It only took a few minutes to reach the area of the spotlight from tower four.

The team stopped and faced the fence of corn. None of the dogs bared their teeth or growled.

Maybe it was just a deer, Cedric thought. He shouldered his rifle and the other three soldiers followed suit, their muzzles aimed at the corn.

"I'm not going in there," Malcom whispered.

Cedric thought about ordering the young soldier to get ahold of himself and go in anyway, but instead he said, "Hold your position." He didn't need a scared kid popping off rounds behind him in the dark.

The gusting wind picked up as they stood there, blowing through the fields violently and turning the wind turbines faster. The branches of oak trees in the distance swayed and creaked.

"Do you see that?" Kelly said quietly. He pointed at the tips of the corn that seemed to be parting like something was moving through them.

"T4, you got anything on infrared?" Cedric asked.

"Negative."

"Something's coming..." Kelly said.

Cedric held up a hand. "Hold your fire."

The wind calmed, and the corn stalks straightened.

"I'm going in," Cedric said. "Agan, you got the balls to follow?"

The big man nodded and followed Cedric into the field, using the spotlight to guide them. Stalks scraped against their skin, scratching his neck and face.

Through the gaps in the corn, Cedric spotted something lying in a fetal position under the glow from the light.

He aimed his muzzle at it and moved his finger to the trigger.

A sudden screech in the distance made him flinch.

"There's another one out there," Agan whispered.

Cedric moved over to the creature lying in the dirt. Something twisted in his gut. It wasn't a creature at all—it was a filthy human. Blood soiled the dirt, but the guy seemed to still be alive, his ribs expanding and contracting slowly.

Agan lowered his rifle.

Cedric went to radio it in. Another high-pitched wail pierced the night.

The call of a monster.

"Help me with him," Cedric said.

Together, the two soldiers carried the injured man back to the road where Malcom and Kelly stood with the dogs. The animals cowered, their tails between their legs.

"Keep it together," Cedric ordered. "There is one of those things, and four of us. You run, you die."

"Fuck it, I'll take my chances," Kelly said.

He let go of the dog leash and took off.

The radio crackled with confused voices. Cedric ignored them as they carefully put the injured man down.

"He's hurt bad," Agan said.

Another screech came, this time from the opposite direction.

Malcom abandoned them then, running after Kelly.

The two remaining dogs both growled and barked viciously.

Gunshots popped through the night as the radio exploded with panicked voices.

"Agan, watch our back," Cedric said.

"Okay, Sarge."

Cedric bent down and rolled the man over gently. Blood covered his side. The bullet had hit him just under his ribs. The man was young, maybe in his thirties, hard to say with mud caking most of his features.

Cedric knew they couldn't carry him back, but he wasn't going to leave him here. They needed to get him up and moving.

Using a gloved hand, Cedric slapped the guy on the cheek, trying to rouse him to consciousness. The man winced in pain, breathing heavily.

"You got to get up," Cedric said. He clamped a hand over the wound and looked up at Agan.

"You cover us on the way back to the gate," he said.

Agan nodded quickly.

Cedric went to help the guy up, but the man grabbed his wrist, squeezing hard. His eyes widened like he was caught in the grips of insanity.

"It's too late…" he mumbled. "You can't go back there."

More gunshots cracked out, and a second Variant screech sounded.

Then came the screams.

Cedric glanced over his shoulder at the gate where Malcom and Kelly were still waiting to get back in. A land mine exploded in the distance, the boom thumping like a grenade.

When Cedric looked back to the two soldiers at the gate, they were gone, shadows sweeping them into the field. A human cry of agony rose like the howling wind.

Agan back peddled. "Sarge," he whispered.

Two Variants skittered up the side of Tower Four. They reached in from opposite sides, surprising Isaac and the other guard.

The beasts yanked them out and tossed them onto the minefield on the other side of the fence. Another boom thumped as the two men were blown to pieces.

The beasts climbed higher up the tower, before perching on the top. Wispy hair blew away from the pale skin of the creature on the left, a female judging from her naked chest. The male one reared his head back and let out a howl.

Several more abominations answered the call.

"We have to go," mumbled the wounded man.

Cedric yanked free of his grip and stood. Dozens of the monsters climbed to the top of rooftops inside the compound.

"How…" he said. "How did they get inside?"

"I came from out there…to warn…" the injured man pointed in the opposite direction of the outpost.

"I came to warn you," whimpered the man.

Cedric hesitated, trying to make sense of things. The guy had to be one of the homesteaders trying to strike out independent from the outposts.

"Sarge, what do we do?" Agan's voice was breaking from fear.

The two Shepherds took off running away from the compound, racing as fast as they could into the cornfields.

Screams of horror filled the night. Cedric imagined the monsters tearing through the outpost, devouring the people inside.

"Sarge," Agan entreated. "What do we do?"

For the first time in his career, Cedric did what he always damned other men for doing. He turned, and he ran away from the fight, following the dogs into the darkness.

At dawn, Kate Lovato walked along the Peaks Island shoreline of Casco Bay, Maine. It was the same thing she did most mornings. The humble house she shared with her husband, Reed Beckham, and eight-year-old son was just five hundred feet from the water's edge, close enough Beckham didn't mind her morning excursions.

When she first started the habit of coming to the water, he wasn't thrilled about it. Their lives before Peaks Island had been fraught with threats, and Beckham had never let his guard down over the years. But they trusted one another, and it would take a miracle for a Variant to get through the secure barriers.

Peaks Island was in the heart of a safe zone, surrounded by advanced sensors, soldiers, sailors, and friends. If anything were to happen, a hidden underground safehouse at the community health center that doubled as her lab provided a final line of defense.

She took a seat on a bench to soak in the clementine sunrise simmering on the horizon. Taking a sip from her steaming mug, she reveled in the small pleasure. The past eight years had been extremely difficult, but despite the odds, they had started to recover and bring back staples like coffee that was grown in Florida. It wasn't as good as the beans from South America and Africa she had enjoyed before the war, but it was better than nothing.

Still, living on an island was a constant reminder of

Plum Island. The secret government labs were ground zero for the bioweapon she had helped design. In the end, the weapon hadn't just killed billions of infected humans—it had created the Variants.

"You did what you had to do, Kate. To save us—to save humanity from the brink of extinction," President Jan Ringgold had reminded her over seven years ago.

Guilt at what her research had brought about consumed Kate to this day.

Most countries were clawing themselves out of complete anarchy after the end of the war. Even in the Allied States, people were still fleeing poverty, starvation, and violence. Peaks Island and Outpost Portland continued to receive refugees on an almost daily basis.

"Morning," came a voice.

She pivoted and smiled when she saw Beckham making his way over. He wore a gray army sweatshirt and camouflage pants. Reaching up with his prosthetic hand, he brushed his thick long hair behind an ear and took a seat next to her.

That hand was a reminder of what Beckham had lost over eight years ago from a Variant acid attack as well as a portion of his leg. But even though his leg and hand might be artificial, the man behind those prosthetics was every bit as strong as he'd been back then. Probably even stronger now.

"Coffee?" she asked, offering her drink to him.

"Sure."

He took a sip and directed his gaze at the water. He was legally blind in his right eye, but he had experienced some improvement thanks to the steroids and pharmaceutical cocktail she had cooked up in her lab on the island.

"You're up early," she said.

"Got a lot on my mind."

"The meeting with President Ringgold?" Kate scooted close to him, feeling his warmth. "Did she tell you why she wants to meet?"

"Nope, but my gut tells me it's political. No matter how many times I tell her that I am not cut out for that life, she encourages me to reconsider." Beckham took another drink. "I think she wants me to challenge Senator McComb."

Kate narrowed her brows. "But McComb is a Ringgold supporter, isn't he?"

"Apparently not as much as she would like. Or maybe he's not supportive of Vice President Lemke's bid for the presidency."

"I'm surprised they haven't tapped you to be Lemke's running mate," Kate said, only half joking. The process had changed and the Vice President wouldn't be selected until after the election now.

He didn't respond, clearly in deep thought. Kate put a hand on his arm.

"You have done enough for your country, Reed. No need to start a second career in politics," she said.

Selfishly, that's what Kate believed, but her husband was a special man, and she knew there might come a time when he was needed off the island.

"What else is bothering you?" she asked, sensing that wasn't the only thing.

"Things have been quiet on the frontier...too quiet."

"Quiet is good. It means the Variants are dying. We can live in peace and focus on rebuilding."

"Quiet scares me," Beckham replied. "In war, it usually means the enemy is planning something. But I'm not just worried about Variants…with elections looming, I'm worried about what happens after President Ringgold leaves office."

He took another drink and paused to reflect. "Her legacy and our country is at risk if the Freedom Party takes over."

"They won't," Kate said confidently.

Beckham handed her the coffee mug back and stood, his prosthetic leg creaking. "I wouldn't be too optimistic. The most recent polls show General Cornelius leading Vice President Lemke by almost four points."

"Polls always leave room for error," Kate said. "And that lead is well within the margin of error."

"Well there are other signs that things aren't looking good for the New America Coalition."

"I know," she admitted. "Vice President Lemke has almost as many enemies as President Ringgold does. Maybe even more."

It wasn't surprising to Kate considering the former admiral of the naval fleet had helped take back the country from Resistance of Tyranny (ROT) eight years ago.

"The biggest issue seems to be over the cities in the frontier," Beckham said. "The Freedom Party is proposing the conscription of all men and women between the age of eighteen and thirty. More and more people think we should try and take the cities back instead of letting the Variants have what once was ours."

Kate hated the thought of sending more young men and women into the meat grinder. Those that were coming of age had been just kids during the war. Parker Horn's daughters, Tasha and Jenny, would almost be of age to serve. Police officer Jake Temper's son, Timothy, and Donna Tufo's son, Bo, would be able to join the military.

She shuddered at the thought of any of them being sent to the frontlines.

For a moment she fell into silence with Beckham, considering the implications of the election just three months away. The areas outside the safe zones had been abandoned after the great war, left for nature to reclaim as the Variants died off. Some human survivors lived in the lawless zones, preferring life on their own rather than in the outposts and cities.

If the Freedom Party had their way, those people would be forced out of the frontier. The cities would be bombed into oblivion, and the young would be sent to fight and die like they had in every other war.

But the human race was still teetering on the edge, and the post-war generation that included Tasha, Jenny, Bo, and Timothy couldn't afford to be wasted.

That's why President Ringgold had taken a more measured approach by sending in Team Ghost and other teams to take out any Variants that threatened outposts.

Fitz was out there now, Kate thought, *doing what he did best—hunting down Variants.*

Beckham broke the quiet between them.

"The Freedom Party is gaining support, especially with voters in the outposts that have been attacked by Variants," he said. "People are scared."

"They should be scared of Cornelius and the Freedom Party. It's basically ROT in disguise, in my opinion. I guess people are forgetting ROT nearly destroyed us."

"I wouldn't exactly compare them with ROT, but I know what you're saying. Some things never change, huh?" Beckham chuckled. "I think politics will outlive the human race. People will still be fighting in their graves. Can't do anything about that."

He brushed his hair back again.

"No, but there is something we can do about that hair," she grinned.

"I kind of like it, to be honest."

Kate kissed him on the cheek. "Whatever you want, my love. But I agree, no politics for now, okay?"

"No politics ever, if I have it my way."

They watched the sunrise for a few more minutes before heading back to their house. Jake, the former New York police officer, shut the door to his house and said goodbye to his son, Timothy.

"Mornin', Jake," Beckham called out.

"Morning!" Jake yelled back. He started off for his guard tower post near the ferry. The vessel was waiting to take early morning workers to the town of Portland, just three miles away.

Kate liked the fact she rarely had to leave the island. She taught school here and ran her small lab. The only times she had to go to the mainland were for groceries or meetings at town hall.

Life was good.

The best it had been in a long time, but there were painful reminders of the old world everywhere. Beckham stopped at a tree that provided a canopy of green over their yard. He took a knee at the grave of his best four-legged friend.

"I miss him," Beckham said.

Kate put a hand on his back. "Apollo lived a good, long life."

Beckham nodded. "He was a loyal dog. The best."

"Yes, he was."

Reaching up, Beckham wiped a tear from his eye. They had just lost Apollo to old age a few months back. They weren't sure how old he was when he crossed the rainbow bridge, but he had passed peacefully, surrounded by friends and family Now he was buried next to the one female dog he had loved, a free spirited mutt he had met when they first moved here..

Kate put an arm around Beckham, and they walked around the house to the front yard. A voice called out across the road. Parker Horn, dressed in nothing but sweatpants, lifted a tattooed arm to wave from his open front door.

It was rare seeing him up this early, but Kate saw what had brought him outside. The big man smoked a homemade cigarette as Apollo's daughter and son ran out of Horn's house barking.

Ginger and Spark darted across the road and over to Beckham and Kate. The four-year-old German Shepherd mixes belonged to Horn's girls, Tasha and Jenny.

Beckham grinned as he knelt to play with the dogs. It was good to see him so happy. She wanted to feel that way, too, but her gut wouldn't let her.

Something was changing on the frontier, and it wasn't just the shadowy Variant forces. With President Ringgold's second term just months away from ending, the country faced the uncertainty of a new leader.

The human race had avoided near extinction once, but this time she wasn't sure they could dodge another bullet if the voters decided to elect Cornelius and support his march back to war.

***

Master Sergeant Joe "Fitz" Fitzpatrick stood at the top of a hill overlooking Ellicott City. Elms and dogwoods blazed with the colors of late autumn. His carbon-fiber blades creaked ever so slightly as he adjusted his weight to pivot for a better view.

It was hard for him to believe he'd lost his flesh-and-blood legs so long ago in Iraq, long before the Variants were even a nightmare on this planet.

But now his prosthetics were as natural to him as his muscles and nerves had once been. Maybe even better. At least, good enough to propel him toward their enemies.

Somewhere out there, an Alpha Variant hid in the shadows with its kin. Team Ghost had the mission to hunt it down and locate the three humans the beasts had kidnapped from Outpost Patapsco Valley just over twenty miles away.

Chances were good all three were already dead, but Team Ghost wouldn't give up until they found them. For the past eight years, they had run missions into the frontier and lawless zones to do exactly that—find and kill Variants and rescue any humans that were snatched by the beasts.

A loose wooden plank on the church next to him rattled. Chips of white paint fluttered away like dust in a gust of wind that rustled his uniform.

"Apollo would've loved a day like this," Fitz said.

The dog had retired several years ago to live out its final days with Beckham and Kate. Fitz had considered asking for Ginger or Spark to be added to the team, but their fate was as pets, not warriors, and the girls had fallen in love with them anyways.

Footsteps crunched over the gravel and Sergeant First Class Jeni Rico joined Fitz at the lookout. She smiled as she chomped on stale gum. Strands of pink hair under the rim of her helmet rustled in the wind. She always found a way to figuratively and literally make things more colorful.

They had fought together and remained lovers for the past eight years. Through all of the battles, heartbreak, and loss, they had found a balance of sorts in their relationship.

But Fitz still worried about losing her every time they came out here. He knew loss well. It haunted him. His brothers had been taken from him by friendly fire in a war long before the Variants. His parents were lost in a tragic car accident.

Over the years he had lost more brothers and sisters in the war against the Variants than he cared to count. A painful stabbing coursed through his gut anytime he thought of Rico falling in battle.

Fitz had been close to the edge many times in his life, especially around the time Beckham found him at Fort Bragg. The man had saved his life by giving him a gun and a purpose. Rico had given him even more.

By her side, he actually had optimism. Optimism that there was something worth fighting for. She had taught him how to strive for a better future for the rest of the world—and for each other.

Their time together also meant she could read him like an open book.

"What's wrong, Fitzie?" she said.

"Just thinkin' of Apollo."

Rico looked toward the lake and then chuckled. "Remember him shaking that dirty ass water all over us after he jumped into a swamp on his last mission."

"Oh yeah," Fitz said.

"At least he's at rest where Beckham and Kate are," Sergeant Yas Dohi said in his stoic tone. The Navajo man stroked his gray goatee that was far longer than regulation length.

"He sure earned his long rest, and I'm glad he enjoyed his golden years in a place free of monsters," Rico said.

Fitz nodded in agreement. "Me, too. He was a good boy."

The dog had hunted more than his fair share of monsters, but there were plenty of beasts that still dwelled in places like this—apocalyptic landscapes that posed dangers with every step.

Telephone poles leaned sideways and lines hung between the poles, draped over the muddy brown water flowing through the street. Brick buildings sported dark windows with shards of glass like the jagged teeth of Variants.

Fitz remembered this city as having a scenic downtown. A perfect place for day trippers to explore the antique and boutique stores before stopping for a beer and sandwich at the brewery.

Would have been a good place to take Rico on a date night, he thought.

"So this is Ellicott City, huh?" Specialist Justin Mendez said, moving to stand beside Fitz.

Mendez's thick black eyebrows arched like caterpillars. He paused.

"Holy shit," he said, raising a scope to his eye.

Fitz signaled for Team Ghost to hunch down.

"You got a hostile?" Fitz asked.

Mendez lowered the rifle. "No, man, it's a '69 Mustang GT," he mumbled. "Damn shame to see a car like that all rusted."

"Jesus, you scared me, man," said Rico, rising back to her feet.

"I had a car like that," Corporal Bobby Ace said.

"Seriously?" Mendez asked.

Ace nodded. "More like a '67 Camaro, but basically the same thing."

"Same thing my ass, old man." Mendez shook his head while staring at Ace.

Ace laughed a deep sound that welled up from his large belly. A scraggly white beard hung from his chin shaped like the machete he kept on his belt. Wrinkles formed canyons around his leathery skin.

Sometimes Fitz was shocked the guy could keep up with the rest of them. His age and weight would have kept him from even being considered for Delta Force back in the day, but men with his fighting experience were a rare breed nowadays.

Team Ghost was lucky to have him.

Ace was an artist with his custom mag-fed Mossberg 500 shotgun and had the killer instinct Fitz was looking for. He selected the corporal to replace men he had lost in an ambush by an Alpha.

Men like Staff Sergeant Blake Tanaka and Sergeant Hugh Stevenson.

Fitz shook off the memory and focused on the final member of Team Ghost. Specialist Will Lincoln held an M4A1 across his chest. He directed eyes as dark as his skin at Fitz. The thin young man had joined the team the same time as Ace.

What his frame lacked in muscle, he made up for in a mind quick and sharp as a Variant's claws. He also provided comedic relief and music in dark times.

"You girls and your cars," he grumbled.

"Girls?" Mendez asked, raising one of his brows.

"Just messin', brother," Lincoln said. "So, ya'll ready to get this hunt started or what?"

"Take in some water, we move out soon," Fitz said.

He looked out over the city again, glad they had been sent here instead of Baltimore. Compared to the bigger city, Ellicott City was in decent condition, even with the flooding. America's urban centers were largely decaying wastelands, destroyed by the effort to push the Variants out of the country, especially on the West Coast.

Most of their missions were to places in the Midwest and East Coast now that the Western part of the country had almost completely been destroyed and abandoned.

Humanity abandoned many of the major cities and left them to the abominations that haunted them, still thirsting for fresh protein. Rumor had reached Team Ghost that the Freedom Party wanted to destroy even more of what remained, including places like this where the Variants still posed a threat.

Fitz was a soldier, but he also had an opinion and had given it to Beckham the last time they talked. Much like national parks had once been, places like this needed to be protected.

He took in a breath before giving the order.

All it takes is all you got, he thought.

"Dohi you take point, Ace you got rear guard," Fitz said. "Stay sharp, Ghost."

It was the usual setup, since Dohi was the best tracker on the team, and Ace had never let anyone or anything sneak up on them.

The team moved out—all business now that they had passed into Variant territory. With the sun still high in the sky, they kept low and close to cover, their weapons shouldered and roving for targets.

Dohi moved slowly, ears perked and eyes moving as he stepped through the ankle-high water. Fitz kept behind him, scanning the interior of the stores and checking every window for any sign of hostiles. Deep within the next store he saw pangs of sunlight reflect off the costume jewelry around the neck of a mannequin.

"Jesus," Rico said. "Thought that was a person at first."

"Nope, but that was," Lincoln said. He raised his rifle, aiming at the spot that had caught his interest across the road. The bottom half of a human skeleton hung out of a window, mold climbing up from the flooded street as if reaching toward it.

Fitz motioned for the team to check it out. When they got to the second-floor window, he stepped underneath to see that the flesh was completely gone. Tooth marks marred the dried bone. Some were snapped like twigs, the marrow sucked dry.

"Guess we know we're in the right place," Rico said dryly.

Fitz looked one last time at the skeletal remains. This was the worst part of tracking down rogue Variants. Team Ghost almost always arrived too late to help.

But they would find the abominations responsible.

According to the reports they'd received, this one was a wily Alpha. Smarter than the average grunt beast judging by how he'd been sneaking in and out of Outpost Patapsco Valley without any of the guards getting a clear shot at it.

Fitz flashed hand signals and the team continued between the brick buildings. A flurry of leaves rustled over the street; flashes of orange and brown, landed in the water, floating away with the slight current at their feet.

The crisp scent of autumn mixed with the odor of must and mold drifted from the buildings. But he didn't detect the sour odor of a Variant.

"We got another skinny," Mendez said. With his rifle, he pointed to a second corpse propped up against a bench next to a toppled garbage can. Flags of ripe flesh hung off the bones.

"Looks fresh," Dohi said.

That sent another stab of dread through Fitz's gut.

Apparently, the Alpha had been hunting in other areas too.

The sooner they killed it the safer this area would be.

The team continued to survey the street. They were coming to the end of the small, historic downtown. A railway bridge crossed twenty feet above the street. On it was painted 'ELLICOTT CITY' in white blocky letters.

A freight train had derailed off the bridge and fallen to the street. The toppled cars served as a dam. Water rushed up against it and trickled between the graffiti-covered cars. Broken crates and steel drums were piled around the train.

Graffiti wasn't the only thing covering them. Dark stains that could only be blood marked the sides like a macabre painting.

"We've got to be close," Fitz said. "Stay sharp."

They moved out in combat intervals and squeezed between the train cars. As Fitz came out the other side, water rushed around his blades and streamed toward the river beyond. Before them lay another bridge, this one for cars.

"Do you hear that?" Dohi asked.

Fitz held up a fist to signal the rest of the team to hold tight. He strained his ears, listening for what Dohi had noticed. Between the gusts of wind, he picked up a quiet chorus of something clinking together. The sound reminded him of wind chimes. Only instead of metal, they sounded almost like wood.

"What the hell is that?" Rico whispered.

The team advanced across the bridge and skirted around the abandoned cars there. The wind chime chorus grew louder.

Fitz tilted his head to listen. It seemed to be originating below them. He leaned over the handrail and peered down at a stomach rolling sight.

Bones strung up beneath the bridge rattled in the wind. Tendrils of red hung from the broken edges and droplets trickled off them.

He didn't need Dohi to tell him these were also fresh kills.

Team Ghost had found two of the human prisoners.

Fitz balled his hand and froze at a scream of sheer agony in the distance. It started off almost animalistic; but by the tail end of the wail he could tell it was human. There was still someone alive out there. At least for now.

Dohi pointed toward a forested area off the road, and Fitz gave the order to pursue the Alpha with a nod. Team Ghost wasn't going home until it had put down this beast.

— 3 —

President Jan Ringgold took a long drink of cold coffee. She was going to need it tonight. Across from her sat Vice President Dan Lemke. Both of them had been waiting anxiously for her Chief of Staff, James Soprano, to arrive at her presidential office in the Greenbrier.

The knock came a few minutes later, and the door opened.

"Evening," Soprano said, wandering over to her desk, carrying a stack of briefing folders.

"I hope you've got good news for me," Ringgold said.

"I haven't looked yet, Madam President," Soprano gently set the stack of folders on her desk and then backed away.

"Thank you," she said to her COS. "We'll catch up shortly."

Soprano exited the room with a nod toward Ringgold and Lemke.

Ringgold began shuffling through the folders. Most contained information about her meetings tomorrow, but she went right for the one with the recent poll numbers for the upcoming election.

"The moment of truth," Ringgold said. She took in a breath and opened the folder. "There we are."

"Well?" asked Lemke.

Ringgold smiled.

The numbers were good. Better than she had thought.

Almost seven points in her party's favor and well outside the margin of error.

"We might just win this thing after all," she said. "Our recent campaign efforts seem to have pushed things further in our favor."

Vice President Dan Lemke leaned forward in his chair. She spun the folder around so he could read them.

"That's because people have a lot to be happy about, Madam President," he said. "You brought us back from the brink over these eight years. We've come a long way from hiding in bunkers and praying during every attack that we would survive for another day."

She leaned back slightly in her chair, looking out the bulletproof window at the trees. The branches swayed in the wind outside, and moonlight cast a white glow on the bark that made them look like skeletal fingers. A cold wave snaked through her body.

Tonight is not the night to be spooked, Ringgold thought.

Ringgold gave herself a moment to relish in some of her accomplishments in the face of this good news. The migration from the West Coast and mountain states during her first term had been risky, but it had paid off. She had been better able to protect their citizens over the consolidated territory and focus on rebuilding important infrastructure to keep them alive.

The economy was rolling along and, recently, it was accelerating. Dormant industries had reawakened. Factories were producing vehicles for both military and civilian use. An old GM plant had already put out three thousand new cars, a fraction of what it had once done, but it was a start.

Farms and orchards across the Allied States were producing enough food again to feed all the country's citizens. Wind turbines and solar energy helped power the farms. The government had even rebuilt part of the electrical grid. Telecommunications engineers were getting close to restoring a cellular network that would support personal cell phone use.

In Texas, several oil operations were back up and running to fuel the expanding economy. The country was using all the resources at its disposal to come back online.

But there were some things she wasn't sure she wanted to return.

Social media, for starters.

She kind of liked the quiet. For one, it made presidential campaigns a lot more straightforward.

The biggest indicator the country was recovering were the relatively infrequent Variant attacks. The beasts were still out there, sure. Some even speculated they were breeding underground, but at least their numbers were manageable, and the damage they did cause was minor, despite it still being a loss of human life.

Lemke stood and tightened his navy tie. The retired rear admiral had helped save the country from ROT. His transition to politics had been surprisingly easy for him after his long tenure of military service.

He was Kennedy family handsome, with thick wavy hair, dimples, and a perfect smile. His charming East Coast accent put even fierce political enemies at ease. He knew when to flash a grin and when to keep a straight face. Best of all, he was loyal and intelligent.

The perfect person to keep the country moving forward.

"You're going to make a hell of a president," Ringgold said. "And I'm going to enjoy watching you from retirement with a mojito in hand."

"I hope you'll be willing to answer my calls, even when you're sipping that drink," Lemke said. "If I'm going to be a good president, it's only because I have you to thank."

Ringgold almost blushed.

"I can't think of any president besides Abe Lincoln that had to deal with such a traumatic war in our homeland the way you have," Lemke added. "And somehow, we still came out of all that with hope for a better future."

"Oh, I see you're already preparing your next talking points for the campaign trail," Ringgold said with a chuckle.

The dimples on his face widened slightly until he looked down at his buzzing government-issued cell phone.

Any humor in his expression immediately evaporated.

"What is it?" she asked.

"Trouble, if I had to guess," he replied. "General Souza at SOCOM doesn't ever call just to shoot the bull."

Ringgold got out of her chair and moved around her desk, forgetting the poll numbers and the stacks of files for tomorrow's meetings.

Lemke took the call in the center of the room, standing behind two couches positioned around a coffee table.

"What?" he asked Souza, furrowing his brow. He flung a glance at Ringgold and then turned slightly, shaking his head.

This couldn't be good. She walked over to the couches but couldn't bring herself to sit. She was too nervous to remain still.

"Understood," Lemke said. "Keep me updated."

He lowered the phone and slowly slipped it into his pocket, pausing like he was nervous to turn and face her.

"Well?" Ringgold asked. "What is it?"

Lemke shook his head. The normally collected rear-admiral-turned-politician looked like he had seen a ghost.

"Outpost Turkey River," he said in almost a whisper. "They've gone completely dark, Madam President."

***

"I'm bored as hell, brother," Horn muttered quietly. He pulled on his jacket cuff. "And I hate wearing this dumb suit."

"Me and you both," Beckham replied. They stood inside the guest lobby of the White House, dressed in suits that needed tailoring.

Most of the people waiting in the room were business folk and politicians that had thrived during the reconstruction period.

Several of Ringgold's security detail stood watching the civilians in the lobby like hawks. Beckham was doing the same thing. It was hard to know who here was a friend and who was an enemy.

A man with a real lip hugger of a mustache stood with his back to a marble column. He wore a cowboy hat, leather boots, and a shiny belt buckle. His gun holster and the holsters on the two bodyguards that accompanied him were empty, their weapons taken by Secret Service.

"Get a load of Chuck Norris over there," Horn whispered. "Who the hell is he?"

Beckham chuckled. "If I had to guess, that's S.M. Fischer, the oil guy."

He had heard the oil tycoon had survived in his

doomsday bunker with a group of personal bodyguards during the war.

Unlike Beckham and Horn, Fischer probably wasn't here to advise President Ringgold. From what Beckham had heard, Fischer would be here to interview the president and vice president.

As one of the wealthiest men left in the country, and with one of the biggest oil fields, Fischer's support would go a long way for whoever he decided to support in the presidential elections.

Maybe I should encourage him to make the right choice... Beckham thought.

Before he could consider the idea thoroughly, a short Latina woman dressed in a business-length skirt, a blouse, and a suit jacket opened a door across the hall. Beckham recognized her right away. Elizabeth Cortez had started off as a staffer for President Ringgold and now served as Chief of Staff for Vice President Lemke.

"Mr. Fischer, the President and Vice President are ready for you," Cortez said.

Fischer took off his cowboy hat as he followed her into an office. He looked at Beckham for a lingering second, perhaps sizing him up.

Beckham's prosthetics and the stories that probably verged more on myth than truth meant he often got looks like that. Most everyone here knew his part in the war. He was also the husband of the woman that had saved the world. Or destroyed it, depending on whom you asked.

"Always last on the list," Horn grumbled.

"You know the drill. The wealthy and powerful always get seats at the table first."

"Yeah, yeah," Horn said. "Somedays I really do miss the battlefield over this boring shit. At least, I had more of an impact and knew why I was there."

"We'll find out soon enough and then go straight home," Beckham promised. He took in a deep breath. He missed the brotherhood that came with serving his country, but he didn't miss the death.

Part of him was glad to be retired and raising a family.

One by one, the other people in the lobby were led into the President and Vice President's offices while Beckham and Horn continued to wait. National Security Advisor Ben Nelson and Ringgold's Chief of Staff James Soprano opened their doors and met with more businessmen and other politicians from the Allied States.

Retired General Cornelius would be doing the same thing at his home base Outpost Galveston, in Texas. The ocean community had become the hub for the Freedom opposition party. He had even organized his own mercenary army there, with over two thousand soldiers. They came from all over, a hodgepodge of armed military contractors, former US service men and women, and militia soldiers from other outposts that had defected to Galveston.

The troops had access to the best weapons, armored vehicles, and even aircraft thanks to Cornelius' strategic alliances with former manufacturers and military contractors.

Not only did Cornelius plan to grow these forces and take back the West Coast and abandoned cities by augmenting them with a conscripted army if he was elected, he intended to use low-yield nukes. His strategy would turn several cities into radioactive craters despite the fact there was little evidence the cities were anything more than hospices for the dying Variants.

Beckham looked at another set of doors that led to the

banquet room where he had married Kate eight years ago. His worries dissolved at the happy memories from that night when they were surrounded by so many friends and family members.

But he also thought of the friends and family members that hadn't survived to see their union. He pictured the faces of Captain Rachel Davis, all of the lost souls from Team Ghost, firefighter Meg Pratt, Sergeant Jose Garcia, Lieutenant Colonel Ray Jensen, and so many others.

No matter how many times he thought of his brothers and sisters, their faces and voices continued to fade away. His mind, like his ailing vision, was another wound from the war. It didn't help that he and Horn weren't the young men they'd been when they were fighting on Team Ghost.

Beckham was forty-two, and Horn was pushing forty.

Another door opened across the hallway, and Beckham glimpsed President Ringgold in the briefing room. She had also aged since Beckham had last seen her. That was just six months ago.

She was under extreme stress trying to keep the country together and ensure her legacy continued with the election of Vice President Dan Lemke.

The retired admiral was the best hope, in Beckham's opinion, for a bright future—a future he was here to discuss today.

She shook hands with S.M. Fischer. The oil tycoon left the office, putting his cowboy hat on as he entered the lobby. He walked over to Beckham and Horn with two of his bodyguards flanking him.

"Captain Beckham?" Fischer asked in a southern drawl that matched Horn's.

Horn stepped up with his arms crossing his swollen

chest and his chin up.

"Yeah," Beckham replied.

Fischer held out a hand. "S.M. Fischer, pleased to meet you."

"I figured that's who you were," Beckham said, shaking his hand.

"Ah, I'm honored to hear that," Fischer said. He glanced at Horn. "And who is your friend?"

"Master Sergeant Parker Horn," Horn said, keeping his arms folded over his chest. He finally reached out when Fischer extended his hand.

"You boys here to meet with Ringgold?" Fischer asked.

"We're here to meet with the president of the Allied States," Beckham replied.

Beckham waited for Fischer to give him the reason for coming over to say hello. Less talking and more listening was the best strategy he had picked up over the years when he wasn't sure if he could trust someone.

"She's an impressive woman," Fischer said. "I'm grateful for the military support she has lent my growing oil operation. They have been helpful in dealing with the Variants terrorizing my fields in Texas, but I'm hoping for more to eradicate this threat once and for all."

Beckham nodded.

"I'm told I can expect even more support from Vice President Lemke," Fischer said.

"He's a man of his word," Beckham replied.

"Glad to hear that. I'm curious to hear what General Cornelius has to say about the diseased bastards though," Fischer said. "What do you boys think of him?"

"I think he would destroy your fields in the process," Horn said.

Fischer stroked his thick mustache.

"What my friend here means is the retired General's strategies might lean more on the reckless side of things," Beckham said. "You *might* get rid of your pests, but the collateral damage your fields would experience might not be worth it."

Fischer lowered his hand.

"He's a good man and served his country during the war, we just see things differently on how to keep the country moving forward," Beckham said.

"I see," Fischer said. He seemed to think on it a moment and then nodded. "I better get going, but it was nice to meet you two fellas."

"Safe travels." Beckham watched Fischer and his bodyguards leave in silence, but Big Horn didn't hold back his thoughts.

"I don't like that guy," Horn mumbled.

"The vice president needs his endorsement. Fischer's company supplies nearly half of the country's oil, and he's got the wealth to fund a campaign all on his own. Like him or not, we want him on our side."

"Don't mean I have to like him though," Horn said.

"That's true, but you could be more polite."

The lobby slowly emptied as the men continued to wait.

"Can we go to the bar for a beer or something?" Horn groaned.

"Shouldn't be too—"

A door creaked open, and Elizabeth Cortez walked into the lobby. "Captain Beckham and Master Sergeant Horn," she said. "Thank you for making the journey."

She reached out and Beckham shook her hand.

"If you'd follow me, please."

They entered the Oval Office where coffee and water had been set out on the tables, but the chairs were empty. POTUS and VPOTUS were not here.

Elizabeth walked over to one of the side doors. Opening it, she then gestured inside to a long hallway. At the entrance beyond, two Marines stood like statues.

Horn flung Beckham a glance, but neither of them said a word as they continued down the passage.

Another pair of Marines stood guard in front of the closed doors of an elevator. Elizabeth typed a code onto a keypad, and the doors whispered open.

Beckham almost hesitated as a memory surfaced in his mind. This was the place Captain Rachel Davis and a small team of Navy SEALs had come to rescue former Vice President George Johnson. They had arrived too late, and the entire Presidential Emergency Operations Center (PEOC) was filled with the infected, including Johnson.

The elevator took them deep underground and Beckham tried to relax. When the doors opened again, a room bustling with activity greeted them.

Military officers and civilian staffers worked at stations facing a wall-mounted monitor the size of a movie theatre screen. It was split into multiple boxes filled with data and live video imagery.

Elizabeth crossed the room to another door. She knocked, then peeked her head in.

"Good afternoon, Madam President," she said. "We have Captain Beckham and Master Sergeant Horn here to see you."

Elizabeth opened the door the rest the way, gesturing inside.

"Thank you," Beckham said.

The door closed behind them, leaving the two retired Delta Force Operators alone with the president and vice president.

"Great to see you, Captain Beckham and Master Sergeant Horn," Ringgold said. "I'm very sorry to keep you both waiting."

She walked around the table. Beckham held out a hand for a shake, but Ringgold went past it, going in for a hug.

"How are your families?" she asked.

"Good, Madam President—" Beckham began to say.

"Jan," Ringgold corrected. "I'm only going to be president a few more months, and I'm starting to train my friends to use my name."

"Ma'am," Beckham said with a dip of his head.

She smiled and shook Horn's hand.

"Everything's good at Peaks Island?" she asked.

"Very good, ma'am," Horn replied.

The vice president had followed behind Ringgold and now stood waiting to shake their hands before taking a seat.

"I called you here in hopes that you would consider running for Senate against McComb. We need your voice and support in the chambers to help Lemke," Ringgold said.

"McComb is weak and I'm worried he might defect to the Freedom Party," Lemke chimed in.

Horn said something under his breath that rhymed with hit, but Beckham ignored him.

"I'm honored, ma'am, but at this time Kate and I would really like to stay out of politics," Beckham said. "I'm happy to help in other ways of course. Advising and maybe even a little campaigning for the party, but…"

"I understand," Ringgold said. "It's something to think

about, although it's not the only reason I brought you in. There are matters that will affect the election more than a Senate race."

"Lay it on us, Madam President," Horn said.

She looked to Lemke. Beckham braced to hear what had them both looking so fatigued and worried.

"There was an attack last night on Outpost Turkey River," Lemke said. "The radio SOS we received said Variants had penetrated the outpost. We lost communications within minutes."

"What?" Horn said, stepping forward.

"We sent a drone a few hours ago and this is what it has sent back," Ringgold said.

Lemke used a remote to click on the monitor across the table. Beckham stiffened in his chair and leaned forward to get a better view of the imagery on screen. With his poor vision in his right eye, he was having a hard time making out the grainy footage at first, but there was no mistaking the empty streets.

"Where is everyone?" Horn asked.

"That's what we're trying to figure out," Lemke said. "The drone did not find a single body of a human, or Variant for that matter."

"Did you ever come across anything like this during your time leading Team Ghost?" Ringgold asked Beckham.

His gaze flitted from the screen to meet hers.

"Not quite on this level, ma'am."

"There were nearly three hundred people living at the outpost," Lemke said. "Gone with barely a trace."

"They're one of the most important agricultural communities we have, too, and they had just recently started to harvest," Ringgold said. "We need this community, and we need to know what happened to them."

"At this point we've only sent in the drone, but we're going to deploy a couple of teams to investigate," Lemke said. "We've got SEALs on deck, already prepared to go. And then if that fails, we can bring in our experts."

Beckham knew what that meant—Team Ghost was going back out there. He thought of Fitz who had spent the past ten years fighting the monsters during the war and post-war. The team had lost more souls since then.

Somehow Fitz and Rico had survived all of the operations, but Beckham feared one of these days he would get a call that Fitz had finally run out of luck.

"I'd like you two to stick around an extra day to monitor the mission," Ringgold said. "We could use your input as this unfolds."

Beckham had promised Kate he would be back by the next morning, but she would understand.

"Absolutely," he said. "We're happy to help."

Ringgold stood and approached the screen, looking at the grainy footage. "I'm worried there is something more sinister going on out there."

Lemke nodded. "Me too, and when word gets out about Turkey River going dark, it's going to fuel the support for Cornelius and his plan to ravage abandoned cities with bombs and a fresh army of young men and women."

"Not my Tasha," Horn muttered.

Ringgold rotated from the screen wearing a mask of concern. "I know you two have already sacrificed so much, but I'm afraid we're going to need your help again to fight this new threat."

A chill passed through Beckham at the thought, and

while he knew this didn't necessarily mean he would need to return to the battlefield, it did mean his days living in peace on the island were numbered.

— 4 —

The screams of agony seemed to ricochet off the trees. Dohi tried to hone in on the direction, but the echo made identifying the location of its source in the treacherous terrain difficult.

Another strong gust whipped through the foliage. Leaves swirled around him and the rest of Team Ghost who had spread out in combat intervals.

Dohi led the way into the thick forest. He cradled his suppressed M4A1, searching for targets. The screams suddenly stopped.

He slowed, stepping on a dead leaf that crunched in the silence.

For a moment he stood there, listening to the woods and the rush of the river not far behind them.

He sniffed the autumn air, but picked up no sour scent from the Variants.

When the wind picked up again, he knew why.

"Christ," Dohi whispered to Fitz. "I think we're upwind from those screams."

"So the Variants smelled us first?" Ace grumbled quietly.

"That's why they silenced the prisoner," Dohi said. "They know we're hunting them.

"Then they'll start hunting us now, too," Lincoln said.

The hunters just became the hunted, Dohi thought dourly.

"Find us that trail, Dohi," Fitz said. "Keep an eye out

for camouflaged beasts, too. It may be light out, but they'll still blend in."

Dohi nodded, not showing his frustration. People normally thought he had some mystical power that allowed him to listen and talk with the woods when he was tracking.

That was nothing more than a stereotypical myth.

Truth was he'd learned not how to listen or talk to the woods, but how to *read* them. All the miniscule signs that led to your quarry were there if you put in the work.

The forest didn't willingly give those signs up. You had to find them.

He crouched to look for any clues. The ground was covered in leaves, making it exceedingly difficult to search for the footprints. Most people made the mistake of trying to track a person or Variant down by looking at things from a single perspective: their own.

They walked, standing straight, and kept their eyes ahead of them. Not very helpful when you were dealing with monsters that could climb, burrow, and even fly, as some across the Atlantic had once done.

An open mind was the best way to come at problems like this. He raked his hands through the leaves, revealing the dried brown grass and patches of dirt underneath them. It would take hours to sift through the leaves if his goal was to find those Variant footprints.

But that wasn't his goal. Instead, he pressed his fingers against the soil. It gave easily. Not unlike the soil around downtown Ellicott City where the flood waters had softened and eroded it.

The rain would've been strong enough to wash the hillside of the blood and little bits of flesh Dohi wanted to look for. What the waters hadn't washed away, the

NICHOLAS SANSBURY SMITH & ANTHONY J. MELCHIORRI

leaves hid. The weather was conspiring with the Variants against him.

A branch cracked somewhere in the distance.

Mendez swiveled on his heels.

Fitz motioned for everyone to keep still. Then he nodded at Dohi who again took point. Team Ghost followed, walking at a hunch, their rifles roving for targets.

Rifle pointing forward, Dohi's eyes scanned the surroundings as he sought another sign, another hint of where the Variants' trail had gone.

He found it on the knotted brown bark of an oak. One of the gray-brown scales had been torn off to reveal a lighter patch of yellow wood, no bigger than his thumb.

Obvious to him, but maybe not to someone who wasn't looking. He plucked something from the bark that turned out to be a chunk of fingernail.

Human from the looks of it.

Dohi motioned them forward, spotting other tree trunks with scratches on them along with saplings that had been split. The casual wear on the landscape revealed the Alpha's preferred travel route. He could practically see a path now.

He pushed forward through the foliage, advancing along the trail at a brisk pace.

This wasn't the first time they had been on a mission to save civilians kidnapped by the Variants, and it likely wouldn't be their last. Most of their recent missions had ended with dead Variants but, in most cases, they were too late to save their prisoners.

The loss of innocent lives weighed heavy on his mind like a dark storm cloud.

He broke into a run, heart pounding. The scratches on

the tree trunks and the depressed leaves and splintered twigs led the team. Around the next oak, a scent hit his nostrils.

Dohi slowed his pace and motioned for Team Ghost to spread out again. Through the screen of trees, he spotted a gray dome propped up by four Doric pillars about twice as tall as a man, each covered by moss.

A rusted iron cross was suspended from the dome giving the structure the appearance of some kind of altar. Bricks lay around it, and huge gray slabs rested on the forest floor where the wind had brushed aside some of the leaves.

The structure was some sort of a rotted chapel. The more Dohi looked between the trees and fallen logs, the more ruined structures he noticed. Most were barely more than a leftover foundation, while others had the remnants of brick walls suffocated by vegetation.

Dohi held his breath to listen.

A screech exploded through the trees. His stomach sank when he realized Team Ghost wasn't the only one studying the area. He swiveled toward the source of the sound, but Fitz found the camouflaged target first. He fired short bursts—bullets chiseled into one of the low-lying brick walls as a shape flung itself down for cover.

Other inhuman shrieks blasted through the forest.

"Eyes up!" Fitz yelled.

Dohi raised his rifle at a hulking figure in the tree branches. Pangs of sunlight piercing through the leafy cover illuminated a creature with throbbing lips and needle-like teeth. Blood vessels pulsed under the mottled green and brown flesh perfectly matching the colors of its surroundings.

Cover blown, it leapt from branch to branch, staying

just ahead of Dohi's aim. When he finally had a shot, it suddenly changed directions.

Dohi fired calculated bursts at the muscled beast and finally hit the target. Blood and flesh flicked out of the exit wounds.

Mindful of his ammo, he fired one last burst as the creature sailed through the air. He jumped out of the way at the last minute, and the Variant walloped the ground next to him, limp and dead on impact.

Another camouflaged creature raced from behind one of the crumbled walls. Ragged black hair twisted in a knot behind its head. It drew back its claws, ready to use them as scythes.

A flurry of rounds cut into the abomination as it made a run for Dohi, spraying hot blood over his fatigues.

"Got you, bro!" Lincoln called out.

"Thanks!" Dohi replied.

The rattle of gunfire echoed around him as he moved to find a new target. His world became the view through his rifle's optics.

Find a Variant. Fire. Repeat.

Surging adrenaline seemed to slow time as he sighted up each shot. Team Ghost had recovered quickly from their ambush. Ace's shotgun boomed as it decimated the bodies of beasts that had gotten too close.

Mendez picked off the Variants still swinging down from the trees, the sunlight hitting their camouflaged skin. Fitz and Rico fended off the monsters further away, winding through the ruins with their suppressed shots.

A final boom from Ace's shotgun announced the death of the last Variant.

The labored breaths of Team Ghost once again claimed the day, the only other sound was the moan of a dying beast that Fitz finished off with a double tap.

"Think that's the whole nest?" Rico asked.

"No," Dohi said. He picked up the muscled arm of one of the dead Variants. The beast was strong, but it wasn't Alpha strong. And the way they'd thrown themselves at Team Ghost likely meant they were cannon fodder—not the leader of this pack.

"The Alpha's probably watching us now," Lincoln said. "Trying to figure out who the weakest link is." He shot a glance at Mendez who spat on the ground.

"Then he'd be looking at you, hombre," retorted Mendez.

Dohi ignored them and searched for tracks. After a few minutes of looking, he located another trail. He motioned the team up chipped concrete stairs. At the bottom of the stairs, dark shapes flitted through the shadowy woods. Two appeared to be normal Variants, loping after another. The third…

"There's the Alpha," Dohi said.

Fitz balled his hand. "Hold your fire, it's got a hostage!"

The beast was a good three feet taller than the others, and slender with ropy muscles. The long limbs appeared insectile, both of them wrapped around a male human prisoner. Mottled patches of gray and black covered the camouflaged flesh.

It turned and bolted with the man. The other two beasts screeched as they followed.

Fitz gave the advance signal.

Dohi had already taken off, fearing that if they lost it now, it would melt into the forest. It was no wonder the creature had been able to infiltrate Outpost Patapsco Valley so easily. The entire outpost was located in woods just like this.

Dohi made up lost ground fast and brought his rifle to aim at one of those slender legs. The first shot found a target, ripping through a muscular calf. The Alpha let out a roar and slammed into the ground, the hostage rolling away into the leaves.

He kept his rifle shouldered, an eye on the other two Variants that had slowed. The Alpha pushed itself back up and hissed, brown saliva spraying Dohi as he approached and fired into the Alpha's side.

Despite the rounds, the creature barreled into Dohi, knocking him to the ground. He lost his rifle and went for his hatchet, pulling it from the sheath just as the Alpha swiped his vest with jagged claws. Dohi planted the blade into its arm, yanked it out, and then struck it in the chin with a crunch.

In his periphery, he saw Fitz engage with the other two Variants, firing at them as they parried their claws with his rifle. Rico soon joined him. They formed a wall between themselves and the person that the Variants had been carrying.

The Alpha let out another roar that nearly deafened Dohi as he tried to pry the blade free from its chin. It brought its fists down, hammering at his chest, and then climbed on top of him.

Suddenly blood sprayed from the Alpha's mouth.

The creature screeched in agony as nerves and muscles and bones gave way to Ace's machete. He hacked at the creature over and over until it finally succumbed to the injuries and died on top of Dohi.

Ace helped push the beast off him and then offered his hand. Dohi took it and rose to his feet, thanking Ace with a nod and a clap on the heavyset man's shoulder.

The other two Variants lay dead next to trees. Lincoln and Rico were already fanning out to hold sentry while Ace bent down to the survivor.

The man crawled away on all fours.

"Relax buddy," Ace said.

Mendez moved over to help.

The man struggled as they peeled off the dried mucus plugs covering his mouth. He sobbed and scooted away on arms covered in bleeding wounds. "They… They killed the others… I saw them… Oh, God! You've got to help me. Help… Help…me…"

"Take it easy," Dohi said. "We're going to get you out of here."

Fitz pulled out his radio to reach command and walked over to Rico and Lincoln. "Help…help…" the injured man kept repeating through quivering lips.

"You're safe now," Mendez said. He and Dohi worked on dressing the wounds. The man was clearly in shock.

Fitz returned a moment later with a sour look.

"Guess we're not going to have a celebratory beer tonight, huh?" Lincoln said.

"Not tonight," Fitz replied.

"Please don't tell us 'all it takes is all you got,'" Mendez said. "I really, really need a hot shower and to hit the rack."

"Yeah, bro," Lincoln said, waving his hand over his nose. "Mendez ain't lying. He really needs a shower."

Fitz frowned. "Sorry fellas, but command has another mission for us," he said. "As soon as we get back to base we're shipping out."

***

"I'm going to be here for another night," Beckham said over the phone. "Maybe more."

"Maybe more?" Kate asked. To her, that meant definitely more, but she had a feeling there was a good reason for the extended journey.

"I'm really sorry, but there's a situation," Beckham said. "President Ringgold has asked me and Horn to help monitor it."

"I just want to remind you that you are retired."

"I remember," Beckham said. "This isn't fieldwork."

A sinking feeling grew in her gut. She recalled that last conversation she and Beckham had shared. How they feared the quiet. The calm before the storm.

Kate knew her husband probably couldn't share details, but she had to ask.

"Is it really bad?" she asked.

"It isn't good, that's for sure." Beckham let out an audible exhalation. "Don't tell anyone, okay?"

"Okay."

"An outpost has gone completely dark and everyone there is missing."

"Where?"

"Turkey River in northern Iowa."

"How does an entire outpost go…"

"I don't know, Kate," he said. "I've got to go, but I love you, and will be home as soon as I can."

"I love you, too, and remember what I said."

"I'm retired. Got it."

Kate said goodbye and let out a sigh. She hated knowing that his instincts might be right. That something was going on out there beyond the walls and gates and sensors.

All those technologies and measures they had relied on

to protect the burgeoning communities around the Allied States had apparently failed Outpost Turkey River.

She prayed there was an explanation and the people living there were okay.

A knock on the door interrupted her thoughts. Javier beat her there and stood on his toes to look out the window in the door.

"It's Jake and Timothy," he said.

Kate nodded, giving Javier permission to let them in.

"Good evening," Jake said. "We come bearing tasty gifts."

Timothy raised an iced cake into the air at his father's goading.

"Wow," Kate said, reaching out. "Red velvet?"

"Sure is," Timothy replied, looking sheepish. The teenager was definitely a notch shier than his father.

"Who told you that's my favorite?" she asked.

"Javier," Timothy replied.

Kate smiled and handed the cake to her son.

"Thank you so much for having us over for dinner," Jake said, stepping inside. He bent down to unlace his boots, but Kate waved her hand. "Keep them on."

"You sure?" Jake asked, polite as usual.

"Of course. Come on in, it's so nice to have you two over."

"Thank you, Doctor," Jake said.

"Kate," she reminded him.

"The table is set!" Tasha called out.

"Sounds like you got some antsy guests," Jake said.

Kate chuckled. "Antsy doesn't begin to describe it."

She moved to the kitchen with Jake and Timothy tailing her. The smell of fresh marinara over spaghetti filled the air. One of Javier's favorites. Tasha and Jenny set the table while their dogs, Ginger and Spark, looked on from the connecting room.

Tasha was old enough to be left home alone to watch Jenny, but Horn preferred they stayed here when he had to leave the island. And Kate suspected the girls preferred it, too. The need to be around others was a psychological vestige of surviving war.

"Come get a plate," Kate said to Jake and the kids.

Jenny and Javier raced over to be first in line. Timothy proved himself the gentleman, allowing Tasha to go first. Kate made a note to keep an eye on those two. Nearly the same age, she saw the looks they'd given each other and recalled her days as a carefree teenager.

"Looks really good," Tasha said as she began to fill her plate.

"Next time, you're the chef," Kate said.

Jenny groaned. "Tasha can't cook."

"She's learning." Kate looked to Tasha with an encouraging smile.

"I bet Tasha is a great chef," Timothy added.

Tasha's cheeks turned red.

"That was Dad on the phone, right?" Javier asked. "When does he get back tomorrow?"

Tasha and Jenny both looked up from their full plates.

"Dad and Parker aren't going to be home for another day or two," Kate informed them. "They have more business to take care of."

"Man…" Tasha said.

"I know, but they will be home soon," Kate said, reaching across the table to place a hand on Tasha's.

"You know, your fathers have been invaluable when it comes to training the security detail," Jake said, looking at Javier and the girls in turn.

"How old do you have to be to join?" Javier asked.

Kate frowned, but wasn't caught off guard by the question.

"Much older than you, buddy," Jake said.

"About my age," Timothy said proudly. He looked at Tasha to make sure she was listening. "I'll be joining up soon."

Jenny tossed the dogs a piece of food from the table.

"I saw that," Kate said, not raising her eyes.

"But dad says…" Jenny began to say.

"His rules at his house, my rules at mine," Kate responded flatly.

"Okay, sorry," Jenny said, bowing her head slightly.

Kate didn't like being harsh but, in a way, she had become a second mom to the girls over the past decade since they lost their mother at Fort Bragg. Horn was a good dad, but there was no denying he carried with him a certain gruffness and wasn't a man of high formality.

And Kate was intent on teaching the kids manners.

"This is really good," Tasha said, smiling as she went to take another bite.

"Sure is," Jenny agreed.

Javier nodded, his long hair falling over an eye. He brushed it away. "My mom is the best cook."

"It beats the pants off the potatoes and beans my dad makes," Timothy said.

Jake laughed. "Never said I was a good cook."

A wild wind blew, and tree branches scraped against the house.

Jenny's eyes went wide and Tasha seemed to tense up at the sound of scratching branches on the window. Timothy reached for her hand. Kate could practically feel the temperature drop around the trio.

They were frozen in fear.

Those scratches along the roof, the wind rustling against the house all could be mistaken for the telltale claws of Variants on the hunt.

Eight years and still the teenagers were haunted by the memories of the slaughter and carnage they'd survived.

Javier looked between them, one eyebrow raised like he didn't quite get why they were so scared. Unlike them, he had been born after the war. He'd been protected from the atrocities they'd borne witness to.

"It's okay," Kate said. "Just the wind."

"I know." Kate could tell the girl was starting to relax again. "Every time, in my head, I tell myself that's all it is. But I can't help thinking that maybe this time it's different. Maybe this time it's a Variant again."

"We're safe here," Kate said. "Don't worry."

"It's hard not to worry." Jenny looked to Kate as she continued. "They teach us about the war in school. I can't help thinking that it might happen again."

"I won't ever let anything happen to you kids," Jake added confidently.

"All I know is that if a Variant does show up here, I'm going to skin the ugly bastard," Javier said, gripping his fork and knife tightly like they were weapons.

"Javier Riley, what did I tell you about that language?"

"If dad and Big Horn can cuss, why can't I?" Javier asked. "I'm going to be a soldier like them, so I got to act like one."

Kate looked hard at him, not giving the boy an inch. The boy was a warrior in the making, that much was sure. She supposed it was inevitable growing up in a household like his and surrounded by a community that had fought tooth and nail to establish itself, but that didn't mean she wanted that future for her son.

"You have a long time to figure out what you want to be." A small smile played on Kate's lips. "Maybe a scientist or a doctor…"

"A soldier," Javier said firmly.

"You have a long time to decide. Either way, no cussing. Especially at the dinner table."

"Fine. Sorry."

She tried not to think about her son following in her husband's footsteps as they continued eating. Javier idolized his father in every way, even growing out his hair and insisting it be as long as his dad's.

The boy finished another bite and added, "I still want to protect people and kill the monsters."

"It's not just soldiers or policemen that protect us," Jake said. "Those doctors and scientists your mom mentioned are even more important. Heck, you can easily find another guy on the street that can learn to stand in a tower like me."

Jake tapped his temple. "But if you've got half the smarts your mom does, you could grow up to be one amazing scientist who saves more lives than I could ever hope to with my rifle."

Kate smiled at the police officer. She appreciated the support in encouraging Javier to think of a different career. Of course, her own career as a scientist hadn't exactly been free from danger.

"So, what happened at school today?" Kate asked, changing the subject.

Timothy was studying the themes and ideas in *1984*. Tasha and Jenny had both taken a math test, and Javier was reading *The Boxcar Children,* which Kate remembered fondly from her own childhood. Knowing they were all getting to have a childhood was a victory in everything they had fought to achieve. Everything they had once taken for granted, and now had worked so hard to earn back.

Peaceful moments like this, when no one was a soldier or scientist or survivor. They were just family and friends, enjoying life, not worrying about a monster hunting them or where their next meal would come from.

It seemed almost like a joke when the distant call of an air-raid siren blared, shattering any illusion that moments of peace were anything but ephemeral now. Spark jumped to his feet, and Ginger's tail curled between her legs.

"What is that?" Javier asked, slowing standing.

Timothy looked at his dad who rose from the table. Tasha and Jenny, too, knew exactly what it was and were already grabbing the dogs to get them ready to move.

"Javier, get the bug-out-bags," Kate said.

"I'm going back to my place to get ours," Jake said. "Grabbing a couple extra weapons, too."

Javier hurried out of the kitchen and ran to the bedroom while the officer left with Timothy. Kate went to the office and grabbed her Glock from the safe. Then she unlocked the cabinet and pulled out an AR-15 and a bag full of magazines.

This was yet another harsh fact of reality. Emergency preparedness began as soon as Javier could walk. The community ran drills all the time, but those were always preceded with an announcement telling everyone it was just a drill.

There had been no warning about the sirens, which told her it was either a surprise test or it was real.

She wasn't taking any chances. Palming a magazine into the AR-15, she then pulled the slide to chamber a round and confirmed the safety was still on.

"Follow me," Kate said in her calmest voice. The girls secured a leash around each dog's collar and took the Shepherds to the front room. Javier was there with the bags.

"I got yours, too, mom," he said.

Kate put her bag over her back, doing her best to remain composed.

Act normal, and the kids will follow your lead, she thought to herself.

"We need to get to the shelter," Kate said.

Javier slipped his hand into her free one and they walked out the front door, greeted by the wail of the air-raid sirens. All along the street, their neighbors poured out of their houses and headed toward the shelter.

Javier held out his free hand to Jenny. She took it, and kept her other hand wrapped in Tasha's. Together, they hurried down the street, following the flow of the crowd. Familiar faces joined them along the way.

Like Donna and her son Bo, the mother and son that Beckham's team had rescued during the war. The boy had looked scraggly and weak when she'd first met him. Since then, he'd grown into a young man with linebacker shoulders and tree trunk calves. Timothy and Jake ran to catch up, both armed with rifles and handguns. The duo ushered people toward the shelter.

"Jake! Any idea what's going on?" Kate called out.

"Something about a blast in Portland," he replied.

"Good Lord," she said.

Kate pushed onward. The scenario felt all too familiar, harkening back to those days when Beckham and Horn were off on some mission and disaster struck at home. Every time the Variants or ROT had attacked, it felt like it could be the end of her time here on Earth.

But this time, with the girls and Javier by her side, she felt they had so much more to lose. They continued down the road in an orderly fashion until the distant pop of gunfire shattered the night. Jenny shrieked, and Javier pulled on Kate's elbow, turning to look toward Portland, Maine.

Another distant explosion bloomed into the night.

The sight of the fireball chilled Kate to her core.

"Run!" someone yelled.

Screams came from all directions and, for the first time in years, the peace on Peaks Island was washed away like a sand castle under the rising tide.

— 5 —

Voices chimed outside of Ringgold's office in the PEOC. Military officers conferred in trenchant whispers and gruff commands.

"Turkey River isn't the only outpost that has gone dark," said President Ringgold. The tremor in her voice caught Beckham off guard almost as much as the news.

"Who else was hit?" Horn asked before Beckham could speak.

Ringgold tapped on one of the monitors on the conference room table, pointing at an old map of the United States. "Outpost Rapid City, South Dakota just went offline and we had almost zero communications before we lost contact."

"That's right on the border of the frontier with the west," Horn said.

Beckham narrowed his eyes at the President. This had to be some sort of a sick joke or perhaps a glitch in communications.

How could two outposts simply go dark?

He thought of their families on Peaks Island. A tingle of worry threaded through his nerves. He simply didn't want to believe that these outposts going dark was because of something widespread.

Something nefarious.

"We're not sure what's happening out there," Ringgold said.

She let out an uncharacteristic sigh and then stiffened. Beckham watched her come back to life, seeming to summon the strength that had gotten her through years of hardship, battles, and war.

"I'll meet you two in the situation room, shortly," she said. "I need to make some calls."

Beckham and Horn both filed into the small conference room in the PEOC. Of all the places in the world, Beckham never thought he would end up in the situation room again.

The white walls were covered with the pictures of former Presidents and a large American flag. This place was normally occupied by Four Star Generals, the Joint Chiefs, POTUS, VPOTUS, the NSA advisor, and the executive cabinet.

Now it was close to empty.

Brigadier General Lucas Barnes was hunched over a laptop near the head of the table, squinting at the screen, his glasses propped up in his gray hair. He glanced up with dark brown eyes that matched the color of his skin and nodded at Beckham. The sixty-year-old General was overseeing the mission to Outpost Turkey River and was in constant communication with General Noah Souza, the Commander of the Special Operations Command (SOCOM).

Beckham recalled the day they had moved SOCOM from MacDill Air Force Base to the Zumwalt Class Destroyer launched shortly before the Hemorrhage Virus ravaged the world. It had been recommissioned as the USS *George Johnson* to honor the Vice President that was killed not far from where they all sat right now.

Across from the Brigadier General was National Security Advisor Ben Nelson, wearing his staple red tie.

He ruffled through a briefing. Vice President Dan Lemke sat at the opposite end with his Chief of Staff, Elizabeth Cortez, behind him.

Ringgold's Chief of Staff, James Soprano, rested his back against a wall, gripping a folder under his arms.

"Looks like you've been hitting the gym," Beckham said to ease the tension.

Soprano smiled. "When you've got a free personal trainer who doesn't let you skip a day, these things happen," he said, jerking his chin at Cortez.

Her face broke into a grin. "You skip plenty of days."

Cortez gestured to two of the empty seats where nametags had been set out for Beckham and Horn. They sat in their respective seats. Cortez continued to stand, glancing occasionally at the door. Even as she stood, she continued tapping her right foot against the floor.

The door opened and President Ringgold stepped in, prompting General Barnes to stand and offer her his chair in front of the laptop.

"That's okay. You sit, General," she said politely. "I'll take my usual spot."

Ringgold sat next to Lemke. Soprano handed her a folder before retreating back to his spot at the wall.

"What's our status?" Ringgold asked.

"We have SEAL Teams 2 and 3 deployed in Operation Snake, with Delta Force Team Ghost on standby," Barnes said in his gruff voice. "Ghost just tracked down and killed an Alpha at Ellicott City. Saved a prisoner too."

"That's our boy, Fitz," Horn said.

Beckham had a feeling Ghost wasn't going to get much downtime to celebrate the small victory. The SEAL Teams were both filled with talented men, but many of them were new and lacked the experience that Fitz and his team had under their belts. He wouldn't be surprised if Ghost was called off standby and deployed in the operation.

"Turkey River went offline approximately twenty-one hours ago and, so far, drone footage has not given us much to go by," Barnes continued. "SEAL Team 2 will land in approximately ten minutes, but SEAL Team 3 will take approximately one hour to reach Outpost Rapid City."

"And the emergency alert system?" Ringgold asked.

"Activated as soon as we got word about Rapid City," said Nelson. "Every outpost and city in the safe zones will be on lock down until we figure out what's going on."

Beckham thought of his family back at the outpost in Portland. He wished he had the chance to tell Kate this was coming so it didn't scare Javier or Tasha and Jenny.

"Bringing up footage from SEAL Team 2," Barnes said. He pushed his headset back into position, talking to General Souza.

The wall-mounted monitor fired to life, splitting into a dozen boxes from the helmet-mounted cams of the SEALs.

"Here we go," Barnes said. "SEAL Team 2 is one minute out from the LZ."

"Do we have any new drone footage?" Lemke asked. He flipped through his briefing folder. "These images make it seem like the entire outpost just vanished. Three hundred people don't just—"

"Three hundred and four," Ringgold corrected.

"Yes, that's correct," Barnes said. "Three hundred and four people don't just vanish."

The Black Hawk carrying SEAL Team 2 crossed over a patchwork of crops and lowered into the compound. The pilots set down in an open area, disgorging the SEALs into the darkness of the night. Their cameras with night vision goggles provided a green-hued view of the agricultural community as the team split up to search for the residents.

Beckham scanned the screens one by one, looking for any sign of bodies or blood or a battle. Anything to indicate what had happened. But all he saw were empty buildings. A school. The post office. Two trading posts. The barracks and offices.

All empty.

Another team moved to the barns and livestock pens located just outside the walls of the main compound. A series of ribbon wire fences looked intact but several of the SEALs stopped at the edge to look through the chain links.

"We got something," Barnes reported, looking up.

He put a palm over his headset to listen.

Beckham strained to see, but there was definitely something on the other side of the fences. Several craters dotted the terrain from what must have been exploded land mines.

"They found the remains of several soldiers, Madam President," Barnes reported. "They're on screen seven."

Beckham was already looking at that screen. The SEAL directed his helmet cam at a crater, roving it back and forth before stopping on what looked a lot like mangled human limbs and a torso.

"The militia soldiers there got caught in the minefields, but not Variants?" Nelson asked.

"Actually, the SEALs think the Variants tossed the

soldiers in the minefields," Lemke said. "There were claw marks on the corpses and tracks indicating such."

"Something doesn't add up here," Nelson said. "The beasts aren't normally that smart."

"Have the other SEALs found anything else?" Ringgold asked.

"Negative, Madam President," Barnes said. "Not a single body."

"What about the livestock?" Beckham asked.

Barnes asked over the comms, and came back with an answer a moment later.

"Gone," he said. "No bodies. No bones."

Beckham used his prosthetic hand to brush the hair back into place on his head, his new nervous tick. Something about it calmed him and helped him think. But it didn't help him make sense of what he was seeing on the screens.

"The Variants took all of them without even stopping for a snack?" Nelson asked. "I've rarely heard of monsters with that kind of self-control."

"You're right," Horn said, speaking up for the first time. "Normal Variants wouldn't do this."

"We must be looking at some kind of twisted Alpha," Beckham said. "Maybe even something else leading them, keeping them under control."

"And there's only one team that can track down whatever—or whoever—is responsible," Horn said.

He glanced at Beckham who agreed with his friend.

"If SEAL Team 2 doesn't come back with anything else, I'd highly recommend deploying Team Ghost," Beckham said. "They have experience with all kinds of Alphas. If anyone can get to the bottom of this, it's them."

Barnes looked to the President for her approval, and she gave it with a nod. She got up from her chair and walked over to the screen as SEAL Team 2 continued the search.

"Yes…" Barnes said into his headset. His features suddenly darkened, and he squinted so hard his forehead turned into a valley of wrinkles. "What… Another one?" he said.

Ringgold turned to look at the General. "What's wrong?" she asked.

Barnes swallowed, his Adam's apple bobbing. "Madam President, General Souza just got word that Outpost New Boston in Massachusetts is reporting a raider attack."

He paused and put his hand over his headset again to listen.

"Christ," Barnes grumbled. "Outpost Portland, Maine, is also under attack."

Beckham's veins turned to ice. He shot out of his chair. "What? How is that possible?"

Images of Kate and the children slammed through his mind.

"We have to get home," Horn said, already moving toward the door.

Beckham turned to follow Horn, then stopped.

A dozen thoughts spun through his mind.

He wanted to believe that people like his neighbor Jake could defend the island and that the safe zone's defenses were prepared for something like this. But between the images they'd just seen of Outpost Turkey River and the reports coming in from other outposts, reality was much more grim.

He couldn't help but think these events were connected.

Were they dealing with a massive coordinated Variant *and* human threat for the first time since the end of the war?

Beckham hesitated. He needed to know more before bailing.

"Boss, come on," Horn urged.

"Hold up," Beckham shot back. He looked to Barnes. "What does General Souza know so far about Portland?"

"Only that they called in an SOS sparked by a raid," replied the General.

"Reed, we can't stay here." The muscles in Horn's jaw moved as he gritted his teeth. "Got to get back there, man."

"Permission to leave, Madam President," Beckham said.

"Get a chopper fired up," Ringgold said to Soprano. The COS rushed through the door, already conveying the president's order to someone outside the situation room.

Beckham and Horn followed her out, Ringgold shadowing them. She stopped just outside. The pain in her features told Beckham she felt partly responsible for this.

But this wasn't her fault.

She had done everything she could to rebuild and protect the country, and Beckham couldn't sit idly by any longer in retirement on an island away from the fight.

It was time to get back into the game.

If it's not already too late, he thought coldly.

***

The custom blue jet circled over S.M. Fischer's ranch and the oil fields in Northern Texas, about ninety miles north of Amarillo. Fischer Fields, his business and his empire. This was home. Always had been, always would be. Passed down through his family, back during the prewar days, it had reached values in the hundreds of millions of dollars.

His wife had loved it here. She had always dreamed of the day he would retire. Enjoying riding horses together along the creeks and trails cutting through their property and ending the days on their porch enjoying the glory of a Texas sunset. But it was not to be.

She had passed from cancer two months before the Hemorrhage Virus.

Now it looked like Fischer would never retire. While he missed her, he was almost glad it had happened before the chaos. If she had survived any longer, she would have risked being torn to pieces or turned into one of those beasts. To Fischer, that was a far worse fate.

Her death to cancer hadn't exactly been peaceful, but at least he had been there holding her hand while she passed in her sleep.

God, did he miss her.

He drowned out the memories by finishing his third beer while the pilots waited for the all clear to land. Another Variant attack had kept them in the sky, and Fischer was anxious to get on the ground.

At ten thousand feet, he couldn't see much of his forty thousand acres of land, especially at night. But in the blanket of darkness below, several geysers of orange flames punctuated the black, spewing columns of smoke that reflected the light of the fire.

Fischer's gut twisted painfully. He was no stranger to a hellish sight like that.

"Oil well fires! What in the Sam Hill is happening

down there?" Fischer asked.

The two bodyguards that had accompanied him to the Greenbrier sat in leather chairs across the cabin. Tran and Chase had both been with Fischer since the war and had never failed in protecting him.

Chase disappeared into the cockpit for a moment, then reemerged. "Sounds like there have been Variant attacks on multiple wells. They went after the engineers again, and our teams are having a hard time capping the wells."

"Second time in a month," Fischer said, finishing his comment with a blue streak of curses. He tried to be a gentleman in most cases but, damn, this was pissing him off.

Using a bottle opener, he twisted off the cap of another beer, wishing it was the head of a Variant. He took a long swig and studied the bottle—another product made at his ranch just like the juicy hunk of steak in front of him.

This hadn't been the first attack on his ranch, and he knew better than to think it would be the last. The Variants were getting more brazen in their efforts.

He was getting tired of losing men and, more importantly, money.

Tipping back the bottle, he took another long swig and then put the bottle down. He caught Tran giving Chase a knowing look. They were right. He should have his senses together.

Three beers gave him a buzz, but anything more could be a detriment to decision making. He looked to Chase and said, "Tell the pilots I want on the ground as soon as fucking possible."

The thin African American man stood again and made

his way back into the cockpit. Tran swiveled his leather chair to look out the window.

"These attacks have to end," Fischer grumbled. "We're wasting time capping oil wells when we should be drawing oil up. These filthy, diseased animals are costing us too damn much."

Tran turned away from the window to face his boss. "I thought President Ringgold was going to send more boots to protect the fields."

"She did, but I don't need two dozen greenhorns." Fischer took another swallow of his beer. He knew he shouldn't, but he was too damn mad. "I need an army to clean the varmints out once and for all. Perhaps General Cornelius will make me an offer I can't refuse."

Tran simply nodded, and Fischer considered asking him his opinion. Most men in his position wouldn't bother listening to hired muscle or soldiers. But Fischer had built his empire by analyzing the opinions of many, from the engineers that worked on the wells to the president of the country.

So far, those opinions weren't helping much.

"Who do you support?" Fischer asked.

Tran shifted uneasily in his chair, apparently caught off guard by the sudden change in topic. Fischer had seen him less nervous when facing Variants.

"It's okay, son, you can talk to me freely," Fischer assured Tran.

"I don't support nuking the cities, sir, but I do support eliminating the Variant threat, especially down there. These attacks are growing more brazen, and I fear the creatures are starting to get stronger instead of weaker."

"Valid assessment," Fischer said. He looked back down at his steak. It was getting cold, and he wasn't going to waste a good sirloin. Meat of this quality was a luxury that only a few men in this country could afford.

While the plane continued to circle, he cut into the seared meat. The red inside practically bled. He took a bit of the rare steak and relished the taste like the Variants might savor the taste of human flesh.

Chase returned from the cockpit. "Sir, we need to wait a few more minutes for teams to secure the tarmac for our landing," he reported. "Apparently, one of those Variant packs is near your ranch."

"What's so damn hard about clearing out two little packs?" Fischer said.

"They're both camouflaged," Chase replied. "Our teams are finding it more difficult than usual to track them down. We've deployed dogs and hunter-killer teams, though. Shouldn't be much longer."

Fischer put his fork down, his appetite ruined. He wiped food out of his bristly mustache with a napkin, and prepared for landing.

Ten minutes later they had the all clear, and the jet began its descent. Fischer looked out his window to search for the flames he saw earlier. Sure enough, the well fires still burned, the deep stores of oil being lapped up by tongues of fire.

The flames might as well have been burning dollar bills.

But how could a Variant start a fire? They had attacked the wells plenty of times, but the wells had never burned like this. Not two at once.

He doubted common Variants had the smarts for starting fires like that. Maybe his men had really screwed the pooch on this one. Or maybe it was something else.

As the jet lowered toward the tarmac, Fischer thought

of his meeting with President Ringgold. She had promised him more men to patrol the oil fields. But a handful more of guards wasn't going to stop the beasts.

When your cattle were being stalked by a pack of wolves, it wasn't enough to wait around at night in hopes you might scare them from dragging a cow away.

No, you went straight to the source. Straight to the wolf's den. You slaughtered every one of them so not a damn one of those dogs came back to bother you or your cattle.

What he needed was an army of hunters. Someone who could be on the offense instead of pressed against the ropes the whole time.

This had to end.

The tires touched down with a jolt. As they slowed, Tran and Chase both unbuckled and moved to the cabinets to grab their rifles. They palmed in magazines, pulled back the bolts to chamber a round, and then advanced to the door.

One of the pilots stepped out of the cabin.

"Sir, your teams have taken down one pack and captured what we think is an Alpha…" he said.

Just as Fischer thought. More than just common Variants.

"It's alive, sir, but barely," the piloted continued.

"Bring it to the tarmac," Fischer said. "I want to see this ugly son of a bitch that's been terrorizing my fields."

"Sir, I'd highly advise against that," Chase replied.

"This is an Alpha," Tran reminded Fischer. "They're extremely dangerous even when injured."

"I know what it is," Fischer shot back. "I want to see it, and I want to finish it off myself."

"Okay, sir," Tran said with a shrug. "But please stay

here until we can secure the area."

Chase opened the cabin door and walked down a ramp to the tarmac. Tran remained in the opening, rifle shouldered.

Fischer pulled out his handgun, his father's old chrome .357. He'd added a new engraving to the barrel. *Monster Killer.*

Maybe it was a little corny, but Fischer wasn't one to mince words. *Monster Killer* was what the weapon was, and killing a monster was what he was about to do.

Pulling back the hammer with a click, he prepared to meet the beast terrorizing his men and fields tonight. Not some pesky, diseased beast, but the *king* of the pack.

A few minutes later, Chase returned with his rifle cradled. "Okay, sir, it's safe to come out."

Fischer followed his men down the ramp. Several Humvees and multiple pickup trucks were parked on the tarmac with the red, double F logo of his oil company.

Soldiers in the mounted gun turrets of the Humvees directed spotlights on the pale, bloody flesh of the biggest Variant Fischer had ever seen. The creature was lying inside a razor wire net, hardly moving.

A dozen men wearing cowboy hats and holding rifles stood guarding the beast. Six German Shepherds barked viciously, their maws dripping saliva.

"Shut them up," Fischer ordered. He hesitated as he approached the monster. The beast was unconscious from what he could tell, both eyelids closed.

"It took a lot of damage before passing out," one of the soldiers said. "Big guy like this, we thought you'd want to see what was responsible for the mess out there. Surprised it's not dead yet."

"But no telling when it's going to wake up," another said.

"It killed four of our men," the first man added. He dipped his cowboy hat at Fischer and spat a hunk of tobacco on the pavement. "Quicker you kill it, the better, sir."

Fischer walked past the man, doing his best to hide his fear of the monster. Chase and Tran both kept near his side with their rifles aimed at the Alpha.

"Don't get too close," Tran warned.

Fischer stopped five feet away from the naked creature.

A wart-covered nose sucked in air, and a scab-covered back rose up and down in long, deep breaths. Crackling came from the lungs as fluid filled them.

He took another step closer, watching the eyes to make sure they didn't open. Then he bent down to study the demon.

Wormy lips hung off a chin that was only connected to the face by strands of gristle. Blood flowed out of small holes in the upper cheek from shotgun pellets.

"My Lord in Heaven," Fischer muttered.

He stood and moved around to check the other injuries. A muscular arm was shredded at the elbow, and a hole the size of an orange gushed blood out of its back. Bullet holes pocked the creature's torso, blood seeping out.

Fischer knew that the Alpha, like all Variants, had remarkable healing capabilities due to the epigenetic changes of the chemical nanoparticles in its bloodstream, but it would take a lot to come back from these injuries, and Fischer wasn't going to give it a chance.

He aimed his .357 at the beast's head.

An eyelid flicked open, a reptilian eye flitting toward Fischer. He stumbled backward as its upper lip drew back to reveal jagged, yellow teeth. The shredded chin and jaw hung loose, a strand of gristle snapping as it opened its mouth wider.

"Kill it," Chase said.

Fischer pulled the trigger, the gunshot piercing the night. The round broke through bone right below the yellow eye.

But the creature didn't die.

A screech of rage followed, piercing Fischer's ears. He glared at the monster in shock as blood burst from the hole in its face.

The Alpha roared and twisted violently under the razor wire, opening up cuts across its entire body, and prompting all of the men with rifles to step back.

The dogs let out guttural barks.

"Jesus Christ," Fischer said. He aimed, held the gun steady, and fired a bullet into the eye. It popped, exploding and leaking blood and goo.

Still, the beast continued to screech.

"Shoot it," Fischer said, gesturing to the soldiers and other men around him. "Open fire!"

A hail of gunfire lanced into the monster, punching through muscular flesh and bone. The monster jerked and twitched in violent fits as the rounds pummeled its body.

Fischer finally held up a hand.

"Hold your fire!" he yelled.

The men lowered their rifles, but the dogs continued to go crazy, barking and pulling on their leashes. The creature let out a final gruesome death rattle, and then went limp, blood pooling from its lacerated flesh.

Although Fischer wanted to think this was the last of his Variant problems, he knew it wasn't. Kill one pack of wolves, another took their place.

There would be more beasts, more Alphas.

Only one thing would end the threat.

"Get that thing out of here," Fischer ordered. He holstered his gun and jerked his chin for Tran and Chase to follow him over to a vehicle to take him to his ranch. He took shotgun and shut the door, watching as his men dragged the monster off the tarmac.

It took ten of them to get it into the back of a pickup truck.

This wasn't going to stop, not with this dead Alpha, and not with the next one either. Fischer Fields needed an army, and Fischer had a feeling there was only one person that could give him the resources he needed.

He rode home in silence, thinking of his upcoming meeting with Cornelius. He was more anxious than ever to hear what the presidential candidate had to offer in return for his support.

— 6 —

"Approaching LZ," reported the pilot.

Fitz tried to stay focused looking out the open side door of the Black Hawk as they circled over Outpost Turkey River. A full moon hung like a gleaming silver disc over the darkened fields. Cloud cover to the west threatened to block out the glow.

The entire team was already on edge after learning about the attack on Portland, Maine, and several other outposts. Having a bit of moonlight to navigate with would help them see, but it wouldn't make the ache go away. People he knew and cared for were in harm's way, and Fitz may as well have been on the other side of the planet.

This wasn't the first time Fitz had been deployed while his friends were in danger, and there wasn't anything he could do about it. The orders came from POTUS.

He pushed aside his worries and patted his helmet to get back in the game.

"All it takes is all you got, baby," Lincoln said.

Fitz nodded back. "Damn right."

"Wish I could have met Sergeant Garcia," said Mendez. "Dude sounded like one hell of an hombre."

"One of the best Marines I ever met," Fitz said.

Ace adjusted the strap on his modified mag-fed Mossberg 500. Metallic clinks rang out as the rest of

Ghost checked over their suppressed M4A1s, inserting magazines and ensuring everything was in working order. A crew chief manned the M240, sweeping the barrel back and forth over the dark terrain.

From what Fitz could see with his night vision goggles, the area was abandoned just like the SEAL team had reported. That was no surprise. SEALs didn't make mistakes.

Neither did Team Ghost.

The chopper passed over the minefield pockmarked with craters from exploded mines. Hunks of a body remained scattered on the darkened earth.

But where the hell was everyone else?

The other people hadn't just disappeared into thin air. Team Ghost had to figure out what the SEAL team had missed.

One thing was for certain, the Variants responsible for this attack were far more sophisticated and far more dangerous than the Alpha they had just taken down in Ellicott City.

"I've got a really bad feeling about this," Fitz said staring out the window.

Rico chewed on a fresh piece of gum. "Tell me about it."

"Good thing we got Dohi," Mendez said.

Dohi remained silent, his helmet down as he meditated.

Ace patted his belly. "Anyone else hungry? Maybe we will find some food down there."

"Chances are better you will end up food if you don't focus," Lincoln said.

"He'd be one hell of a meal," Mendez laughed.

"Cut the shit," Fitz said. "There were three hundred

people living there, and aside from some poor, torn-apart soldiers we have no idea what happened to them, or where they went."

"Maybe it's tied to those raiders that have been hitting the other outposts," Rico suggested. "Could be some ex-military dudes that know how to cover their trail."

"Cover a trail from SEALs?" Lincoln said with a shake. "I doubt it."

"I'll find them," Dohi finally looked up, eyes smoldering.

The rest of the team simply stared at him and then Lincoln burst into his contagious laugh.

"Dude, that was creepy." Lincoln continued laughing for a few seconds.

"Jesus." Fitz reached over and smacked Lincoln on the side of his helmet.

"Sorry, man," Lincoln said.

Mendez chuckled under his breath, and when they had finally finished, Fitz handed out orders.

"I've got Alpha with Ace and Lincoln. We'll search the interior of the outpost," he said. "Rico is leading Bravo with Dohi and Mendez on the perimeter."

After confirming Lincoln and Mendez were done goofing off, Fitz told the pilots they were good to go. The chopper descended, kicking up waves in the dried grass in the middle of a field inside the outpost's perimeter fences.

"All it takes is all you got, Ghost," Fitz said.

The wheels of the Black Hawk hit the ground with a jolt.

"Ace, you're on point," Fitz said. "Lincoln, rearguard."

Ace hopped out of the chopper first, his combat shotgun pressed tightly against his shoulder. Fitz followed with Lincoln close behind. He crept forward at a crouch, roving his rifle over the buildings at the edge of the field.

An eerie shiver crept down his spine. He couldn't attribute the feeling to just the rotor wash hitting his back as Bravo exited the chopper next. It felt like he was being watched from the many windows of the office building and school across the field.

Fitz waved at Rico, and she smiled back, her way of saying she loved him without words.

I love you too, Jeni.

Dohi led her and Mendez out the front gate, past the guard towers. It never got easier fighting with her, and every mission Fitz worried about losing her, but they had both decided long ago to stay together. Of course, neither one of them wanted to give up serving on Team Ghost either.

There wasn't anywhere he would rather be.

The chopper lifted back into the sky, leaving Team Ghost alone.

Fitz flashed hand signals for the team to spread out. He doubted the Variants had stuck around for an ambush, especially after the SEALs had sifted through the base. But with the monsters, he had come to expect the unexpected.

Soon the thrum of rotor blades evaporated into the whispers of wind gusts tickling through the trees scattered through the outpost. Somewhere a wind chime tinkled, letting out a ghostly metallic ring.

The place looked like an idyllic town just like where Beckham and Kate lived on Peaks Island. The kind of place where your neighbor always had your back, whether you needed help with a flat tire or to borrow some sugar.

The lived-in animal odor of the barns drifted toward them, but there was no more livestock to be found, just as the SEALs had reported.

They pushed toward the town and stopped outside a one-story brick building with a sign out front that said 'TOWN HALL.' Ace held up his fist as they approached.

Dried blood spray appeared like dark shadows through Fitz's night vision goggles, covering the brick walls and the sidewalk. He noticed something else in the torn-up lawn.

Next to spent shells and bullet casings were a scattered array of boot prints in the soil. Those seemed to belong to the people caught mostly unaware, barely able to defend themselves.

And beside those marks were long, even gouges in the soil. Talon-marks. The SEAL teams had reported similar findings throughout the town; blood stains and claw and talon marks were everywhere. But strangely, the SEALs hadn't found any talon marks or blood outside of the outpost's perimeter where Bravo was searching.

Fitz hoped Dohi could clear up that mystery.

Ace looked back at Fitz, waiting for his next command. Fitz held up a finger, asking him to wait. Something in the air had caught his attention. He looked up at the dark sky, sniffing the wind.

He picked up the faintest odor of rotten fruit. Not so strong as when a Variant was nearby, but strong enough he didn't discount it. Or maybe the smell was nothing but Fitz's mind playing tricks on him, priming him for what he expected to encounter.

He looked back at Lincoln and pointed at his nose. Lincoln seemed to understand the gesture, pausing and taking a big whiff before he gave Fitz a nod.

So I'm not crazy.

Where the hell was this smell coming from?

Fitz gestured for Ace to proceed to the open door of the town hall. The wooden door was hanging off a single hinge, flapping in the wind. Alpha team gathered around the front entrance. Fitz held his breath, listening for sounds from inside.

Nothing.

Fitz gestured for Ace to go in. He went afterward, with Lincoln watching their backs. They found themselves in a wide room with folding chairs scattered across a wooden floor.

At the front of the room was a table that had collapsed, legs broken. A handful of other seats were tossed about behind it. Long streaks of blood crossed the floor. Dark, crusted handprints marred the walls beside gaping holes punched into the drywall. Scratches along the floorboard showed clear marks where the Variants had been.

The single bathroom and a door leading to a kitchen told Fitz this place had served not just as a place for town meetings, but also a location for community gatherings.

They crept into the kitchen next. Flies clouded the room, buzzing relentlessly. On the counter lay a half-dozen opened glass jars reflecting the moonlight shifting in through the nearby window. A large mixing bowl was filled with the source of the smell—a putrid mix of rotten moldy fruit.

Fitz moved past the scattered pie tins and spilled cans of fruit preserves littering the floor. He noticed a knife on the ground with dried blood crusting the edge. Maybe a desperate, last-ditch weapon.

The three-man team advanced on to another house, and then the school, and finally an office building.

Every place showed some signs of struggle, but if they

ignored the blood, it was as if they'd walked into a town where people had just vanished doing their daily chores: baskets full of half-folded laundry and sinks with dishes still soaking in water.

Fitz cursed, trying to think outside of the box. They were basically doing the same thing the SEALs had already done.

He went back to the road to look for tire tracks, wondering if it was possible that collaborators working with the Variants had brought in large vehicles to ship these people somewhere.

But he didn't see any major tracks. He shook his head. No way they would have missed something that obvious, anyway.

Ace led them toward a storehouse in the center of town when the sound of crunching glass broke over the wind chimes.

Fitz instinctively ducked low, signaling for Ace and Lincoln to do the same. They took cover against the wall of the warehouse.

Another crunch came. It could have been a wild animal. Maybe a raccoon slinking through garbage. But if it wasn't...

The sound came from behind a house across the street. He signaled for Ace to take one side while Fitz and Lincoln took the other.

They rushed over to the house, running as quietly as they could, then rounded the corner. He leveled his rifle, ready to squeeze off a burst into the wart-covered face of a beast, but there was nothing except for a patio with broken pots spilling dirt and plants positioned across the rail.

Only a few fragments of glass remained in the sliding

doors, gleaming in the moonlight, making them look like the maw of some angry monster.

Ace appeared on the opposite side, and Fitz motioned for him to go inside the house. Lincoln and Fitz went through the broken sliding door next.

Toys were scattered over the floor, and a playpen, torn apart, lay in the corner. Bloodstains covered the carpet amid dried brown footprints that looked as if they'd belonged to Variants.

The living room opened up into a hall with toppled bookshelves. Ripped book pages fluttered in the breeze coursing through the place.

At the end of the hall, broken windows opened to the view of the trees outside. Drapes danced along the frame.

He went to turn when something or someone jumped through one of the windows.

Fitz gave Ace the go ahead with a nod, and all three of them stormed over the trampled books and fallen bookshelves, charging down the hall, then leaping out the window back onto the lawn.

Gravel on the driveway crunched under Fitz's blades as he pursued.

Ahead of them, the contact had just disappeared around the side of another house. Fitz pumped harder, rocketing forward. He made it to the backyard, getting a good glimpse of his target for the first time.

It was a man, covered in dirty, ragged, blood-stained clothes.

A rifle hung over his back.

He looked like he might be a raider.

"Stop!" Fitz said, shouldering his rifle. "Stop, or I'll shoot!"

The man kept running.

Fitz gritted his teeth. The last thing he wanted to do was actually kill what might be their only clue.

The man looked over his shoulder, then started to run faster as Fitz took off after him. Lincoln had already sprinted down the sidewalk, keeping out of sight. The athletic soldier quickly caught up and tackled their contact like a linebacker.

A crunch sounded, followed by a muffled grunt.

Fitz slowed his pace and aimed his rifle as Lincoln wrestled the guy to his back.

"No!" the man yelled. "Let me go!"

"Who are you?" Fitz said.

The man snarled, baring coffee-stained teeth, but they were all intact, which told Fitz this guy was probably not a collaborator.

"I asked you a question," Fitz said standing over the man.

He signaled to Ace who helped Lincoln get the guy upright. Dried mud covered nearly every inch of the guy's face, including an eye. But even through the grit, Fitz could see the deep wrinkles carved into the man's skin.

No matter how many times Fitz demanded that the old guy tell him who he was, he got nothing but incoherent babbling.

Exasperated, Fitz tried another tactic. "My name is Joe Fitzpatrick and I'm with Delta Force Team Ghost. We're here to figure out what happened and to help any survivors."

That seemed to snap the man out of his fugue. He looked down at the ground. "I'm a coward."

"What?" Fitz said.

"I am a soldier. A *good* soldier…"

Lincoln and Ace shot each other wary glances.

"You were posted here?" Fitz asked, flipping up his NVGs. "Were you defending the outpost against the attack?"

Now the wheels seemed to be turning in the old man's head again, he lifted his head slightly at Fitz's shoulder where the Team Ghost patch was: a skull next to pistols emblazoned against black fabric.

"We never saw it coming," the man muttered.

Then he lifted his head fully to meet Fitz's gaze, one eye blinking through the mask of grit. It was then Fitz saw the mud covering half his face wasn't masking a second eye—the soldier only had one eye.

"I'm Cedric Long," he said. "I know Captain Beckham."

"Well, goddamn, ain't that something," Ace said.

Fitz vaguely remembered meeting the one-eyed soldier at the White House years ago, but this was not the man he remembered.

"I'm sorry," Cedric mumbled. "They came out of nowhere. They were just…there. All at once."

"How?" Fitz asked.

"I don't know," Cedric said, starting to rock. "I ran. I ran, and I didn't look back. Escaped with one other guy. But the beasts found us, too. Took him… and… and…"

He bit his bottom lip and started to shake. "I forced myself to come back the next day and that's when I saw them."

"Saw who?" Ace asked.

"The townspeople," Cedric whispered.

Fitz looked at Lincoln and Ace in turn.

"Are they alive?" Lincoln said.

Reaching forward, Fitz put a hand on Cedric's shoulder, but the man flinched and pulled away like he had been burned.

"It's okay," Fitz said. "I'm not going to hurt you, but you have to tell us what you saw. We need to know where everyone went."

Cedric's remaining eye glassed over as if reliving some horrifying memory.

"They were alive when I saw them," he choked. "But I think they had wished they weren't."

The CH-47 Chinook hit turbulence on the final stretch of sky to Portland, Maine. The vibrations through the bulkheads and howling wind didn't distract Beckham from his thoughts. He sat strapped in a seat next to Horn who seemed to be shouting every ten minutes over the comms.

"Do we have a SITREP?" Beckham had asked.

Each time the pilots would come back with a negative.

The grid at the outpost was down. No one was answering from the bunker where their families should have been. And even though the first transmissions reported raiders, the lack of communication since made Beckham fear it was a Variant attack, coordinated just like the others.

He pushed aside those morbid thoughts.

Kate and the others were alive, and they were safe in the bunker. They had to be. He could feel it in his bones.

His concern for his family occupied his thoughts, but he couldn't shake the soldier instincts in him. He continued to wonder if there was a coordinated human collaboration effort going on with the Variant forces outside of the safe zones. And whether it had something to do with the election.

Brutal memories flooded his mind of the Great War of Extinction, when Lieutenant Andrew Wood, the former Commander of ROT, had made a deal with the devil by infecting several SZTs with the Hemorrhage Virus.

But Beckham couldn't bring himself to believe General Cornelius would stoop so low to join forces with the Variants to win the presidency.

Cornelius wasn't Wood. Not even close. Beckham had met the man multiple times, and he loved his country. He just had a very different idea on how to protect it.

"ETA thirty mikes," reported one of the pilots.

Beckham and Horn watched the assault team as they made their final preparations. Ringgold had sent some of her best—a twelve-strong team of Army Rangers from the 75th Ranger Regiment who had been reassigned from Fort Benning and now posted near the White House. The men and women joining Beckham and Horn came from First Battalion, Alpha Company. They called themselves the Iron Hogs. From the stories Beckham had heard about them, they had more than earned that moniker, and he was glad to have them along.

Armed with suppressed M4A1s and equipped with night vision goggles (NVGs) they would have no problem taking down whoever or whatever was responsible for this attack.

Especially with the help of Captain Beckham and Master Sergeant Horn.

The retired Delta Force Operators were doing something they hadn't done in over a year—heading into battle.

The Rangers didn't glare at his prosthetics like he had experienced in the past with some greenhorns. They all knew who he was and how he had lost an arm and leg.

"Good to have you with us, Captain," said Lieutenant David Niven.

"Damn honor," the team Sergeant, a woman named

Candace Ruckley, agreed.

"Honor's mine," Beckham said. "And let's be clear: this is your mission. Your team, your orders. Horn and I are just glad to have you all along, especially since our families are down there."

"We'll do our best to keep them safe, Captain," Niven said.

Horn grumbled as he tried to loosen his vest. "Fucking thing doesn't fit."

"Too many beers," Beckham said, trying to cut the tension.

It worked for a split second and Horn grinned.

All trace of jocularity vanished as they made their final preps on approach to the island and outpost.

"We got multiple fires ahead," said Lieutenant Niven over the comms. "Still no contact with anyone on the ground. Making two passes to ensure we got a clear LZ."

"Check your gear, and check your buddy's gear," Ruckley said. "We're going in hot."

The Chinook sailed over the border of Outpost Portland. Two major fires raged in the heart of the historic downtown. Peaks Island, however, appeared dark on the horizon. No fires, or lights for that matter.

Horn palmed a box into his M249 and opened the feed tray cover to lay the belt in. Beckham loaded his M4A1 carbine. Then he checked his Sig Sauer.

"What's the OPORD, Lieutenant?" Beckham asked.

"I'm splitting us into two teams," Niven said. "I'll take Alpha Team to Portland. Sergeant Ruckley will take Bravo to Peaks Island."

Beckham nodded and clapped a hand on Horn's shoulder. The man was holding it together, but Beckham could tell worry was eating at him. Horn had suffered the

NICHOLAS SANSBURY SMITH & ANTHONY J. MELCHIORRI

loss of his wife at the beginning of the outbreak eight years ago, and now Beckham knew that same fear.

The chopper lowered over a park at the outpost and Niven hit the button for the rear loading ramp. The ramp hissed open, revealing the orange glow of distant fires. Alpha Team filed out into the night.

As soon as they were clear, the pilots pulled away.

Horn and Beckham stepped up to the open door on their final leg to the LZ on Peaks Island. He spotted the school where Kate taught classes below.

The Chinook headed for the eastern side of the island, between the forested area and the city. They set down in a field north of Brackett Ave with a slight jolt.

Beckham flipped his night vision goggles over his eyes, charged his M4, and was the first out of the troop hold. A wind swept into him, carrying the scent of smoke, but he didn't detect the sour smell of Variants.

The team fanned out across the field and most of them went prone while the chopper pulled away into the black sky. Beckham and Horn crouched down, scanning for hostiles. The wind died down, but the overgrown grass swayed in the breeze.

An eerie silence claimed the night, interrupted only by the sound of chirping bugs and a creaking of tree branches. There were no air raid sirens like he'd expected. They must have been cut. Their absence sent another chill of fear through him.

Ruckley flashed hand signals and the team moved out, hurrying down the side of the road to the bunker at the healthcare center in the middle of the island. She had studied the map well on the ride and knew exactly where she was going thanks to Beckham's guidance.

A transmission broke over the comms, and Beckham

slowed his pace.

"Bravo 1, this is Alpha 1, we've got mass casualties here," Niven reported. "Looks like a bomb went off. Over."

That explains the fires, Beckham thought. He looked toward the mainland where the flames continued licking the night.

"No sign of hostiles," Niven added.

"Copy that, Alpha 1," said Ruckley. "Negative on hostiles here, too. Over."

The team pushed on, moving into the outskirts of the residential area and deeper toward the more populated area. A cat darted across the road and into the brush, but the team didn't even flinch.

Ruckley cut through a backyard to Upper A Street, continuing diagonally toward Hermann Avenue. The group of Rangers moved across a dirt field and approached a broken-down abandoned house that the teenagers often used to drink and smoke cigarettes.

Horn had found Tasha here a few days ago with Timothy. A few weeks before, they had been caught doing the same thing at a rundown park maintenance building, forcing Horn to have a stern conversation with Jake Temper about their two kids.

Ruckley balled her fist. The team moved to cover and hunched down. Beckham did as ordered, but he was itching to move, and Horn was no different. The man stayed in a half crouch, ready to leap.

"Where the hell is everyone?" Horn whispered.

Beckham remained silent. Hopefully the answer was inside the bunker, which could fit the entire town's population of sixty-two. But in the seconds that passed, he started to worry they weren't going to find anyone—

that Peaks Island had suffered the same fate as Turkey River.

They waited another few beats to look for hostiles, and seeing none, Ruckley gave the signal to advance on the Healthcare Center.

Beckham and Horn ran along the shoulder of the road near the center of the pack of Rangers. They moved to the back entrance, finding it wide open, and the windows shattered.

Bullet holes marked the door and frame.

Ruckley again balled her first.

Horn didn't heed the command and went right in before she could stop him. Beckham followed his friend into the open door and moved into a hallway, checking his corner and running the wall behind Horn.

They cleared the entrance hall, and then moved to the stairwell that led to the basement where Kate's lab and the bunker had been built inside an old Cold War fallout shelter.

His heartbeat accelerated.

They took up position on either side of the doorway and exchanged a nod. Beckham saw Ruckley stalking down the hall with her rifle shouldered. He couldn't see her features, but knew she had to be pissed.

Horn had put the team at risk by charging forward.

But it was too late to back up now.

Beckham gave Horn a nod and moved into the stairwell.

A body lay at the bottom landing.

Horn directed his rifle at the man and moved slowly down the concrete steps. Beckham followed him down, his prosthetic blade clicking on a step.

"Jake?" Horn said, lowering his rifle.

He hurried down to the landing and bent down next to Jake Temper. The man sat with his back to the wall, hand gripping his gut, head slumped against his chest.

Beckham moved past them to check the next corner, his blade and boot nearly sliding in the puddle of blood. But it wasn't just the blood that made his heart skip. The blast door was blown open.

"I tried to stop them," Jake mumbled, his voice so low it sounded like a whisper. "Flanked them from behind…"

Beckham moved back to the fallen officer.

"Stop who?" he asked.

"They had masks." Jake shook his head. "I don't know who they were, but they were trained…" He let out a moan and winced. "I hit two of 'em, but they had armor."

"Take it easy," Beckham said.

"Where are my girls?" Horn asked.

"They're gone…" Jake whispered, blood drooling down his chin.

Horn shot up.

Beckham also stood and looked up at Ruckley, "We need a medic."

She nodded, and Beckham put a hand on Jake.

"Hang on man, we're going to get you help," he said.

Jake managed a nod. "I'm sorry…" he said. "I'm sorry I couldn't."

"You did all you could, Jake." Beckham stayed with the officer until the medic came, and then he followed Horn into the bunker.

Bloody footprints led down the stairs and into an interior living space furnished with couches and two tables. The red tracks moved into the hallway past the other communal areas, a storage room, a kitchen, and the bedrooms.

Beckham moved faster, fearing that their families had been kidnapped or worse. They cleared two more rooms and stopped at the glass walls of the secured lab.

The open spaces were clear.

Not a person in sight, or a sign of a fight.

"No one's here," Horn whispered.

Beckham moved back to the storage room and opened the door. He had helped with the retrofitting of the fallout shelter and was one of a few people that knew there was a second exit here, just in case the occupants needed to escape.

The large room was full of shelving units supporting canned goods, water, and medical supplies. He navigated through the aisles to the back where the escape door was normally hidden behind a shelf. His blade again slopped through a puddle, but this time it wasn't blood—it was peaches and tomato sauce. The broken bottles and dented cans were scattered on the floor.

Someone had moved the shelf, and in a hurry. The hatch was still open.

"They must have escaped while Jake ambushed the raiders in the passage, before they blew the door open," Beckham said. He jerked his chin and Horn followed him back the way they had come.

When they reached the landing, Ruckley's medic was trying to resuscitate Jake.

"Oh no." Beckham hurried over and bent down.

"Jesus," Horn said putting a hand on Beckham's shoulder as Beckham watched the medic work on his friend of over ten years.

Beckham wanted to scream.

The police officer had survived the virus and monsters only to be killed by some raiders. But instead of screaming, Beckham said a prayer, and made a promise to the fallen officer.

I'll find Timothy and I'll take care of your boy.

Giving Beckham a moment, Horn waited impatiently at the top of the stairs. Several of the Rangers stood sentry in the hallway as Ruckley spoke to Niven over the comm channel.

The report made Beckham's blood freeze.

"Multiple causalities at town hall, including children," Niven reported.

Horn didn't waste time with words and started off for the exit. Beckham moved to follow, but paused and looked to Ruckley.

"Come on, Sergeant" he said. "We have to find our families."

***

Kate squeezed Javier's hand as she pulled him along through the woods. In her other hand she held the strap tight for the AR15 hanging over her back.

"Don't look back," she told him.

They led the other twenty escapees away from the bunker. The other half of their group had already scattered to hide in the darkness, but Kate had decided not to go back to the town. She wanted to put as much distance as she could between them and the raiders.

Ginger and Spark led her deeper into the forest, away from civilization. Leaves and sticks whipped past her face as she stumbled through the dark.

"Ouch," Jenny said.

"Keep moving," Tasha whispered.

Trying to keep track of the kids, while simultaneously

navigating her way through the forest was almost impossible, especially with only moonlight to guide her.

The dense canopy of autumn leaves allowed only faint beams to pass through. All around her the silhouettes of others faded in and out of the shadows.

These people were not trained military professionals, and they were all frightened, which made the journey slower and noisier.

Every breaking branch, every crunch of fallen leaves made her think the raiders had caught up to them. In her head, she could still hear the shots from Jake's gun and the return fire as she led the group away from the bunker.

If they hadn't had that door, and if Jake hadn't sacrificed himself, she feared they would've all been dead by now.

"My dad, we have to go back for my dad," Timothy said, his voice louder than before. The teen was a wreck. He had to have known what those echoing gunshots outside the bunker meant.

"We've got to keep moving," Kate said. "That's what your dad told us to do, and we've got to listen to him, okay?"

It was everything Kate could do to keep her own mind on track.

Someone yelped to her right and hit the ground. Kate ran over to them to see Donna pushing herself up. Bo reached down, but she cried out in pain when he tried to help her.

"It's my ankle," she cried.

"Come on, mom," Bo said. He finally helped her up with the aid of a neighbor, and the group continued moving, making far too much noise.

"Please, everyone, you need to be quiet," Kate said,

loud enough for them all to hear, but hopefully quiet enough that none of the raiders could.

She might as well have been telling the ocean to stop sending waves to the shore. All she could do was pray that the couple of people with guns at the back of the group were ready if the raiders caught up to them.

Without the constant threat of Variants on Peaks Island, people had started to take their security for granted, despite the work Jake, Beckham, and Horn did to train these people. But the last thing they had expected were raiders with training and weapons to match.

She hoped someone would respond to the SOS, but it had gone out hours ago, and still nothing. Beckham was at the Greenbrier, and she had no idea what the situation was in Portland.

Kate pushed forward, heading for shelter. She remembered a three-story building out here where Tasha and Timothy had been caught smoking cigarettes.

The cement and cinderblock structure had once been used as a park management resource building, but she didn't know exactly where it was.

"Tasha," Kate whispered. "Do you remember where the old park management building is? The concrete one?"

"I don't know—" Tasha said. "I can't see anything out here."

"I know how to get there," Timothy responded. "Follow me."

He veered away and Kate motioned for everyone to follow them in the drip of moonlight. Bo picked his mother up, and carried her.

The crack of gunfire rang out in the distance, and Kate crouched down with everyone else. She turned to quiet Ginger and Spark.

"Help me with them, Javier," Kate said.

While her son calmed the dogs, she held up her rifle, searching for a target. She was used to saving lives, not taking them. If she was backed into a corner though, given no other choice but to protect herself, the kids, and the rest of the people around her, she knew what choice she would make.

"I don't see anyone," Timothy said. He motioned for Tasha and Jenny to get behind him and then brought up his own gun. A few other people sobbed behind a cluster of bushes, but Kate saw more of their friends taking off through the woods.

She searched for Donna and Bo just as more gunfire lanced through the darkness. Muzzle fires flashed through the branches. Several pained screams echoed between the trees.

Another burst illuminated a raider. She lined up her rifle, but the man took off before she could fire a shot, pursuing the small pack that had broken off from their group.

Another volley of rounds blasted through the branches.

"When I tell you, get up, and run," Kate whispered.

Javier nodded, and Tasha and Jenny did as well.

Kate waited for another blast of gunfire, and then said, "Run."

The kids swarmed around her as she moved deeper into the woods, throwing her rifle over her back again. She grabbed Javier's hand tight and nearly pulled him off his feet. The dogs raced ahead, but she could still see them in the moonlight.

She wanted to call out for Bo and Donna, but couldn't risk making noise. Kate took off through the woods, branches scraping her face, and thorns cutting her pants.

"Are we close, Timothy?" she panted out.

When she got no response, she turned around, but didn't see Timothy.

"Timothy," she said quietly.

"He went back," Tasha replied.

The pop of a pistol sounded.

Oh no... Kate thought.

Timothy had gone to avenge his dad.

A hand pulled on Kate's sleeve as she tried to think.

"There," Tasha said. She pointed through a gap in the woods at a structure. There was a single window on each wall of each floor and an empty doorway. The wooden door had long since rotted away, leaving only hinges.

"Go, go," Kate said.

They bolted for the structure. She made sure the kids got in first, ushering Javier in after them. Other escapees broke through the trees, heading toward their direction. Spark and Ginger growled beside Kate, staring out into the woods. The fur on their hackles stood straight, their tails tucked beneath their legs.

More people came out of the woods. A woman ran toward Kate, blood streaming from her shoulder. Her right arm hung beside her.

A handful of other people were close behind, children in tow. A baby wailed from where it was tucked in against the chest of one of the men.

She scanned them all, realizing Bo and Donna weren't among them, and Timothy was still out there.

"What do we do?" someone asked.

Kate had only a second to decide.

"We hold here," she said. "Everyone with a weapon, get ready. If you see a raider, shoot them, but make sure it's not one of our people."

The kids and women huddled into the corner of the earth-covered floor and comforted each other. Some stared with wide eyes at Kate and the door.

"Go upstairs," Kate said. "It'll be safer up there."

And easier to defend, she added inwardly, still praying it didn't come to that.

She counted no more than twelve people that had joined them. So many were still lost out there, scattered by the chaos. Her heart ached, thinking of how frightened Donna, Bo, and Timothy were right now.

But there was nothing more she could do for them.

Kate positioned herself with her AR-15 so she could keep an eye on the woods without being seen. Time seemed to slow to an agonizing lurch as she waited. The screams and yells were growing distant and the gunfire more sporadic.

She felt the adrenaline starting to fade. Exhaustion taking over.

They'd run for so long. Both tonight and well before they'd ended up on Peaks Island. She had always thought they had found safety and security here. That they could forge new lives, rebuild society.

And instead these raiders had shattered everything they had fought so hard to build.

A flurry of gunshots pierced the woods, some of them more of a whistle than a crack. In less than a few seconds, all hell seemed to break loose.

Muzzle flashes lit up the black but then, seconds later, everything went dark again.

Kate strained to see what was happening. A muffled scream sounded. More whistles followed. Then a scream of agony and what sounded like a tree limb snapping.

"Someone's coming," said the man next to Kate.

"Hold your fire until you get a good shot," she replied. Her grip tightened around her rifle. She signaled to another man with a shotgun, and he inched forward.

Kate lined up the sights on the figure.

Another shape appeared.

Then a third.

They definitely held rifles and were advancing low and slow like soldiers.

The question now was whether they were raiders or friendlies.

The only advantage she had was the element of surprise, and the fact they outnumbered the three men.

She steeled herself, thinking of Javier and Tasha and Jenny and all the others upstairs. Closing an eye, she aimed and moved her finger to the trigger. The crosshairs hit the chest of one of the men.

"Kate!" yelled a familiar voice. "Kate, Tasha, Jenny!"

"Timothy?" Tasha called out.

The teenager ran forward, his pistol still in his hand. Two men followed close behind, and when Kate saw the prosthetic leg, she knew it was Beckham and Horn.

She ran out into the night, doing all she could to not drop to her knees and sob out of joy and sadness.

— 8 —

Over an hour had passed since Fitz discovered Cedric. Bravo Team had continued on their mission to uncover what the outpost soldier had seen in the forest. They had moved slowly due to the minefields and other security measures that in some cases weren't marked at all.

Now they were at the edge of the eastern cornfields, and Dohi studied the fence of trees in the distance. A storm cloud passed over the moon, and the glow retracted from the landscape like the tide receding into the ocean.

A chill ran through Dohi as he considered what Cedric had told Fitz about seeing the people from the outpost. The part about them being partially buried in the forest reminded him of an old Navajo folk story about humans that were pulled into the ground by evil spirits.

Rico stepped up to his side.

"What cha' thinkin'?" she asked.

You don't want to know…

Instead of telling her he said, "I'm worried about mines between these fields and the forest, but I don't know any other way."

The terrain separating them from the line of trees was covered in foliage, and he didn't see any warning signs.

"Let's keep moving through the corn," Rico said.

Dohi didn't like that either, but they had no choice.

He moved into the field, doing his best not to rustle

the plants. But the task was nearly impossible. A minute into the trek, a sound crackled that sounded suspiciously like the popping of joints.

He held up a fist to listen.

The wind shook the tops of the stalks, and he waited for a shriek to erupt and a Variant to come charging at him.

Raising his rifle, he moved his finger to the inside of the trigger guard.

Come on, he thought. *Show yourself.*

Squawks and caws suddenly exploded in the distance. A murder of crows took flight, climbing into the air. Their cacophony rose with them as they circled against the full moon before finally settling somewhere to Bravo's south.

After waiting a few minutes, he continued forward. The leaves on the stalks scraped against his face and snagged on his skin. He scanned the area while he moved, waiting for a Variant to come bursting out with claws spread and sucker lips smacking.

Eventually he could see trees growing near the edge of the corn. A good sign that meant he wouldn't have to lead his team through any potential minefields.

The wind shifted as he moved. Stalks smacked against each other, creating a whispering chorus of scratching leaves. A blast of carrion odor drifted on the air.

There was definitely something out here.

He halted at the edge of the field. White moonlight bled across the space between the field and the tree line. The smell of rot only grew worse as they pushed into the dark forest.

Elms and oaks towered above Dohi, their branches swaying. Weeds protruded from the carpet of leaves that had already fallen here. Judging from the scent wafting through the crisp air, they were close to whatever Cedric had seen.

Dohi stopped when he heard a scratching. Rico and Mendez heard it, too, and fanned out, keeping low.

They continued slowly through the dense woods. Dohi avoided the rotting logs and dense patches of leaves as best as he could. But even the best covert operative couldn't help but make noise in a place like this.

A gurgling creek sounded as they crested a hill. Dohi halted at the top to scan the terrain and almost froze at the sight of gray-fleshed Variants, still partially blended with the forest.

He quickly went prone.

Rico crawled up next to him.

"Alpha 1, Bravo 2 here," Dohi whispered. "We got contacts. Lots of them."

"Hold your position," Fitz said. "We're on our way."

The Variants were hunched and focused on the ground. Their talons cut into the carpet of leaves. They were digging, throwing fantails of dirt behind them.

It was clear this was the source of the odor.

Dohi peered through his optics to see what they were digging up from the dirt. His heart climbed to his throat when he saw what looked like a human half-buried in a crater of dark earth.

It might've been a man, but Dohi could hardly tell. Most of the skin from his chest had been flayed off, revealing bleeding muscle and bone. Some strange webbing was wrapped around his face, masking his eyes.

Strings of long, greasy black hair protruded from between those webs. Blood trickled from bruised, broken lips. A few cords from that webbing seemed to go up the man's nostrils and into his mouth, giving him a decidedly inhuman appearance.

The man let out a moan as the Variant pulled on him, ripping his flesh.

All around him, the same scene played out. Men and women covered in wounds. Their heads wrapped in that same strange netting, like bloody oversized spider webs. Almost as if the blood vessels inside their bodies didn't know they were supposed to grow under their skin and had suddenly erupted from the people's faces.

Judging by the Variants' frantic attempts to dig them out, the monsters were in a hurry to get the people out of here, which told Dohi this was all recent.

No wonder the SEALs hadn't found anyone.

The people were underground all this time.

Dohi winced as one of the Variants began tugging on a woman. Red webs covered her eyes but her mouth was partially free.

She let out an agonized moan as the beast sunk claws into her shoulder and tried to yank her from the dirt. It got her halfway out.

The Variant squawked in frustration, shredding her shoulder in the process. Her moan turned into a pained scream only partly muffled by the webbing.

"We got to do something," Rico said. "Alpha could take an hour to get here."

Dohi motioned for her to move back down the hill to send a transmission to Fitz. She hurried away and Mendez joined Dohi at the crest of the hill.

They were far enough away that the creatures hadn't detected them, but Dohi kept his finger near the trigger just in case. He cringed as more people were pulled from the ground.

The Variants began dragging them away. In minutes, the first disappeared over another crest, leaving nothing but blood-covered leaves and dirt behind.

This was the evil sight that had caused the soldier Fitz had found to go mad.

All these people half-buried in the middle of the woods with some kind of strange netting growing around their heads was enough to steal the breath of any hardened warrior, even Dohi.

So many questions circled his mind as the minutes ticked by. Most pressing was what they were going to do now. Alpha was still on their way but one by one the Variants finished digging the people out and took them over the small hill.

Dohi listened to the convo over the channel.

"Alpha 1, Bravo 1," Rico said from the bottom of the hill. "Variants are moving out with hostages. Pursue?"

There was a beat of silence over the channel.

"Track them," Fitz said, "but do not engage."

"Copy," Rico whispered back.

The last few Variants disappeared with their prey.

Dohi rushed down the hill and toward the creek. He cleared it in a single jump. Mendez and Rico shadowed him. They started climbing up the hill, passing the tunnels where the civilians had been dug out.

But as they made their way up, Dohi noticed something else in the freshly upturned soil. Slimy red tubes pushed up from the dirt like broken blood vessels from a wound in the earth.

They looked like the same growths he'd seen on the people's faces. Whatever those tubes were, they gave off a smell that was nearly as bad as a Variant.

He led Bravo up to the top of the next hill where he

shouldered his rifle, ready to fire. Rico and Mendez spread out between the trees to cover the vantage.

But he didn't see the beasts.

Shafts of moonlight pierced the forest canopy on the other side.

Not a single one of the creatures or even the hostages was in view. He had seen camouflaged Variants vanish before, but not humans.

Dohi set off to continue the search, wondering if they had gone back underground. He searched the trees, too, just in case any of the beasts had climbed up as lookouts.

Seeing none, he followed the only evidence he could find.

A trail of splattered blood.

It didn't go far and stopped at what looked to be dark, wet soil, as if someone had just filled in a hole.

The pieces started to coalesce in his head. But even as they came together, he had a hard time believing them.

"Shit," Rico whispered, her gaze on the trees. "We lost them."

"I'm not so sure about that," Dohi said. He bent down and prodded the ground with a finger.

"This shit is creepin' me out," Mendez said quietly. He glanced up at the trees towering above them. "Where the hell did they go?"

"Alpha 1, Bravo 1," Rico said. "We got—"

The ground trembled before she could finish. Dohi tried to retreat with Mendez and Rico, but he was hit by a blast of soil that knocked him down.

He landed on his back as a pack of mud-covered Variants spilled out of the hole like ants from a broken mound. They dispersed around him, needle-pointed teeth grinding together, joints clicking as they prepared to attack.

Gunfire burst from Rico and Mendez as Dohi scrambled away. He got to his feet and then turned with his rifle leveled. A trigger squeeze sent bullets punching through the closest Variant. Blood and flesh sprayed out the exit wounds.

The body of the monster flopped to the ground, but another crashed into Dohi. He pushed the creature off and pulled his buck knife, jabbing it through its meaty throat.

Rico and Mendez fended off the others when three more Variants burst from the hole. Dohi rolled to grab his rifle, but a Variant leapt onto his back. It slammed its claws into his helmet, and his head thudded against the ground, blurring his vision.

He rolled to his back, slashing at the beast with the knife still in his hand.

Another hammering fist crashed into his helmet. The blow knocked his night vision goggles off kilter with a crack. Growls and gunfire sounded like they were coming at him from inside a pool.

You have to get up!

Something hot and wet hit his face, followed by what could only be the rancid breath of a Variant. A moment of clear vision allowed him to see the jagged teeth behind wormy lips inching toward his own face.

The beast pinned him down to the soft earth.

All sense of weight suddenly subsided, but it wasn't until his hand scratched the vertical wall of a tunnel that he realized it wasn't from the beast letting up.

He was falling!

Dohi tried to brace himself but hit the ground hard a

moment later, pain radiating through his back. The beast landed a few feet away with a thump.

Above him, moonlight streamed in the hole they had broken through.

The gunfire and screeches sounded even more distant now, but he wasn't sure if it was from his pounding head or because the team was retreating.

No, they wouldn't leave you.

The thought filled Dohi with adrenaline, and he managed to reach up with a trembling limb to put his goggles back into place. When he brought them over his eyes, he saw darkness.

The damn things were busted.

"Rico, Mendez!" he tried to yell, but his strained voice was lost in the din of combat above. Not only that but his earpiece and mic were also busted.

Son of a bitch!

He struggled to move, his muscles tensing at the sound of a snapping joint, followed by a snarling maw. Dohi pulled his knife and prepared to fight when more popping joints and smacking lips filled the dark cavern.

Dohi and the beast that had fallen with him weren't alone.

***

"We have to hold here until it's clear," Beckham told the civilians huddling upstairs. He hated leaving Bo and Donna out there, but without knowing where they could possibly be, he had to hope they would just hunker down and wait.

"I want to go home," moaned Jenny.

"Soon," Kate said, reassuringly. She walked over to

Beckham who remained to the side of a window, looking out in the darkness with his NVGs.

He couldn't see any hostiles out there, but there were bound to be more. He and Horn had followed their gunfire into the forest and managed to take down three of the raiders before the other two fled.

Ruckley's team was out there hunting them, and Alpha team in Portland was still securing the area. So for now, Beckham and Horn had to keep holding position.

Javier hugged him around the waist.

"I knew you'd come back, dad," the boy said. Beckham patted him on the back of the head and listened to an incoming transmission.

"Bravo 7, this is Bravo 1, do you copy, over?" said Ruckley.

"Copy Bravo 1, this is Bravo 7," Beckham replied.

"Can you move your injured and meet back at the rally point?"

Beckham looked back at the others. Several had gunshot wounds, and others had injuries that would slow them down.

"Affirmative, Bravo 1," Beckham said. "We've got a lot of people that need medical attention. We'll be slow moving, but we can make it."

"Copy that," Ruckley said. "We'll be ready for you."

Horn suddenly went rigid by the door. He pointed to his eyes and then held up two fingers. Beckham turned to Timothy. The teen hadn't left his corner by the stairs. They still hadn't told him his father was dead, but Beckham had a feeling he already knew the truth.

"Timothy, I need you to tell everyone to stay put for a second," Beckham whispered. "Do it as quietly as you can."

Timothy nodded, then crept up the stairs.

"Boss, they got a hostage," Horn said. He paused and added, "Make that two."

Beckham's stomach sank.

"They're headed this way," Horn said.

"We know you're hiding in there!" boomed a voice. "You shoot, and we shoot your people."

"You're out numbered and surrounded!" Beckham shouted back. "Put down your weapons and let the hostages go."

"Not a chance, asshole!" replied the raider.

Beckham looked at Horn who snorted and yelled back, "Which one of you wants to turn into a spray of pink mist first? You got one minute to decide."

Brash and garish, Beckham expected no less from Horn. He gave his friend a nod, and then slunk to the building's single open window in the back, concealed from the raiders' view, and slipped his rifle out.

Beckham pulled himself through after, landing hard on his blade. Slowly, he made his way to the cover of the woods.

"We want passage off this island," one of the raiders called out. "Give us a boat and we will let your people go."

"That's what you want?" Horn said.

Beckham was almost behind them now. He paused a second, glassing the duo with his optics. He recognized the hostages instantly.

Donna and Bo. The teenager was taller than his captor, but he wasn't fighting back.

Beckham saw why.

The raider had a pistol pressed to Bo's temple.

"Radio your army friends and tell them we're free to

go," said the captor. "Do it, or I'm going to off this kid and his bitch mom."

Bo moved, which earned him a pistol whip to the face.

Donna screamed, "Leave him alone!"

Beckham moved faster, knowing he had just moments to save them. He was about twenty meters away now, and the raiders still hadn't noticed him. These grunts weren't that bright, but whoever had coordinated this attack likely had military or police training.

The attack was far more coordinated than others and made him worry again it was part of something on a much wider scope.

"All right, boys, I'm coming out," Horn bellowed, keeping the raiders' attention on him. He took a step out of the doorway and raised one hand. His rifle swung down slightly on the other, giving the impression he was going to let it go.

Beckham snuck behind a bush and got into position.

"Go on now," one of the raiders said. "Drop it all the way to the ground."

Bo kicked at the raider hard enough the impact of his boot on bone echoed. The raider's handgun wavered, pointing upward, as he reached down to his shin. The timing could not have been better.

Beckham took his shot. The man crumpled, and the second raider looked nervously around, trying to figure out where the shot had come from.

Horn started to swing up his rifle, and the other raider pushed Donna aside and fired at Horn. The big man dove to the ground and scrambled away.

By the time Beckham had his rifle on the raider, he had grabbed Donna again.

"Shit," Beckham whispered.

"I'll kill the bitch!" the raider shouted. "I'll fucking kill her!"

He turned his gun on Bo and fired a shot, but Bo leapt behind a tree. Beckham lined up the sights on the raider, but he couldn't get a clear shot with Donna still in his grips.

Instead, Beckham moved away from his position and charged. He propelled himself forward from the bushes, feeling the springy bounce of his prosthetic blade. The raider took three wild shots at Horn and then at Bo as Beckham hit him from behind.

The guy sprawled forward, releasing Donna. Beckham used his helmet to slam the guy in the nose. A sickening crack sounded.

The second head butt did the trick.

The raider went limp in the dirt, knocked out cold.

Bo held a gun that he must have grabbed from the dead raider. He aimed it at the unconscious man, but Beckham slapped the gun away as he pulled the trigger.

The bullet lanced into the dirt next to the raider's head.

"Hey!" Bo shouted.

"We need him alive," Beckham said.

"But he was going to kill me and my mom," Bo shot back.

"He will get what's coming to him, but first we need to find out who he is, and who the other raiders are."

Beckham moved in front of Bo, not giving him the chance to fire on the downed raider. "Lower the gun," he said.

Bo spat on the ground but did as ordered. He moved over to his mom and wrapped her in his arms.

"You okay, mom?"

Beckham studied her in the green hue of his night vision, checking for injuries. She was shivering, her bottom lip trembling, but she managed a nod.

Bo looked down at the raider again before helping her to the building.

"Bravo 1, this is Bravo 7," Beckham said into his headset. "We found the last two raiders. Bringing one back."

"Copy," Ruckley replied.

Beckham pulled zip-ties from his vest and bent down to the crumpled raider.

Horn trotted over and picked the guy up over his shoulder. The civilians flowed from the building, fanning out around them.

"Stay close," Beckham said. "We're going back to the bunker."

He took point with Ginger and Spark on either side. Having the dogs with him was a comfort, much like having Apollo back in the day.

Beckham kept his optics trained on the terrain. They might have eliminated all the raiders in this pack, but he didn't know if there were more out there.

Timothy walked up alongside Beckham carrying the pistol his father had given him on his sixteenth birthday. Before Jake had given it to his son, Beckham had helped him carve an engraving on the barrel that read, *Never Stop Fighting.*

The young boy had already used the gun to kill a raider in the forest when Beckham and Horn had discovered the boy, and so far he seemed to be taking his first kill pretty well.

But having him up here was no good in his emotional state.

"Timothy, fall back and watch the kids, okay?" Beckham said.

"Sure," Timothy said. The teen dropped back to the center of the pack.

Horn was on rearguard, making sure they weren't being followed. He and Beckham were both used to skulking through the darkness with a team of trained operatives. But now they might as well have been shepherding a herd of cattle through the woods and praying the wolves around them somehow didn't notice.

Fifteen minutes later, Beckham spotted the entrance to the bunker. Several Rangers stood sentry, and he motioned for the group of civilians to come out of hiding.

Ruckley met him on the sidewalk, returning from her own search.

"Good to see you, Captain," she said. Her tone didn't mask the frustration of Horn and Beckham going AWOL earlier.

"I'm sorry about taking off," he said. "I didn't mean to put you and your team—"

"All that matters is everyone's okay," she said.

But everyone wasn't okay, Beckham thought.

He looked over his shoulder and saw Timothy a safe distance back.

"Where's Jake?" Beckham asked Ruckley in a whisper.

"Who?"

"The man we found on the stairs. Is he out—"

"We moved his body out of view, don't worry."

Beckham exhaled, unable to hide his emotions.

"I'm sorry for your loss," Ruckley said. She walked away and began handing out orders to her soldiers. The Rangers helped the injured into the bunker.

"I'll meet you inside," Beckham said to Kate.

"But dad," Javier protested.

"Please go with your mother," Beckham said.

Kate led Javier inside with Horn and his girls.

Beckham walked over to Timothy. The teenager's face went white like he knew what was coming, even though Beckham hadn't uttered a single word.

"No," Timothy said. "No...please..."

He moved away from Beckham and in through the doorway.

"Wait up," Beckham called out.

Timothy pushed the group and made his way into the hallway. Beckham ran after him, nearly tripping. The boy made it down the stairs and into the bunker before he finally caught up with him.

In the first section, medics and a couple of nurses from Peaks Island were treating those who had already made it to the bunker.

"Where's my dad?" Timothy said, in a voice shy of a shout. He searched the beds, and then stopped near a large olive canvas curtain separating the triage into sections. Beckham put a hand on his shoulder.

"I'm sorry, Timothy, but your dad didn't make it," Beckham said. "He died saving you and the others."

"No," Timothy choked. He pulled back the curtain to reveal another section filled with cots covered with white sheets. All anonymous victims of the raiders, masked by those sheets, with only the point of a nose tenting it up at one end or their feet at the other.

Beckham put a hand on Timothy's arm, but the boy pulled away and set off through the space.

"No, no, no," he murmured, turning back to Beckham. "Which one is he?"

"You shouldn't see this," Beckham said.

Kate joined them in the room and helped Beckham sort through the dead. They found Jake at the back of the room, while Timothy was still searching the other cots.

He looked up and caught Beckham's gaze, then hurried over to his side.

Beckham held the sheet down.

"I want to see him," Timothy said.

Kate and Beckham exchanged a glance, and then Beckham pulled back the covering.

"Noooooo," Timothy moaned. He nearly collapsed over his father, wrapping his arms around his dad's shoulders, tears streaming down his face.

Kate rubbed his back in the way she used to comfort Javier when he was scared at night. Beckham placed a hand on Timothy's shoulder.

"Your dad was a great man," he said.

Timothy nodded, keeping his head on his dad's chest.

Beckham had seen so many of his brothers-in-arms perish fighting the Variants, but this was something even more heartbreaking. To see Timothy suddenly alone in this world, losing the man that had been his anchor, that had helped see him through since before Operation Liberty during the first months of the war eight years ago.

How many other children were orphans because of these raiders?

Beckham's sadness erupted into anger.

He managed it by clenching his jaw, and stayed there beside Timothy, seething with rage but doing his best to comfort the teen.

A transmission over the headset Beckham still wore made him flinch. Lieutenant Niven's voice came over the channel. "We've picked up the enemy's trail, and we're going after them," he said.

Beckham looked at Kate. Even though she couldn't hear the transmission she must have recognized the gaze in his eyes. With a nod she gave him permission to do what he did best—hunt and kill monsters.

Fitz broke through the final row of corn and stopped at the edge to look at the dense forest of oak trees. The canopy of leaves blew in the wind, masking the distant sound of gunfire.

Rain drops bit his face as he kept moving.

He had run all the way from the center of Turkey River after the SOS came in over the comms about a Variant attack, covering nearly three miles in the past thirty-two minutes.

It wasn't a record pace by any means, but with his gear, and the threat of mines, he couldn't run much faster, especially without letting his guard down.

Leaving Cedric didn't help matters, and Fitz wasn't sure he would be where they left him when they returned. But there was no way in hell he would bring the guy back out here.

Lincoln kept up with Fitz, but Ace fell behind, stopping every few minutes to breathe.

"Go on," he called out, hands on his knees. He raised one of them, waving to proceed without him. "I'll…catch up."

Fitz and Lincoln didn't waste time. They kept moving into the dense forest, following the sound of gunfire, and the ethereal screeches of dying monsters.

A half mile later, they came up on a hill that blocked their view of the forest. Fitz balled his hand, and slowly moved up the slope, leaves crunching under his blades.

Ace finally caught up behind them, panting like a wild boar.

"Holy shit," Fitz said, staring at the scene of carnage.

Rico and Mendez stood in the middle of it, surrounded by a red halo of dead beasts.

"Come on!" Fitz said.

He hurried down the hill and set off across an area of holes seeping the Variants' noxious, rotten odor, but stronger, like it had been distilled and hyper-concentrated.

"You okay?" Fitz whispered.

Rico and Mendez both nodded but kept their rifles up, still roving the barrels for contacts. Lincoln and Ace joined them, weapons also up.

"Where's Dohi?" Fitz asked, keeping his voice low.

Rico simply pointed at the ground.

Fitz crept to the edge of a gaping hole and peered over the edge. The full brunt of the carrion smell made his eyes water.

Moonlight illuminated a patch of the tunnel covered in webs of strange tissue stretching across the soil. He bent down for a better look.

A Variant the color of an earthworm came bursting from the tunnel, knocking Fitz backward. Vessels bulged under its skin, ropey muscles tensing.

Fitz brought up his rifle and shot it in the head.

The beast fell limply to the floor of the tunnel, landing with a thud.

The other team members huddled around, all of them looking down.

Fitz tried Dohi on the comms. Nothing came back but static.

He pushed his NVGs away from his eyes and flicked

on the tactical light mounted to the bottom of his gun barrel. The others did the same, angling the light into the tunnel. The drop to the bottom appeared to be about ten feet.

"We're going in there, aren't we?" Lincoln said.

Fitz nodded.

"Shit."

Fitz and Rico helped lower Ace down first. Then Rico dropped in with Mendez and Fitz following. Lincoln came last, his boots smacking against the mud-filled tunnel floor.

Maybe it was an illusion, but the red vines and webbing looked like they were actually pulsating. Fitz moved quietly, taking it all in.

The tunnel appeared to have a diameter of about ten feet and seemed to travel north, winding so he couldn't see the end. The southern end was blocked by piles of fallen soil and rock. While the walls and ceiling were curved, the floor seemed to be pounded nearly flat.

What in the hell kind of twisted Variant engineering was this?

He had seen tunnels, especially in Europe. The worm Variants had burrowed under the cities. But as far as he knew, they'd never made it across the Atlantic. And from his experience, they didn't leave behind this webbing.

No, this was something entirely different.

The only tunnels he had seen in the states were manmade. This...this was beyond anything he experienced.

A wail broke the silence, and a Variant came bounding into the tunnel. Five tactical lights hit the beast as it moved, digging claws into the red tendrils stretching over the walls and ceiling like a spider web.

It practically galloped toward them on the ceiling, using the tendrils to move.

"Ace, take it down," Fitz ordered.

"I got this ugly son of a…" Ace said, his voice silenced by the boom of his shotgun.

Bits of the tendrils flew away with the shot as the Variant leapt away unharmed. He pumped the weapon and fired again. This time the buckshot found a home in its skull, erasing all former human features in a fine pink mist.

The corpse slammed against the muddy floor, kicking up wet muck.

An angry roar echoed through the tunnel from seemingly all directions. The team turned to search for the source.

Ace bumped into Mendez.

"Watch it big guy," Mendez said.

"Get out of my way, dude," Ace shot back.

"Take it easy," Fitz said. "Watch your zones."

That smell of rotten fruit seemed to waft off the red webs covering the walls as their beams flitted through the black. He had no idea what it was, but it sure as hell looked like something Kate would be interested in seeing in the lab.

Right now, though, lab samples could wait; Dohi could not.

The roars faded away, leaving them in silence.

Fitz waited another moment before giving the advance sign.

They followed the winding tunnel, darkness swallowing them except for the patches illuminated with their beams. Every surface was covered with the same gruesome webbing. The hairs on the back of Fitz's neck stood straight, almost as if they were passing through an electric current.

Variant shrieks echoed, but sounded distant, like they were moving away from the team. The monotony of the massive tunnel was interrupted for the first time with an intersection. The team halted, the faint echo of their movement fading away into silence. Fitz heard something dripping to the right.

"Which way?" Rico whispered.

A human scream to the right provided their answer.

Ace took point, and the team moved in behind the large man and his shotgun.

The tunnel they entered next looked like it had been dug by a group of human-sized moles. It was wide enough for them to walk through three abreast and tall enough no one had to duck down. The red vines were even more dense, covering every surface, even the ground.

Now Fitz was almost certain some of those webs were pulsing. He caught Rico and Mendez studying the webbing, but Ace's shotgun never strayed from pointing straight ahead.

The tunnel curved back and forth slightly, bending just enough to prevent them from seeing what lay beyond each turn. The squawks and growls carried through the narrow passage, but the echo made it difficult to determine distance.

Whatever this strange place was, there was no doubt that they had uncovered how the Variants entered this outpost. The sensor systems wouldn't have caught anything invading the place from underground.

Ace curled around another corner, then swiftly turned back, signaling contacts.

Doh? Fitz mouthed.

Ace shook his head.

"Watch your fire zones for hostages," Fitz whispered.

They inched around the corner, picked out targets and, all of them but Ace, opened fire. The suppressed barks of their rifles echoed as they cut down several beasts that had been taken off guard.

Those that survived the initial onslaught didn't turn around to attack like Fitz had expected. Instead, they bolted into the darkness.

Fitz flashed an advance signal.

The beasts ran up the sides of the tunnel and scurried across the ceiling, their claws and talons digging into the dirt around the webbing.

Variants faded in and out of their beams, disappearing around the corner.

The team slowed as they approached. Ace went first, moving into a straighter tunnel.

"Clear," he said.

Fitz went next, spotting dirt falling from the ceiling like sand trickling in an hourglass. He directed his flashlight beam on the feet of a Variant just as it disappeared up a vertical tunnel.

For a fraction of a second, he debated climbing up the webbing to pursue the beast. If the webbing could hold a Variant, it could sure as hell hold him. But that would also expose him and the team to even more untold danger.

Variants had the advantage when it came to climbing. And trying to fight a Variant that had the upper ground in a place like this was even more of a nightmare than this mission had already turned into.

Another human yell echoed down from the chimney-like tunnel. It didn't sound like Dohi, but if it was a civilian being taken away, then there was a damn good chance that's where the Variants had Dohi, too.

"Ace, get—"

A loud rumble interrupted Fitz. The tunnel seemed to shake. Fitz's blades nearly slipped from under him. Then the ceiling of the tunnel behind them began to collapse, dumping rock, webbing, and dirt.

"We have to go up!" Fitz yelled over the din.

The other end of the tunnel was collapsing too. They would be buried alive down here if they didn't move. This must have been what happened to the half-buried humans Rico had described finding on the comms. The tunnels the Variants had transported them through had broken down around those people.

And Fitz didn't want to be next.

Dirt showered him as he moved. Some of the webbing came loose, slapping over his face. He had to pry the sticky red strands off.

God only knew what was waiting for them up top, but Fitz decided facing a few swinging Variant claws was better than choking on dirt for the last few minutes of his life.

Ace slung his shotgun and started climbing. Mendez followed with Fitz and Lincoln covering them. The collapsing ceilings were closing in from both sides.

To Fitz it was like being trapped in the throat of a giant creature trying to swallow them whole. He followed Lincoln up into the vertical shaft, using the webbing. Lincoln moved fast, quickly ascending, but Fitz strained to propel himself up.

His blades weren't so good for finding footholds. He managed to get purchase by jamming them in the side of the wall. Then he levered himself upward and stabbed them in again.

The walls thumped below him, dust booming up into the shaft.

Fitz coughed but kept moving.

A hand reached down, and he looked up to see Lincoln. He reached for the man's fingers, but they were still short by more than a foot.

The ground beneath Fitz rose, threatening to swallow his feet, the rumbling earth shaking his bones. Dirt started to break free from the vertical tunnel.

Rocks and dirt clods smacked into his face and body. He tried to take that last step up, pushing to close the gap between his fingers and Lincoln's.

His blade wouldn't budge. He'd embedded it too far into the dirt wall and now had to bounce on it, trying to break it free. The dirt around the blade moved, but he couldn't get it out.

Fitz grunted and shoved down on his blade with all his strength, digging a small cavity in the wall. He yanked it free, then lunged upward. His fingers met Lincoln's and the man pulled him up, the earth rising around him as the tunnel collapsed inward.

On all fours above ground, Fitz gasped for air. He wiped the dirt covering his face, seeing they were in the woods.

"Anyone got eyes?" Fitz managed between pants.

"Negative," Ace said.

Fitz listened for a second with the others, desperate to hear the cries of the Variants or the screams from the hapless humans they had kidnapped.

"Dohi," Fitz tried one last time over his comm channel. "Dohi, do you read?"

Static came back again.

Fitz looked back down at the collapsed tunnel and considered the reality of their situation. They had lost their best tracker and a good friend.

They had no evidence he was alive. No tracks, no discarded equipment, or a transmission. He picked up dirt and let it filter through his gloved fingers, his heart filling with dread.

Parts of the red webbing stuck out of the ground where the tunnel had collapsed. He pulled out his knife and sawed off a handful of them, then stuffed them in his pack. They weren't taking Dohi back with them, but they weren't going home empty handed.

This shit was weird enough to warrant sending it back to a lab for analysis.

"Bag some of this shit up," Fitz said. "We'll need a chopper to come back for Cedric anyway, and we can send some of this back with him. I have a feeling Kate is going to want to take a look at this immediately."

Maybe there was some clue as to what this was and how the Variants had used it and the tunnel to take out Outpost Turkey River. And maybe, just maybe, it would help them find Dohi at some point, even if it was just his body to bury.

"We going back with these samples?" Lincoln asked.

Fitz wanted to say yes, but emotions had to take a back seat to duty.

"We aren't going back until we find Dohi and figure out what the hell is going on," he said.

The team huddled around the hole, none of them saying what they were all likely thinking.

For now, Dohi was on his own.

All it takes is all you got, brother, Fitz thought.

***

The Portland Sheriff Department dual cab truck cut through the night without headlights, but soon the passengers wouldn't need their night vision goggles. Beckham glanced at the dashboard and confirmed it was almost morning.

They had been pursuing the raiders for the past hour, and he was getting anxious the farther they drove from Portland. The driver of the truck ahead of them reported he could see one of the raiders, but Beckham still hadn't laid eyes on the person.

Ruckley stared in the front passenger seat, her gaze seemingly glued to the dark road.

"We're outside the safe zone now," said the driver. "This is Variant country."

Beckham saw the posted warning signs by the road, and Horn readied his M249 in the back seat next to him.

"Can't this truck go any faster?" Horn grumbled.

Beckham strained for a better view as the road curved ahead. Frankly they were lucky they had caught up to this raider crew at all. The assholes had gotten a head start, but several citizens from Portland had followed them and relayed the information to the Rangers.

A voice sounded from Ruckley's radio, and she pressed the receiver to her ear.

"Wilco," Ruckley said. Then she spoke over the channel to the rest of the team. "Bravo, we're turning around. Now."

The brake lights of the pickup truck in front of them fired, glaring red as it stopped.

"What the hell are you doing?" Beckham said.

"Lieutenant Niven has called off the chase," Ruckley said. "He doesn't want to risk going into a Variant hot zone."

"Fuck this," Horn said. "Keep going! This is bullshit!"

Horn was still a pressurized boiler about to explode and Beckham didn't have to know Ruckley as well to see she was just as angry about their orders.

Enough anger and frustration radiated off them all to keep the truck cab hot even without the use of its heater. Beckham was also steaming. They had let the raiders that killed Jake and slaughtered countless citizens get away.

Keep cool, Reed.

Beckham still wasn't sure what the death count was. But he guessed it was going to get worse when the sun rose and they sent out patrols to locate missing residents in Portland and Peaks Island.

"The piece of shit raider we captured on Peaks Island is mine," Beckham said.

Ruckley glanced into the back seat again. "I've got orders to bring him back to command, Captain. Can't stop you from interrogating him first, of course."

"I just need a few minutes."

Horn nodded. "That's all it's going to take."

The two-truck convoy raced down the highway with their headlights on now. Beckham tried to focus on how lucky their families were to be okay after the bloodshed. But he couldn't help feeling that their luck was running out.

They rode in silence for the first half of the trip back, but Ruckley broke it by turning around from the front seat again.

"These raiders could have been collaborators," she said. "Maybe they had something to do with what happened at Turkey River."

"In Iowa?" Horn replied. "That's a hell of a long way for Variants and collaborators to coordinate attacks."

"Captain, you got any ideas on what's going on?" she asked.

"I was thinking the same thing Horn, actually," Beckham said. "But usually collaborators don't use bombs and hunt down civilians just to kill them. They kidnap people and take them to lairs to feed their Variant masters."

"Maybe they just knew we wouldn't follow them there," said the driver.

"I guess they were fucking right," Horn snorted.

Ruckley turned back to the front seat and lowered her helmet to listen to another message over a private channel.

"Copy that," she replied, clearly frustrated.

Beckham expected her to fill them in, but she didn't say anything. He didn't push the issue. Niven's reason for turning them around was by the book, and Beckham and Horn couldn't do shit about it.

They sat in silence for the rest of the ride. Twenty minutes later, they turned onto an off-ramp on the outskirts of Portland. Razor wire fences marked the barrier into the inhabited part of the city.

None of the defenses had stopped the raiders.

Smoke billowed from fires in the heart of the safe zone.

For so long, he'd told Javier and Kate they were safe here.

Now, he had to tell his son he'd been wrong, and explain what had happened.

Come on, Reed. You're lucky you get to explain it to him at all.

There were others that wouldn't get the same opportunity.

Timothy was now an orphan, and Jake would never get the chance to talk to his son again. The thought sent another surge of anger roaring through Beckham, just as their pickup pulled up in the town's square.

Dozens of troops and emergency response personnel were on the ground, recent arrivals to help secure the area and help with the cleanup.

White sheets covered the dead in front of Portland City Hall. The first bomb had gone off right outside the glass windows. The front wall was nothing but rubble, glistening with shards of broken glass and pieces of the metal plating where the roof had caved in.

A second bomb had gone off inside the medical clinic after the raiders had taken what they wanted there. As if stealing medicine weren't bad enough, they had destroyed the city's emergency facilities, leaving the residents of Portland without a working medical center when it was needed most.

Sick sons of bitches, Beckham thought.

The military had already put up a makeshift tent, and Beckham saw several doctors and nurses working on patients through the open flap. Kate was inside, but that was no surprise.

Beckham and Horn followed Ruckley and the other Rangers toward the police station without stopping.

Multiple generators powered lights set up around the staging area, casting a carpet of light over the devastation. Beckham stepped over broken glass and charred metal, and his blade splashed into a puddle of blood.

He looked down to see a severed hand missing several fingers. The remaining finger still wore a wedding ring.

The rest of the body was under a sheet a few feet away judging by the stump of a wrist sticking out. A group of civilians carried off the dead and loaded them into the back of a pickup truck.

One of the men dropped a corpse and bent over, vomiting on the street.

Beckham felt sick to his stomach, too.

All of this senseless death and for what?

The raiders could have taken what they wanted.

Why slaughter so many innocent people?

There had to be more to this story and, in a few minutes, he was going to talk to the one person that knew the answers.

Lieutenant Niven stood outside the police station talking on a handheld radio. He looked at Beckham as he approached.

"Yes, Captain Beckham is here," Niven said into the radio. "Yes, I'll let him know."

Beckham halted, anticipating more bad news.

"Captain, Master Sergeant," Niven said in turn. "That was Command. Got an update from Team Ghost at Turkey River. They found some of the missing townsfolk. Apparently, the Variants dug tunnels and used them to get inside the perimeter without being detected."

"And that's how they got the people out, too, without leaving a trace aboveground," Beckham said, more of a statement than a question.

"Sounds that way," Niven said. He paused a moment, looking tense.

The pit at the bottom of Beckham's stomach started to give way. "There's something else, isn't there?"

"Sergeant Yas Dohi is MIA."

"Son of a bitch," Beckham whispered. Things kept

getting worse. "What about the rest of Team Ghost?"

"They're back at the outpost waiting for reinforcements," Niven replied. "Sounds like Master Sergeant Fitzpatrick sent a sample of webbing from the tunnels that he wants the white coats to look at."

"Boss," Horn said, jerking his chin. He was anxious to see the raider, and so was Beckham.

"We'd like to have a chat with the prisoner," Beckham said.

"Be my guest, but don't rough him up too much," Niven said. "I need him in one piece for Command."

Horn mumbled something under his breath and followed it up with a snort.

"Sergeant Ruckley, escort them please."

"Yes, sir," she said.

Beckham followed her into the lobby. A lantern lit the desks and closed office doors beyond the reception area. They proceeded to the hallway and down a stairwell which led to the cells in the basement.

A single Ranger stood guard outside the main door.

"Sergeant," he said.

"Open it up," she replied.

The man unlocked the door and stepped aside.

Ruckley went first and stopped two strides in.

"What in the actual fuck?" she said.

Beckham moved past her, stopping at the sight of the raider curled up on the floor. Flesh had melted away from his face. The rancid smell forced Beckham to hold a sleeve to his nose.

"Guard!" Ruckley shouted.

The Ranger that had been holding sentry duty rushed in.

"What the hell happened?" Ruckley asked.

The man shook his head. "I... I don't know, he was fine when I checked thirty minutes ago."

Beckham and Horn moved over to the old school barred door. The lock sizzled, and strands of a clear hardened material hung from it like strands of solid glue.

"The hell..." Horn said.

"Don't," Beckham said to the guard who held up a key.

The Ranger backed away.

"Variant acid." Beckham was intimately familiar with the gunk that had taken his leg and part of his arm. It only took a small amount to do extreme damage.

Horn pulled his skull bandana up over his nose. "Dude must have had some hidden away, and it backfired."

Niven joined them in the basement a few moments later. He paced and put a hand on the back of his head. Then he looked to the guard and yelled, "How the hell did this happen, Rollins?"

"I'm sorry, sir," Rollins said. "I thought I searched the guy really well..."

"Fuck, fuck, fuck," Niven said. He stopped pacing, straightened, and drew in a breath. "What a goddamn mess."

Beckham didn't know what to say. All he knew was the only man that could have answered their questions was dead.

Sick to his stomach, he left the Rangers in the basement and hurried up to the medical tent with Horn. Over twenty people, some of them gravely wounded occupied the cots.

Kate was busy working with two doctors on a guy in the middle of the room. The man was laying still on a table and, judging from the sheer amount of blood on the ground, he was in pretty bad shape.

Beckham took a seat on the curb to wait. "I want to talk to Kate before we go find the kids," he said.

Horn pulled out a cigarette. "I figured as much."

Frantic voices came from inside the tent, and from the words Beckham picked up, it sounded like some unlucky patient was going into cardiac arrest.

Horn took a drag on his cigarette and offered it to Beckham, but Beckham waved it away. The distant glow of a new sunrise warmed the horizon.

Despite the view of a new day, his heart continued to pound from anxiety. There were too many questions in his mind.

"Hell of a few days," Horn mumbled. "Things could have been worse though."

"It could still get worse, Big Horn. I got a bad feeling about all of this."

The voices in the tent trailed off, replaced by the sporadic moan or cough of a patient. Kate stepped outside a few minutes later, removing her surgical gloves and tossing them into a bin. Then she pulled her surgical mask down and let out a long sigh before she saw Beckham.

"Kate," he said.

"Reed," she hurried over and threw her arms around him. "Did you catch them?"

"No, and the raider from the island is dead."

Kate pulled away with a confused look. "What? How?"

"He had Variant acid. Must have backfired when he tried to use it to escape."

"What was he doing with that?"

"Good question," Horn said. He blew the smoke skyward.

"Do we have a death count yet?" Beckham asked, looking at the tent.

"No but it just went up by one," Kate replied without turning. "We just lost McComb."

"McComb?" Horn said. "As in *Senator* McComb?"

"He was speaking at city hall when it was hit by the bomb," Kate said.

Beckham swallowed with realization. He knew it could just be a coincidence that the Senator was here during the attack, but it was hard to believe when looking at the bigger picture.

This definitely wasn't a random raider attack. These guys weren't just here to steal shit and sew a little chaos. They had known about the location of the bunker on the island, which meant they had an inside source, and they had known McComb was going to be here.

They also had a clear connection to Variants with the acid, which led him to believe they were collaborators.

"Maybe that prisoner told us more than we thought," he said.

"The acid?" Kate asked.

Beckham nodded. He grabbed her and pulled her tight, looking at the rising sun. Earlier, he could have bought the raiders weren't working with the monsters and that they were escaping into the Variant zone just to hide.

But not now.

In this world, Beckham had learned coincidences were never *just* coincidences. Whoever these guys were, they were connected to the monsters, and he had a feeling the only way to unravel this mystery was to return to the hell where the demons dwelled.

— 10 —

The road sign pocked with bullet holes made S.M. Fischer smile every time he drove past.

Is this heaven? No, it's Texas.

Whoever had hung it years ago had scratched out the word "Iowa" and replaced it with the Lone Star State. Nothing against the Midwest or Iowa, but there wasn't anything like the Texas Panhandle. Fischer would have happily shaken the hand of the fellow that had mounted the sign.

He drove his truck solo this morning, but his men weren't far from sight. Three pickups led the way toward the site of one of his damaged oil derricks.

It was one of those mornings that he needed time to think and contemplate. He had started it early, getting up before dawn to map out his day.

He turned his black dual-cab Ford F350 down a rust-colored dirt road and eased off the gas to give the truck ahead some room.

The golden glow of the morning sun continued to rise in a cloudless ocean of blue. He took in the sights cautiously, recalling why he had stayed here after losing his wife.

When he was a child, his parents had sent him to a good Christian boarding school back east. They had a second home in upstate New York where he had eventually met his wife.

During the summers, he had returned to the ranch where he spent dawn to dusk outside riding horses, driving dirt bikes, and hunting for wild hogs with his father's .357. That same handgun was still nestled in his hip holster.

Those were some damn good memories.

Now he felt like most of his time on the ranch was spent hunting for Variants.

Rolling brown hills rose to the west, but the land to the east was flat and green. Portions of old fences lay on their sides beside the dusty road. He didn't bother having them fixed. There was no point in keeping cattle out here anymore. The Variants would kill them all, and he didn't have the men to watch the herds.

The three-thousand heads he did own were in barns not far from his house. The only way the monsters could get to them were through electric fences and his guards.

They had tried in the past, and they had failed every time.

But after the attack on several of his derricks the other night, he was starting to wonder how long they could hold them back. The Alpha had been a smart son of a devil. Who knew how many more were out there like it that would encroach on his land in search of food?

The convoy of pickup trucks pulled off the dirt road, parking along the shoulder. Fischer maneuvered behind them and then killed the engine. He jumped out, and his most trusted guards, Tran and Chase, got out of the truck ahead. They both wore black fatigues and black baseball caps with the red double F logo.

Tran carried an SR-25, and Chase had an M4A1. They nodded at Fischer and flanked him on the walk to the fence. The derrick was on the other side of a hill.

The dozen men started out on the path, their rifles up and ready just in case any Variants had returned to finish what they started.

At the crest of the hill, Fischer saw that there had been no need to return.

He had grown up earning his keep by working on the derricks during the summers when he was back from college, long after his days of playing were over. His father had, in turn, paid for his education.

He knew enough about the technology to know when his engineers were right or when they were just being lazy.

This time, they were right. The derrick was done for.

"Son of a bitch," he said, spitting into the dirt.

The skeletal oil derrick was completely blackened and bent at the top.

That brought his count from ninety-five derricks down to ninety-three. It wouldn't hurt production dramatically, but he couldn't afford to keep losing more. Employing so many men and investing in tools and weapons to fend off the Variants rang in at a heavy price.

At least they had capped the wells before too much oil was burned off.

"Did we recover any bodies?" Fischer asked Tran.

Tran shook his head.

"I doubt we will," Chase said. "My guess is they're just bones now."

He glanced at his watch and then took one last look at the derrick before turning away. He needed to scope out the other one and then get back to the ranch to prepare for his meeting with General Cornelius at noon.

"Tran, ride with me," Fischer said. Before his meeting,

he wanted to talk to Tran again about his thoughts on the General.

The four-pickup convoy headed back on the road to the second damaged rig. This one was in plain sight from the road. After putting the truck in park, Fischer used a pair of binoculars to survey the damage.

"We got this one capped faster," Tran said from the passenger seat. "You think we can get it back up and running?"

"Maybe," Fischer replied. "I'm just not sure if we can recoup the cost, especially since the engineers say they've got about a fifty-fifty shot at getting that thing functional. Might be better to just strip it of parts and..."

His words trailed off when he saw movement.

"Sir?" Tran said.

"You see that?" Fischer whispered, a chill running through him. He zoomed in on movement on the right side of the derrick.

Something was hunched over.

Tran rolled down the window and brought the scope of his SR-25 up to an eye.

"Oh shit," he muttered. "It's a Variant."

Fischer opened the door and exited the vehicle.

"Sir," Tran said, meeting him at the front of the truck. "You should stay inside.

The other men all got out, shouldering their rifles and aiming at the beast in the distance. Fischer calmly reached out to Tran.

"Relax, and give me your rifle," he said.

Tran reluctantly handed it over, and Fischer pulled the bi-pod down. He positioned it on the hood of the truck and lined up the sights on a gruesome scene that made him cringe.

Two human corpses lay in the dirt. But it wasn't the dead engineers the Variant had all but consumed that repulsed him—it was the charred right side of the creature.

Blistering black flesh peeled back to reveal bulbous red tissue the color of a ripe watermelon. The burns extended to the head, covering most of the skull and patchy, melted flesh that had once been its ears.

No wonder it can't hear us, he thought.

"It's not going to miss this, though" Fischer said aloud. He steadied the sights, aiming for the head, moved his finger to the trigger, and pulled. The round found a home in the creature's skull, blowing out a spray of burned flesh.

The monster collapsed over the body of the dead engineer.

Fischer pulled the rifle off the hood and handed it back to Tran.

"Put the bodies of the men in the back of my truck," Fischer ordered.

He got back in his F350 and waited as his men worked, forcing himself to watch them carry the remains back with them.

Chase was right.

There wasn't much left but bones.

A few minutes later they set off for the ranch. Fischer still wanted to have that talk with Tran about General Cornelius, but a new sight caused him to delay those plans again.

"Is that a chopper?" Tran asked.

Fischer looked at the dashboard clock. It was only ten in the morning. He wasn't late for his meeting.

Cornelius, or whoever this was, was early.

Fischer sped around the other trucks and pushed the pedal down, increasing the speed to eighty miles an hour. The vehicle and its oversized wheels easily handled the rough terrain.

They hit smooth gray concrete over the next hill, and he gunned the engine to one hundred miles an hour. The mile long stretch of road had cost him a pretty penny, but he liked to greet his guests with smooth roads to remind them where they were when they arrived, and what they were leaving when they departed.

The Fischer ranch was a castle in the middle of what had once been the Wild West. The property, with its many barns and multiple buildings, was more than fitting for his oil empire, and it was equally fitting for a meeting with the man many thought would be the next President of the country.

Soon, Fischer would make his own determination.

The chopper landed in the field on the other side of the circular drive. Fischer parked and watched the men getting out of the bird. Keeping low, they hurried under the blades, all but two of them wearing fatigues.

He spotted Cornelius among them. The tallest, with a mane of white hair, the General was the type of guy that stood out in a room, commanding attention. He wore a crisp uniform that seemed immaculately clean for the current state of the world.

Dressed in jeans, cowboy boots, and a cowboy hat, Fischer was hardly ready for a meeting with the potential leader of the country, but he honestly didn't care all that much. He wasn't the one asking for money today.

Fischer got out of his truck and considered telling his men to drive it, with the bodies, away, but it was too late.

"Mr. Fischer," Cornelius called out.

Fischer walked out to meet the man, smiling but not too widely. He was a businessman and didn't want to look over eager. Entering negotiations with a poker face was one of the first things his dad taught him.

"You're early, General," Fischer said. He reached out and shook the man's calloused hands.

"My apologies, but a lot happened last night and I wanted to meet with you before I head out east," Cornelius replied.

Fischer motioned for Cornelius to follow him toward the house.

"Perhaps if you get elected you could move the government down here," Fischer suggested. "Then you wouldn't have to leave the best state in the Allied States and you would have prime access to the most productive oil fields to fuel your small army. Don't tell me you aren't interested in them."

Cornelius let out a laugh. "Perhaps, but I've got a lot of other things on my agenda first. Although, you're right. My plans include cooperation with Fischer Fields."

A waft of rotting flesh drifted through the air. Cornelius put a sleeve over his mouth and nose as he passed the truck with the corpses.

"Sorry about that," Fischer said. "We were surveying the damage to my derricks and found some of my men that had been out there a while."

Cornelius lowered his hand. He didn't seem disturbed by the gory sight.

"I'm sorry for your loss, Mr. Fischer," said the General. "You weren't the only one that got hit. Something is happening at the outposts and safe zones. Things that I'm sure President Ringgold wants to keep quiet."

Fischer remained standing by the pickup, his curiosity piqued.

"Ringgold is a smart woman," Cornelius continued. "I like her and Vice President Lemke. They're good people, but they've proven they don't have the strength to protect the country."

Cornelius looked back at the corpses in the truck. "Letting the Variants take over the abandoned cities is a strategic failure. Those cities are ticking time bombs waiting to explode. It's negligence like that is leading to the increase in attacks, like the ones on your ranch."

There was anger in the general's voice. Fischer had heard about the general's temper.

Anger wasn't necessarily bad if it was controlled. But if the general was the type that let emotion get in the way of a sound decision, that was a problem. Someone leading the country needed to be cool and levelheaded, especially when facing threats like this.

"That's why I'm here to make you an offer in return for your support," Cornelius said, the edge no longer in his voice.

Fischer didn't speak too loudly. He didn't want his men to hear the offer just in case Fischer didn't end up accepting it, although he had a feeling whatever it is was, it would beat what little Ringgold had done to protect his oil fields.

***

The morning after the attack, Kate had gone straight to the lab to test the samples rushed in by a helicopter from Outpost Turkey River. Horn and Beckham were outside with several Rangers, and the kids were back at the shelter for survivors in downtown Portland. Knowing Beckham was close and her family was safe helped her focus on the questions.

There were hundreds of thoughts on her mind about the attacks, but she tried to keep them all about science. Her job wasn't to figure out who the raiders were or how the attack on Portland and Peaks Island was connected to the other attacks—her job was to find out what was going on in those Variant tunnels.

A musty odor hung in the lab, contrasting sharply with the sterile hospital smell that usually pervaded the space. Half of her working area was strewn with individually wrapped pipette tips, syringes, and broken beakers.

Muddy boot prints tracked across what had once been a clean white-tiled floor. Kate brushed aside the cardboard boxes of disposable syringes where they lay scattered on a lab bench.

Normally, she would've been bothered by a single pipette negligently left on a lab bench instead of in its stand or a stray disposable nitrile glove left hanging outside a trash can. But today she had no choice but to work in the filth, hoping that the raiders hadn't taken everything she would need for her experiment.

Perusing drawers and cabinets with doors askew, she searched for cell culture supplies. She pulled out a plastic sleeve of cell culture dishes. She could've sworn she had had more in stock.

In the freezer, all her one-liter bottles of red liquid cell media were gone. As were the bottles of bovine serum to supplement that media.

What in God's name did raiders need cell culture supplies for?

Maybe they'd mistaken them for medicine of some

kind. Thankfully she still had a few half-used bottles of media with serum already added in her 4-degree Celsius refrigerator.

Cell culture dishes and handheld electronic pipettes at least had not been stolen. Most of the antibiotics she kept on hand for adding to cell cultures were gone, of course. No surprise there.

That was okay. As long as she was extremely careful, she could minimize the risk of contaminating her culture dishes.

Sitting on the bench in front of her was a cooler-sized Styrofoam container with the samples that had been sent to her from Fitz. She lifted one of the ten milliliter plastic tubes from the container.

The red matter in there—whatever it was—had apparently been living just fine in dirt tunnels bored through the ground by the Variants outside of Outpost Turkey River.

If this stuff had been living in those tunnels, what harm was a little bacteria from the lab anyway?

Looking across the lab space to the smaller room where the biosafety cabinets were, the place looked empty. Not for a lack of debris and lab supplies. But Kate found herself thinking of Doctor Pat Ellis, her old laboratory partner. He'd been with her for several years before he met his tragic end.

There was still a hole in her heart for the man who'd been both a close and valued coworker and friend. Now she had to do this alone.

She missed Ellis, but especially today. All the death and destruction had peeled back the scabs of time, reopening old emotional wounds.

She took the plastic culture dishes and pipettes to one

of the biosafety cabinets, inserted them under the protective glass sash. A bottle of pink, pre-warmed liquid cell medium went in next.

"Let's see what Team Ghost found," she whispered to herself.

Holding the plastic sample tube in one gloved hand, she unscrewed the cap with the other, placing it on the metal surface inside the biosafety cabinet.

Images of the scenes inside the medical tent flashed through her mind. Still fresh, she could practically feel Senator McComb's pulse stopping under her fingers again, smell the coppery scent of blood, and hear the cries of the wounded and the frightened.

She blinked away the memories and exhaustion, willing herself to wake up. The dregs of adrenaline that helped her through the night faded. She needed every bit of brainpower left in her reserves, and it had been so long since she really sat in a lab like this to work on Variant-related research.

But history had a vicious way of repeating itself.

She used a pair of stainless-steel forceps to pull a thin strip of the red webbing from the plastic tube. Dangling in the air above the cell culture dish, it could have been a thinly sliced chunk of steak for all she knew.

Her fingers trembled as she held the forceps, examining the sample.

You got this, Kate.

But in her mind's eye, she saw Timothy standing over his dad again. That look on his face. The pain no child should have to endure. Losing both parents like this. Growing up alone.

The trembling in her fingers traced down the length of the forceps, and the red webbing nearly slipped out.

Holding her breath, she gently deposited the tendril into the cell culture dish. Next, she filled the dish with cell media from one of the bottles in the refrigerator that hadn't been stolen. Hopefully it would get the tendril to grow, using a pipette.

She continued the process. It was work that any decent lab tech—or even a novice student in biology—could do. Yet now, it felt like the hardest thing she had done in her life.

But Kate worked through the pain and anguish like she always did and managed to set up all the samples. She would let them grow and observe their phenotypical changes and behavior. Once she placed the cell culture dishes back in the incubator, she prepared a microscope slide with another razor thin piece of the webbing.

Kate found it hard to believe that this living material had covered those tunnels like Team Ghost had described. When she'd first heard of it, she had figured it must be some kind of fungus. That would explain how it could evidently grow so fast, especially in an underground environment like that.

Now she wasn't so sure.

She took the prepared slide over to an inverted light microscope. Peering through the scope's eyepiece showed her doubts had weight. Most of the tissue seemed to be made of long, striated cells. Clearly mammalian. Between them grew other spidery cells that connected to each other through tendril-like growths that looked suspiciously like dendrites.

If she didn't know any better, she would say those spidery cells looked like nerves. And all the others around them might be myoblast or fibroblasts—muscle cells or connective tissue cells.

Cells like that didn't grow outside of an animal or human though. At least not that she knew of. With the Variants, it seemed all the rules of nature had been broken or bent.

The trick was figuring out how the cells grew like that, and if these cells had some kind of secrets that would help them find Dohi or prevent another Turkey River event, then she was determined to uncover them.

She made a note to check her supplies for the antibody kits she would need to perform proper tissue characterization assays on these cells. It might be a few days before she got the proper supplies if she was missing anything.

Team Ghost would need her results to have some idea of what they were dealing with in the tunnels. Dohi likely didn't have time to wait for robust experiments. Assuming he was still alive.

Whatever clues might be in these samples needed to be found now. There was no time to do every experiment in replicate and put each hypothesis through a battery of tests.

She would have to go with her gut on this one. Move forward with her hypothesis and verify later. So for now, she would operate as if these cells were indeed a mixture of nerve and muscle cells.

But if they were, the question was why?

And, nearly as important, what kind of creature grew these types of cells?

The dark round spots of nuclei inside them were readily apparent and there was no thick, square-like cell wall holding them together. Definitely not plant or fungus derived like she had originally thought.

As she studied the cells, she noticed something

peculiar. Some of the nuclei were actually dividing in front of her eyes. And as they did, so too did the cytoplasm—all the gooey parts inside the cells.

That couldn't be possible…

She blinked, half-tempted to pinch herself to make sure she wasn't dreaming, taken by exhaustion. Sure enough, when she stared back through the eyepiece, she saw that the cells were in fact dividing.

They weren't just dividing—they were growing. Odd, considering the slice she'd prepared for the slide wasn't in perfect physiological conditions like the cell culture dishes in the incubator.

Mammalian cells just didn't do a good job growing unless they were in the right temperature, humidity, oxygen levels, and nutrients. Yet here these were, not only dividing, but spreading across the slide rapidly.

"This can't be…" she whispered.

Ellis would have loved seeing this.

She stored the slide in a culture dish and kept it on the table next to the scope, too afraid to simply discard it. Before she threw it out, she made a mental note to douse this thing in acid or burn it, just to make sure it didn't start growing from a landfill or something. Then she went back to the incubator, pulled out one of the cell culture dishes, and placed it on the microscope's stage.

She didn't even have to look through the eyepiece to see that the cells within that dish had already adapted to their environment. The tissue sample pulsed wildly, contracting and expanding randomly throughout the strand.

When viewed through the scope, the images there only confirmed her suspicions. Those cells she thought were myoblasts were moving. Just like cardiomyocytes, the cells that automatically contracted and released to maintain a person's heartbeat.

What frightened her even more was seeing that as the cells pulsed, they continued to divide. It looked like she was watching a tumor grow in time-lapse images. Only instead of taking weeks or months for the tumor to become malignant and spread, it was happening in seconds.

Kate's stomach sank as she peeled herself away from the scope. The Variants had tested her knowledge and understanding of biology from the very start. Now it was as if they were toying with her and torturing her with the unknown.

But she would not be tricked.

If these biological samples contained the clues that would stop whatever happened at Outpost Turkey River from spreading, she would crack the code.

11

Everything hurt.

That was the first thing that made its way into Dohi's dulled consciousness. Sharp pain radiated through his elbows and throbbed along his spine. His mind seemed to be trapped in a dark pool.

Maybe his body, too.

He couldn't see anything but black.

Fear joined the pain, and adrenaline churned through his vessels.

The grogginess fogging his mind faded, and he felt his limbs again. Something was dragging him over the ground. The rush of blood helped activate his senses, and the memories flooded him with the events at Outpost Turkey River.

Variants had ambushed him, and he had fallen into a tunnel.

Everything after that was a haze.

There was no easy way to tell how long he'd been out or how far he had been dragged. His headset and night vision goggles were busted to shit. His rifle had been lost in the fray.

Slowly he felt near his hip. At least his M1911 was still in its holster. Thankfully, so was the tactical light on his utility belt. If he stood any chance of escaping, he would need both.

That was going to be very difficult judging from the

huge claws wrapped around one of his ankles. While he couldn't see the beast, he could tell right away this was no ordinary grunt Variant.

At least not judging by the heavy thwack of its footsteps and the bellowing, huffing breaths it let out.

Suddenly the creature let out a high-pitched squeal and a series of clicks.

A Variant answered in the distance.

The abomination dragged him deeper into the tunnel. The squawks and clicking of joints echoed.

Without the luxury of sight, Dohi concentrated on his other senses.

The rotten fruit odor of the creatures overwhelmed him, especially the stink of the monster dragging him along. If he let his fingers relax, tracing along the tunnel floor, he could feel the moist earth and more prominently the stretchy webbing that he'd seen before he'd fallen into the tunnel.

Every time he made contact with the organic material it made the hair on his arm stand straight. The air itself left a biting, cruel taste on his tongue, making his stomach roil. Almost as if he had taken a long swig of chunky spoiled milk.

He tried to focus on counting the number of Variants but the agonized cries of the other human captives made the task difficult. He guessed there were at least half a dozen grunts marching in front of the monstrous knuckle-dragger pulling him along.

Maybe he was thinking about this the wrong way— maybe this was a break and the bastards would take him right to their nest. If he could escape, he would have the location of this lair and the rest of the people from Outpost Turkey River.

But escaping was going to be next to impossible down here.

He went back to using his internal compass to try and track the path just in case he might have an opportunity. The path seemed to wind and curve so much, it was difficult to maintain any semblance of proper orientation.

The longer he was dragged, the worse of a beating he took. His mind struggled to maintain focus, and he couldn't tell if he'd gone unconscious again or if time passed differently in the inky darkness.

In truth, he had no idea how long he had been down here.

A piercing scream suddenly echoed down the tunnel, followed by the unmistakable splatter of blood. The clamor of squawking Variants exploded through the murk.

Something primal roared in Dohi. Pure instinct, ingrained by years of evolution, prepping him for a flight or fight response.

Another human scream blared, cut short by a tearing sound.

Then a thump. Like a body falling, followed by another, lighter thump. Dohi imagined a headless body hitting the ground and a horde of Variants consuming the meat.

A moment later, the monstrous creature pulling him halted.

Dohi tried hard to control his breathing.

The beast gave him a single tug, inching him forward slightly.

Another human shrieked.

That's when he made his move.

With all his strength, he yanked his boot free from his

captor. The monster was caught off guard and jerked backward as Dohi pulled his M1911 from its holster and with his other hand pulled out his tac light.

He flicked the flashlight on and spun on his captor, bringing the handgun to bear in concert with the light's beam.

Time seemed to slow.

The tunnel around him was nearly twice as tall as Dohi, and the beast before him took up most of that space. An ape-like face with exaggerated, pointed features rotated in his direction. Huge nostrils flared, and its lips tore back to reveal a set of curved fangs. Large, bat-like ears fanned off the side of its face, and its wide, webbed claws were caked in dirt.

Dohi had expected the creature to stare him down— or maybe, if he was lucky, throw a clawed hand in front of its eyes to shield itself from the sudden blinding light.

But this Alpha didn't even move away from the beam. It was then he realized its milky white eyes weren't even looking at him. Suddenly the high-pitched squeals and clicks made sense. The beast was using echolocation, perfectly suited for the tunnel.

Dohi didn't waste another second and pulled the trigger.

Click.

"Shit," he muttered.

The beast simply tilted its head, not realizing how lucky it was that his gun hadn't fired. Muscles rippled down the length of its body, and some kind of viscous goo coated its smooth flesh.

Claws large enough to go straight through Dohi's chest and out the other side protruded from its fingers. Thin tendrils sprouted from its spine. Each of those fibers seemed to prod at the webbing along the tunnel wall.

The beast released another high-pitched shriek.

Now he was fucked.

Dohi quickly pulled the slide back to chamber a round and pulled the trigger as the beast homed in on him. Two rounds buried in its barreled chest.

He kept the beam aimed on the creature as he fired. Blood and bits of clear goo flecked off in the light.

The other Variants in the tunnel dropped their human captives ahead. In the glow of his beam, he noticed humans stuck in the red webbing. The strange growths seemed to spread out of their open mouths and eyes.

Dohi had no time to make sense of the horrific scene. The Variants charged around the Alpha.

One of the monsters flung itself into the air, claws outstretched.

Dohi fired twice into the creature's center mass, sending it sliding across the tunnel floor. Two more trampled over their dead comrade, and Dohi took them out in quick succession and then put a round in the Alpha's skull, sending it hunching against a wall.

He quickly pushed himself up and limped away, changing his magazine while he moved. Every step hurt, each tremor rocking through his bruised bones.

Palming in the mag, he turned and raised the gun and light at the pursuing Variants. He squared off another shot that slammed into the head of the lead monster.

Two more darted past and he took them both down with shots to their T sections. The giant Alpha roared behind them and then lumbered forward on all fours, using its wide claws to help propel itself forward like a gorilla.

Dohi sent another shot straight through the chest of the last grunt Variant. The beast crumpled, tumbling headfirst into the webbing. The Alpha careened forward stomping the dead into the mud while letting out another piercing screech.

The long fibrous growths tracing along the red webbing tensed.

Dohi could almost feel the air explode with electricity.

He pulled the trigger again, sending a bullet punching into the Alpha's chest that resulted in a raucous roar. It seemed to absorb the impact.

Another trigger squeeze and the slide locked.

The pistol was empty, and he was out of magazines. He had lost his buck knife in the fall with his rifle. All he had to defend himself with were his hands.

Those fight-or-flight instincts kicked in again.

This time he chose the latter of the two.

Dohi ran using his light to guide him through the tunnel. Webbing snagged at his boots and shoulders, and he broke through the sticky vine-like growths. The earthen corridors branched. He took random turns, no idea where he was headed.

Grunts and squeals resounded through the tunnel as the beast used echolocation to track him. But even when Dohi was far out of what he judged as the beast's effective sonar range, the monster still pursued.

That left only a few other possibilities. Scent being one of them, but he couldn't help but wonder if the webbing also had something to do with it being able to track him.

He pictured those fibrous growths sprouting from the Alpha's spine and tracing the webbing. Running wasn't going to help him escape either of those things.

He stopped around another bend and placed his hand

between the gaps in the webbing. Easily his fingers pressed through the muddy soil.

Maybe...

He turned around and stretched the webbing over himself. Then he slowly squirmed backward into the mud. With his hands, he smeared it over his body in cold, wet globs. As best he could, he dug out a shallow cavity in the wall.

The stomping of the Alpha grew closer. Squeals erupting down the tunnel.

Mud slopped around Dohi's shoulders, and he squeezed it over his helmet, into his hair, and over his cheeks.

Another high-pitched shriek echoed down the tunnel.

He flicked off his flashlight and stuffed it into his pocket. He was almost certain the Alpha couldn't see, but he didn't want to take any chances.

The ground trembled.

The beast wasn't far.

Dohi sucked in a deep breath and closed his eyes. The tunnels were already steeped in darkness, but he couldn't help the natural instinct to make every bit of him disappear in that mud under the web.

The clicking grew louder. The beast couldn't have been more than a yard or more away now. Massive feet slopped along the muck, and a rolling growl sounded.

Dohi could smell rancid breath, but he kept his mouth clamped shut, the air still in his lungs.

A sniffing followed the growl.

It knows I'm here. It knows.

Another whoosh of rank breath rushed past Dohi's mud-covered face.

The creature was right in front of him.

Was it toying with him?

His lungs burned, but he held the same breath inside. If he let it out, the beast would tear out his guts.

As the seconds passed his heart thumped harder.

Could it hear that?

The creature growled again.

Then it stomped away, taking off down the passage the way they had come. Dohi waited a few more moments before slowly letting out a breath. He gulped down a mouthful of the tunnel air. Musty and rotten as it was, air had never tasted sweeter.

He stayed in the mud behind the webbing until those clicks and squeals finally went silent. After another fifteen minutes had passed, he emerged from the mud and squeezed back through the gaps in the webbing. He pulled his fingers over his face and through his goatee, flaking the mud away.

With nothing but a flashlight to find his way out of here, he set off, knowing what he had seen had to be relayed to command before another outpost was attacked.

The very future of the country could rest on his escape.

***

The late afternoon sunlight filtered through the trees the day after Team Ghost lost Dohi. They remained at Outpost Turkey River where they had received a resupply in the evac that had taken Cedric Long to command for questioning, and the samples Fitz collected for Kate.

Fitz wasn't leaving until they had recovered Dohi. Every passing hour, he knew the chances of finding him alive were shrinking.

But Dohi was the best tracker on Team Ghost, a veritable bloodhound. If anyone could survive underground in the Variant infested superhighway it was Dohi.

Fitz checked his team as they continued the search for their lost brother.

Mendez was on point. Lincoln had rearguard, his gaze roving the skeletal trees. Fitz and Rico were between them. Ace wore a large black backpack that held a rugged computer system and battery connected to the long gray tubular instrument he carried.

The tube looked like an old-fashioned bazooka, except that it had an LCD screen glowing up toward Ace. He held it over the ground in front of him like a minesweeper.

When command had learned of the team's situation, they had offered the perfect solution. Along with fresh ammunition, a group of Army engineers had dropped off an R2TD, or Rapid Reaction Tunnel Detection system developed over a decade ago by the US Army. It used ground penetrating radar to detect tunnels as well as the sounds and activity of people or machinery underground.

Before abandoning some of the cities to Variants after the great war ended, the device was widely used by squads just like Team Ghost.

While operating the device was easy enough, discerning the signal from noise on the detection screen Ace was staring at was more of an art than a science and would require communication with two Army combat engineers.

"Overwatch 1, Ghost 1," Fitz whispered. "Anything?"

"Negative, Ghost 1," Lieutenant Scott, the engineer assisting them, replied. "We'll ping you if we see something. Over."

For all the magic that the engineers had promised them this R2TD system could accomplish, they had found precious little to show for it. Fitz looked over at Rico with a raised brow. An unspoken question: Can you believe this?

She shrugged back.

For far too many hours, they'd been scouring the forest with only the rustle of the trees to keep them company. They hadn't found a single tunnel. Nothing to take them to Dohi or the escaped Variants.

He was halfway tempted to try something drastic. Start setting up explosives to blow holes in the earth. Maybe cave in some tunnels and get the beasts to show themselves.

But that was his frustration speaking and it could end up killing Dohi and any other prisoners below ground.

Slow and steady saves lives, Fitz thought.

They approached the crest of another rolling hill, far past the outskirts of Outpost Turkey River's safe zone. Every step they took was another pulling them deeper into enemy territory.

Ace froze, his eyes on the screen. He motioned to Fitz to join him.

If Fitz wasn't mistaken, the strange deep blue and black colors appearing in a semi-circle on the screen were what the engineers had told them they would see if they had indeed found a tunnel.

Fitz studied the image for a second, making sure what he was seeing was real.

Lieutenant Scott chimed back in over the channel. "Ghost 1, Overwatch 1. You have a positive read. Tunnel depth approximately one meter down and three meters in diameter directly below your position. Appears to lead twenty degrees east from current course."

Fitz signaled to Mendez to adjust his route and follow Scott's directions.

Sure enough the signal on Ace's radar screen remained strong. Fitz followed, finally confident that they had a trail of some kind.

They still didn't know if this was the tunnel that Dohi had gone down, but without any other leads, this was the best chance they had of finding some clue as to where their brother had gone.

Ace stopped again, and Fitz checked the screen. Strange shapes emerged there. Green, globular things, almost like spirits.

There were Variants under their feet, and possibly human prisoners, too.

"Ghost 1, slow down," Scott said over the comm channel.

"Any idea how many targets are down there?" Fitz asked.

There was a slight pause before the Lieutenant replied. "Ghost 1, by my estimate, you've got six to eight contacts."

Fitz did the math. Getting the scoop on six to eight Variants would be tough, but doable. Especially if a couple of those contacts turned out to be captive humans and not Variants.

"Ghost 1," Scott began, "I'm seeing something strange. Is there any issue with the R2TD system? Like one of the power supply cords damaged or something?"

Fitz and Ace gave the cables and system a cursory glance. But neither of them was as technically familiar with the system as the engineers.

"Negative," Fitz responded. "At least, as far as I can tell."

"I'm getting some really weird readings," Scott replied.

Fitz looked at the screen. A flash of white seemed to illuminate the circumference of the tunnel on the radar readings. "Is it this halo-looking thing you're talking about?"

"Correct, Ghost 1," Scott said. "If you're seeing it, too, that means it's not just an imaging artifact on my end."

Fitz wasn't sure what the engineer meant by artifact, but he didn't like the sudden nervousness in the man's voice.

Fitz peered back over his shoulder. The woods around them were mostly silent. Not even the call of the crows that lived in the canopy. Only a few dried leaves brushing against each other.

"The electromagnetic induction system that the R2TD uses can also detect other EM signals," Scott said.

"In English, please," Fitz said.

"Electrical wires, communications equipment, all that stuff. If there's power going through a cable, for instance, it'll give off a signal like that."

"And light up the whole tunnel?"

"Negative," Scott said. "Ghost 1, something's happening below you. The entire tunnel is exploding in electromagnetic activity. Like, the whole thing is wired or something."

Fitz wracked his mind trying to come up with any explanation that made sense.

"That webbing," Rico whispered. "You think—?"

She had no time to finish the thought. A huge green amorphous shape appeared on Ace's screen. Fitz saw it only for a brief second before the ground erupted, soil and grass flying around them.

The force of the blast sent Ace flying backward. He hit a tree trunk, his helmet cracking against the side and knocking him unconscious.

Fitz managed to level his rifle up as the cloud of dirt fell back to the ground. A beast appeared at the lip of the hole and jumped out, blood seeping out of the dirt-covered flesh.

The monster looked like some muscular mix of a bat and a gorilla. Long fibrous growths stood out of its spine like a porcupine's quills. It let out a series of shrieking clicks, bulbous head swiveling on its neck.

"Take it down!" Fitz ordered.

The rest of Team Ghost fired as he pulled the trigger.

The beast propelled itself through the torrent of gunfire, barreling straight toward Ace who was still limp on the ground.

Rico tried to move in closer, chewing up the creature's flank. Lincoln and Mendez followed suit, battering at the creature with gunfire.

The beast started to slow, wounds stitching its side. A long groan erupted from its wormy lips as it reared back a meaty fist tipped with knife-like claws.

"Behind us!" Rico shouted.

Fitz twisted as six grunt Variants emerged from the hole.

He didn't even need to yell at Mendez and Rico to turn their focus on the beasts.

Fitz finished his magazine, scoring several more hits on the Alpha.

"Help!" Rico shouted.

Lincoln turned to provide covering fire while Fitz

changed his magazine. In the seconds it took him to pull out a fresh one and palm it home, the Alpha had reached Ace.

More blood sprayed from the rounds buried in its flesh, and yet the creature still advanced, bending down with a talon tipped claw.

But to Fitz's surprise, the blades didn't curl around the fallen member of Team Ghost. Instead they grabbed the long, tubular portion of the R2TD. The beast crunched into the metal, and the device fell apart like it was nothing more than a Lego model.

For a moment, the creature stood there. It let out a breath almost as if it was relieved, blood trickling out of its gaping nostrils and weeping down the front of its chest.

Then it collapsed, the ground trembling from the impact.

Fitz checked his six, seeing the other members of Ghost had cleared the area. Crumpled Variants lay in the dirt.

Rico and Mendez stepped between the fresh corpses of the smaller Variants while Lincoln followed Fitz over to the beast. Another transmission hissed over the comm channel, and he could finally make out the Lieutenant.

"I lost the signal," Scott said.

Fitz kicked the dirt near the shattered machine and reported the loss. Then he made his way over to Ace, who began to stir, lifting a hand toward his head.

"You good?" Rico said.

Ace managed a nod.

"You sure?" Fitz said, crouching.

"I've taken worse hits in my day, boss," Ace said, as Fitz and Mendez helped him to his feet.

"So what do we do now that we don't have R2TD to guide us?" Lincoln said.

Fitz found himself missing Apollo right now more than ever. The team could use the dog's nose, and he considered requesting the army send fresh canine reinforcements to help their search.

But even if they did, that would just take up more time that they might not have to find Dohi.

Fitz walked over to the Alpha and nudged the enormous clawed hand. The beast didn't move. Blood seeped from its body, soaking the ground.

He stared at it for a moment, wondering what had compelled it to go straight for the radar system, as if it possessed some kind of preternatural intelligence.

"You hear that?" Mendez whispered.

The scratching came a moment later, and Fitz nodded. He ordered Rico and Lincoln to watch over Ace, then gestured for Mendez to fall in with him.

They moved around the side of the Alpha, guns pointed at the hole in the ground where the Alpha and its minions had appeared. A dark shape moved out of the dirt there. Soil-covered fingers clawed at the lip of the hole pulling a body up covered in mud.

Nothing but the white of the creature's eyes showed.

"Hold your fire!" the creature said in an all too familiar voice.

Fitz lowered his rifle and blinked to make sure his eyes weren't playing tricks on him.

"Dohi?" Rico said.

She bent down, and together with Fitz, they grabbed Dohi and helped pull him onto solid ground.

"Dude, where the…" Lincoln said.

He and Mendez looked down in the hole, aiming their

rifles into the darkness.

Dohi sat up on his knees and wiped his face with a sleeve.

As much as Fitz was thrilled to see his friend, Dohi smelled like he had just crawled out of a sewer.

"Water," Dohi choked.

Fitz quickly handed him a water bottle.

The rest of the team were all grins, but they didn't give away their position by calling out in celebration.

Dohi finished off a drink, wiped his mouth, and then looked at the Alpha.

"That monster almost ended me," he said.

"What the hell is it?" Fitz said.

"Some new kind of Alpha," Dohi said.

Ace staggered over like he was drunk with blood dripping down his forehead. He cradled his shotgun and stood over the hole, guarding it with the others while Fitz opened a channel to command.

"Hotspot 1, this is Ghost 1, requesting evac. We've got a brand-new specimen for you."

"Copy that Ghost, sending a chopper to the outpost. Over."

"We got to haul ass back there," Lincoln muttered when Fitz shared the news.

"Who's got the rope?" Rico asked.

Lincoln looked at her and then the Alpha.

"You got to be kidding me, we're taking it with?" he grumbled.

"Yeah, and you're going to pull it first," Fitz said.

Mendez chuckled. "You're such a baby, brah."

"You help him," Fitz watched as the grin on Mendez's face soured.

Working with Lincoln, he helped secure the rope

around the Alpha's legs.

"Damn, look at these paws," Lincoln said. "Huge."

"All the better for digging, by the looks of it," Mendez said.

"Let's move out," Fitz said. He led Team Ghost off in silence toward the evac zone back in the walled off outpost. It was slow going, and the team took turns dragging the monster that was basically a tunnel-digging machine.

Fitz held his questions for Dohi, trying to keep quiet, and also give the man some time to collect his thoughts.

"Glad to have you back, brother," Fitz said.

Dohi hardly reacted, his eyes glazed like he was in a trance.

An hour and a half later the distant thump of a bird sounded.

Lincoln and Mendez dragged the Alpha out toward the landing zone, while the rest of the team scanned the shadows for hostiles. If the Variants were going to attack, this would be the time.

But the beasts remained hidden, and the chopper set down, the crew hopping out to help load the Alpha. The crew chief passed a new headset to Dohi.

After Dohi drank another bottle of water, Fitz finally figured it was time to ask him some questions, the most obvious one coming first.

"How'd you find us?" Fitz said.

"I followed the gunfire and the screams."

Fitz was so tired he hadn't even considered it. Of course Dohi would have come toward the sound of gunfire, but why had the Alpha come after the R2TD?

That was a question far above his pay grade, but looking at the beast slumped on the floor of the chopper, he imagined someone would be able to figure it out.

For now, Fitz was counting his blessings.

They had Dohi back, and they had killed a beast that might just hold the key to the mystery behind the tunnels and recent attacks.

Today was a victory.

He would savor it as long as he could.

12

"I've got to figure out what's going on," Beckham said to Kate.

"I understand why you have to go," Kate said. "Hopefully President Ringgold will be able to give you answers."

He had expected Kate to protest, but if the bags under her eyes were any indication, she was too exhausted.

Voices outside brought him to the window of the historic brick and stone hotel that was now serving as a shelter for the survivors of Peaks Island.

The room his family had been assigned was small, but nice, with two bedrooms, a large bathroom, and a kitchen. It wasn't their comfortable home back on Peaks Island, but it would suffice until they could return.

Outside a platoon of Marines patrolled the streets. They had deployed all across the country at affected outposts per President Ringgold's orders. Beckham felt much better about leaving now that they were here. Especially since Kate also had Sergeant Ruckley and her Ranger team assigned to protect the lab.

Kate pinched the bridge of her nose.

"Headache?" he asked.

Kate nodded and sighed. "Tired."

Beckham was, too, but at least he could sleep on the ride to command.

"You promise you'll try and get some sleep now?" he asked her.

She placed a hand on her forehead. "If I can...but not until tonight. I've got to get back to the lab. I just wanted to see you off and make sure Javier and the kids are okay."

Beckham hated seeing her like this, but she had duties to their country just like he did, and she took them just as seriously.

"Has that sample that Fitz sent back been helpful?" Beckham asked, anxious to hear about it.

"Helpful is a generous word. I've only had the day to analyze it, but so far, I've got more questions than answers."

"Do you at least have some idea what that stuff is?"

Kate pulled her hand away from her head. "This is going to sound crazy, but it looks to me like mammalian muscle and nerve cells. They seem to spontaneously grow at an alarming rate... Faster than even cancer cells."

Beckham knew just enough about science to know that was weird. "I didn't think cells like that could just grow outside an animal's body."

"Normally they can't," Kate said. "There are a whole bunch of reasons why they shouldn't be able to grow like they are. Most obvious is the lack of nutrient and oxygen delivery, along with a working immune system."

"So you're telling me those tunnel walls are alive?"

He thought she was going to shrug, but after a slight hesitation she nodded.

"Not literally," she said. "The cells are. Those vines are. But not the tunnels. Still, the longer I examined the cells under the scope, the more red and white blood cells

I found. There seemed to be small vesicles, too, to deliver those cells."

She stepped closer to the window. "Whatever this growth is, it's unlike anything I've ever seen before."

"This has to have something to do with Outpost Turkey River, don't you think? The missing people."

"Probably. My guess is the Variants are using people as food and energy, like fodder for the cellular growths. Hard to tell right now though."

Beckham swallowed hard at the implications.

"With the sheer number of nerve cells in there, I'd have to guess it's some kind of massive sensory organ or something," Kate said. "How exactly it works—or why—I'm still not sure. But that's what I hope to find out. Only way to do that is go back to the lab."

She gave Beckham a hug, holding him tightly for a moment.

"It feels good to have some work to do," she admitted with her head to his chest. "Spending time in the lab has made me miss Ellis even more though. He was a close friend, no denying that, but I could also use a hand or two on these experiments. It's a lot for one person to do."

"I'd be surprised if Ringgold doesn't already have plans to send help your way. If she doesn't, I'll request it."

"I wouldn't say no to that." She pulled away and took in a deep breath. "I just hope whatever is happening, we can stop it."

"Dohi is alive, and the Alpha the team killed might help us figure out what's going on. Everything is going to be okay."

"Maybe for us, but not for everyone. Not for Timothy."

Beckham brooded at her words.

She was right.

Timothy's life would be forever changed.

"We'll take care of him," he said.

Kate simply nodded.

"We survived the war," Beckham said. "We'll survive whatever this is."

Whatever this is… he thought.

The limited intel he had right now wasn't much, but it led him to believe that the attacks at the outposts were the start of something much bigger and widely coordinated. That's exactly why President Ringgold had requested his council at command to meet her and Team Ghost.

But it wasn't just soldiers that would win this new fight. The work Kate was doing in her lab was also important.

The thump of a chopper sounded in the distance, and a Black Hawk crossed over the city, putting down in a green space a few blocks away.

"My ride is here," he said. "I better get moving so I can say goodbye to Javier and the kids."

He walked away from the window to grab his rucksack and rifle, but she grabbed his prosthetic hand.

"Reed, we still haven't talked about Senator McComb," Kate said.

"I know…but that can wait. For now, the more important thing is figuring out who is behind these attacks and what those tunnels are used for."

"But what if President Ringgold asks you to run for Senate again? With McComb gone, she'll be even more desperate to find a good candidate."

"I won't make a decision without talking to you first, I promise."

He threw his pack over his shoulders and slung his rifle. Then he opened the door and reached for her hand. She gripped his prosthetic on the walk to the stairs. Several doors were open along the way, one of them to the room Donna was sharing with her son.

Beckham paused at the open doorway. "You guys doing okay?"

Donna managed a half smile, but he knew it was forced. She limped over to the door, her ankle wrapped. Bo wore a tank top that showed off his muscular body.

He seemed fine, despite the bandage on his head.

The two had been through so much in the past decade. Once again, they were victims of war, and if it weren't for Beckham and Horn, they would have ended up like Bo's father, Red.

A memory of the large man fighting the Bone Collector on Plum Island flashed through Beckham's memory—the same beast that had killed Staff Sergeant Alex 'The Kid' Riley.

"Your ankle okay?" Beckham asked Donna.

She directed her dull eyes at him and nodded.

All of the torment she had suffered had taken its toll.

Beckham wasn't sure if Donna would ever come back from the darkness, but he believed there was still hope for her son. Bo still had a sparkle in his gaze. Like most kids, he was resilient.

"I heard that raider died in the police station." Bo crossed his arms as he continued, "You should have let me take care of that piece of garbage in the woods."

The spark Beckham had seen a few moments before

seemed to grow. But instead of the optimism and hope Beckham had expected, it was replaced by rage.

"We needed information from him," Beckham said.

"Did you get any?" Bo asked.

Beckham shook his head. "Unfortunately, no."

Bo snorted and muttered under his breath.

"I've got to go, but I'll see you both soon," Beckham said. He nodded at Donna and then did the same to Bo. The teenager nodded back and walked away, fists still clenched, knuckles white. "Just wanted to make sure you were doing all right."

"Let me know if you need anything," Kate said. "I'm right down the hall."

"Thank you," Donna replied. She slowly shut the door, whispering something to Bo that Beckham couldn't make out.

Kate frowned and Beckham let out a sigh. They made their way down the stairs to the lobby. The place was packed with their fellow refugees, all friends and neighbors, from Peaks Island.

Beckham said hello to a few people but hurried outside. Horn stood on the sidewalk smoking a cigarette, a rifle slung over his back.

"Where are the kids?" Kate asked, holding up a hand to shield her tired eyes from the sun.

Horn pointed with his cigarette at the park across the street, "Figured I'd let 'em run a bit."

Laughter came from behind several trees in the park. The sound was the last thing Beckham had expected to hear, but it was a welcome one.

He followed the drifting giggles to the park with Kate and Horn. On the other side of the trees, they found Javier, Tasha, and Jenny playing with Ginger and Spark.

The dogs rolled in the grass and chased a bone Javier threw.

But not everyone was enjoying the sunshine and dogs.

Timothy sat on a bench, staring into the distance.

"Better keep a close eye on him while I'm gone," Beckham said.

Kate folded her arms across her chest, looking at the young man with concern. "I will. He's staying at the shelter until things are secure on the island, and then we'll have to figure out if he's going to stay with us."

"Like I said, we'll take care of him," Beckham said.

Horn flicked his cigarette on the ground. "He's welcome to stay with me, too."

"We'll figure it all out." Beckham shrugged his pack higher on his shoulder. "I've really got to get to the bird now."

"How long you going to be gone?" Horn asked.

"Hopefully not more than a day or two." Horn smothered the cigarette with a boot. "You sure you don't want me to come?"

"I want you to stay here and keep watch over the home fires," Beckham said.

"You got it, boss."

Javier spotted them then and came running over. He wrapped his arms around Beckham.

"Look after your mom for me while I'm gone."

"I will, Dad."

Javier ran back to the other kids, and Beckham made his way over to Timothy. The teenager looked up as he approached.

"How you doing?" Beckham asked.

Timothy didn't reply.

"I'm really sorry about your dad."

Timothy didn't respond to that either, but he did look at Beckham's fatigues, rucksack, and weapon.

"You going somewhere?"

Beckham pointed to the chopper waiting in a field a few blocks away. "To SOCOM on the USS *George Johnson*."

"Can I come?"

"You have a more important role here," Beckham said. He jerked his chin at the kids. "I need you to look after everyone like your dad did."

Timothy glanced around. "I want to fight, not play babysitter."

Beckham understood where he was coming from. Just like Bo, Timothy wanted to fight back. Wanted revenge for what he'd lost. But neither of the boys were ready or even trained to fight the raiders or Variants.

"When I get back, you, me, and Bo are going to sit down to talk about your futures," Beckham said. "Until then, please watch after things here for me. Okay?"

"Yeah, okay," Timothy replied. He got up and followed Beckham over to the group that had huddled around the dogs.

"I'll see you all soon," Beckham said. He finished his goodbyes, patted Spark and Ginger, and then he set off for a new mission.

The pilots and crew chief waited for him in the grass outside the Black Hawk, eating a snack of local produce a few citizens had brought them.

"Captain Beckham, good to have you with us," said one of the pilots. He climbed back into the cockpit, and the crew chief jumped into the open troop hold.

"Captain," he said, handing him a headset.

"Thanks," Beckham said.

A few minutes later they pulled into the air.

Beckham looked out the window to the quaint city below, seeing the hotel turned shelter for refugees from Peaks Island and the Marines and Rangers patrolling the area.

Several Humvees and a MATV sat parked in front of the police station. Despite all their firepower and armor, they hadn't been able to stop the raider from burning his face off with Variant acid.

Debris piles and the charcoaled ground outside town hall evinced the night's destruction.

Beckham closed his eyes and rested his head on the bulkhead.

There were so many questions in his mind; hopefully, in a few hours, he would start to get some answers.

But first, he needed sleep.

***

President Jan Ringgold flew under the cover of darkness in a stealth Black Hawk like the one she had used to escape the attack on the Greenbrier almost eight years ago.

Tonight, she wasn't escaping anything, but her nerves were still tight like back then. Over the past several days, the situation had escalated from one outpost going dark to three outposts going dark, and three more attacked by raiders.

Her generals and intelligence officers were still piecing things together. By the time she reached command she hoped to have a better idea of what the hell was happening out there.

She had been in politics long enough to know one

thing—these attacks would have a dramatic effect on the upcoming election. The violence gave General Cornelius and his Freedom Party plenty of ammo to accuse her administration of being unable to protect the country, which meant more ammo to support bombing the cities and conscripting an army of kids to fight.

Last week, Vice President Lemke had been ahead in the polls. This week the polls would tell a different story. Fear was a powerful motivating factor, and there had been plenty of reasons for fear to spread through the citizens of the safe zones.

She opened her briefing folder to see more numbers. These weren't polls; they were the number of troops she had at her disposal. Before she left, she had requested the current count from her staff.

Now she stared at them.

These can't be right...

Twelve thousand and change wasn't much.

There were ninety-eight outposts, varying in size. If her math was right, and she deployed all the troops equally, there would be just over one hundred and twenty for each outpost to join the current militias there.

Hardly an army.

The Navy and Air Force had about the same numbers combined with just shy of fifteen thousand. But that wouldn't help at the outposts except by pulling the Special Ops teams like the SEALs.

She didn't like it, but Cornelius had two thousand of his own men and women in his private army that could be deployed should the need arise. But she wasn't sure how cooperative he would be given the current political climate and certainly didn't want to rely on them if she didn't have to.

Next she looked at the current estimate of Variants in the frontier and living in the abandoned cities. The number seemed like a lot, but it wasn't a surprise.

Sixty to sixty-five thousand.

The estimate had actually gone down since she saw it last, with scientists arguing the creatures were starving to death and killing each other. There was almost no evidence of any breeding, which was another good sign that their numbers would continue to drop.

The beasts didn't seem like a huge threat until now, and that's why she hadn't destroyed the cities or sent in precious troops to wipe them out. Plus, there was still the hope that someday humanity could reclaim those urban centers, once symbols of their economic and cultural strength.

The idea was to let the creatures die naturally, and only go after the Alphas that ventured out to cause problems at the outposts. The plan had worked well until two days ago.

"ETA fifteen minutes, Madam President," said one of the pilots.

Ringgold put her briefing folder back into her pack, trying to suppress her worries. She was packing light, expecting to stay on the USS *George Johnson* only twenty-four hours or less.

Vice President Lemke had remained behind at the Greenbrier's PEOC. He and Brigadier General Lucas Barnes had insisted she stay there, but she wanted to talk in person to the teams most familiar with the situation.

The soldiers on the ground were always more knowledgeable than the generals about what was *really* happening, from her experience.

Men like Captain Reed Beckham, whom she trusted

more than all of her generals combined. He had served his country in a way few men in the history of the country had served, and now she needed him for a new mission.

With the death of Senator McComb last night, it was time for the former leader of Team Ghost to carry the torch into the halls of Congress.

She also needed his wife, Kate, to figure out what was going on in the tunnels. The couple had done more for America than anyone she knew, and once again, she was asking for their help.

"Prepare for landing," said one of the pilots.

Ringgold looked out the porthole window. She knew she was over the ocean, but she couldn't see the stealth destroyer in the darkness. Clouds drifted across the horizon blocking out most of the moonlight and the stars.

A few moments later the wheels touched down with a soft jolt.

The crew chief across from her opened the door, and two of her Secret Service agents helped her onto the deck. A group of Marines ran over to escort them.

General Noah Souza, the SOCOM Commander, waited for her outside a hatch. He was a handsome man with a square jaw, sharp nose, and even sharper green eyes.

"Madam President, good to have you with us tonight," he said in his rough voice.

"Thank you, General. First things first, take me to that Alpha."

Souza looked at her security guards, but quickly focused back on her. "Yes, Madam President, but I'll warn you, it's pretty gruesome."

"I've seen plenty of dead monsters," she said.

"That makes two of us," Souza said. "Follow me, Madam President."

They went to the lower decks where two Marines stood guard outside a hatch marked with a biohazard symbol. When they saw her, both men came to attention.

"At ease, gentlemen," she said.

Souza gestured toward the hatch and the Marines opened it to a cold dark room. One of them switched on a light, revealing several metal tables. A corpse lay on the center table, covered mostly by a white blanket.

Huge arms hung over the sides, talons protruding out of thick fingers.

Footsteps echoed down the passage and a man wearing a white lab coat with slicked back hair joined them.

"Madam President, I'd like to introduce you to Doctor Jeff Carr," said Souza.

Ringgold shook the man's hand.

"Nice to meet you, President Ringgold," Carr said. "I take it you want to see our new specimen."

"Indeed, I do."

Souza nodded at the two Marines. They entered the freezing room and Carr followed without hesitation. He pulled reading glasses out of his breast pocket, put them on, and then placed a pair of protective goggles over those.

"Let's give President Ringgold a look at our new friend," Carr said.

The Marines pulled the blanket back to reveal the grotesque ape-like face of a monster without eyes. Crusted blood lined its wide nostrils, and saggy lips hung over curved fangs. But it was the bat-like ears fanning off its face that sparked her curiosity.

She stepped closer. "Doctor, tell me what in the devil I'm looking at."

"A new Alpha Variant, Madam President."

Ringgold kept her gaze on the beast while Carr put on surgical gloves. Then he grabbed a scalpel off a tray and used it to push up a flap of skin covering a tendril on its back.

"This Alpha has strange attributes unlike any I've seen, and I've seen a lot," he said glancing up for a moment. "The huge claws' purpose seems clear enough: digging."

He focused back on the tendril. "But these are more interesting. They have some kind of fibers in them. According to Team Ghost, those fibers seem to interact with the webs in all those tunnels. I'm told Doctor Kate Lovato is working on identifying and studying those samples."

"She is," Souza confirmed.

"I'd like to talk to her," Carr said. "Get her opinion on what we're dealing with."

"And what's yours?" Ringgold asked.

Carr looked down at the corpse for several moments before glancing at her. "I think we're dealing with a deadly new threat that's been evolving underground right beneath our noses."

— 13 —

"Beckham!" shouted Rico.

She got up from the metal table and ran across the mess hall of the USS *George Johnson*.

Fitz pushed himself up fast—a bit too fast. Pain flashed across his back, reminding him of the injuries and damage his body had never quite had the chance to recover from. The soreness quickly faded, replaced by joy at the sight of his friend and mentor. He and the rest of Team Ghost followed quickly after Rico toward his old friend, anxious to talk to the man that had once been the leader of the Delta Force Team Ghost.

Beckham walked toward them with a slight limp on his way to embrace Rico.

Despite his limp and the prosthetic hand, Beckham looked pretty good to Fitz, if not a bit older. His perpetual five o'clock shadow had streaks of gray on his chin, and his hair was much longer. But his uniform was filled out well with hardened muscles.

"Captain, it's great to see you," Fitz said. He reached out to shake Beckham's hand but Beckham wrapped him up in a hug like he had Rico.

"You know you're not supposed to call me Captain," he said. "I'm a civilian now."

"You'll always be the leader of Team Ghost to me." Fitz smiled and patted Beckham on the back. "I've missed you, my friend."

"I've missed you too, brother."

They pulled away and Beckham looked Fitz up and down. "You look good," he said. "Still got that baby face."

Fitz stroked his chin and smirked. "Still can't grow a beard, but Rico doesn't seem to mind."

"Not a fan of facial hair on myself or others," Rico said with a grin. That got a laugh from the rest of the team. "No offense, of course, Captain."

"None taken. Kate doesn't seem to mind."

"How is Kate and the rest of the family?" Rico asked. "And Big Horn and his girls?"

"The family is okay. So is Horn and his family...but we lost Jake Temper and twenty-two more people across Peaks Island and Portland in the attack."

The grins on Team Ghost's faces all vanished. Fitz said a mental prayer for Jake and the other victims, then quickly regained his composure.

Now was not the time to grieve—now was the time to prevent this from happening to anyone else.

"The raiders bombed Portland, too," Beckham added. "Senator McComb was one of the victims."

Fitz reached back up and stroked his chin nervously this time. Not only had they lost one of the best men Fitz had ever known, but they had lost a Senator aligned with the New America Coalition agenda.

"I can't believe it," Rico said, shaking her pink-streaked hair.

"How in the hell did they get past the defenses?" Lincoln asked.

"I suspect they had an inside source. They posed as civilians and drove right through gates in pickups,"

Beckham replied. "Another group took a boat to Peaks Island."

"And they all got away?" Mendez asked.

"The only raider we captured killed himself with Variant acid before we could question him," Beckham said.

Lincoln reared back.

"Those people are worse than the monsters," Mendez said, brows crunched together.

"That's because they're working *with* the monsters, aren't they?" Rico asked. "That's the only explanation that makes sense to me."

"I think you're right," Beckham said. "They seem to be connected somehow, and that's why I'm here. To find out and plan an offensive before they strike again…"

Fitz got the sense that wasn't the only reason Beckham was here. It was an open secret that Ringgold had been recruiting him to run for office, and with McComb's demise, he suspected the meeting with Ringgold wasn't just a coincidence. But Fitz saved his questions for later. There would be plenty of time to catch up in private.

"You hungry?" Rico asked.

Beckham shook his head. "But I'll sit with you guys."

He sat across from Dohi. "How are you feeling, brother?"

Dohi shrugged. "I'll live."

"Not going to lie, I thought you were Variant chowder," Ace said with a chuckle. His upper cheeks above his long white beard turned red when none of the other members found his statement amusing.

"Anyone ever tell you that you look like Santa Claus with those rosy cheeks?" Lincoln said.

Ace shrugged. "A skinnier version, yeah."

Fitz frowned. The big guy really needed to learn when to joke and when to keep his mouth shut. So did Lincoln for that matter.

Picking up a fork, Fitz went back to eating his roast beef and mashed potatoes.

"On the flight here, I read your report on those tunnels," Beckham said. "Most men would never have made it out alive."

"Those people down there... I hope they didn't survive, because if they did... Let's just say hell couldn't be any worse," Dohi said.

Beckham leaned forward. "We've all seen some pretty horrifying stuff and, before this war is over, we're going to see more. As painful as it is to talk about, that's why we need to figure out what these tunnels are and more about the Alpha you killed."

I just hope it's not too late, Fitz thought.

"Officer on deck!" came a bellowing voice.

The sailors and soldiers all stood as General Souza and an entourage walked into the mess hall, boots clicking on the deck.

"Briefing room in fifteen minutes," said Lieutenant Brian Festa, the liaison officer—LNO—from SOCOM.

Fitz grabbed his tray and followed the rest of the enlisted troops and sailors out of the mess in a hurry. By the time they got to the briefing room, the place was packed.

Fitz and Beckham went to the front to stand at a table with General Souza and President Ringgold. Secret Service agents flanked them, along with a middle-aged man in a lab coat that Fitz had never seen before.

While more people filed into the room the President shook hands with Beckham. They turned away from the crowd, speaking somewhat quietly within their group. Fitz was close enough to catch some of the conversation, something about Senator McComb and attending one of her speeches before he made up his mind.

When Beckham turned around, Fitz could tell by the look on his face he wasn't happy. Fitz's suspicions about the Senate race seemed to be right.

"Alright, people, let's get started," General Souza said. He swept a commanding gaze over the men and women in front of him. "We've got a hell of a situation on our hands, so I'm going to cut right to the chase. Three outposts have gone dark from Variant attacks, and three more were attacked by raiders."

He motioned to Lieutenant Festa. The shorter man with puffy thin hair stepped over to a wall-mounted monitor. A map of the country came online. He tapped the touch screen and pulled up a five-state area.

"Outpost Turkey River, Iowa; Outpost Rapid City, South Dakota; and Outpost Kansas City, Missouri, have all gone dark," Festa said. "Our recon teams discovered the Variants used tunnels to avoid our defenses."

Hushed voices broke out in the room.

"Quiet," Souza said.

Festa waited a moment and then continued. "Three more outposts were attacked by raiders, but they were all on the East Coast. Needless to say, we believe these attacks are all connected."

Souza picked up when Festa paused. "The pattern of these attacks suggests there is some sort of connected network here in the Midwest. We still don't know how the Variants are communicating over such large areas or with the human collaborators."

Festa touched the monitor again, this time bringing up

a map of the northeastern seaboard.

"The raider attacks hit outposts in the following areas," Festa said. "Portland, Maine. New Boston, Massachusetts. Providence, Rhode Island. Casualties are still coming in, but we're already in the hundreds."

More voices broke out around the room. The numbers were chilling. After years of only the stray Variant attacks and random raiders, the news was beyond devastating to the men and women that had fought for peace.

Especially President Ringgold.

She stood at the front of the room, stiff and proud. But the pallor that had overcome her face belied her confident posture. She was clearly horrified at what was happening in the final months of her administration. Her entire legacy was at stake, not to mention the future of the country.

"We expect casualties to continue rising, and we're also preparing for more attacks," Souza said.

Fitz studied the map on the wall-mounted screen, trying to come up with a theory of what was happening. Unless the Variants had evolved to use radios, and their transmissions were somehow encrypted, he had no freaking idea how they could be coordinating over such a large territory.

"We now believe many of the Variant kidnappings over the past few years weren't for food," Souza continued. "Personally, I believe these kidnappings were to create a small army of raiders that were utilized the other night to inflict terror."

Fitz wasn't surprised. He had met a few collaborators in his day. Most were batshit crazy after being held hostage by the monsters.

The General paused and looked over at the man in the

lab coat. "This is Doctor Jeff Carr. He will be working with Doctor Kate Lovato to figure out exactly what we're dealing with, starting with the Alpha Variant from Outpost Turkey River and the other samples our teams have retrieved."

"Thank you, General," Carr stepped up to the monitor and brought up an image of the beast that the Navy had stored in a freezer a deck below their feet. Fitz had already seen it up close and personal but seeing it on screen still sent a chill up his spine.

"This is an Alpha that no one has seen before now," Carr said. "Based off our field reports and my research, it seems to use echolocation to find prey. We also believe that the fibers attached to its spine may have something to do with the strange webbing found in the tunnels our recon teams found.

"We're not quite sure what the purpose of those fibers are. If you should meet one in the wild, any observations are appreciated. Other than that, all I can say is that you should expect the unexpected with these new monsters."

President Ringgold stepped up. "I was hoping the worst days of humanity were behind us," she said. "But again, we are faced with another threat to our species."

Fitz felt a sense of déjà vu and could almost guess what was coming next.

"I've decided to send in recon teams for more intel before we mount an offensive or reach out to our allies for help," Ringgold continued. "General Souza is in the process of putting together teams, and I've authorized the deployment of our main fighting force to be evenly distributed to the ninety-eight outposts to help guard them from future attacks."

Fitz appreciated her proactive approach but wondered

if she knew something he didn't. Deploying *all* of the troops?

"Operation Shadow will start in a few hours," Ringgold said.

She swept her gaze over the hardened soldiers, sailors, and Marines.

"Make no mistake, ladies and gentleman, this new threat may be the greatest we have faced since the first days of the Hemorrhage Virus," Ringgold said. "It will be up to you to help stop it before we lose everything we have fought to rebuild."

Fitz and Beckham exchanged a glance as two old friends and warriors. Both of them knew exactly what this meant.

No rest for Team Ghost.

They were headed back into the fray.

***

Dohi knelt in the knee-high grass. The blades were already golden, dried by the onslaught of cooler weather striking Outpost Duluth in Minnesota. Between the crushed stalks of grass were the unmistakable taloned footprints of the Variants.

Just like General Souza had feared, the Variants had continued their assaults, reaching all the way into northern Minnesota. This was just the latest attack, occurring only hours after their briefing on the USS *George Johnson*.

Team Ghost stood in the overgrown practice baseball and softball fields at the University of Minnesota Duluth. The campus had been retrofitted over the years into a fortified outpost, complete with chain-link fences, razor wire, and all the electronic surveillance equipment the military had given them.

Unlike Outpost Turkey River and Outpost Rapid City, the defenses had held, and only a handful of monsters had managed to get inside before they were repelled and forced to retreat.

The emergency alert system the Ringgold administration had provided to all of the outposts had helped, too, and this one knew trouble was coming from the quick acting alert.

But Dohi had a feeling it was really the two platoons of Army Rangers working with the militia that had saved this place from falling.

A group of Rangers were helping treat civilians across the field, some of which had lost loved ones in the fighting. The sobs and cries of pain drifted in the blustering winds.

White sheets covered the bodies of the deceased in neat rows.

Dohi and Team Ghost made their way across the field.

"Who's in charge here?" Fitz called out.

An Asian man with broad shoulders looked over his shoulder and then walked over to Fitz.

"That would be me," he held out a hand to Fitz. "Sergeant Randall Chung with the 3rd Battalion."

"Master Sergeant Fitzpatrick with Team Ghost." Fitz gestured at the other men and Dohi nodded.

"Glad to have you with us, Master Sergeant," Chung said. He sighed and gestured to the bodies. "We did what we could, but we couldn't stop all of the Variants once they tunneled in."

"Wish we'd gotten here sooner," Mendez said.

Chung adjusted his chin strap. "You guys have any

idea on where all these beasts are coming from?"

"That's what we're here to find out," Fitz said.

Dohi walked over to a hole near home plate while Fitz and Chung spoke. He flicked on his tactical light and shone it down into a passage covered in the glistening red webbing.

The nightmares of what he had seen in those tunnels at Turkey River flashed through his mind. He felt a pang of nausea as images of the half-buried people with tendrils growing from their mouths and out of their orbital cavities passed through his mind.

"You, okay, bro?"

Dohi looked back at Mendez who stood with his rifle cradled. They rejoined the rest of the team at the tail end of the conversation.

"Did the Variants escape with any people?" Fitz asked.

"None that we know of, but we haven't accounted for all civilians yet," Chung said.

"Did you see any Alphas?" Fitz asked.

"Caught one." Chung pointed toward the opposite side of the field where the Rangers had dumped the remains of the beasts.

The team made their way over to corpses riddled with bullet holes, their gray flesh even paler in death. Unseeing reptilian eyes staring up at the cloud-covered sky.

Dohi checked the barreled chest of an Alpha. It was the same type that he had fought at Outpost Turkey River.

"Have your men started searching the tunnels yet?" Fitz asked.

"No," Chung replied. "We've been too busy cleaning up this mess. But we've got an R2TD setup and ready to go to look for others."

Chung motioned to one of the red brick-covered buildings.

"Thomas, Watson, get the R2TD over here," he called.

Two of the Rangers began setting up the equipment.

"You all used one of these before?" Chung asked.

"I got some experience," Ace said.

"Then be our guest. It'll be more effective to have you guys on this one than us. I want to make sure we're prepared for another attack."

Ace jogged over to the two Rangers. They strapped the pack over his back and handed him the tube-shaped radar device.

"If we're going to prevent this from happening again, then we need to find out where these tunnels are coming from," Fitz said. "That's the only way we can launch an effective offensive."

"Whatever it takes," Rico said.

"Man, we're going underground?" Lincoln mumbled.

"You ever stop complaining?" Mendez gave Lincoln a questioning glare.

"I mean…not really," Lincoln smirked.

A cold wind howled over the open field, a harbinger of the winter that was only weeks away, silencing the team. Dohi thought he heard something else on the wind. Like the distant moan of someone in pain.

Maybe it was just his mind playing tricks on him. Those images of his time in the tunnels flashed through his thoughts again.

He did not want to go back underground again either but, if Fitz gave the order, he would do whatever it took, just like Rico had said.

"Good luck," Chung called out.

Fitz led the team toward the edge of the university

campus. Chain-link fences and razor wire marked the border. Two of the town's militia soldiers pulled back a mechanized gate to let Team Ghost through.

Ace studied the screen of the R2TD as they marched south, following the curve of Lake Superior into the city of Duluth.

Houses lined the streets around them. Most seemed to have been vacant for years. Broken glass stuck up in shards around rotted window frames. Some were burned down to their foundations, now nothing more than piles of charcoaled debris.

Ace led them between the lawns of abandoned structures until they reached a wide park with tall trees. Canopies of leaves the shades of fire rustled in the wind.

"Tunnels end here," Ace said, looking up from his screen, perplexed.

"Not quite," Dohi said.

He bent next to a hole in the ground about as big as his waist. Several braided ropes of red tissue protruded from the edge and stretched across a creek.

Taking off a glove, he then traced his fingers over the rope of red webbing. Electricity practically flowed to his hand. The individual threads within the organic cables pulsed slightly, pushing back against his skin.

"They didn't dig under the water," Dohi said. "Maybe they were smart enough to know they'd risk collapsing the tunnel."

"That webbing…" Mendez started.

"Keep following it," Fitz said.

Dohi lifted his rifle to his shoulder again. He pushed into water that rose up to the middle of his shins. The bank on the other side of the creek crested slightly. He scurried over the mud, still following the red tendrils.

There they led back into another opening. Talon prints marred the ground between the carpet of dead leaves. But something else made his heart climb into his throat. He aimed his rifle into the darkness of the tunnel opening. Wind howled out of the Variant-made cavern. Somewhere in there he thought he heard a groan.

Get ahold of yourself, Dohi.

The groaning continued, and now he was almost certain this wasn't the wind.

God, he might be going mad.

He wondered if what he'd seen in those tunnels was coming back to haunt him in a bad way. He hated to admit it, but maybe he should have sat this mission out. If he didn't get his head on, he would become a liability to the other members, but he also didn't want to let them down.

Fitz held up a fist. He pointed to his ear, then at the tunnel. Ace lowered the R2TD device.

So maybe Dohi wasn't so crazy after all. The others had also heard the noise, and if someone was groaning in there, that meant they were still alive.

Fitz signaled for them to turn on their lights. Then with another gesture, he sent Dohi forward. He moved inside without hesitation, his light illuminating braided red cables that spread into the webbing. Claw marks marred the walls and a trail of taloned footprints led deeper.

The pained, animalistic groans grew louder as they advanced.

The closer he got, the more inhuman it sounded.

Dohi crept along, following the curve in the tunnel, heart pounding harder with each step. He rounded the corner and swept the passage with his light. The shadows fled as the beam hit webbing that had grown together in a mass of strange flesh.

"What in the…" Dohi paused.

Red ropes climbed out of this creature's ears and open mouth.

It wasn't human.

Not Variant either.

Dohi moved closer, shining his light to see it was a deer.

More of the red webbing grew from open wounds. The chest slowly rose and fell, blood-covered fur glistening in the light. Every time it exhaled, it let out a haunted groan.

The Variants did not discriminate when it came to live prey, and it seemed that their wide taste in food extended to their use of living creatures for whatever *this* was.

As the rest of Team Ghost filtered in around Dohi, their lights filled the tunnel. Other animals hung from the walls. Webbing grew from all of them. Some of the creatures were nothing but skin and bones, their fur falling away in large clumps.

Dohi said a prayer for every animal that the Variants had done this to as he moved deeper. Heat swelled in his chest. This was an abomination of nature.

He had read Kate's report on the flight and understood that such fast-spreading growths needed sustenance. The Variants seemed to be turning humans and animals into fuel.

Team Ghost pushed along through the darkness.

Fitz pulled out his knife and ended the suffering of the deer and other living animals behind them. Dohi flinched at each sound and walked faster at the sight of columns of light in the distance.

A way out of this hell.

Dohi followed the light to a ramp of scree that led into the sunlight. This was the end of the tunnel. He made his way up on the side of a hill overlooking Lake Superior. The vast freshwater body stretched all the way to Michigan.

The rest of Team Ghost joined him, fanning out to follow the Variant footprints that scattered in all directions. Whoever or whatever was organizing these monsters knew what they were doing. There was no easy path forward.

Except...

Dohi dropped to a knee. A slight glint caught his eye. A flash of scarlet peeking out from the black soil near his boots. He hooked a finger on the red tendril and pulled it up. More of the red webbing unearthed itself as he pulled on the organic cables.

The more fibers that Dohi pulled up, the more certain he was that these tendrils would lead them to something. But when Fitz signaled for Ace to use the R2TD system again, they found no more tunnel systems. It seemed that while the fibers continued on, the tunnels were only dug when the beasts were close to the outpost.

"Might want to tell command what we're finding," Dohi said. "If I had to guess, the Variants don't just tunnel all the way from one part of the country to another."

"No, shit," Lincoln said. "That would be impossible."

Rico reached out toward the webbing Dohi had in his gloves.

"This reminds me of something I saw on the National Geographic channel once," she said. "The world's largest living organism—at least at that time—was a mushroom.

It covered like 2000 acres of forest in Oregon. Most of it all just tiny filaments underground."

Lincoln bent down to pull up another strand. "Don't look like mushrooms to me."

"You missed the point," Rico said.

"Come on guys, keep digging this shit up so we can see where it leads," Fitz ordered.

The team worked for an hour to peel the fibers up, taking them south and deeper into the woods. Finally, as the light of day began to wane, Fitz called off the search.

"Let's get back to the outpost," Fitz said. "We'll pick this trail up at first light."

While they walked, Dohi looked southward, past the tree-covered horizon, wondering where those webbings would lead.

"Seems like the Variants can collapse those tunnels at will," he said.

"Makes sense to me," Rico said. "If those things are like muscles fibers or whatever Kate said, then maybe they can force the tunnels to contract."

"They dig the tunnels just far enough away so they can attack unseen, then poof," Mendez said. "They yank the tunnels closed after they exit back out the other end."

"And still leave the fibers behind in this massive network," Dohi said. "Hold up a second."

He pulled out a map from his pack, studying it in the waning light.

"The tunnels—or at least the webbings—head this way," Dohi said, tracing the direction they had followed over the map. "And the ones from Turkey River…"

Fitz's eyes widened, seeming to understand where he was going with this. "From New Chicago, reports said the tunnels were headed northwest. And from Kansas City, almost straight north."

"Well shit," Mendez said. "I failed geography but even I know where that leads. It's got to be New York."

Dohi laughed, a rare act. "Not even close, man."

"I know, I was kidding," Mendez chuckled.

"Only you weren't, dumbass." Lincoln looked over Dohi's shoulder, glancing at the map.

Dohi shook his head. "You guys never stop do you?"

"So what are you thinking?" Fitz asked.

"I'm thinking if you triangulate all of these tunnels, we know where this web might have originated from," Dohi said.

He jabbed a finger at the map right over Minneapolis.

"All the networks we've discovered head that direction, and if these fibers need a lot of people to grow, there is probably more than enough food for them there."

"The Midwest outposts are rife with people," Rico added. "Highest number of kidnappings before all this started, too."

"Goddamn you guys are smart," Mendez said.

"I guess we know where we're going next," Lincoln grumbled. "Back underground, huh?"

Dohi had a feeling he was right.

— 14 —

Kate soaked in the astringent smells of the laboratory on Peaks Island. The stinging odor of the freshly sanitized whitewashed tiled floors and black lab benches never failed to energize her.

Fluorescent lights buzzed on with the flip of switches.

The lab itself wasn't exactly cavernous, but working alone in here made the place feel like she was the last person left on earth. She had barely seen Beckham before he'd been sent off to SOCOM and her time with Javier felt like little more than an exchange of a few words before bedtime over the past forty-eight hours.

As much as she knew she should rest, and spend time with her son, her country needed her again. No one else in the world had her experience and expertise researching Variants.

Fortunately, she was getting the help she needed. Today she was receiving support staff and the body of an Alpha that Team Ghost had retrieved from Outpost Turkey River.

She worked fast to get the lab in tip-top shape for the new arrivals. When she finished, she checked on the cell culture experiments with the samples from the webbing.

Once again they had grown to the limits of the large plastic flasks she had placed them in. It seemed they grew out of each smaller cell culture plate and flask in a matter of minutes. The only limitation on their growth was the amount of nutrient media she placed in the containers.

She turned at the intercom's buzzer.

Sergeant Ruckley stood behind the glass wall, near the intercom system.

"Doctor Lovato, the new staff just landed and will be here shortly," she said.

Kate gave a thumbs up sign and went right back to work.

One by one, she checked her smaller samples before moving onto the riskiest experiment she had setup. No laboratory she knew made much use of cell flasks larger than a liter or two. Even that was on the big end of things.

When she saw the webbing would outgrow its container so quickly, she had put in a strange request with her suppliers that had thankfully been answered: she needed a fifty-gallon fish tank.

The tank now housed a monstrous cell growth at the back of the lab behind a plexiglass window. Strangely, the cells no longer looked like the well-organized red webs, but rather lab grown meat.

She walked over to check the mass of red cells. They seemed to throb and pulsate within the equipment. For the next thirty minutes, she examined the growth, wondering if she should move it into a bigger enclosure. If they got any bigger the tank could fracture.

A sudden knock against the lab's door caused her to jump.

This time Beckham stood behind the glass.

"What in the hell is that?" he said, staring at the fish tank.

"That's what I'm trying to find out," she said loud enough for him to hear through the window.

She peeled off the nitrile gloves she wore, tossing them into the trash. Then she removed her lab coat and joined Beckham outside the lab.

"How are you?" Beckham said, tugging on her hand.

"Tired. You?"

"We have a lot of work to do."

Kate had a feeling that could mean a number of things, but she didn't ask. She simply wrapped him in a hug.

"You know that doesn't exactly answer my question," she said.

"I'll be fine."

The click of footsteps pulled her away.

Horn stood next to a tall man with dark, slicked-back hair. The newcomer approached with an extended hand.

"I'm Doctor Jeff Carr," he said.

Kate took his hand. "Doctor Kate Lovato."

"A pleasure to meet you," Carr said. "The president has spoken very highly of your work. Your reputation certainly precedes you in...what's left of the scientific community," he finished with an awkward grin.

Kate had stopped worrying about her reputation years ago. It was evenly split between hate and love after her scientific developments killed billions of those initially infected by the Hemorrhage virus, only to create the deadlier Variants.

"Welcome to my humble lab," Kate said. "I'm happy to have you here to assist with the work."

"Assist?" Carr's eyebrows rose as if he was dismayed. "I thought this would be more of an egalitarian, team-based approach."

"Oh, of course," Kate said, suddenly looking a little uncomfortable.

Carr peered back down the hall and waved at the cadre of people surrounding a cart there. Kate moved for a better look, confirming it was indeed the cart used in a morgue to transfer corpses. This one had a plastic dome to keep the contents sealed.

"Bring the subject in," Carr said, waving.

Kate stood aside as the team pushed the cart toward the lab entrance. Carr led the procession inside.

He peered around the room, a discerning scowl on his face until he pointed to a corner.

"It's one ugly SOB," Beckham said.

The lab team filtered in and out of the room, bringing in boxes of supplies and equipment. Carr surveyed them, barking orders at the techs.

"Is he always like this?" Kate said in a conspiratorial tone to Horn and Beckham.

"Definitely takes some getting used to," Beckham said.

Horn exhaled sharply. "Guy like that probably likes the smell of his own farts. There's no getting used to that."

"That's just great," Kate said. "I hoped an extra hand around here would make this a little easier, but…"

"Well you got an entire team now," Beckham said.

The techs continued to unload equipment. The potential of their productivity had increased an order of magnitude, assuming cooperation with Carr wasn't difficult.

"The extra hands will help determine the Alpha's connection to the webbing faster," Kate nodded.

"Sooner we can figure out how it's working, the sooner we can shut it down," Beckham said.

"Doctor Lovato," Carr interrupted from the other side of the lab. "What's this monstrous thing growing in your cell culture room?"

Beckham and Horn shot a glance at the aquarium.

"I was going to ask the same thing," Horn said. "Looks like what happens after I used to eat McDonalds."

"Very funny, Big Horn." Beckham groaned, shaking his head.

"That's the webbing," Kate said.

Beckham motioned for her to join him in the hallway. He jerked his chin at Horn, too, and they all retreated into the shadows. If Kate didn't know any better, she would say her husband appeared nervous.

"This better not be more bad news," Horn said.

Carr shot them a raised eyebrow, peering curiously at them as the team of techs continued flowing in and out of the lab with equipment.

Beckham began in a hushed voice. "Ringgold asked again about running for McCombs seat."

"Brother, you're retired. Being a politician...well, damn, that's the kind of stuff we told each other we'd never do," Horn responded gently.

"I know."

Beckham reached for Kate's hand. "And I'm sorry. I am. I know we said we'd talk about it first but, with everything going on, we're inches from anarchy in this country and inches from losing everything you and I and Team Ghost worked so hard to achieve. I can't stand by, sitting here on Peaks Island, while everything crumbles."

Kate pulled her hand away. "We're a team, Reed. There are people who need you here. Timothy. Bo. *Your son*."

A grimace cut across Beckham's face. "I haven't forgotten them or you or my friends. I'm just afraid that if we can't stabilize the political situation, things will only get worse for everyone."

Horn clapped a hand over Beckham's shoulder. "You know I respect you and look up to you, but I want it on record that I think this is the dumbest idea you've ever had."

"I have to run for Senate," Beckham firmly stated.

"You don't *have* to," Kate shot back. "We've got plenty to do around here."

"*You've* got plenty to do. You've got a whole team to help you in the lab now, and you've been plenty busy with experiments since the raiders' attack. I promise you won't even miss me while I'm campaigning."

"You know that's not true," Kate looked away.

Beckham leaned against the wall. "I'm sorry, Kate, but if I don't run, who will?" He looked at Horn. "Clearly not Big Horn."

"God damn right," he said with a snort.

"You know politics can be just as dangerous as any mission with Team Ghost," Kate suddenly responded. "Ringgold has enemies. Look at what happened to Senator McComb!"

"She's right," Horn said. "With people angry as they are, who's to say another crazy R.O.T. group shows up and tries to take you down?"

"Or maybe they already have," Kate said, thinking of the raiders.

"My whole goal in running is to ensure that doesn't happen," Beckham said.

"Still think this is the wrong move." Horn kicked his toe against the tiled floor. "But damn it, you're Reed Beckham, and you haven't got us killed yet, so I guess I gotta support you."

Beckham offered him a measured grin and looked to Kate.

"You know I support you, too, whatever you do," she said. "But that doesn't mean I like it."

"I'll take that for now." He held her hand again, and this time she let him. "I'm sorry I basically agreed to this before talking to you first, but—"

"We can talk later. I better get back to the lab." Kate glanced over her shoulder. "I don't trust Carr in there."

"One last thing," Beckham pulled her back.

"Ringgold wants me at a rally with her tomorrow, which means I've got to leave first thing in the morning," he said.

Kate sighed and shook her head. "I'll see you at the shelter when I get off work."

"I'm sorry, Kate," Beckham said.

"Me too, but what can we do?"

With that Beckham and Horn left the corridor and she returned to her office. The techs had a nearly complete autopsy suite ready. Atop the table lay the abomination still covered by the plastic dome.

The beast underneath did not disappoint her expectations. The ape-like face with bat-like ears were even more gruesome than she had imagined.

Long spines stuck out from under the back. They appeared both delicate and dangerous, not unlike a stack of fencing sabers.

Carr stepped up next to her. "It's a beauty, right?"

"Sure is," Kate said. "Got any idea how it interacts with that webbing yet?"

"I have a few ideas."

"Let's get to work then."

Carr hesitated, suddenly not as ambitious as he was

when he got here. Perhaps he had heard some of her conversation with Beckham and wondered if she was up to the task.

"Sure you don't need a break?" Carr asked. "You seem a little tense. I don't want it to hamper our work."

"Nothing hampers my work." Kate tossed a set of goggles to him and put some on herself.

"Well do not let me hold us back then," Carr said. "Please, lead on, Doctor Lovato."

***

"Gather round, boys!" Fischer yelled.

He stroked the sides of his freshly trimmed mustache as his security guards and hired hunters approached. Over fifty men dressed in camouflaged fatigues with automatic weapons and high-powered hunting rifles stood on his property this morning.

Another group had just parked in a gravel lot full of pickup trucks and dust-covered SUVs. Every security guard on the Fischer Fields payroll was here tonight, plus the hired help they had brought in to hunt.

There were also the ten soldiers President Ringgold had sent to help secure the oil fields. The men had arrived yesterday in a pair of rusting Humvees, led by a man named Sergeant Ken Sharp. He and his boys had seen plenty of action, and Sharp was a Native Texan, which Fischer appreciated.

But just ten men and some shitty equipment that looked like it had come from an Army surplus store?

It just reaffirmed the fact her administration wasn't serious about protecting his fields. And if the government wasn't going to take care of the Variants in the area, he was going to do it the way they used to in the Wild West—with blood and bullets.

Word had spread fast across the Allied States, and the men were all talking about what was going on: raiders and mysterious Variant tunnels popping up across the Midwest.

Texas was a long way from the heart of the trouble, but everyone here knew it was just a matter of time before the Variants and their human collaborators hit the Lone Star State.

Fischer had no doubt, the increased Variant activity was a sign of a growing threat. Something more dangerous than anyone in the government was letting on. While he wasn't sure what sinister Alpha or Alphas were behind it, he wasn't going to stand idly by and wait for their attack.

There was one old adage that had always proven true in matters of personal and business interest: the best defense was a good offense. Dealing with Variants was no exception.

His most trusted soldiers, Tran and Chase, agreed with his decision to hunt the diseased monsters on his property.

Now it was time to break it to everyone else.

"That's the last of them," said Tran.

Chase swept his gaze over the crowd from under the bill of his Fischer Fields baseball cap. The two lead security agents flanked Fischer on the deck overlooking his backyard where the men had gathered.

Blazing sunlight bore down on the hardened faces of men that in some cases had been fighting the monsters for eight years or more now.

Fischer may have been standing over them, but he felt

like he was one of them.

He instinctively put his hands on his chrome belt buckle holding up his fatigues and filled his lungs with the dry breeze.

"As many of you have heard, the Allied States are under attack," Fischer bellowed. "The Variants are going after the outposts, taking those homesteaders underground into God only knows what kind of hell on Earth."

The men all seemed to stiffen, their gazes locked on Fischer.

"Several outposts in the east got hit by raiders that some suspect might be human collaborators," he continued. "With human enemies and the monsters fighting on all fronts, I'm afraid we can't count on someone over a thousand-and-a-half miles away to save us."

Hushed conversations broke out in the crowd, but the ten soldiers present remained quiet, not reacting to his words at all.

"That's why we're all here," Fischer said. "I've got my own backup plans."

He looked at part of those plans in the distance. Multiple industrial barns that housed his cattle sat in rows about a quarter mile away on the eastern edge of his property. Electrical fences surrounded the metal buildings. The only way in was a gate guarded by two men at all times. More guards patrolled the inside. They were there now, walking with their shotguns and rifles.

The expensive redundancy had protected his livestock for years now, and it had worked for his oil derricks, until recently.

"We're going to plan B today," Fischer said. "We're

not waiting for the Variants to come to us anymore. Instead, we'll find the holes they are hiding in and…"

Fischer reached for a bag Chase held and pulled out a stick of TNT.

"We will blow the dirty bastards out of their nests like the varmints they are."

Several of the men in the crowd grunted their approval. But they weren't all convinced. A former sheriff's deputy that now worked for Fischer spat a blob of tobacco on the dirt and said, "How do we know where the devils sleep?"

"Our friends here helped with some of that," Fischer said, gesturing to the Army soldiers. "I also paid good money for a private tracking team to dig up my own intel."

He nodded in the direction of two men in the crowd. The older guy, a man named Aaron Galinsky, had short-cropped hair and was former Israeli military. His partner Eric Welling had hair to his shoulders and looked as if he had stepped straight out of the Australian outback.

"I got a pretty good idea where the demons sleep," Fischer said. "And if we have our way, they're never waking up."

"You're asking us to put our lives on the line," said another man. "What's in it for us?"

"I will be paying very well," Fischer replied. "Every man that goes out with us will receive triple hazard pay. Bonuses will go to anyone that kills a Variant. Bag an Alpha and you get five grand."

"Well what are we waiting for? Let's get out there!" yelled Galinsky.

Welling laughed, and several men in the crowd joined in.

Fischer smiled at the change in enthusiasm. If there was one thing that could change a man's heart real fast, it was a wheelbarrow full of cash.

"You've all trained for this," Fischer said. "Going to be like shooting fish in a barrel."

He nodded at Tran and Chase who both dispersed into the crowd to hand out maps and assignments. An hour later the sixty plus group had split into six teams of ten. They loaded up into their pickup trucks and SUVs with their weapons slung and spirits high.

Three of the teams would head thirty miles to the hills in the southwest, and the other three would head with Fischer to the hills in the southeast. All signs pointed at those areas being potential nest locations, from tracks to the direction of most attacks.

Fischer got into his pickup truck, riding shotgun with Chase behind the wheel. Tran hopped in the back of the dual cab with Sergeant Sharp and, soon as the door shut, they were off.

The convoy took the road past the barns of cattle, chickens, and pigs on the way out. Fischer Fields provided almost five percent of the nation's meat, something else he was damn proud of. But that was a small contribution compared to how much oil he was producing for the country.

As of now, his fields were supplying over 25 percent of the nation's refined petroleum products.

The fact he couldn't get more government help in protecting them was maddening. It was also the reason he was leaning toward supporting General Cornelius in the general election.

Chase raised a hand out the window to several guards patrolling the interior of the electric fences as they passed the barns.

"How many men did you pull off sentry duty?" Fischer asked.

"Half, but don't worry, there are still plenty," Chase said.

Fischer looked at the blazing sun. The Variants were far more likely to attack when the sun had sunk beyond the horizon, just about now, but he still worried about leaving so few men to guard his livestock.

He tried to relax on the ride to the foothills. The beauty of the open fields and blue skies helped. The ride took them through the flat country, past several of the oil derricks, where more of his workers monitored the extraction and others guarded the precious resource.

Fischer pulled out his map and then put on his reading glasses. He studied the potential nesting areas for a few moments before turning to Sharp.

"Sergeant, which site do you think is the most likely to be an active nest?" he asked.

Sharp seemed to tense at the question, which gave Fischer his answer.

The Army soldiers had no idea.

"Hard to say," Sharp replied, hoping to sound confident.

"Did you or did you not confirm the presence of Variants at these locations?"

"We did," Sharp said. "But we did not confirm numbers."

"In other words, you didn't get close enough."

Sharp said nothing.

Fischer turned back to the front seat, suddenly questioning how useful these maps would be. The other teams were heading to the location marked by Welling and Galinsky. Now he wondered if he should head to the location the two professional trackers were going.

"So we don't know if any of these are live tunnels?" Fischer asked.

"We confirmed the presence of bones just outside several," Sharp replied. "However, since we didn't get close, we couldn't see how fresh the kills were. It's always hard to say with bones anyways, because the Variants don't leave much behind."

Fischer gave the Sergeant that. The beasts stripped everything clean. The best way to tell if a tunnel or hole was active was their feces.

Dust billowed up ahead as the convoy of vehicles hit a gravel road. Chase eased off the gas to give them some room. The next road was paved and took them past several more derricks. Over the next hill, they got their first view of their target.

"Here we go," Chase said. He followed the other vehicles to a staging area off the road where he parked next to one of the Army Humvees.

Fischer jumped out and went to the back bed of the truck to pull out his M4A1. Tran grabbed his SR-25, and Chase slung his carbine.

Sergeant Sharp spoke to his men while they charged their weapons.

In total, thirty men gathered outside the vehicles, including the ten soldiers. Sharp told a Corporal and PFC to take point, and they set off toward the clumps of hills a quarter mile away, fanning out into the grass.

Tran and Chase remained close to Fischer, but let him lead the way. He kept behind Sharp, eyeing the foothills. The mounds of brown earth were covered in vegetation and trees unlike a lot of the surrounding area. Plenty of places for Variants to hide.

The soldiers fanned out ahead into two teams, weapons up and roving.

Fischer followed his team across the field, heart thumping with excitement. Being out here, with these men, made him nostalgic for the hunts he had gone on as a kid.

Only this hunt was far more dangerous than going after wild boars.

The two groups peeled off, filing down separate tracks. Fischer kept behind Sharp.

Underbrush scraped across his fatigues, and his boots crunched over small rocks. Fischer spotted the first evidence of Variant tracks in the dirt ahead.

Sharp pointed them out, but then continued on up a hill and through the spindly vegetation. Skeletal limbs from dead trees reached out like grasping fingers.

Most of the vegetation on the other side of the hill was dry and brown. The lack of leaves and underbrush made the tunnels easier to spot.

Sharp stopped to look at his map, and then pointed to the next hill on their right. The group peeled off into two smaller teams and moved toward the holes.

Fischer was one of the first to reach it and stopped about ten feet away. He aimed his barrel at the entrance of the shadowed cavern.

Sure enough, several animal bones were scattered just inside the lip of the dirt hole. He bent down with Sharp and they directed their lights inside, revealing more bones scattered on the dirt floor. Raking his light, Fischer saw no sign of fresh Variant feces.

"This must be an old one," Fischer said.

Sharp gestured toward the group that had veered off

to check another cavern. Two of his soldiers had crouched down in front of it for a better look.

By the time Fischer got there, they had ducked inside. The rest of the group waited outside, weapons angled at the entrance.

A radio crackled, and Tran pulled it out from his pouch.

"FF1, this is FF2, do you copy?" came a voice.

Fischer waited anxiously for the report from his team at the other location.

"Copy FF2, this is FF1 what you got?" Tran replied.

"Nothing, FF1, we've got dead tunnels. You have better luck than us?"

"Standby FF2," Tran said. He put the radio back in his pouch and moved over with Fischer to get a better look inside the tunnel.

The soldiers were already returning, and they were carrying something.

Fischer didn't need his flashlight to see one of the items was a helmet with the FF logo. The men crawled out of the hole with gear and several bones of the final missing derrick engineer.

"Looks like an old nest," said the soldier. He looked down at the helmet. "At least we finally found his remains."

Fischer nodded, happy that the family would have some closure now, but disappointed he wasn't going to get to use any of his TNT.

He spat on the ground and turned his back to look at the dead terrain.

"Where the hell did you bastards go?" Fischer muttered.

15

Beckham hated getting dressed up almost as much as Horn did, but today he found himself in a sharp navy-blue suit with a red tie. Suits were for businessmen and politicians, he had been told as a young man.

You're going to be a politician, he thought. *You're going to have to get used to this.*

He wasn't the only one that didn't like what he was wearing. President Ringgold had complained about the bulletproof vest Beckham had insisted she wore today.

She sat in a chair next to the Vice President for an interview with a reporter across the lobby in a hotel in Outpost New Boston, not far from the site of the raider attack. The President had insisted on moving the rally here.

Ringgold was probably telling the reporter the same thing she had said to Beckham.

"I will not be intimidated," she had said. "I will not be scared off by these cowards."

Beckham waited by a window near the hotel's entrance. Outside, hundreds had gathered in the street. Most held New America Coalition signs, but not everyone seemed so enthusiastic.

He scanned the faces with his normal paranoid mindset.

Any of them could be enemies.

Raiders and collaborators.

The assholes had penetrated several outposts, including this one, and he feared they would try again.

Beckham let the drape fall over the window and made his way back into the lobby. President Ringgold and Vice President Lemke were still talking to a female reporter from the New Boston Globe paper.

The Globe was one of several institutions of journalism that had made a comeback over the past few years. With television and civilian cell phone service still a thing of the past, printed news was one of the only ways for average citizens to get their information.

Which made this interview very important.

He waited patiently for it to conclude and then walked over.

"There you are, Captain," Ringgold said. "I've got to talk to you."

Beckham stepped over. The middle-aged reporter seemed to measure him up with a sweeping gaze before she finally walked away with her bag.

Ringgold got out of her chair and motioned for Lemke and Beckham to follow her to a conference room off the lobby. Two Secret Service agents shadowed them to the door where they stood sentry.

"Close that, please," Ringgold said.

Beckham closed the door, anticipating more bad news.

"Team Ghost reported in late last night," Lemke said. "They think they know the epicenter of the Variant activity."

"Minneapolis, Minnesota," Ringgold said.

"Really?" Beckham said. "That's a heck of a long ways away from some of the outposts the Variants attacked."

He paused to think a moment and then said, "What does SOCOM think about this?"

"Honestly, we're not sure yet, but we're going to find out," Lemke said.

"Operation Shadow is continuing with the deployment of six teams, including Team Ghost to figure out what we're dealing with," Ringgold said. "All the teams so far have reported similar findings around the attacked outposts. Variants used tunnels to get under the defenses."

"When our teams followed the tunnels out, they eventually disappeared, and they were left only with the remnants of webbing to follow," Lemke added.

"Now we're sending Team Ghost to Minneapolis, and the other teams to five other targets where the webbing seems to lead," Ringgold continued.

Lemke handed Beckham a folder.

Inside were the names of the targets: Minneapolis, Minnesota; Chicago, Illinois; Lincoln, Nebraska; Kansas City, Missouri; Indianapolis, Indiana; and Columbus, Ohio.

"These are the other likely locations of the civilians abducted from outposts," Lemke said. "If these people were taken to any of these locations, there could be hundreds of others under these cities."

"The teams are heading out shortly, and I wanted you to know," Ringgold said. "But I won't be mentioning this to anyone out there. For now, the mission stays under wraps. I don't want there to be any chance of it leaking to collaborators."

The suggestion made Beckham tense up even more. In the past, rival campaigns might have sent spies to listen to speeches. Now they had to worry about traitorous human collaborators working with the Variants.

"I'm just waiting for a leak to happen though," Ringgold said. "I'm sure Cornelius will find out, and push even more for nuking these sites, regardless of the potential innocent lives we could lose."

"Nuking the city might not even destroy the nests anyways," Beckham added. "The creatures are resilient. More so than cockroaches. I wouldn't be surprised if those tunnels go pretty deep under the cities."

"Precisely," Ringgold agreed. "And of course, most people supporting Cornelius' Freedom Party agenda don't realize this."

"I've also been trying to bring more attention to how many people are still scratching out a living outside of the outposts, in cities like Minneapolis," Lemke said.

"Yeah but Cornelius does not care about them," Beckham said. "In his eyes, and the eyes of his supporters, the people outside the outposts have made their choice. They're nothing but collateral damage."

"Or human collaborators," Lemke said. "That's their new line. Anyone behind the lines are working with the Variants."

"Bull fucking shit." Beckham winced a second later. "Sorry for my language."

"It's quite all right," Ringgold said with a grin.

"Hopefully you mentioned this stuff in your interview with the Globe," Beckham subtly inquired.

Lemke nodded and looked to Ringgold.

"Actually, that's what I want to talk to you about," she said, pausing for a moment. "I'm hoping you'll talk today, not just to the crowd, but to the reporters."

"You're a national hero," Lemke said.

Now Beckham knew why the reporter had studied him like that. She was sizing him up for a potential interview.

"All due respect, but I'm not good at talking to crowds, and I've never liked journalists," Beckham said. "No offense to the profession, but as a soldier, I'm used to saying less than more."

Ringgold sighed and looked at Lemke.

Beckham hated the fact his past could be used for the election, but he knew it was necessary to save lives.

Especially if it could stop the cities from being nuked.

"Look at page five of your briefing folder," Lemke said.

Beckham flipped to recent poll numbers.

"The tide has changed." Ringgold began tapping her foot unconsciously. "Citizens are blaming us for what's happening at the outposts."

She stepped forward and put a hand on his shoulder. "I know what you might be thinking, but you're not a political pawn. You are a patriot, and your country needs you and your wife again."

"And we will serve until our last breaths," Beckham said.

"I know," Ringgold said with a kind smile. "We better get out there."

"Thank you, Captain," Lemke said.

Beckham hesitated before following the president and vice president back to the lobby, his mind racing. By the time he joined them, James Soprano and Elizabeth Cortez had arrived.

"Ready?" Cortez asked cheerfully.

"Always," Ringgold said with a smile.

Soprano handed the President her speech, and they set off with a team of Secret Service agents. They moved in a cordon around the POTUS and VPOTUS as soon as they were outside, joining more agents posted on the sidewalk.

Brick and stone buildings framed the historic street where they would give their speech and ask these people for their support. Beckham spotted snipers posted on rooftops and knew there were even more he couldn't see behind darkened windows.

The military was also here, with an entire Marine platoon on this block alone. Security was tight, and everyone that had come to see the two speak had gone through metal detectors.

But there were other ways in and more weapons than guns.

He fiddled with the buttons on his suit, cursed under his breath, and told himself to relax as he followed the leaders of the country.

Talking in front of people scared him more than facing a Variant. Coupled with his nerves about threats in the crowd, he was practically sweating bullets.

Elizabeth Cortez took the stage first, heading to the podium that sported the New America Coalition logo. She tapped the microphone. Static broke from the speakers.

The crowd quieted.

"Good afternoon, and thank you for coming out today," Cortez said. "President Jan Ringgold and Vice President Dan Lemke are here to talk about everything the administration has achieved and hopes to achieve with another four years of the New America Coalition."

Beckham sensed the tension in the woman's normally peppy voice. He didn't blame her. Only about half of the crowd responded positively with claps and applause.

Cortez smiled after a pause and said, "But you didn't come here to see me, so without further ado, I'm honored to present President Jan Ringgold."

Beckham clapped and was relieved that most everyone joined in. He watched the President walk up to the stage and step up to the podium.

"Good afternoon ladies and gentlemen, and thank you for taking the time to be a part of our movement," Ringgold said. She set her speech out on the podium and looked over the crowd.

"Today, I'm outlining a vision for our future. A vision that builds on our history of achievements and victories. A vision that includes all of you," she said. "I know many of you are scared. You've heard about the recent attacks, and you might be wondering how can I stand up here and talk about achievements during these trying times."

"Damn right!" someone shouted.

Ringgold recognized the man with a nod. "I understand being scared and being mad. I have done everything in my power to protect our country and will continue to do so in the face of evil."

Another man yelled out in the distance. "You failed us!"

The crowd broke out in a storm of voices.

Ringgold waited for them to quiet down.

"Please," she urged. "Give me a few minutes of your time and, when I finish, I will stick around to personally answer your questions."

The citizens seemed to calm down, and she continued after a brief pause.

"The Variant threat is still out there. We believe they are planning something, but at this point I don't believe in destroying our cities and killing the people living there or killing the people the Variants have captured."

"Nuke the cities!" someone yelled.

Another shouted. "We have to do it!"

"No, we don't," Ringgold said. "In a few moments, we're going to introduce you to someone that will explain why we don't and why doing so will cause far more harm than good."

Beckham knew she was looking in his direction, but he was looking at two men dressed in dark brown jackets. One had a scruffy beard, and the other had a face marred by a long scar. Their emotionless features stood out to him.

Neither of them seemed to be reacting to Ringgold's speech in a positive or negative manner. Their faces remained stern even when others exploded in enthusiastic cheers or angry jeers.

Beckham relocated down the sidewalk for a better look, keeping his hand low, near the Sig Sauer he had holstered under his suit jacket. For the next few minutes, he drowned out Ringgold's speech and focused his senses on the crowd.

Vice President Lemke joined President Ringgold on stage, wearing a dimpled smile.

The two onlookers still remained stern faced.

Beckham moved again and was able to see they wore muddy boots and pants with rips in the side. Suspicious, but not all that much different than what a lot of people were wearing.

Lemke went into his speech, talking about his new proposals to spur the safe zone economies and reignite global trade, but Beckham was hardly listening.

He started off into the crowd, carefully maneuvering around families that had come out to see the President and Vice President. Several people holding New America Coalition signs moved and blocked his view of the two suspicious men.

Beckham made his way around the campaign signs and then paused just as the two men spotted him. The one with the beard jerked his chin to the other, and they promptly turned and began their way out.

The crowd cheered at Lemke's speech as Beckham moved faster. By the time he got to the sidewalk across the street, the two men were practically jogging.

"I promise our brave men and women will identify and destroy this new Variant threat!" Lemke said to the roar of the crowd.

Beckham flagged down two Secret Service agents and pointed at the two men. Using his radio, one of the agents called in reinforcements to stop the men before they could escape.

The crowd quieted behind them.

"Now I'd like to introduce you to another brave man that has fought for our country against overwhelming odds since day one of the Variant threat," Lemke said.

Beckham paused as two Secret Service agents and a pair of Marines rounded a corner at the end of the block and told the two fleeing men to stop.

The bearded guy reached inside his coat pocket and pulled out a plastic canister the size of a water bottle. The other guy took off running.

"Drop it!" shouted a soldier, aiming his rifle.

The other soldier pursued the runner with a Secret Service agent around the next corner. People at the rear of the crowd turned to look, but Lemke was still speaking, his voice booming. Most of the people at the front and middle still hadn't noticed what was happening.

"It's my honor to present Medal of Honor recipient Captain Reed Beckham," he said. "Please join me in welcoming this hero today!"

Beckham took off in the opposite direction of the stage.

"Captain Reed Beckham!" Lemke said again.

Murmurs flowed through the crowd, but Beckham wasn't listening. He watched in horror as the bearded man tossed the contents of his canister at the soldier. Fluid hit him in the face and he cried out in agony, dropping to his knees. Gunshots followed as the Secret Service agent took down the assailant with multiple rounds.

Beckham drew his weapon.

Screams rang out in all directions, and Beckham glanced over his shoulder as the President and Vice President were whisked off the stage by security.

Seeing they were safe, he continued toward the violence, navigating through the crowd until he reached the downed soldier. The man twitched on his back, his sizzling features erased by Variant acid.

Next to him, the body of the collaborator lay in a pool of blood, his eyes roving. They flitted to Beckham as he approached.

The dying man gasped for his last breaths through black teeth.

"Adios, Reed," he said.

Then he was gone, his eyes rolling up and his chest flattening.

16

The C-27J Spartan shook as the plane entered another patch of rough turbulence. Fitz held onto the cable above his head, bracing himself. The sounds of groaning and flexing metal resonated through the cabin along with the throaty drone of the engines.

Fitz looked around at the rest of Team Ghost as they finished putting on the rub that would hopefully mask their scent from the Variants.

Mendez closed his eyes. His lips moved in silent prayer. Dohi's jaw was set and expression stern, almost as if he were a marble statue. Rico popped another bubble, and Ace and Lincoln checked their weapons.

Fitz could feel the electricity of tension in the air. Soon they would be jumping out of the back of the Spartan 17,000 feet above Minneapolis in the dead of night. The mission would leave them alone for several days and nights behind enemy territory.

This wasn't Fitz's first rodeo, but he couldn't help but feel this mission was more dangerous and different than all the others.

"Five minutes until drop," the crew chief reported, standing near the rear door. A tether hooked to his harness kept him attached to a metal loop on the bulkhead.

"Alright, y'all," Fitz said, looking at each member seated around him. "Call signs are the usual. I'm Ghost 1 and Alpha team leader with Ace and Lincoln. They're Ghost 4 and 5. Ace is our designated R2TD operator. Rico, you're Ghost 2 and Bravo leader with Dohi and Mendez. They're 6 and 3, respectively."

The team responded with a chorus of grunts and nods.

"This is a HALO jump," Fitz continued. "So we won't be pulling chutes until three thousand feet. There's no telling what's down there. Stealth will be key to avoiding detection. Keep your wits about you and stay low."

He looked at Rico with those last words, and she nodded, giving him a wink. Just enough to let him know she understood what had gone unspoken between them: *Be careful.*

The aircraft bucked again.

"If we encounter civilians, we mark their location and move on," Fitz said. "Our goal is to extract intel, not people."

"What if we find a shit ton?" Lincoln questioned with raised brows.

"You mark it, dummy," Ace responded.

"*Pendejo*," Mendez said. Fitz had since learned that roughly translated to dumbass or idiot. He'd had about enough of Ace and Mendez's bantering.

"Cut the shit already!" Fitz snapped.

"He's right," Rico said. "You guys need to quit the jokes and focus."

Fitz waited a moment before continuing. Now that he had their full attention, he said, "Our DZ is a softball field. Rally point is a hundred yards east, place called Bohemian Flats park. If you land outside the DZ, head straight to the rally point."

The team nodded in response.

"Our two main targets are the University of Minnesota

and downtown Minneapolis," he added. "Satellite imagery confirms some recent Variant activity in both locations, so maintain radio silence on the surface unless it's an absolute emergency."

"Approaching target!" the crew chief said. "Oxygen on!"

Rico spit out her gum into her palm and slapped it on her helmet. She hesitated before putting her oxygen mask on to look at Fitz. "Stay safe, Fitzie!" she said.

"I love you," Fitz mouthed in reply.

Her dimples widened. "I love you, too."

"Cute shit!" Ace yelled.

Rico rolled her eyes and strapped her oxygen mask over her face. Fitz did the same thing and secured his visor.

"Door open!" the crew chief said, as he hit the mechanism to open the rear door.

Air blasted in, wind slamming the team. Fitz could barely hear anything over the roar filling the troop hold.

With a hand signal, the crew chief gestured for them to approach the rear door. Fitz waddled toward him. The weight of all his gear for this multi-day mission and the heavy MC-5 parachute strapped to his back dragged him down. Ace had it the worst with the R2TD system over the front of his chest plus his shotgun and suppressed M4A1.

Dohi was first in line with his fingers wrapped tightly around the harnesses strapped over his chest. The crew chief held his arm bent at the elbow and then made a chopping motion.

Go time, Fitz thought.

Dohi stepped out first and immediately disappeared in the blackness. Next went Ace, then Lincoln. Rico followed with Mendez, leaving just Fitz on the platform. He paused there briefly.

Beneath the scattered clouds lay a carpet of black. No lights punctuated the city. No fires. No signs of life at all. Even with the assistance of his night vision goggles, he saw only dark except for the blinking strobes of his team's IR tags far below.

The crew chief motioned for Fitz to drop and he moved over the edge into freefall. For the first few moments, he felt nothing but the weight of his pack and gear. Then the wind took him: pulling, tugging, and slamming his body like an angry ghost.

He fought back, battling the forces lashing his body until he brought his arms tight against his sides. Maneuvering into a nosedive he rocketed toward terminal velocity.

The adrenaline chugging through his body seemed to lessen, and instinct took over. This was the part of jumps he could normally enjoy. The feeling of weightlessness and freedom.

But there was no joy to be found in a dive like this knowing what they were headed toward tonight.

Craning his visor, he saw the last two blinking IR tags showing Rico and Lincoln catching up to him. The Spartan continued onward, abandoning them to gravity and the Variants.

The IR tags below started to coalesce, just as they were trained. After another couple thousand feet, Fitz made it over to Dohi, Ace, and Lincoln, who were already into stable arch positions to slow their fall.

Not long after, Rico and Mendez found them, breaking out of their nosedives and into arch position, too. For now, the team moved into formation, bodies spread out, arms and legs bent enough to guide them through the air.

If all went well and the stars aligned, the Variants would never know they were even here.

Fitz shifted his wrist enough to see his altimeter watch. Just a few thousand more feet to go before they deployed their chutes. The Navigation Aid (NAVAID) showed they were still on target.

Low opening free-falls like this were not forgiving when it came to mistakes and, once they hit an altitude of three-thousand feet, there was precious little time between deploying their chutes and landing without busting their bones, especially with the weight of all their equipment.

Fitz watched the numbers shoot down on his watch. They were seconds from deployment.

He motioned for the team to spread back out. The team gracefully fanned apart, giving each other ample room to deploy their chutes without tangling their lines or colliding.

When Fitz was comfortable with their distance, he reached up and yanked on his cord. His chute exploded open behind him, pulling hard on his body. The harnesses tightened around his shoulders like a giant hand from the back.

The dark chutes of the other Team Ghost members bloomed around him one by one.

All except for Mendez. His chute came out like a snake, twisting around wildly. Somewhere, somehow, something had gotten tangled just enough that the chute couldn't fully deploy.

Mendez whipped around like he was trapped in a cyclone.

Fitz adjusted his chute, positioning himself closer to Mendez's position. But the other soldier was being pulled away wildly.

"Can't get control!" Mendez yelled over their channel.

"Cut to reserve!" Fitz shouted back.

Mendez reached to release his chute but thanks to the malfunction of his first chute, he'd been tossed far from the landing site showing on Fitz's NAVAID.

An enemy world of whites and greens came into view. The concrete jungle rose up to meet their boots, growing nearer by the second. Fitz was close enough to see highways littered with charred vehicles, and skeletal buildings blown to pieces from the failed Operation Liberty.

Fitz's heart climbed into his throat. If Mendez's reserve chute didn't pull soon, he would end up smeared across the concrete.

"Deploy!" Fitz cried.

The reserve chute shot out of Mendez's pack in the distance. He was far from the Mississippi River now, pushed off course and headed past the snaking 35 West interstate toward downtown.

Fitz breathed a sigh of relief.

But his relief was short lived.

"Mother of Jesus!" Mendez said. "I've got hostiles across my LZ!"

Fitz glanced at the NAVAID. The rest of the team was still on their way to the DZ near Bohemian Flats. They would land in the open fields and make their way to the park on the river, giving them plenty of open space to cut loose and leave their chutes.

But Mendez was headed right in the middle of the urban hell.

The ground was approaching quickly, and there was no way for Fitz to make up enough distance now to reunite with Mendez.

"Ghost 3, I want you to get as close as you can to Gold Medal Park. It's a mile west of our DZ," Fitz said. "Post up there if the streets aren't safe."

"Copy," Mendez said.

His chute disappeared behind a screen of buildings framing the highway.

The tattered grass of the old softball fields spread before Fitz. He eyed the landing zone and prepared to do a two-stage flare. Seconds later, his blades hit the ground and he ran out the momentum, all the while looking for movement in the field.

His chute floated down behind him as he ran forward and slowed. Coming to a stop, he quickly shed his harness and chute.

Around him, Team Ghost completed their descents, chutes falling to the ground like deflating balloons sucked to the grass. Fitz crouched down, raising his rifle while his team shed their harnesses and chutes. The team collected their jump gear, and Fitz looked for a place to stow it. He thought the base of a tree at the field edge would work, but something in the back of his mind told him to hold off. Wishing they had time to bury the gear properly, Fitz gave the signal to move out to the Bohemian Flats park.

A wall of trees lined the perimeter of the park except where a pedestrian path stretched across the river toward the university campus. All the vegetation seemed sapped of life, dry and brown.

Even the overgrown grass had died off, crunching beneath their feet.

A mobile construction office trailer sat at the near

edge of the park, beside the pedestrian path. Its door hung open and the windows were all broken. It wasn't perfect, but it would do as a storage spot for their jump gear and, once inside, he could break radio silence to check on Mendez.

Turning, Fitz scanned the shadows in the forested area. Nothing moved in the darkness. He checked the rest of his team as they finished stowing their gear.

Their discarded chutes caught the wind rustling through the grass, flapping and creating a muffled scratching sound. But that wasn't the only thing Fitz heard.

Distant groans and clicks echoed over the park.

Somewhere out there, the Variants were on the prowl.

Beyond the trees, a beast suddenly screamed, freezing Fitz in place. Scanning the pines, Fitz knew the monsters were close, and he wondered if they had heard the chutes snapping open at such a low altitude.

Fitz signaled them to form up on him, then gestured for Dohi and Ace to take point and head for the construction trailer. Team Ghost moved out, rifles coming up quickly, probing the darkness.

Their advance wasn't easy with the extra bulk of the HALO gear. They walked with clumsy gaits trying to manage it all toward the construction trailer. None of this stuff was supposed to be carried once they had hit the ground.

Ace pushed the door open, cleared the space, and then gestured for the team to go inside. Once everyone was in, Lincoln shut the door, and the Team stowed their chutes and oxygen supplies under the desks in there.

Fitz directed the rest of the team to watch out the windows for hostiles. He hated to make any sound, even inside, but he had to know if Mendez was alive.

"Ghost 3, Ghost 1, do you copy?" he whispered into his mic.

Static filled his earpiece.

"Ghost 3, Ghost 1, do you copy? Over."

The channel remained silent.

Fitz pictured the Variants ripping Mendez to pieces. The imagery filled him with dread. He could do nothing to help his teammate.

"Ghost 3, I say again, do you copy?" Fitz whispered a final time.

The only response he got was the wind rushing through the blinds of the office trailer and the constant noise of the distant Variants.

Dohi and Lincoln glanced at Fitz. Rico signaled to him that she had eyes on a hostile, and it was headed into the open fields.

The comm channel suddenly fired with a voice.

"Ghost 1, Ghost 3. I'm holed up, but I think they got my scent," Mendez whispered back.

"Location?" Fitz asked.

"Inside a condo at the corner of 11th and South Washington."

"Can you make it to Gold Medal Park?"

"Negative. At least not yet. Soon as I set foot outside this place, I'm toast."

"Keep your head down. We'll come to you."

Rico pointed at the tree line.

Fitz heard the clicking of joints and looked out the window as Variants emerged from the darkness. The pack prowled on all fours, their tongues lashing against their sucker lips.

A brute led them down the slope toward the fence

along the river.

Team Ghost was being surrounded, just like Mendez.

Dread welled up inside his gut as Fitz considered their next move. They would have to split off in order to save Mendez.

And that meant sending Rico off with Dohi.

Fitz cursed his anger, but managed to separate his feelings like all the other times they had run into issues like this.

"Rico," he whispered. "After we get out of here, I want you and Dohi to go after Mendez. Then sweep downtown, find any signs of the tunnel origins and the webbing."

He turned to Ace and Lincoln next.

"We're going straight to the university. But first, we take down this pack," Fitz said.

The Variants swept the area, changing direction, as they approached the trailer, while another pack emerged at the edges of the park. They were closing in.

The leading monster skittered over toward the mobile office, stopping about one hundred yards away to sniff the air. Its bony back went rigid like an angry cat, confirming it had picked up their scent.

It let out a screech that sent the other beasts into a frenzy.

The creatures bolted toward the trailer. If Team Ghost fired now they might be able to hold them off for a little while, but more would be drawn to their location.

An idea simmered in Fitz's mind.

He grabbed an oxygen tank from their HALO equipment and moved toward one of the broken open windows. He heaved the football-sized tank as far as he could. It sailed silently over the heads of the Variants before thudding into the ground.

The noise drew their attention and several creatures galloped over.

Taking a breath, Fitz raised his rifle and moved his finger over the trigger.

"Everyone down," he whispered.

The team crouched, and Fitz fired.

A round flew from the suppressed barrel and hit home, puncturing the oxygen tank and sparking against its shell. The spark was enough to ignite it, and the tank ruptured, exploding.

A low boom echoed over the park. The fireball bloomed overhead. Flames rolled over the bodies of the Variants, burning away their flesh.

"Open fire," Fitz said.

Team Ghost angled their suppressed rifles out the window, and they slaughtered the rest of the beasts. As the last of the Variants hit the ground, Fitz motioned for the team to abandon their shelter.

"All it takes is all you got," Fitz said. "Good luck, Bravo team."

"Good luck," Rico responded back.

Fitz suddenly experienced the same dread that came on every mission where they had to split up. Watching her venture out into enemy territory without him now was one of the hardest things he'd had to do on any mission.

While her skills in the field were unrivaled by most soldiers, all it took was one mistake, one errant Variant claw, and that was it. All he could do was hope for the best and trust she would make it back alive.

"Let's move," Lincoln said.

Fitz nodded and set off with Ace and Lincoln in the

opposite direction of Rico and Dohi. It wasn't ideal, but it would hopefully save Mendez's life.

An old military adage surfaced in his mind as Fitz ran on his carbon fiber blades.

No plan survives first contact with the enemy.

"Ain't that the truth," he whispered.

17

Normally the underground laboratory on Peaks Island smelled strongly of antiseptic cleaning solutions and crisp filtered air, but not today.

Instead the air had an almost tangy, gamey bite to it and with Kate's full white bunny suit, it seemed as if Kate were running a full-scale butcher shop in a fabrication cleanroom.

A surgical mask clung to her face and goggles pressed against her forehead. She leaned over a laboratory bench in the cell culture room. Beside her was Doctor Carr.

The scientist hemmed and hawed as he peered over the acrylic cylinder nearly a foot in diameter lying between them. A mess of smaller tubes hung off the end of the clear cylinder, providing the nutrient-rich media that kept the tissues inside of it alive.

To the untrained eye, the mass of red inside looked like chopped up hamburger meat, which might have been horrifying to someone like Big Horn, but Kate found it fascinating.

"You think this bioreactor is enough to contain these tissues?" Carr asked, pointing to the acrylic tube.

"Nothing's escaped yet," Kate said. "And it's not like these tissues have a mind of their own."

"They grow extraordinarily fast, though. How long until they outgrow the bioreactor?"

Kate glanced at the window separating the cell culture

room from the main portion of the lab. The handful of techs Carr had brought with him were working in there. Some peered through microscopes. Other pipetted samples into tubes for PCR or other quantitative analyses.

"The cells, as fast as they grow, still obey the basic laws of physics and nature," Kate said. "They only grow so long as we're feeding them. If I cut off their nutrient supply, they go dormant."

"Dormant?" Carr asked. "Not just into a senescent state?"

"From my observations, that's not the case with these things. It seems like there's nothing they like to do more than divide, and they're damned hard to kill."

"Strange. Almost as if they're cancerous."

Kate pressed a finger to the acrylic tube with the cells throbbing inside it. The acrylic was warm to the touch. "All the phenotypic analyses I performed before you arrived confirmed my initial suspicions. These cells are a mix of white blood, nerve, and muscle cells."

"Did you test for any cancer markers?"

"No," Kate replied. "Didn't have the bandwidth by myself."

Carr's brow furrowed beneath his goggles. He seemed agitated. "I suppose I can allocate one of our team members to look into it."

"I'd appreciate that. Knowing what kind of cells we're dealing with is great, but there's something else beyond cell phenotype that we need to figure out."

"I am already one step ahead of you, Doctor Lovato."

Carr wheeled over a cart from a corner of the cell culture room. He pulled back a blue sheet covering the top.

"This is from the autopsy," Carr said.

He waved a hand over a long slice of tissue from a metal tray. The tissue had been isolated from one of the spindly growths jutting out of the Alpha's spine.

"Excellent," Kate said. "So far, every cell culture that I've grown looks like this."

She gestured to the mess within the bioreactor.

"Once I grow these cells on their own, even if it's a piece of intact webbing obtained from the field, they invariably grow into a blob of tissue with no organization."

"These tumorous monstrosities look nothing like nerve cells or the webbing," Carr said. "I suspect it has something to do with a lack of external stimulus."

"That's what I was thinking." Kate rotated the bioreactor to get a view of the chunky tissue floating around within. "Normally, the cells in our body depend on microenvironmental cues to direct cell behavior. The cells I've been growing in here have no directional cues."

"Yes, yes, this is very basic biology." Carr picked up the tray with the Alpha spindle and placed it next to the bioreactor. "And that's all correct, I have the key to this dilemma right here."

Carr held up a small box-shaped device with dials. A few wires stuck out of the sides attached to metal clips.

"My hope is to show you how we can induce the web-like growths you've seen with the external stimulus missing from your cell cultures," he said.

"And how is that?" Kate asked.

Carr began attaching the metal clips to the exposed nerves in the Alpha spindle. An electric wire then went between another batch of nerves, and he handed the free end to Kate.

"Connect this to the webbing samples within your

bioreactor," he instructed. "It should stimulate an electrical signal."

Kate wormed the wire into a valve and pushed it through the liquid media until it made contact with the tissue mass inside the bioreactor. She could've sworn the tissue recoiled at the touch.

But that was impossible.

This thing couldn't feel or react, right?

It was just a bunch of mindless cells.

"Is it embedded in the tissue?" Carr asked.

Kate jostled the wire. She was feeling more like an assistant than a full-blown scientist with Carr demanding these things of her.

"Cut the suspense and tell me what you're thinking," she said.

Carr started to mess with the dials on the box. "This here is a controller. I've attached electrodes to one end of the Alpha spindle. I'm hoping to apply an electric stimulus to it."

Now Kate could clearly see where he was going with this. Her eyes traced the spindle then the wire that led into the bioreactor. "You're going to stimulate a nerve response from the Alpha into the tissue."

"Precisely." Carr smiled confidently. "I believe that these Alphas exude the electrical stimuli necessary to direct the proper hierarchical growths of the webbing. The spindles and growths jutting out of the Alpha's spine likely serve as antennae."

Carr initialized the controller. It buzzed to life.

"From those antennae, I believe the Alpha spreads a signal that tells the webbing to grow, using it to communicate with the Variants around it," he said.

"How did you get all that from one autopsy?" Kate

asked, unable to contain her skepticism on this simple solution.

If she had learned one thing from the Variants, it was that the more you thought you knew about them, the less you actually did.

Still, she hoped Carr was right. Figuring out how this webbing worked and, most importantly, what the Variants were using it for would greatly help Team Ghost and all the others stuck in the field with these monsters.

"If this works, we should see the tissue begin to pulse, just like reports indicate in the tunnels," Carr said. "And after that, the tissue will begin to self-organize into web-like formations."

"Let's try it out."

Carr turned the dial on the controller. The Alpha spindle contracted. Clearly the electrical signal was having some effect.

The spindle soon began to shiver, and Carr had to grab hold of the tray to keep it from shaking the spindle off the lab bench and onto the floor.

"This is not exactly what I expected. The muscles within the thin spindle are reacting far more violently than one would anticipate. In fact, I wouldn't have thought, given the proper connections, we'd see any reaction at all based off the footage of the Alpha."

Kate monitored the cells within the bioreactor. They didn't seem to be doing anything yet.

"Are you sure you have that wire connected properly?" Carr asked.

Kate adjusted the wire to ensure it was embedded deep within the mass of tissue. She could feel the resistance as she tried to push it through the robust cells.

"It's definitely in there good." Kate bent to eye-level

with the bioreactor. "Wait, I see something."

"What? Are they forming webbing already?"

Kate narrowed her eyes. The tissue was pulsing. But the cells weren't forming webbing. Instead, the tissue seemed to be bulging. Almost like a flexing muscle.

"It's not thinning out and forming a spider web," Kate said. "In fact, it looks like it's doing the opposite. Something isn't right."

"Likely the electrical stimulus. I'm turning it up."

"No," Kate said. "I think—"

But it was too late. Carr had already turned the dial, increasing the voltage. The Alpha spindle thrashed like a snake missing the head. It bucked out of the metal pan as electricity flowed through it and into the bioreactor.

The tissue inside went wild. Sections ballooned and deflated, pressing against the clear acrylic walls containing it. Pieces of tissue spread out in jagged spikes, pushing into the tubes feeding the cells liquid media.

Kate turned off the pump, afraid adding pressure to the system would rupture it. But the tissue didn't seem to care. Part of it migrated into the tubes leading into the main bioreactor.

The tubes popped off, unable to contain the intense pressure of the tissues pushing on the liquid. Pink cell media sprayed over the lab bench and floor.

Fractures spread through the acrylic. Before Kate could do anything, the plastic split and the throbbing mass of red tissue expanded.

"Turn off the controller!" Kate yelled at Carr.

He didn't react in time.

The tissue inside exploded, sending red globules throughout the space. The meaty hunks smacked against the walls and peppered the scientists.

Frozen in place, Kate simply stared. Then she reached up to wipe off the chunks from her goggles and the front of her suit.

Carr did the same thing, cursing.

"Next time, maybe you should be a little more cautious, and listen to me," Kate said somewhat angrily.

If Carr had heard her, he didn't seem to react.

"Doctor?"

She turned to see bits of tissue dripping off him.

"I'm just trying to think of where I went wrong," he said quietly.

"I think you had the right idea, but you can't rush science. You should know that."

A few of the lab techs were gawking at them beyond the window to the cell culture room. Carr waved them in and ordered them to start assisting the cleanup. Kate and Carr exited the room to exchange their lab garments for clean suits, goggles, and gloves while the techs worked.

When Kate and Carr were changed, they reentered the cell culture room.

"Instead of going big right away, we need to start small and work our way up," Kate suggested. "Something definitely happened with the electrical signal, and I want to figure out if we can control it."

Carr slid the controller over to her on the table. "I'll let you drive this time."

Kate prepared smaller plastic plates full of tissue to scale down the experiment. This time, even if there was an accident, there wouldn't be much more than a tiny splash. She attached the spindle and the electrical wire to the small tissue samples.

They slowly went through the samples, testing different voltages and amperages. But each time, all they succeeded in doing, if the tissue reacted at all, was frying the cells within the plate.

"Something isn't right," Kate said, after running through another exhaustive experiment. "We're missing a key component. Not a single tissue has formed a webbing of any kind. And in fact, they all seem to be reacting negatively to the external stimuli."

"I must admit, I'm completely stumped," Carr said.

Kate stared at the last plastic plate full of barbecued tissue. The tiny cells held so many secrets, and still she couldn't unveil them.

With Team Ghost in the field and the threat of more raider and Variant attacks looming over her, she knew she didn't have the luxury of time now. She had to solve this mystery.

Slowly or quickly.

It had to be done.

The question was how.

***

Fischer had spent much of the day out in the field, sweating away with his men on their hunt for the Variants. He had come back for supper to find breaking news on his laptop. Having internet access had cost him a hell of a lot of money, but being up to date on things going on across the country was worth every penny.

The attempted attack at the New America Coalition rally in Outpost New Boston was shocking even with the other attacks on safe zone outposts. The thwarted assassination attempt in plain daylight was the most brazen thing he had seen in a while.

Such an incident proved to Fischer yet again that

President Ringgold and Vice President Lemke did not have even their own security under control. If collaborators could sneak into an event like that, Fischer wasn't sure there was any safe place left in the country.

At least not under the leadership of the New America Coalition.

He closed his laptop and grabbed a cigar. Moving over to the windows, he glanced out at the star-filled night sky.

In a strange way, he was surprised that out in his little corner of Texas, it looked just as pretty tonight as all those nights before the Great War of Extinction. Back then, he didn't have to compete with the light pollution of a big city clotting his view of the Big Dipper and all the other constellations swirling above.

Now he didn't have to compete with anything at all.

It was just him, mother nature, and the monsters.

He lit his cigar and took the first puff as several pickup trucks drove away from the compound, their lights chasing away the darkness. Chase and Tran were heading out with Sergeant Sharp to use the infrared scanners now that it was dark in one last attempt to locate the monsters.

All the money he'd paid for good intel on the Variants' whereabouts might as well have been burned in an open field.

The pesky fuckers seemed to have abandoned ship. Fischer Fields had lost enough guards and workers to the beasts, not to mention costly equipment. All of it had set back their operations considerably.

Fischer blew out a puff of smoke, hoping that maybe those creatures were smart enough to know he was hunting them now. That maybe they'd run for their lives.

But that was probably being too optimistic.

Optimism had never served him nor his fields well.

Realism was much better.

Hope for the best, prepare for the worst, he thought.

That was why he was skipping whiskey with his cigar tonight. Until his teams returned with an all clear, he wasn't going to crack open a bottle. The Variants were as sneaky as they were deadly, and he wasn't going to assume that they'd simply run off without a fight.

A knock on his door sounded, and he turned to see Maddie holding a plate and a glass of water. The fifty-year-old housekeeper doubled as a cook, maid, and friend. She had taken damn good care of him over the past two years.

"Good evening, Mr. Fischer," she said. "Would you like to eat in here or in the dining room?"

Fischer gestured toward his desk. "I'll eat in here tonight. Thank you, Maddie."

He almost always ate at his desk when he didn't have company. Sitting in the large dining room by himself was damn depressing and reminded him of how much he missed his wife.

Maddie set the food down and he took a seat at his desk.

"Thanks," he said again.

She nodded and closed the door behind her quietly.

Although he didn't feel much like eating tonight, he dug into the warm meal of mashed potatoes and broiled chicken. Food wasn't just for pleasure. It was for fuel. And if he had Variants to deal with, he was going to need a hell of a lot of fuel to keep him fighting.

He continued reading more reports on attacks at other outposts as he chewed.

"Holy shit," he whispered.

By the time he finished eating, he had read about

another six attacks.

He stood and looked outside.

What the hell is happening out there?

He took his plate back to the kitchen and set it in the sink.

"Thank you," he said to Maddie, who was washing the rest of the dishes.

"You're welcome, sir."

The news of the Variants had him on edge. He took another cigar out from his humidor and looked out the window.

A carpet of moonlight spread over the fields and the livestock barns on the eastern edge of his property. Opening the window, he lit the cigar and took a deep inhale. Then he blew the smoke outward. The breeze rustled his sweat-stained fatigues. Crickets chirped outside, their calls rising into a steady chorus.

He loved that sound.

Fischer took a seat in his leather recliner, putting his feet up when the insects were silenced by a gunshot.

He froze.

Two more gunshots pierced the night.

Something was wrong.

A siren blared from the guard post on the south side of the property. He got out of his chair and walked to the windows holding the smoking cigar.

The radio on his desk crackled behind him.

"Mr. Fischer, this is Tran. Do you copy?"

What the Sam Hill is going on?" Fischer replied.

"Where are you, sir?"

"In my goddamn office. What's going on?"

"You need to get to the bunker as soon as possible," Tran said. "We think we found the Variants, sir."

Before Fischer could reply Tran added, "They were underground all along."

"Underground? Where?"

"Here, sir! The guards at the livestock barns were the ones who reported it, and now they aren't responding."

"Turn on the floodlights," Fischer said.

The lights clicked on one at a time, and Fischer's cigar fell from his mouth at the sight of a fight.

No…

A slaughter.

Dozens of Variants streamed out of a broken-down side door in one barn, chasing cows into the grass. The screams of the livestock filled the night as the monsters tore them to pieces and fed on their fattened flesh.

Other beasts ripped apart the guards that had been patrolling outside. The men hadn't expected an attack to occur from within the barns and were completely unprepared.

A man was retreating into the eastern corner of the electric fences. He backed up, trying to reload his rifle.

"Oh my god," Fischer whispered.

A Variant dropped to all fours and bolted after him. The man climbed the barbed wire fence. He managed to get over the top but so did the Variant.

With nowhere to go, the soldier chose the electric fence over claws. It fried him and sent him flying backward into the livestock fence.

The beast dug in on the smoking flesh.

"Sir, we're almost back!" Tran said on the radio. "If you're not in the bunker, you need to go. Now!"

Fischer smelled smoke and looked down, seeing the cigar had burned into the carpet. He picked it up and smothered it in a glass ashtray. Then he hurried over to grab his M4. He slung it over his back and then went to his cabinet. Opening the doors, he pulled out his Remington 3200 double-barreled 12 gauge.

With his .357 already holstered, he was ready to go.

Two pickup trucks pulled up outside, skidding to a stop. Men jumped out and fired at the beasts around the barns.

"Son of a bitch," Fischer said. He hurried out of his office and into the hallway.

"Maddie!" he yelled.

The woman stumbled into the hallway. "Sir, those things are out there!"

"Grab the rest of the staff and take them to the bunker right now!"

She nodded and took off down the hallway toward the basement. The bunker there was built to survive a chemical, biological, or nuclear attack. There was enough food and water for his whole staff to live on for a year or more.

Fischer had spent almost a year inside it when the Variants had first overwhelmed the country, and he didn't like the idea of returning to it now.

Halfway down the hall Maddie stopped and turned.

"Aren't you coming?" she said.

He plucked another cigar out of his breast pocket.

"I'm not comin'," Fischer said. "I've got some unfinished business with these bastards."

"But sir!" she called out.

"Go to the bunker, and don't come out until you're given the all clear!" he yelled over his shoulder.

He took off in the direction of the gunfire. The wail of the siren, chatter of automatic weapons, and pop of small arms reminded him of the first days of the Great War of Extinction.

He promised himself if this happened again, he wouldn't run and hide. If he was to die, he wanted to do it standing up, not crouching like a coward.

Bringing up his shotgun, he ran through the living room and to the back doors. He opened it with one hand and stepped outside on the deck, his ears assaulted by the sounds of battle.

"Sir, what are you doing?" someone called out.

Chase ran up the wood steps, his baseball cap splattered with blood. Tran was right behind him, his bicep slashed open. The rest of the men were still holding position near the pickups.

"Mr. Fischer, we *need* to get to the bunker," Tran said. "There are too many of them."

"And leave these men and my livestock out here to die? *Hell* no," Fischer said. He moved over to the railing of the deck and set his shotgun against the side. Then he unslung his M4 and palmed in a magazine.

"Fall back!" he shouted. "Everyone, fall back to the deck!"

Tran and Chase both reloaded their weapons, trying to convince him to change his mind, but nothing they could say would work.

The other men all ran up the steps and joined them on the deck. Fischer lined up his scope and zoomed in on the closest fenced off area, about fourteen hundred feet away. It was quite the distance, but he was a good shot and there were enough targets he figured he would hit something.

He centered the sights on a beast with its maw buried in the belly of a squirming cow. He pulled the trigger, firing off a burst. One of the rounds found a home in the creature's neck.

The monster skittered away a few feet and then crashed to the ground limp. Two other Variants tried to drag a calf away. Fischer killed one with a headshot and then aimed for the other beast, trying to get a clear shot.

He found it a beat later and pulled the trigger. The second Variant slumped to the ground, and the calf pushed itself up and huddled behind another cow.

Fischer sighted up a third creature and brought it down with a shot to the leg. He finished it with shots to the back and side.

The men next to him took down several more, but the rest of the Variants ripping his men and livestock apart behind the first barn were too far to hit.

The beasts retreated back into the barn with their kills. Several more shots rang out from the men around him, but they became more sporadic until finally stopping. After a few seconds, the only noise was that of the wailing siren.

"Shut the thing off," Fischer said.

Tran brought up his radio and called their command post. The noise rose and fell one last time. Fischer brought the scope to his eye and zoomed in on the distant fences, seeing the Variants had also retreated in those areas.

Soon the screams of the massacred animals and men went quiet and the chirp of the crickets resumed.

"Anyone got eyes on those shits?" Fischer continued to scan the area.

Everyone reported they saw nothing.

"Think they went back underground?" Chase asked.

"We'll have to send a couple scouts to find out," Tran replied.

"Where is everyone else?" Fischer said, looking around. He didn't see Sergeant Sharp or any of his soldiers. He didn't see his trackers, Galinsky or Welling, either.

"They went to help put the fires out," Tran said. "The Variants attacked several of the derricks, too."

"And you didn't think to mention that earlier?" Fischer said with an angry snort.

"I'm sorry, sir, but my goal was to make sure you were safe," Tran said.

Chase nodded. "We figured Sharp had that under control."

"I highly doubt that," Fischer stated.

He didn't want to believe it, but there had to be another Alpha out there. Something smart enough to have coordinated this multi-location attack. He cursed through gritted teeth, trying to think of what to do.

The livestock were obviously lost, but maybe he could still save the derricks. One thing was certain: if he didn't do something, Fischer Fields wasn't going to make it through the night.

18

Dohi had spent the better part of the night slowly working his way toward Gold Medal Park in Minneapolis with Rico. The last report from Mendez confirmed he was still holed up in the condo.

But now Dohi was starting to worry. He hadn't heard anything from Team Alpha either. They were supposed to be working their way across the other side of the city to the University of Minneapolis.

The good news was the team had prepared to be out here for at least two or three days. As long as they didn't go beyond that, they would be fine.

He took a drink of water and followed Rico through a burned-out pub with exposed brick walls. Charcoaled stools and tables littered the floor. Shards from broken bottles and the bar mirror hid under the debris, making each step dangerous.

Progress just to get to this pub had been painfully slow. They had taken a detour much further south than Dohi would have liked before they had headed north again. Prowling Variants had forced them inside. Even from their hidden location, he could hear their clicking joints and howls as they hunted.

Dohi tried to drown out the noises and the smells.

The rotten fruit odor wasn't the only thing contributing to the malodorous, bombed-out city. Mold climbed up the walls from puddles of stagnant water along the floor.

In the back of the bar, a refrigerator lay open, its contents a mess of black fur and spiky growths. Crumpled beer cans were adhered to the floor in sticky piles of unrecognizable brown gunk.

At Rico's command, Dohi positioned himself near a back door and snapped his night vision goggles back on. According to his map, this exit led to an alley. The main thoroughfares were too dangerous, and Bravo hoped to avoid some of those monsters by creeping along in the shadows instead as they made their way to Mendez.

Rico shouldered her M4A1 and gave him a nod. Dohi wrapped his gloved hand around the handle and twisted it, pushing the door open a couple of inches.

Distant growls of Variants filtered in, but none sounded close. He waited there to be sure, counting the passing seconds, not making another move. Just peering into the darkness outside with his NVGs, studying the green and white sliver of alley.

Shadows moved in the street beyond the carcasses of cars and trucks.

Dohi signaled to Rico and she gestured back for him to exit. He eased the door open further and stepped into the alley, clearing both sides before signaling for Rico to follow.

She moved and they navigated the scree from devastated buildings side by side. A cool wind cut into them and another distant Variant howled. More of the beasts answered the call, the shrieks rising into the night like a flock of birds taking to the air.

Every hair on the back of his neck stood straight. A single mistake would bring the hordes on them. There was no way he and Rico could survive that.

He swallowed his fear and pushed on, squeezing between an overturned dumpster and a brick wall. Scattered bones lay on the other side, blackened and broken.

Once he got to the end of the alley, he knelt behind the bumper of a car that had slammed into a nearby wall. Inside the front seat sat a picked-over skeleton.

All around him came the scrapes and scratches of other beasts searching the picked-through graveyard. Most of the creatures were starving and desperate, which made them even more dangerous.

Rico pointed at a rusted Humvee. It took him a moment to spot the Variant. It crouched nearby, angling a wart-covered nose in the air.

Dohi rotated so he had the creature in his sights. A suppressed shot now would rupture the silence of the night unless it was timed with a howl. If not, it would draw every Variant within the neighboring blocks on his position.

He waited, hoping that it would simply go on wandering listlessly into the night.

But he had no such luck. The creature seemed to catch a whiff of something and dropped to all fours. He moved his finger to the trigger, waiting for a shriek or howl to mask his shot.

The creature bounded across and he prepared to squeeze the trigger, but the Variant seemed to drop through the street.

Dohi eased off the trigger.

It took a moment for him to realize what had happened.

There was an open manhole in the middle of the street. From there, an animalistic cry exploded. The clicking of joints grew louder, and other cries from Variants responded.

The starving, filthy beasts began to pour out of shops and skittered down the sides of buildings. Others leapt from broken windows.

They rocked into each other as they stormed toward the open manhole. One by one, they squeezed into the hole, vanishing into the darkness.

All Dohi and Rico could do was press themselves against the wall, shrinking behind the car while the stampede rattled the ground. It might have only lasted a minute, but to Dohi it felt like an eternity.

Eventually the last of the beasts made it into the underground hell.

Dohi made a mental note of their position. Once he made sure their path ahead was clear, he led Rico away.

They began winding their way over the sidewalk, avoiding other corpses and ducking between crashed vehicles. The area had been hit hard, most of the buildings were nothing but husks or crushed piles of debris.

But there was still one building standing. US Bank Stadium towered over the block in the distance, standing between them and Mendez. Jagged panes of black, grime-covered glass stood around the top of the once enclosed stadium.

The roof had been entirely blown away, and chunks of melted scaffolding jutted down from the opening. A low moan seemed to radiate out of the stadium like the building was groaning in pain.

Dohi balled his fist and listened.

The sounds definitely seemed to be coming from inside the stadium.

"Sounds like people," Rico said quietly.

Images of the tunnels in Outpost Turkey River surfaced in his mind.

These sounds were all too familiar. One din of countless voices blended together in a macabre soup. The cries from people who were in so much pain, they would beg for death.

Rico set off toward the rusted cars, buses, and military trucks in the parking lot. The moaning grew louder, almost as if they were approaching a waterfall in the jungle.

On the other side of the abandoned vehicles was a quarantine and evacuation checkpoint. Decaying fabric still flapped from huge collapsed tent poles. The canvas on the rusted cots in the lot had mostly rotted away, and boxes of military first aid supplies lay on their sides, their contents long since raided.

Dohi snuck through the area until he reached one of the wide-open gates of the stadium. Rico joined him, roving her rifle back and forth for contacts.

Once inside, they crept between piles of debris littering the corridors. Dohi imagined what it had once looked like with vendors selling cold beers and hotdogs in the wide hall. He could almost smell the popcorn and peanuts in the air and hear the cheerful chatter of throngs heading for a Vikings game.

Now the place was anything but celebratory.

Gloom filled the dark passages. Long dark stains painted the walls. Everywhere Dohi looked was another sign that the civilization he had grown up in no longer existed.

The groans and moaning became louder.

Rico motioned for Dohi to hurry up.

They prowled up stairs that would take them to the seats overlooking the arena floor. Near the top, a sudden clink of talons against concrete sent them both ducking into the shadows.

Pale flesh from a Variant streaked past.

Dohi slipped into a stairwell and took it to the entrance of a seating area marked 211. He stopped in the open corridor, the moaning echoing off the walls.

Rico took point and crouched at the end. Dohi followed her, heart flipping when he got a view of the field.

Much of the roof had caved in, dumping bent scaffolding onto the football field. Holes leading to underground tunnels littered the space like oversized ant colonies and flowing from the black lips of earth were dozens of Variants.

They used the scaffolding that had fallen from the roof into the center of the stadium as a ladder to move around the stadium.

Red webbing covered the metal platforms. Those pulsating vines stretched out of the network of tunnels and straight up to the scaffolding. Humans consumed by the growths hung from the spider web of metal.

Dohi zoomed in with his rifle at webbing growing from eye sockets, open mouths, and virtually every orifice of their bodies. Most of the people appeared to be utterly desiccated, looking like browned and leathery mummies.

But others retained some color to their skin. They were still breathing and writhing ever so slightly.

Alphas like the one he'd seen in the tunnels climbed up the network, their tendrils dragging along the organic cables. They pawed at the humans, opening up new wounds. Red webbing extended from the wounds of the weaker-looking prisoners.

Dohi swallowed the bile climbing in his throat and knelt behind the seats, trying not to throw up. This was Outpost Turkey River all over again, only worse. The nightmarish tableau had him wanting to hide.

A tap on his shoulder brought him back to attention. Rico pointed to the top of his helmet, and he nodded back.

They stood to capture the scene with their cameras. Dohi raked his back and forth to get a sweeping view of the place before they retreated to the outer corridors.

The hallway around the stadium's perimeter took them to the north side where they would continue on to find Mendez. As much as Dohi knew he needed to focus on the path ahead, he couldn't get the sounds or images out of his mind. They were like tattoos seared in his thoughts.

We will save them, Dohi thought, trying to reassure himself.

But in his heart, he knew most of those people were beyond saving. Bombing the stadium would have been more merciful than unhooking them from the network of red webbing.

He finally managed to get his wits and made it to the north side of the stadium without encountering any of the beasts. Only a block or so separated them from the condo building Mendez was waiting inside.

Thinking of his brother did help Dohi refocus from what he had just seen, but with every step away from the stadium, he felt like a magnet was tugging on his bones.

There was no denying the connection he felt to this place. While it was probably just in his mind, he couldn't help but feel like he was a prisoner to the nightmarish webbing just like the people in the stadium.

Rico suddenly yanked on his arm and pulled him behind a car. As soon as they ducked down, Dohi saw why.

An army of monsters were huddled down on the next block, surrounding what had to be a fresh kill. He zoomed in with his rifle, his heart thumping at the possibility it was Mendez. The body of several humans came into view through the mass of diseased flesh.

From what little clothing these people still had on, he could tell they weren't soldiers. Probably more of the prisoners that these Variants had plucked from the webbing. He was surprised he hadn't seen more of this.

The Variants swarmed, fighting over the scraps, and tore the three humans apart frantically. Screeches sounded over the squawking beasts, but they weren't coming from down the street.

Dohi glanced over his shoulder.

"Oh, shit," he mumbled.

Rico turned to see what had him spooked.

Hundreds of Variants flooded out of the stadium and around the quarantine area. Their numbers were so great, the ground rumbled beneath them, their clawed hands pounding the cracked concrete.

"We have to find cover," Rico whispered.

Dohi nodded and followed her toward the closest building. They ducked inside, and moved behind the booth of an old pub. The stampede grew louder, and he poked his head up for a glimpse of the beasts, freezing when he saw their armored flesh.

The sight of these monsters sparked a memory. These were no ordinary Variants…these were juveniles, a new generation of monsters.

But how was that possible?

There had been no reports or sightings of more than a few juveniles over the years.

"Hell…" he whispered.

Rico pulled on him and keeping low, they bolted for a bathroom while the ground vibrated from the heavy armored feet of juvenile Variants.

"What did you see?" she whispered.

Dohi shook his head. This nightmare kept getting worse. Seeing the offspring of the monsters meant the beasts were doing something no one believed they were still capable of doing.

Breeding on a mass scale.

"Dohi," Rico whispered.

"Juveniles," he said. "Those were all juveniles."

Rico's jaw hung open. "You're sure?"

He nodded. "Should we break radio silence and tell Fitz?"

"He probably already knows," Rico said. She pulled the gum off her helmet and plopped it in her mouth, chewing as the tiles rumbled under their boots.

"Mendez isn't the only one that needs rescuing now," she whispered. "We're screwed, too."

***

President Ringgold changed her mind about their destination as she boarded Marine 1 from Boston to the Greenbrier.

"Take us to Peaks Island instead," she ordered.

COS Soprano gave her a confused look, but he knew better than to argue after almost eight years of service. The Secret Service agents, however, protested the change, saying it would be too difficult to secure the area in time.

"I think we're good," Beckham said. "We have Lieutenant Niven and the Iron Hogs on the ground. They'll make sure the LZ is secured."

The lead Secret Service agent approved the plan after Ringgold agreed to call in a second team of Marines, and the VH-60N White Hawk helicopter took off for the island.

After the events in Boston, Ringgold wanted to see some friendly faces and learn more about the work being done in the lab there. If anyone could figure out what kind of strange biological phenomena were taking place in those tunnels, it was Kate Lovato.

Ringgold tried to relax on the flight, but her mind and heart were with the men and women on dangerous missions across the country. In six major cities, teams had deployed to gather intel and, if history repeated itself, many of them would not come back.

She prayed for their safe return. All of the men and women had the skills and experience to accomplish their goals, but she couldn't shake the worry that she'd sent them on a suicide mission.

The pilots received the all clear at a few minutes past eleven in the evening. They'd been hovering off the shore at Peaks Island, and now Marine 1 lowered from the sky.

A few minutes later, they touched down in an open field. Ringgold looked outside to see the silhouetted Marines had formed a perimeter. There were probably more prone in the weeds and in the tree line, their sniper rifles ready to fire on any threats.

Beckham hopped out first, and then offered his prosthetic hand to her. She took it and, keeping low, followed him and the rest of her team across the grassy field.

Several Humvees waited for them. Ringgold climbed in one with Beckham and three Secret Service agents. The convoy tore down a dirt road toward the healthcare center that doubled as a bunker and a lab. If she recalled correctly, this was where the raiders had concentrated their attack.

"The facilities survived?" Ringgold asked.

"Mostly," Beckham replied. "All the supplies we lost were replaced. But we can't replace the lives we lost. Jake Temper died trying to protect people there."

"I'm sorry, Reed," Ringgold said.

She had met the New York Police officer and his son Timothy a handful of times. Her heart hurt just thinking about all the deaths in the past week. In the past, heartbreak had proved to be good motivation, but her aging heart couldn't shatter much more without giving out entirely.

"This is it," said the driver. He parked the vehicle outside the health center, and a group of Marines fanned out to form a new perimeter.

Once it was secure, a Secret Service agent opened her door and led her toward the building. Another agent moved next to her, his eyes roving at all times. Beckham joined them, moving fast.

At the side door to the building, a large man stood with a machine gun resting on his shoulder and a cigarette in his mouth.

"Guess your first political rally didn't go so well huh, boss?" he said to Beckham.

"It could have been worse," Beckham replied.

The man tipped his baseball cap up at Ringgold. "Madam President, very nice to see you tonight."

It was then she saw the face of Master Sergeant Parker Horn.

"Good to see you, too, Master Sergeant," she said with a faint smile as they strode past.

Horn patted Beckham on the back, but stayed outside, smoking his cigarette and watching the surrounding darkness for threats.

The two Secret Service agents continued into the building, leading Ringgold and Beckham into a well-lit hallway. The top floor was being used as a command post for the Iron Hog team of Army Rangers. Crates and boxes were stacked neatly in the hallway.

She passed a room they had turned into an operations center.

Backtracking, she stopped in the doorway. The former office was full of radio and surveillance equipment. Screens glowed blue over the faces of soldiers sitting there. They were so intent on their work that it took a moment before one of the officers noticed her and shot up at attention. The others all burst up from their seats and stood stiff as boards.

"At ease, everyone," she said. "I wanted to thank you. I really appreciate you working overtime tonight to make sure the island is secure."

"Thank you, Madam President," replied a sergeant.

"How's it going, Ruckley?" Beckham asked the woman.

"Island's locked down, Captain," she said. "No one is getting past our defenses."

Ringgold was accustomed to the tired looks of warriors, but there was clearly some resentment in a few gazes tonight. Not that she blamed them. What was happening across the country was too reminiscent of the final nightmarish stages of the Great War of Extinction.

Almost as startling, half of the Rangers in this room were in their early twenties, which meant they were hardly even teenagers during that first war.

First war, she thought.

She backed out of the room. Soprano and one of the agents went inside the office, but she followed Beckham and the rest of the security detail down the stairs to the lab.

Until Boston, she hadn't really thought about the possibility of another full-fledged war again.

Considering this new reality made her heart thump.

She had to find out what was going on, and stop it before it was too late.

"This way, Madam President," Beckham said. He gestured through an open steel door to the bunker and a living area. They crossed the space and moved into a passage. At the end, glass walls provided a glimpse into a full lab.

Kate was working behind the protective glass with Carr and the technicians. But Ringgold's eyes gravitated instantly to a clear fish tank full of what looked like a living hunk of meat in a pink bath of liquid.

The red, squirming tissue looked like the heart of a monster.

"What in God's name is that?" she asked.

"Good question," Beckham said. "Kate tried to explain it to me, and I still don't think I understand."

He hit a button on the wall, buzzing the lab.

Everyone inside turned around toward the glass walls. Kate smiled behind her visor and raised a finger to indicate they should wait one moment.

Ringgold continued scanning the room. Technicians

worked at all kinds of equipment, their faces buried in what they were doing. She recognized the microscopes but was less familiar with the contraptions that had hoses sticking out of them or the large racks of devices with blinking lights that seemed to be humming.

Atop a cart in a corner of the lab, a woman sliced into the exposed muscle of a monstrous limb from an Alpha. The technician then took a chunk of what looked like muscle and deposited it into a glass jar.

Footsteps sounded back in the bunker hallway and Ringgold turned to see Soprano speed walking through the hallway.

"Madam President," he said, panting. "I've got news about that collaborator we took into custody at the rally."

"What is it?"

"He gave us the potential location of other collaborators."

"Where?" Beckham turned to join in the conversation.

"Luray Caverns in Virginia," Soprano said. "SOCOM is already putting together a strike team to check it out."

Beckham looked at Ringgold. "I want on that team. That bastard called me out by name. If this is something personal, I need to be there to stop it."

"It's too dangerous," Ringgold replied. "Chances are this is a trap. Those caverns could be filled with Variants or who knows what else."

Beckham stood straighter and drew in a breath.

"Madam President, you asked me to run for Senate to protect my country," he said. "I can't do that without knowing who these collaborators are."

"There are other soldiers to do that, Reed, you already gave more than enough of yourself," Ringgold said.

"Please, I promise no live fire. I just want to go for

support. I'll bring Big Horn with me."

She had never heard Beckham so insistent on something before. That only reinforced her feeling this was a bad idea. But she trusted him. When it came to military matters, he knew what he was doing.

"Okay," she agreed.

More footsteps echoed at the end of the hallway drawing her attention to what was probably another problem. Two more Rangers joined them, including Sergeant Ruckley.

"Madam President, we have Vice President Lemke on a line for you," she said, handing over a satellite phone.

Ringgold took it in a tired hand. Another call this soon after the first couldn't be because the vice president wanted to chitchat.

"Talk to me, Dan," she said.

"Got more bad news. Fischer Fields is under attack."

Ringgold looked back over the lab, the news sinking in. She was hoping for the tycoon's support but doubted she would get it now.

"How about the reinforcements we sent them?" Ringgold asked.

"I'm not sure they will be enough," Lemke replied. "Sounds pretty bad."

"Keep me updated."

"Yes, Madam President."

Ringgold shook her head and handed the phone back to the Sergeant.

She had to stop what was happening out there before it spread to every free inch of the Allied States, and they lost everything she had spent the past eight years trying to rebuild.

— 19 —

The sun dipped on the horizon, disappearing behind the overgrown trees along the Mississippi River. Fitz looked out the window of the Walter Library at the University of Minnesota campus, eyeing the packs of Variants hunting outside.

Hours ago, the creatures had swarmed the streets, forcing Team Alpha to take cover here. He set up guard shifts, so they could all get some sleep while they waited, but Fitz hadn't been able to rest. From the looks of it, his men hadn't fared much better.

Ace leaned against the wall next to the window, clearly struggling to keep his eyes open as he watched for threats. Lincoln lay nearby, his head propped up behind his hands on the floor.

Fitz wasn't happy about hiding in the mildew-covered building full of rotting books. They needed to get out there and identify the location of the Variants and any prisoners. But roaming packs had forced them into shelter.

Added to that, Fitz was on pins and needles not knowing how Team Bravo was doing. He still didn't know if Rico and Dohi had linked up with Mendez yet, or if they were even still alive for that matter.

This was the most difficult part about dating Rico. Not knowing how she was, or if she was hurt. Sometimes he could block out the worry by keeping himself busy. But when the only companion in his mind was boredom, he couldn't help thinking of all the terrible things that might have happened to her.

Every second that passed, he considered breaking radio silence. But he decided to trust Rico would transmit if there was an emergency.

He checked the window again as the last of the packs moved out of the area. Ace nodded from his location at another window.

It was time to move.

Fitz nudged Lincoln with a boot. They gathered their gear and headed toward the entryway to the computer lab. Ace led them into the main corridor of the library, passing toppled shelves bleeding soggy, mold-covered books. Leaking water from the ceiling pinged on the floor.

Somewhere ahead came the scratching and growling of Variants. Their rotten fruit odor rose over the pungency of the rotten books.

A chill ran through Fitz, and he held up a fist.

He suddenly got the sense he made a vital error in judgment, and the Variant packs had flanked them. Shadows stretched over the library's floor as several beasts sniffed their way into the room.

Lincoln and Ace took cover next to Fitz behind a standing bookshelf. He watched through a gap in the books as three of the thinnest Variants he had ever seen prowled through the shelves, looking for something to eat.

They hadn't caught the team's scent yet.

Fitz motioned for Lincoln and Ace to hold their fire.

One of the creatures picked up a book and then tossed it aside, hitting a second beast. It snapped back and growled, an eye seeming to bulge from a sunken socket.

The third beast had stopped to chew on an arm covered in open wounds oozing blood and pus. The creatures were all covered in bite and scratch marks.

They were cannibalizing one another, he thought.

Fitz maneuvered for a better look, his right blade letting out a slight creak.

The munching Variant glanced up. The sucker lips snarled back, rows of needle-sharp teeth glistening in saliva.

Fitz waited a beat, hoping that the Variant would write the noise off and turn away. But he had no such luck.

The growling Variant crept toward the team. Fitz looked for a quick escape but, with the beasts around them, there would be none.

They didn't have any way out of this mess except—

Fitz signaled to Lincoln.

"Fuck this," Lincoln growled. He stepped out from their hiding spot and fired a burst. Rounds punched through the creature's chest, sending it spinning backward. It crashed in a tangled mess of limbs.

The remaining two bounded over to their dead comrade, each letting out a furious shriek. Lincoln ended their short-lived assault with two more bursts.

All three beasts bled out into the pool of rain water and wet pages of novels that would never be read again.

But the damage had been done.

The suppressed shots and screeches had attracted the attention of another pack. Fitz didn't need to tell his team to run. Fighting inside the close quarters would be suicide. If they were going to make a stand they needed a better vantage.

Or you could hide, Fitz thought.

A pair of Variants exploded out of a doorway ahead of Ace.

Fight it is, then.

The older man blew off their heads with perfectly aimed shotgun blasts. Other shrieks came from the hallway behind them. Lincoln laid out a wall of cover fire.

The crash of metal clanged from the hallway. Fitz followed Lincoln and Ace out to see three more Variants vaulting out of a doorway.

Windows cracked in the back of the library as other creatures flanked their position.

Team Alpha was already surrounded.

Ace took on the Variants in front, and Lincoln focused on those in back with Fitz. A few got close enough they managed haphazard swipes. Bullets chewed into the diseased flesh of the monsters, dropping them easily.

Once they were all down, another flurry of screeches filled the halls.

"Changing," Fitz said.

Lincoln slapped in a new magazine, and Ace reloaded his rifle.

As Fitz charged his rifle, he noticed broken-open ceiling tiles and the red webbing they had seen in the tunnels. He signaled for Lincoln and Ace to continue down a stairwell.

The group headed toward the bottom floor of the library where manmade tunnels would lead to other buildings on campus. These had preceded the Variants, built for students to transit in warmth during harsh Minnesota winters.

Red webbing covered the walls down here and the scent of carrion intensified. The Variants had made themselves at home.

Fitz ran onto a dirt-covered floor and looked over his shoulder at the stairs. They had to flick on their tac-lights to pierce the suffocating darkness. The roars of the Variants boomed from the upper floors of the library. He whirled to scan the basement.

Growls and grunts came from across the dark space. The noises sounded like there was something more than the garden variety Variants occupying this area. He identified the familiar high-pitched staccato notes and an ear-splitting clicking that the Alphas made.

Now he wondered if it was the noise they had made that drew all of the packs, or if it was this creature commanding them like some crazed conductor.

If that was the case, then they wouldn't be able to escape the constant barrage of attacks until the Alpha was dead. They had to take it down.

Fitz signaled toward the manmade tunnel that led from the bottom floor of the library to neighboring university buildings. The webbing was dense here, some of it stretching across the passage.

Other Variant-made tunnels branched off the main passage, more of the webbing coating the dirt and rock walls like cobwebs. Clicking joints echoed, preventing Fitz from getting a good read on the location of the other packs. He knew one thing—they were coming for Alpha Team.

The soldiers pressed deeper into another passage where he finally saw movement. A massive shape lumbered down the dark corridor.

"That's the Alpha," Fitz whispered to his team members.

Lincoln aimed his rifle but the abomination rounded a

corner. A flood of smaller Variants suddenly rushed in to cover their leader's escape.

Lincoln took a knee, and Ace hugged the wall. Fitz moved between them to get an open firing zone in the narrow passage. The sinewy monsters crashed under the wave of gunfire, clogging the tunnel with bodies.

"Conserve your ammo!" Fitz yelled. He had already gone through several magazines, and only had four left, plus his sidearm, and they still hadn't collected the intel they needed to relay to command.

They had to get out of here.

He turned, seeing more shadows moving in the space.

Dread filled his gut.

In an effort to try and escape, he had trapped them down here in a network of Variant-infested tunnels.

Shit, shit…stay focused, stay calm. All it takes is all you got, Fitz.

As the Alpha Variant escaped, it seemed to be sending more Variants at Team Ghost. Suddenly one of the creatures pounced from a branching tunnel and rammed into Lincoln. He crashed to the ground pushing up at the beast as the wormy lips peeled back, saliva roping off its teeth onto Lincoln's face.

Fitz grabbed its head and twisted it with a violent snap. The claws meant for Lincoln's face slid along the floor, tearing into the pulsing webs of tissue.

"Thanks," Lincoln said, as he rose with Fitz's help.

Turning to fire, rounds and shotgun blasts chewed into more Variants advancing on them.

Almost as soon as they finished off that batch, another creature exploded out of the darkness. Lincoln cut it down with a flurry of rounds that sent it sliding across the web-covered floor.

Fitz motioned for them to head into a branching tunnel, trying to find a way out before the Alpha could send another wave.

They needed something to change the paradigm. It took him a few minutes of running for his mind to think back to Outpost Turkey River, and that gave him an idea.

The R2TD system had attracted the Alpha, which had seemed more interested in destroying that piece of equipment than any of the humans around it.

From what Fitz knew, the beast used echolocation to navigate through its environment. Those huge bat-like ears were hypersensitive to sound. And the pings of the R2TD device must be in the right frequency range for the beast to pick up.

More Variants hurled themselves out of neighboring tunnels ahead, and Fitz stopped to take them down. He yelled while firing, "Activate the R2TD system."

"What?" Ace shouted back.

"Turn it on!" Fitz screamed. "Lincoln and I will lay down covering fire."

"You fucking crazy?"

"If you want to get out of here, do it!"

Ace took off the device and flipped it on. A low hum emanated from the machine as they waited for the next pack of monsters.

Instead of the squawks from the grunts, a roar blasted from one of the nearby tunnels. The sound of footsteps echoed as the creature was drawn to the machine like a bug to a light.

"Where's it coming from?" Lincoln said.

Fitz turned just in time to see a giant shape filling the wide corridor.

"Behind us," he said.

The Alpha ran at a hunch, bat-like ears fanning out the sides of its head. The muscular arms pumped as it moved and the spindles of tissue stuck out of its spine toward the surface of the webbing on all sides of the tunnel.

The three men opened up on it with their weapons. Rounds blew out hunks of meat, slowing the advancing monster. It stumbled under the hail of lead, letting out a series of pained screams.

It made it a few more strides before collapsing to the ground. Using its claws, it dragged its broken body toward them.

Fitz lined up his aiming reticles over the creature's bulbous head. A final shot blasted away the bone and flesh of the creature's blind face.

For a moment, Fitz thought he had a chance to gather his breath again, but new sounds boomed down the tunnels.

More Alphas.

A new trickle of adrenaline surged through his vessels. Fitz signaled for Ace to set the R2TD system down. The device would attract all the nearby Alphas. He had only intended to eliminate the one, but if they could clear out more, then he would take that opportunity.

The questions were how many more they would have to take out, and did they have enough ammo?

Another beast lumbered into the tunnel with hands clamped over its ears. It let out a pained howl that was answered by the boom of Ace's shotgun.

The abomination crashed not far from the first.

Another Alpha joined the fight, then a third and a fourth.

Holy shit, Fitz thought. He hadn't expected so many of the beasts to be prowling these tunnels under

Minneapolis. It only proved to him that this place was important, undoubtedly an epicenter of Variant activity.

By the time Fitz directed Ace to turn the R2TD off, seven corpses clogged the tunnels. The clicking of joints and shrieks seemed to retreat.

"Let's get out of here," Lincoln whispered.

Ace picked up the dormant R2TD system, and Fitz used the back of his hand to clean flecks of blood from his face. He took point and led them back to the main tunnel system.

Other tunnels intersected with the sides of the main corridor. Fitz spotted the desiccated remains of animals in several of them. Everything big and small had been strung up, sharing a fate like those deer they'd seen in Duluth.

In some instances, Fitz even saw dead Variants hanging from the red webbing.

Whatever this stuff was, it pulsed more wildly here. Fitz could practically feel the electricity coming off it and into his own skin. The deeper into the main tunnel system they went, the faster his heart beat, as if his own body knew what he was heading into before he did.

After using the R2TD weapon like that, he was certain that they had taken out all the Alphas within a generous area from their location.

If his memory served him correctly, they were nearing the Northrop Performing Arts Center. The air became more humid the deeper they moved.

Advancing through these tunnels seemed like walking through the blood vessels of some giant beast. Fitz realized that wasn't so far from the truth.

The tunnels were, in a way, part of a living monster, and the Delta Operators were like parasites. These growths of living tissue seemed to be the way the monsters organized themselves, creating a kind of hive mind network.

He didn't know exactly how it worked, but he had a feeling they were getting close to uncovering that secret based on the ferocity of the Variant defenses they had encountered.

He balled his fist as a deep roar boomed in the distance. The thunderous voice rattled his bones, resonating in his marrow.

Lincoln and Ace both had their hands on their helmets, staggering back and forth until the sound died away.

Fitz brought up his rifle, trying to blink away the stars bursting before his vision.

"What was that?" he stammered.

Ace shook his helmet. "I don't know, and I don't want to find out."

Lincoln shrugged and shouldered his rifle. "If something's going to try to kill us down here, I'd rather get this shit over with."

***

Kate rolled over in bed, instinctively reaching out for Beckham, and feeling nothing but sheets. She shot up, remembering that he had left shortly after midnight for the USS *George Johnson.*

"I'm just going to monitor the mission and will only go in after the team has confirmed it's safe," he had said.

Horn had gone with him, entrusting her security, and the kids, with Sergeant Ruckley and her Army Rangers, as well as the Marines.

Kate got out of bed and walked over to the window, taking in a deep breath of the crisp morning air drifting into the temporary housing.

Letting out a yawn, she went to her bag of clothes. She had slept, but not well, since Beckham was gone.

With the end of the Great War of Extinction, she had gotten used to seeing him every day and feeling the warmth of his body at night.

For the past few weeks, she hadn't seen much of him at all, and she feared that wasn't going to change anytime soon. Especially with the new scientific studies she was embarking on and his decision to take on a role with the government.

It seemed their quiet lifestyle on the island had come to an end.

"Mom," Javier said, rubbing his eyes in the doorway. "Do you have to work again?"

"Yes, honey, I'm sorry."

Javier frowned. "When is dad coming back?"

"Soon."

"I want to go home," Javier sighed. "I don't like this place."

"Don't you like hanging out with the other kids?"

"I guess, but Timothy seems really mad and so does Bo."

"I imagine it's going to be hard for Timothy for a while. Just keep trying to be there for him, okay?"

Javier nodded. "He does like playing with Ginger and Spark."

"Good, you guys should take them to the park and play today."

"Okay," Javier said, his spirit lifting. "As long as Tasha and Jenny are cool with it. Maybe they'll want to play soldier with me."

Kate nearly winced.

"Why don't you play scientists instead?" Kate asked. "You know, some of us are quite happy as scientists."

Javier sunk his hands into his pockets. "If I don't become a soldier, then I'll be a scientist," he said. "I just want to help people when I get older."

Kate smiled at that.

"You can start by helping Timothy and being there for him in his time of need."

"I know, and I will."

Javier went back to his room to get ready for the day.

When she was good to go, she started a pot of coffee. While she waited for it to brew, she watched Javier eat his breakfast, wondering what his future might hold. Her gut told her his future might very well be decided in the next several days by scientists and soldiers.

One of them waited outside her door now.

"Morning, Doctor," said Michael. The fit young soldier raised a fist and Javier pounded it.

"Hey, Mikey," Javier said.

"Sup, champ?"

"Not much, just another boring day ahead."

"Tell me about it." Michael glanced at Kate. "No offense, doctor."

She smiled and walked down to Donna's room, stopping to knock. Turning back, she kissed Javier and gave him a hug.

"Have a good day, honey."

Donna stepped out of her room, at that moment, with a smile aimed at Kate. "Don't worry," she said. "I'll take good care of him."

"I know you will, thanks, Donna," Kate replied.

Michael led her downstairs where a full escort of soldiers waited in the hotel lobby. Security had been tight since the raid on Peaks Island and Portland. Because Ringgold had identified her and Carr as VIPs, they could barely use a bathroom without having to check in with someone.

A Humvee took her to the piers, and a private boat took her to Peaks Island and the lab. Carr was already working, his eyes pressed against a microscope within the cell culture room.

Kate donned a white bunny suit, mask, and goggles, then stepped into the lab. The familiar chorus of chirping and humming laboratory equipment greeted her.

Lab techs filtered in and out. The team that Carr had arrived with was big enough to keep the place staffed twenty-four hours a day. It bumped up their productivity and allowed Kate a night of rest so desperately needed without feeling too guilty.

One of the techs handed Kate a summary of the experiments they'd conducted through the night.

"Anything particularly interesting I should be looking at?" Kate asked, beginning to skim the report.

"The cells tested positive for cancer markers," the tech replied.

"Ah, that certainly helps explain the unrestrained growth of the cells and why the vessels feeding the tissues are so patchy."

The tech nodded and walked away.

Kate took the report with her to where Carr worked, trying to wrap her mind around the implications of these new findings. Oftentimes in tumors, blood vessels grew too fast to form properly. Instead of allowing blood to flow through them normally like a garden hose, vessels growing in tumors acted more like those sprinkler hoses with all the tiny holes in them used to water lawns.

But that didn't help her to understand why they couldn't get the masses of tissues in their bioreactors and cell culture plates to form the same organized webbing structures that Team Ghost had seen in the tunnels.

"Good morning, Doctor Lovato," Carr said, when she joined him at the microscope. "I trust you've read the most recent data."

"I have, and what it tells me is that we've still got a long way to go."

"That we do." He sighed and turned to look at her. "I've tried making sense of the phenotypic data in comparison with the abhorrent bulk behavior of the tissue, but it just doesn't fit together."

"What have you tried since I was gone?"

Carr pulled out the cell culture plate he'd been examining on the microscope tray. "I'm incubating tissue samples from the autopsied Alpha with the webbing samples."

"Mind if I take a look?"

"Be my guest."

Carr replaced the cell culture plate, and Kate pressed her face to the eyepieces. The nerve and muscle cells from the webbing were a disorganized mess. They certainly looked like the cancerous mass that the tech had reported they were.

But on the other side of the dish, separated by a thin semi-permeable membrane, the cells isolated from the autopsied Alpha spindle were still growing. They appeared neat and organized, stretching in long networks like the nerve and muscle cells Kate would have expected in mature healthy tissue.

The cells appeared to be doing exactly what they were supposed to do. As if something was directing their growth. It hit Kate maybe that was exactly what was happening. If so, she had been looking at things backward.

"Let's have the team run GTPase activity assays on these samples," Kate said. "I want to know the signaling activity levels in both cell populations."

"I don't know if—"

"We ran your experiments with the Alpha spindle, and they didn't work," Kate said, looking over at Carr who stood by her shoulder. "It's time to try something else."

Carr gave the order to the techs. They started running the assays in the other part of the lab. If the results proved her instincts right, then they were going to have to adjust their understanding of the cellular interactions they thought had been dictating the tissue behavior so far.

It took a couple of hours, and once the experiments had completed, Kate and Carr studied the results on a computer monitor. The staff had already analyzed the data and transferred it to graphs that showed the relationship Kate had been expecting.

"My goodness, this is...not what I expected," Carr said.

"Increased GTPase activity indicates higher levels of cell signaling with an especially high concentration going on in the webbing cells," Kate stated.

"I can see that. What's strange to me is that there is far less signaling going on in the spindle cells."

"Precisely," Kate said. "My guess is that the cell signaling is stronger in the webbing because the Alpha spindles function differently than we expected. The spindles are more like an old TV's antenna than a radio station's antenna."

"You mean they are meant for receiving signals instead of transmitting them?"

"Yes, the GTPase activity is just as high in the webbing in dishes that both have and don't have the spindle cells," Kate continued. "If you look at a cell culture that only has spindle cells, there is very little GTPase activity, meaning the Alpha spindle cells don't do anything without signals from the webbing cells."

"That certainly supports your hypothesis." Carr gestured to one of the larger bioreactors with the masses of tissue growing in them. "Guess it's time to take these tests to the next level."

Kate nodded and helped carry one of the football-sized clear tanks with the webbing tissue to a table in the middle of the cell culture room. Carr set up one of the Alpha's spindles like they did last time, complete with a controller to apply voltages to the tissue. This time, he set the electrode to apply an electrical field to the webbing tissue instead of the Alpha spindle.

"Ready?" he asked.

She nodded.

He turned on the controller.

Kate held her breath, anxious to see if she was right.

The invisible current of electricity passed through the mass of webbing tissue and, unlike the other tests, it didn't bubble or expand. Instead, it pulsed evenly like a heartbeat. At the other end of the bioreactor, connected to those webbing tissues, was the Alpha spindle attached through a port in the bioreactor.

The spindle seemed to contract smoothly and didn't quiver or jump around like a fish on land. Even when Carr pressed their luck by increasing the voltage, the tissues continued to perform the same way. There appeared to be little difference in the behavior of the different tissues.

"It's working," Carr said, as a smile slowly started to spread across his face. "You're right. Whatever signals are being transmitted through the webbing are passing through the Alpha spindle. And this time, nothing appears to be going crazy."

"This is how the tissues are *supposed* to behave."

"So the Alpha is taking signals from the webbing, but the webbing tissues haven't changed form at all. It's still a mess instead of self-organizing into the spider web tendrils."

Kate frowned. "That's what I was afraid of. We've only got half the equation here."

"There must be something else that transmits commands through the webbing..." Carr seemed to think on it for a moment before turning to look at Kate. "I don't think the Alphas are at the top of the food chain, Doctor Lovato."

"I think you're right. All this reminds me of the monsters from Europe that had morphed into bug and reptile-like creatures. They had fairly complex social structures."

If there was something else out there that could control the Alphas, and coordinating Variants and collaborators, it had to be more intelligent and frightening than anything they had encountered yet.

Her stomach sank.

Team Ghost was out there in enemy territory. They could come face to face with this monstrosity and, this time, there was nothing she could do but warn them. If she wasn't already too late.

"Come on," she said, turning toward the exit. "We have to notify command."

20

Two elements of a platoon from SEAL Team 3 sat inside the briefing room of the USS *George Johnson* listening attentively to General Souza and his LNO, Lieutenant Festa, discuss their mission, dubbed Operation Renegade.

Beckham and Horn watched from the back of the room, their backs to a bulkhead.

The eight SEALs sat ramrod straight, faces covered by black paint, only the whites of their eyes showing. Horn, on the other hand, was slouched and staring off into space. Beckham gave him an elbow to the side.

That did the trick.

Horn stood up straight and folded his arms over his chest.

"The drone we sent over the target shows no recent Variant activity," said General Souza.

Beckham had already studied the maps and satellite imagery, but this new image on the wall-mounted monitor was much more recent. He took in the fiery canopy of trees and the mostly abandoned parking lot outside the Luray Cavern buildings.

"Infrared scans came back negative for human and Variant contacts," Souza added. "However, these scans can be unreliable. Past experience shows Variants can mask their heat signatures, and there is evidence to suggest recent human activity in the area."

Lieutenant Festa brought up a new picture of two roads leading to the caverns.

"Fresh tracks indicate vehicle movement on both Highway 340 and Cave Hill Road," he said.

"If our source is telling the truth, this could be one of the most important missions in figuring out the collaborators' connection to the Variants and their attacks on the outposts," Souza said.

Malcom Winters, the Chief Petty Officer in charge of the SEAL team, cleared his throat. "What about other human populations in the area?" he asked. "Any friendlies we should be aware of?"

"This is Variant territory, so anyone out there is living off the grid and should be considered hostile until proven otherwise," Souza replied.

"Roger that," said the chief.

"Any other questions?" Souza asked.

The SEALs shook their heads.

"Beckham, Horn?" Souza looked to the back.

"No, sir," Horn said.

"Not right now, sir," Beckham added.

"Good, let's get topside. I want to bag and tag these fuckers before sunset."

The SEALs filed out of the room. Beckham and Horn started to follow but, before they left, Souza called out to them.

"Hold up, Captain," he said.

The general directed his LNO to shut the hatch, indicating whatever he had to say wasn't good. Beckham's thoughts instantly went to Team Ghost.

"We just got word from Doctor Lovato before this briefing," Souza said.

Beckham's heart flipped. He pictured another raid on

Peaks Island sweeping away Kate and Javier and the other kids.

"What's wrong?" Horn got out before Beckham could respond.

"Nothing's wrong at the outpost. It's what Doctor Lovato found in the lab. She thinks she's figured out what the red webbing is for."

Beckham knew she would come through.

"It's some sort of communication network," Souza said. "They think the Variants are using it to coordinate the attacks by sending signals to the Alphas we've seen."

"If this is true, then maybe the collaborators are tapped into this network, too," Beckham said.

"It's unclear if humans can tap into this network or if they'd be relying on communication through Variants. Either way, we need an immediate answer to this," Souza said, crossing his arms. "That's why Festa is coming along on this mission."

"Sir…" Beckham's words trail off, realizing he would be out of line to tell the Commander of SOCOM that it was a bad idea to send his LNO.

Instead, he said, "Have you heard anything from Team Ghost?"

"Negative, they've been radio silent since the HALO jump," Souza said. "Hopefully, we'll hear something soon."

"I hope so, too, sir."

"I need to get back to command to monitor Operation Shadow," Souza said. "Good luck out there."

Festa opened the hatch, and Souza hurried off in the opposite direction. The rest of them took ladders to the deck of the destroyer. The SEALs were finishing up their gear check outside the open troop hold of a V-22 Osprey.

Clouds crossed over the morning skyline, blocking out the sun. Beckham didn't like going in during daytime, but they didn't have a choice.

There was no time to waste.

A group of ten Marines filed out of the hatch in full combat kit, carrying suppressed M4A1 carbines. They loaded straight into the Osprey.

"We got more people joining the party out there?" Horn wasn't very good at hiding the skepticism in his voice, and Beckham shot him a look.

"They're going to help with intel extraction and prisoners," Festa said. "And they'll make sure I don't become Variant feed."

Beckham cracked an uneasy grin as he grabbed his M4 and Horn picked up his M249. They followed the Lieutenant into the troop hold where they took seats and waited for the SEALs.

If all went well, the support crew wouldn't have to fire a shot while the SEALs cleaned house.

Horn settled into the seat next to Beckham.

"Reminds me of the day this all started, riding one of these to San Nicholas Island," he said.

Beckham swallowed and looked down at his boot and blade. The memories brought back physical and emotional pain.

"Sorry, boss, I know you remember," Horn said, resting a hand on Beckham's shoulder. "We lost a lot of our brothers that day."

"Hard to fathom what's happened since then."

"Tell me about it. I think of Sheila every damn day and what could have been."

"She would be damned proud of how you've raised your girls," Beckham said, looking up. "You're a hell of a father. The best."

Horn drew in a breath and forced a smile.

The SEALs moved into the hold and sat down. Some of them traded looks with Beckham, but nobody spoke. The V-22's engines growled to life, and the rumble vibrated through the bulkheads. Beckham put on his headset and closed his eyes. The flight would take three and a half hours, plenty of time to get some desperately needed shuteye.

A nudge to his arm woke him up sometime later. He blinked away his grogginess.

"Better wake up, boss," Horn said. "Command is reporting contacts in the drop zone."

Horn tapped his headset, and Beckham snapped alert, listening to one of the pilots over the channel.

"Please advise," the pilot said.

"Standby for orders," was Chief Winters reply.

Across the troop hold, Festa was talking on another channel.

Beckham couldn't hear what the LNO was saying over the engines. He strained to look out the windows, seeing nothing but clouds.

"We're ten minutes from target," said one of the pilots over the comms.

"Alright listen up," Festa said. "Our drone operators are reporting movement in the area. Two pickup trucks and a van."

"Are they headed to or from the target?" asked Winters.

"To the target," Festa said.

"If you don't want them to hear us coming, we better put down far outside the DZ," Winters said.

Beckham agreed.

"Moving in on foot is risky, but it's your call, Chief," Festa said, looking to Winters.

"Why not just land and go in guns blazing?" Horn rumbled.

"That's not how we do things, Master Sergeant," said the SEAL Chief.

"He's right," Beckham agreed. "We haven't even confirmed they're collaborators."

"Who the hell else would they be?" Horn said. "You heard what General Souza said. Anyone out here has to be treated hostile until proven otherwise."

"I'm all for lighting up these bastards if they are collaborators, but I don't want to kill some random stranded survivors," Winters spoke.

"Me either," Festa said. "Plus, we need the collaborators alive for intel."

The voice of a pilot came back over the open channel. "Sir, we need to make a decision soon."

"Let's go low and sweep them," Beckham said. "See if we can get them to stop. If they aren't collaborators, they might still have good information for us."

Winters agreed after a short pause.

"Let's get it done," Festa said with a nod.

He went up to the cockpit to talk to the pilots while Winters relayed the plan to his team and the Marines. The nervous sounds of pre-combat stretches and gear checks echoed through the space as the craft lowered through the cloudy sky.

"I don't like this boss," Horn said. "What if they are collaborators and start shooting?"

"Then we take them out," Beckham answered.

Horn looked at the M240 near the back of the aircraft.

"Targets in sight," said the primary pilot. "They are

heading north on Cave Hill Road."

The Osprey continued to descend and the back door opened. A crew chief grabbed the M240 and set it up, manning the weapon.

"They spotted us," confirmed one of the pilots. "One pickup just veered off onto a dirt road through that forest, but the van and other pickup are still heading north."

"Cut 'em off," Festa replied.

"Stranded survivors my hairy ass," Horn snorted.

The Osprey curved through the sky as it moved to intercept the vehicles. Beckham glimpsed the sea of orange and red leaves in the forest canopy. A brown road curved through it like a polluted river.

The crew chief on the M240 aimed the barrel downward and Horn moved over, tapping him on the shoulder.

"Step aside, bub."

The crew chief gave him a glance, but a nod from Festa made him get out of the way, allowing Horn to grab the weapon.

"Both vehicles just turned off the road," reported the primary pilot. "They're still heading for the target area."

The aircraft turned again, cutting low over the trees. They were close enough Beckham could see the truck and van driving perpendicular to the Osprey.

"Fire a warning shot," Festa told Horn.

Horn squeezed off a burst in front of the pickup, but instead of stopping, two men stuck rifles out of the windows and opened fire.

The M240 barked to life in Horn's grip.

As the Osprey curved with the vehicles, Beckham caught a better view of where they were headed. They sped toward a parking lot outside the various buildings once used for cave tours. Beckham figured the collaborators were using them as housing now.

Horn fired another burst from the M240. Sparks and smoke exploded from the front of the pickup truck. The vehicle jerked, grinding to a stop from blown tires. The van swerved around, slamming into the ditch.

"Take us down," Festa said over the comm. "Get ready, everyone."

The aircraft's wings tilted up as it slowed, and the Osprey began a vertical descent toward the road. The wheels thumped against the asphalt.

"Go, go, go!" Winters yelled.

The SEALs stormed down the ramp and fanned out with their weapons shouldered. Beckham joined Horn who was aiming the M240 at the van.

As soon as the SEALs were out, the Osprey lifted back into the sky, circling overhead. The SEALs spread into a wide semi-circle around the vehicles, and gunfire quickly rang out.

Several rounds slammed into the bulkhead and Beckham ducked down.

"Eat this, assholes!" Horn yelled as he fired at the vehicles. Beckham straightened to see multiple hostiles had jumped out of the truck and van. The men were clumped around the damaged vehicles, shooting at the SEALs.

Gunfire lanced across the road, and Horn rained more rounds down at two men kneeling in the ditch. They both collapsed, blood painting the grass.

"Nice shooting, Big Horn," Beckham said.

The collaborators outnumbered the SEALs, but they were no match for the warriors and Horn on the M240.

One by one the bastards hit the dirt.

"Fox 1, this is Eagle Eye 1, all hostiles down," Winters reported over the comm channel. "Requesting permission to proceed to target."

"Permission granted, Eagle Eye 1," Festa replied. He ordered the pilots to put them back down a safe distance from the vehicles. The wheels touched the pavement again, and this time most of the Marines piled out to help secure the area.

The SEALs advanced toward the caverns and the buildings, veering off into two smaller elements to explore both locations. Horn gave up the M240, and the crew chief took over.

"On me," Festa said.

Beckham, Horn, and two Marines walked down the street with the Lieutenant after a perimeter had been set up. Within five minutes, the entire scene had been locked down.

One of the Marines jogged over to Festa.

"Nine hostiles dead and one alive, sir."

Festa gestured toward the Osprey with a thumb. "Get the bastard into the troop hold."

Two Marines dragged a man out of the ditch. His pants were stained red from a wound. A cobweb of a beard clung to his grime-covered face and dreads hung over his shoulders.

The collaborator snarled like a Variant as the Marines hauled him off. Even from a distance, Beckham could smell the man's fetid odor.

Festa motioned for Beckham and Horn to join him and their Marine escort. They set off for the parking lot the SEALs had crossed, toward the entrance of the caves and the buildings surrounding it.

The Osprey took off again, pulling away to avoid any potential enemy fire. Beckham kept his rifle cradled, scanning the forest, buildings, and surrounding areas for any hostiles.

The crisp autumn air rustled the hair sticking out under his helmet. He filled his lungs as suppressed gunshots sounded in the distance.

"Eagle Eye 1 engaging two hostiles," Winters reported.

Festa balled his fist. Beckham took cover behind an abandoned car with Horn and waited while the SEALs raided the buildings across the parking lot.

Cleaning house, he thought.

And clean house they did.

Winters came back online a moment later. "Fox 1, Eagle Eye 1. All hostiles eliminated. We're checking for booby traps."

"Fox 1, Eagle Eye 2, we've cleared the building," said the SEAL in charge of the second team. "It's a freaking gold mine. Better have a look, Fox 1."

Festa stood and nodded. The Marines took point, weapons at the ready. They moved into the building and found the room where the SEAL fire team waited.

Computers, radio equipment, and crates of supplies were stacked against the walls across from bunk beds.

"Get it all on the Osprey," Festa ordered.

"Guess that prisoner wasn't lying," Horn mumbled.

"Yeah but how did he know my name?" Beckham moved to a table with maps to start the search for any connection they had with him or Kate.

"Pack these up," Horn said to one of the Marines.

"Fox 1, Eagle Eye 1, we found some of that red webbing in the caverns," Winters said.

"Copy that, Eagle Eye 1. I'm on my way," Festa said.

Beckham scanned through the maps and papers as quickly as he could.

"Captain, I'd like you to join me," Festa said.

"Big Horn, you keep going through these," Beckham said.

"What, and let you have all the fun?" Horn snorted. "Y'all got this under control, right?"

The Marines nodded.

"Come on then," Beckham said.

A SEAL led them out of the building to the entrance of the caverns. They hiked down a stairwell into the underground lair. A brick path led them into a damp open area with huge stalactites.

It took them another ten minutes to get to the other SEALs.

"Should be right up here," said their escort.

Beckham examined the red vines stretching across the walls and hanging from the jagged ceiling. He continued around a corner and spotted Winters and another SEAL with their weapons raised upward.

"Look at this shit," Winters called out.

Festa halted in front of Beckham, both of them looking up.

Strapped inside the webbing were four Variants, their flesh shriveled and eye sockets sunken. Even their sucker lips looked deflated, but their chests slowly expanded and deflated.

They were still alive.

"What the hell are they doing up there?" Horn asked.

"I've never seen anything like this," Winters said in a low voice.

Beckham didn't quite understand it, but maybe this

was how the collaborators were communicating with the other locations. Through the monsters.

"I think I have an idea..." he was cut off by a distant boom.

The men all turned back the way they had come.

"What the hell was that?" Horn asked.

"Eagle Eye 2, this is Eagle Eye 1, what's happening up there?" Winters said into his headset.

"The van!" came the reply. "It blew!"

"Winters, take care of these Variants and meet us topside," Festa said.

Winters aimed his suppressed rifle and fired off bursts into the heads of each beast while Beckham, Horn, and Festa took off with the SEAL that had led them into the cavern.

It took them ten minutes to get back to the road. When they did, they were greeted with billowing smoke and the scent of caustic acid.

The scene of chaos seized the breath Beckham held in his lungs.

A Marine limped away from the road, his flesh melting off his bones. SEALs ran over to help drag the injured men away from the destroyed vehicle. It hadn't just been packed with explosives; it had contained a major supply of Variant acid.

The sizzling fluid had hit four Marines. Their skin bubbled and sloughed off their muscles as they writhed on the ground. A SEAL helped pull an unconscious Marine into the grass. When he got there, he suddenly let go of the body and held up his hands, screaming in horror as his gloves melted.

Beckham and Horn ran over to help.

"We need evac, Lieutenant!" Horn yelled.

He bent down with Beckham next to a Marine that had lost his legs in the blast. Beckham immediately tied tourniquets around the shredded stumps of the man's thighs while the injured man mumbled about his mother.

"It's okay, we're going to get you out of here," Beckham reassured the unfortunate man. He looked up for Festa. The lieutenant appeared paralyzed a few feet behind them.

Beckham gave the order for evac into his headset, but the pilots wouldn't authorize the landing without Festa.

"Snap out of it, Lieutenant! We need your authorization!" Beckham shouted.

Horn grabbed Festa by the arm and squeezed. That got his attention. He spoke into the comm, and the Osprey came swooping back down to the ground.

SEALs, Marines, and the two crew chiefs helped haul the injured into the troop hold. Others carried equipment and boxes of documents from the building.

Beckham and Horn carried the man that had lost his legs. They set him down gently on the deck.

The screams of the injured echoed as the door clicked shut. A medic hurried over and set down a pack.

"Hold on, brother," Beckham said. He looked over his shoulder as the medic worked to dress the wounds and improve Beckham's hastily applied measures.

At the back of the aircraft, the collaborator rocked back and forth, chained to the bulkhead. The filthy man watched the chaotic scene with a satisfied smile behind his crusty beard.

Winters stormed back there and wiped the grin off his face with a punch to the jaw. Then he pulled out his MK3 knife. Horn joined him, rolling up his sleeves on the way.

"The son of a bitch had a detonator on him," said the

medic. "Blew up the van when we went to search it."

Beckham gripped the injured Marine's hand, squeezing and trying to help him stay conscious while the medic worked to stop the bleeding.

"Where are the Variant leaders hiding?" Winters yelled. "Tell me their fucking location."

The collaborator spat blood into the SEAL's face and smiled again.

"I will tear your fucking eyes from your face," Winters yelled, angling his knife at one of the man's eyeballs. The collaborator twisted away and Horn grabbed his chin to push it back toward the blade.

"Tell us where the Variant leaders are!" Horn shouted.

Winters pushed the blade against the man's cheek, drawing blood. His eyes flitted from Horn to Winters.

"Captain, can you help me with this?" said the medic.

Beckham helped him wrap a dressing around one of the bloody stumps, but a thud drew his eyes up for a moment.

Horn grabbed the guy by the neck, squeezing, and slammed the collaborator's head against the bulkhead again.

The man's eyes bulged and his lips spread to reveal his black teeth. He said something and Horn loosened his grip.

The man coughed, and then looked in Beckham's direction with blood shot eyes.

"They're everywhere!" he yelled. "You can't stop their reckoning!"

21

Dohi took a sip of water and brought up his binos to focus on the condo where Mendez was holed up.

"You see him?" Rico whispered.

"Negative," Dohi said quietly.

Two scraggly Variants prowled around the abandoned cars in the parking lot separating them from the building. He saw more moving inside.

Dohi was worried they were never going to find Mendez. Not alive anyway. It had taken them an entire day and night just to get here. They had spent the previous evening inside a bathroom after the juvenile hordes had funneled out of the stadium to feed on the humans that the older Variants had brought home for dinner.

He had never seen Rico pray before, and he had a feeling Mendez was doing the same thing.

The Variant activity was worse than a cockroach infestation in the slums, and the presence of juveniles changed the entire game. But at least they had all returned to the stadium for now, leaving only the diseased and starving older monsters out here.

Rico signaled for Dohi to advance across the street. He snuck between the cars and behind a bus resting on deflated, rotted-out tires. The entrance to the condo building lay only a few yards away. Beyond the broken doors was a lobby filled with ornate columns and a dried-out fountain.

Dohi peered through his optics, glassing the lobby. Two starving Variants meandered around a stairwell, but otherwise the coast was clear. Those dying beasts would be no obstacle. He motioned to Rico, and then began creeping toward the condo's entrance, passing several vehicles.

A hiss broke the silence. He swiveled to his left, but was already too late. The Variant leapt out of a vehicle with a tongue slithering around its sucker lips. Dohi barely dodged the attack and brought his rifle up to parry a set of claws.

A pop sounded from above. Blood painted Dohi's face and helmet. He blinked and used a sleeve to wipe the gore off his face as the creature crumpled at his feet. He spotted a rifle barrel sticking out of a condo window on the fifth floor.

Guess that answers whether Mendez is alive.

Dohi didn't waste a beat. He charged into the condo lobby, taking out the two lethargic Variants with single shots. Rico followed him up the stairs, but a pack of emaciated Variants came leaping down toward the landing.

"Move," Rico said.

Dohi jumped to the side as she fired two bursts, splattering the wall with gore.

Four more Variants staggered in the hallway on the fifth floor, moaning like the undead. They could have been mistaken for zombies. Their bodies appeared to be more skeleton than flesh.

Dohi took them all down with single shots to the head before they got close enough to swipe with a claw.

A door swung open down the hall, and Mendez stepped out, looking at the corpses and then smiling his handsome grin.

"Took you long enough," he said. "I was starting to think you guys left me for dead."

"Been hell getting here," Rico said, picking up her step as she headed toward him.

Dohi sounded relieved when he said, "Good to see you, brother."

"I don't think you know how good it really is," Mendez said. "Thought I'd never make it out of this shit hole."

"Frankly, it's still going to be tough with us three," Dohi said.

"I think I should break radio silence now," Rico said as she grabbed her radio. "See where Alpha Team is."

Dohi nodded. "I agree."

"Don't let me hold you back." Mendez and Dohi stood guard while she bent down to transmit a message.

"Ghost 1, this is Ghost 2," Rico said. "Ghost 3 is safe and sound. Over."

The reply came a few beats later.

"Good to hear your voice Ghost 2," Fitz replied over the channel.

Rico smiled at his reply.

"Rally point is the Northrop building at the university campus. Meet us..." Fitz paused. A moment later he added, "Meet us in classroom B2 on the basement level."

Rico glanced at her watch. "Copy, Ghost 1. On our way. ETA two to three hours if all goes as planned."

She let out a sigh of relief and patted Dohi on the shoulder.

In that moment, he envied what Rico and Fitz had. A

relationship they could cling to and find comfort in. Love in a world filled with horror and loss.

But then again, Dohi didn't want the worry of a relationship. He saw how Fitz and Rico loved each other, but he also saw how they worried about one another.

The only woman he had ever loved had died during the war eight years ago, and he had never allowed himself to get close to anyone again. Fearing he would lose them, too.

Another sip of water, a hand signal from Rico, and Dohi went back to business, taking point out of the rear entrance of the building. They crept down the stairs and out into an alley that would take them straight toward the riverside.

As soon as he opened the door, Dohi picked up the rotting fruit scent.

A platoon-size group of Variants digging through the scattered trash looked up from their search. Each snarled, revealing a mouthful of teeth evolved to shred flesh.

Dohi and Rico strode out, unleashing suppressed fire into the ranks of the beasts. Mendez joined the fight on their left flank.

Most of the creatures went down easy, but the healthier beasts moved fast.

One flung itself up onto the alley wall, then lunged, throwing itself through the air. Dohi caught it in the chest with a burst, killing it before it even landed.

The remaining Variants scattered, making single shots difficult. Dohi switched to automatic to keep them back. By the time they were dead, he had burned through two precious magazines.

"How much ammo you got?" Dohi asked Mendez.

"I only fired the shot that saved your ass."

"Good, we're going to need it," Rico said.

The trio set off between rusting vehicles and piles of debris from battle-damaged buildings. They didn't stop until they got to the steel fences of the St. Anthony's Falls Visitor Center.

The center overlooked the rumbling falls in the middle of the Mississippi. Mendez and Rico took seats, both covered in sweat. She lifted her binos and scoped the dormant black smokestacks of the University of Minnesota steam plant across the river.

After a brief rest, Dohi again moved in front of the group. He traversed a stone arch bridge leading Mendez and Rico toward the opposite shore. Dark bloodstains covered the bridge halfway across.

Crossing here was already dangerous with no cover, and seeing others had died trying made him jumpy. The group ran all the way across and bolted for the shelter of trees in the park on the other side. From there, they cut through the area and used the cover on the side of a rough asphalt road to advance.

Distant howls cut through the morning.

Dohi balled his hand into a fist, and all three of the soldiers crouched down in the swaying grass. He waited there for several minutes listening to the wind, sensing something out there.

But nothing moved.

Traipsing around in Variant territory had him on edge every second, and his frayed nerves were paying the price.

Rising to his feet, Dohi motioned for the team to continue. They jogged to train tracks covered by mud and foliage until the University of Minnesota campus buildings sprouted into view. Blackened husks of vehicles clotted the streets between the brick-faced buildings.

Variants climbed over fallen trees leaning over the roads. Normally the limbs might have cracked under the weight of a beast, but not these famished creatures. Their wart-covered faces were sunken around their skulls, and their eyes bulged, scanning frantically across the ruins for food.

Through his binos, Dohi spotted more of the thin red spindles stretching out of the debris in the distance. The scree framed the road, some of it scattered over the asphalt. In the center of the street, red vines curved out of an open manhole.

If the webbing aboveground here was any indication, then he had a feeling they were about to uncover more of what he had seen in the stadium when they went underground.

He led the team around several Variants fighting over rats. Some had reverted to chomping on their own flesh. The variety of scents helped mask Team Ghost as they made their way toward the rally point with Team Alpha.

A Variant sat perched in front of the theater like a statue. Dohi considered taking it out but decided in favor of stealth, heading for the side entrance. He made his way to the loading docks where two semi-trucks were parked. The back doors were open as if someone were still moving cargo in and out of the building.

He stopped to listen and then gestured for the others to join him. They hurried around the trucks, up a ramp, and into the Northrop building.

From there they crossed a storage room full of soggy, collapsed cardboard boxes and wooden crates nearly devoured by termites. He moved through an open door into a hallway where his hair stood on end, energy practically radiating off the red webbing growing on the walls.

He stepped onto the tissue and continued forward. Skeletal remains hung from the walls. From the looks of it, these animals and humans had been dead for a long time.

A quake suddenly vibrated through the building. Dohi shouldered his rifle, ready for something to come charging but, after a few seconds, the quaking stopped. The webbing contracted and relaxed, seemingly beating in concert with his heart.

Clicking joints echoed down the corridors along with the tapping of claws against tile. Intense waves of a fetid odor swarmed into the passage.

The sounds faded away and Dohi signaled for the others to duck low. They found shelter behind a door leading to a dressing area furnished with broken chairs and powder stains. Shattered mirrors lay amid a pile of rotting costumes, webs growing over the once colorful outfits.

A few more seconds of silence passed.

"What are we doing?" Mendez asked.

Dohi couldn't explain why he took cover here. Something felt off, and his gut told him to wait. Rico went to move, but Dohi stopped her.

"Hold on," he whispered.

Mendez and Rico both crouched and brought up their rifles, clearly on edge now. They remained there for several minutes, listening, but the beasts remained silent.

Dohi finally decided he was being paranoid and went to give the forward signal when a vicious roar exploded through the corridors. The thunderous voice seemed to rattle through the webbing and right through Dohi, awakening feelings of primal fury and hunger. Adrenaline churned through his blood vessels.

What is happening to me?

The roar subsided with the vibrating.

Dohi blinked away sweat dripping into his eyes. That ungodly roar must have had something to do with whatever Fitz had discovered down here.

Rico gestured for them to advance. They crept past a few corridors filled with sleeping Variants. Another turn into a wider corridor, and then a final door led them to the rally point.

They entered a classroom where Fitz, Ace, and Lincoln huddled in the darkness. The men all rose, and Fitz strode across the room and wrapped his arms around Rico, pulling her close to his chest. The others greeted each other quietly with smiles.

After the short reunion, Fitz signaled he would take point.

"Wait," Dohi whispered. "Do you know about the juveniles?"

Fitz raised a brow. "What juveniles?"

"We saw them last night at the stadium," Rico whispered. "Hundreds of them."

Lincoln and Ace both stepped closer.

"Hell no," Lincoln muttered. "I don't believe it. No way those diseased fucks are breeding again."

"It's true," Dohi said. "I saw it."

Lincoln shook his head, and Ace did the same.

"You're sure?" Ace asked.

Dohi and Rico nodded.

"Do you have footage for command?" Fitz asked eagerly.

"No, we hardly escaped," Rico said.

"But you know they're in the stadium?" Fitz asked.

"Yes," Dohi responded.

"Fuck," Fitz said. "I think this is worth breaking radio silence for, but first I want to show you guys what we found. Might as well send it to command, too."

"What did you find?" Rico asked.

"Something more unbelievable than the juveniles. You'll have to see it yourself."

He led Team Ghost out of the classroom and up a set of stairs to the main auditorium. The scattering of Variant claws came from all directions. Squawks and shrieks filled the performing arts center.

Team Ghost crept behind the back row of seats, staying low in the shadows. Webs covered the stage and roped down from the ceiling, stretching from the balconies above them toward a monstrosity on the stage.

Holes in the ceiling let the meager moonlight bathe a monster unlike any Dohi had ever seen. Hundreds of vines connected to a bulbous red abomination on the stage.

The body looked somewhat humanoid, with limbs as big and wide as a redwood tree. Flesh drooped over its body in huge pink folds, making it look like a gigantic brain.

Dohi assumed the creature's real brain was located somewhere in a squat and flat head with unblinking eyes the size of a giant squid's.

The creature moved, pulling on the hundreds of red fibers and stretching them like cords. It let out a long groan while the webbings attached to its chest contracted. The movement caused a chain reaction among the vines stretched out into the auditorium.

Variants suddenly burst onto the stage and swarmed the monstrosity's body like worker ants on a queen. They shoved hunks of flesh into the open massive maw with fanged teeth.

An old Native American saying came to Dohi's mind.

No river can return to its source, yet all rivers must have a beginning.

He had found the beginning of this river in the tunnels below Outpost Turkey, and now he saw the source was more terrible than he could have imagined.

The abomination seemed to be the ultimate evolution of Alpha Variants, a creature so powerful and strangely intelligent it had spread itself across the country through the growths of those webs, devouring every living thing in its path.

"That's what we came here for," Fitz whispered. "We have to get this info back to command and Doctor Lovato."

"Fuck that, I say we kill it," Ace said quietly.

"How we going to kill that thing?" Lincoln whispered. "It's got a freaking army protecting it."

Dohi agreed with Ace this time but, he knew if they did kill it, there was no way Team Ghost would get out of here alive.

***

A gunshot split the Texas sky, and a Variant making a run for the hills hit the dirt in a puff of dust and blood splatter.

Fischer lowered his rifle and took in a breath of smoky air.

"That's the last one," said Tran.

Fischer scanned the area around the derrick to confirm he was correct, and then motioned for his men to gather around. They had held the beasts back from this derrick, protecting it for the past few hours while the sun rose over the burning Texas oilfields.

The exhausted team of eleven men huddled in the dirt like a football team that had just lost a game in overtime. The face of every soldier was covered in streaks of soot and blood from the ten-hour battle.

Fischer reached up and wiped his cheek clean, his hand coming back with blood. He wasn't even sure if it was human or monster. The fighting had killed many on both sides.

While his men had cleared this area, there were still Variants out there threatening the other derricks. He feared his engineers would stop the burning oil only to have the beasts come back at night to attack them again.

Assuming the engineers would even risk their lives to do that.

He no longer blamed his men for fleeing.

Fischer scanned the bodies sprawled in the dirt and grass around the derrick they'd saved. Protecting this one had cost them gravely. Amongst the corpses of the beasts were several people that had succumbed to their wounds. Fischer and his men hadn't been able to reach them to provide aid.

One of Sergeant Sharp's men lay on his back, his hands still around his neck where a Variant had ripped open his jugular vein. Lifeless eyes stared up at the oily black clouds streaking the light blue sky.

Fischer bent down to close his eyelids.

He stood and faced the others after letting out a quiet sigh. The fatigued and injured men awaited his orders. The way he saw it, he had two options.

Tell them to retreat to the ranch or continue hunting the beasts.

If they chose the latter, they would likely be on their own from here on out. Sergeant Sharp had fought valiantly and impressed Fischer in his commitment to the oil fields, but his request to command for reinforcements had been delayed multiple times, despite losing half his men.

"Any word on those reinforcements?" Fischer asked, just to be sure.

Sharp frowned. "They said they're working it, but that it's a shit sandwich out there."

Fischer had a feeling that was going to be the response.

We're on our own, indeed.

"What do we do now, sir?" Tran asked.

Fischer took another moment to think before replying.

"These attacks aren't random," he said. "We've known that for a while now. I thought we killed the Alpha causing most of our problems, but now I'm certain there are multiple Alphas. We're going to have to kill them all if we want to save Fischer Fields."

None of the men replied, and even Chase, who was normally gung-ho for whatever Fischer suggested, looked at the dirt. The two engineers, armed with weapons instead of tools, both avoided eye contact.

"I'll understand if you want to stand down," Fischer said. "But I'm going out there to find and kill them. I haven't given my blood, sweat, and tears for this land to let it be taken over by the beasts."

He walked over to the truck, ignoring the hushed conversations behind him. If no one came with him, he wouldn't be surprised, nor would he be mad.

These men had already proven their loyalty and bravery by standing with him for the past ten hours.

"I ain't letting my men die in vain," came a voice.

Fischer turned back to the group.

Sergeant Sharp stepped forward. "I'll keep fighting, but we're going to have to get dirty if we want to find those Alphas."

Several other men exchanged glances.

Tran wiped grime off his face with a sleeve. "I'm with you, sir. I got nothing else to lose."

"Me, too," Chase said.

"You're probably going to need our help," said someone at the back of the group. The two-man team of trackers Fischer had hired also stepped out.

"That is, so long as you keep payin'," said Eric Welling. He brushed his long hair from his eyes to look at his partner, Aaron Galinsky.

The former Israeli military soldier chomped on tobacco. He spat a glob in the dirt. "We'll find the beasts in the tunnels," said Galinsky.

"Hell yes," Fischer drawled.

He pulled a cigar out of his vest pocket. While he had been saving it for a victory, he decided to go ahead and smoke it just in case he never returned from the tunnels. He knew the odds of coming back out weren't good.

"Grab some food, water, and ammo," Tran said. "How about we move out in fifteen minutes, sir?"

Fischer nodded as he lit the cigar and took a puff. He shed most of his gear into the back of his pickup truck, keeping only his body armor and the vest. Then he stuffed fresh magazines into the slots.

He looked back at the bed of the truck for the crate of TNT. He placed a few clusters of sticks into his vest, and Chase did the same.

"Here, sir, better have a drink," Tran said. He offered

a bottle of water, and Fischer downed half of it.

"Thanks."

The men loaded up the bodies of the fallen into the back of one of the other trucks. Fischer walked over to help Sharp and two of his soldiers pick up the private with the torn neck. They gently put him into the back of a pickup.

"RIP, kid," Sharp said. He crossed his chest and looked up to the sky before heading over to his Humvee.

Fischer stayed there a moment, looking down at the young man that had given his life in the fight for the oil fields.

"I'm sorry," Fischer whispered.

Sharp patted the side of his Humvee, indicating he was ready to roll.

"Alright, let's move!" Chase yelled.

Welling and Galinsky climbed into their rust-pocked Toyota pickup. The oversized tires kicked up dirt as it peeled away.

Fischer followed in his pickup, leaving behind the grisly scene of the battle. He glanced over at Tran and then back at Chase.

"I appreciate you boys sticking with me," he said. "I'll make sure you're rewarded for your loyalty."

"I appreciate that, sir, but what I really want is a vacation," Tran said, with a slight smile.

Chase smirked at the suggestion. "The Caribbean sounds pretty damn nice right about now."

"Hell, I'd be happy going anywhere there aren't monsters," Tran said.

"Once we get rid of them here, I'll take you boys on a nice trip in the private jet and we can be on the beach."

"I'm assuming this is a BYOB beach?" Tran said.

Fischer chuckled.

"I almost feel bad for the beasts now," Chase said. "Any monsters standing between me and an ice-cold beer with sand between my toes is going down faster than a ten-dollar hooker."

Fischer laughed again, but the laughter trailed off faster this time. He gripped the wheel tighter and turned onto another road. The lead truck gunned it toward the livestock barns.

The trucks drove past the ranch and Fischer snuck a glance, almost too scared to look at his house. But it didn't appear to have sustained any damage.

He would check on Maddie and the rest of his staff later in the bunker. If they had stayed inside, they would be fine. For that he was at least thankful. But his prized herds of cattle and other livestock were likely all dead by now.

The three trucks parked on the dirt road outside the fenced off barns. Fischer hopped out, and grabbed his rifle from the bed of the pickup. Sharp walked up to the fence, staring at the blood-stained grass on the other side.

Not a single animal or human was left inside.

"Where did all the bodies go?" Tran asked, looking back.

"Variants took 'em all underground, of course," Galinsky said.

"Let's go," Fischer said. He led the way to the open gates and moved toward the first barn. The side door was broken off and laying in the dirt.

Chase and Tran shouldered their weapons and slipped inside the dark barn. Fischer went next, using a hand to swat away a swarm of flies. The buzzing sound echoed inside the hot room, and he brought up his bandana to keep out the reek of rotting flesh.

It hardly helped.

Crimson blots of gore marked the walks, and blood pooled across the dirt.

Just like outside, Fischer didn't see a single body.

Welling and Galinsky moved ahead of the group toward the tunnel opening at the far side of the room. They passed several pens, the troughs red with blood and the hay speckled with dried flesh.

Galinsky bent down at the edge of the tunnel and spit out another glob of tobacco. Then he looked up and motioned for Fischer.

Keeping his bandana over his face, Fischer stepped up to the edge of the tunnel that sloped downward. Red webbing grew on the walls inside, but it was the limbs, hunks of meat, and a full calf stuck to the wall that caused him to rear back.

"What in the holy hell," said Tran.

Chase bent down, a sleeve covering his face from the smell.

"Jesus Christ," Sharp said.

Fischer looked down at the red sticks of TNT in his vest. His gut told him to just toss them inside and blow the hole, but in his head, he knew the only way to prevent another atrocity like this was to find the Alphas and make them pay.

"Mr. Fischer." Sharp looked over at him before he tossed a pair of night vision goggles over. "You're going to need these, sir."

Fischer tightened the bandana around his face, put the goggles over his eyes, and then pulled out his .357, taking a second to look at the barrel. It was time to hunt some monsters.

22

Ringgold had returned to the White House after leaving Peaks Island. For the past day, most of her time had been spent in the PEOC with her staff, monitoring Operation Shadow and the attacks across the country at places like Fischer Fields.

There simply weren't enough soldiers or resources to support every request for reinforcements.

Those requests were taking up the majority of her attention since most of the teams in Operation Shadow were still radio silent, including Team Ghost. The only good news so far was from SEAL Team 3. They had just wrapped up their mission in Luray Caverns in Virginia. But even that mission had come at a cost.

She took the elevator up from the PEOC to meet with Captain Beckham and Lieutenant Festa for a full briefing on the raid. From the sounds of it, they had a lot of wounded in tow and a prisoner.

Her heart raced to know what else they had found in the caverns.

The elevator doors opened, revealing Vice President Lemke waiting in the hallway with his Chief of Staff, Elizabeth Cortez.

"Good afternoon, Madam President," they both said.

"Walk with me," Ringgold replied.

Lemke and Cortez took off on her flanks down the carpeted hallway.

"The Osprey just landed," Lemke said. "All wounded are being treated, but we lost a Marine on the flight and another three back at the target."

The news stabbed at her.

"What else do we know?" she asked.

Lemke shook his head. "Not much, but Captain Beckham and Lieutenant Festa will be here shortly for a briefing."

Chief of Staff James Soprano marched through an intersection at the end of the hallway at a brisk pace.

"The situation room is ready," he said. "Elizabeth, I could use your help with something."

"We'll be there shortly." Ringgold halted at the row of bulletproof windows framing the hallway. The view revealed the lawns and the Osprey that had landed on the other side of the gardens. A medical team carried the wounded off in stretchers.

A pair of Marines hauled off a man in brown clothing, his hands cuffed beyond his back. Lemke stepped up for a better look.

"That must be the collaborator," Ringgold said.

"The team also extracted communication equipment and other intel," Lemke pointed out.

She followed his finger toward a group of Marines unloading crates from the troop hold.

"Maybe something in there will give us the key to how the collaborators and the Variants are connected," Ringgold said.

She turned away from the windows and hurried to the situation room, anxious to see what the team had discovered at the caverns. Most of her staff was already at the long table, but Brigadier General Lucas Barnes and

National Security Advisor Ben Nelson entered a moment later.

"Any updates from Operation Shadow?" Ringgold asked.

"None of the six teams have reported in yet," Barnes replied. "I'll be frank. I would have expected one of them to have made it out by now."

The door opened again, and a short man in fatigues with puffy thin hair entered.

"Lieutenant Festa," she said.

"Madame President," he said politely.

Beckham and Horn followed him into the room, both of their fatigues soiled in blood. She skipped the formalities and cut right to the chase.

"What happened?" she asked.

Beckham and Horn both looked to Festa.

"The collaborators were working with the Variants out of the Luray Caverns," he said. "But it wasn't like collaborator dens we've discovered in the past, ma'am."

"I think we finally know what the red webbing is used for, but we need to talk to Kate to confirm it," Beckham said. His hard features had new creases, and that made Ringgold worry.

"See if you can get her on the line," she said to Soprano. The COS nodded and moved out of the room.

"We went through some of the intel on the flight, but the collaborator isn't saying much," Festa said.

"Has he said anything helpful?" Lemke asked.

"Just that the Variants are everywhere and something about a reckoning," Festa replied. "Whatever the hell that means."

Beckham cut in. "We know more about the collaborators from the maps and plans we recovered, and it's not good, Madam President."

"They have been planning all of this for a while," Horn added.

"Planning what exactly?" Ringgold asked. "Do you mean the attacks on the outposts?"

From the looks on their faces, she could tell that was not the case.

"Hitting the outposts was just the beginning," Beckham said.

"The van we stopped outside the caverns was packed with explosives and Variant acid," Festa said. "We recovered a map that had Outpost Norfolk circled."

"That's where my next rally is going to be," Ringgold said.

"*Was*," replied Beckham. "We're calling it off."

"Holy shit," Barnes said. "You're sure about this?"

Festa nodded again. "Positive, General. The time and date of the rally was found scribbled on a piece of paper taped to that map. This isn't a coincidence."

Barnes straightened his collar, clearly nervous. "Madam President, if this is true, I would highly advise canceling *all* future campaign events and going underground until we know for sure what the Variants and their puppets are planning."

"Absolutely not," Ringgold said. "I'm not spending my last few months in office by hiding in a bunker. I will never do that again."

She thought back to the Raven Rock complex when she was still Secretary of State. There were days she never thought she would see the sun again.

No, she would not be going back into a dark bunker to ride out whatever the hell the Variants were scheming.

"I will not sit by and watch them destroy everything our administration has worked so hard to rebuild."

"All due respect, Madam President, but they are already destroying it," Barnes said. "We need to consider a new strategy, depending on what the teams find...assuming any of them survive their missions."

Beckham glanced at Ringgold, fear in his gaze.

"I will authorize the use of low-yield nuclear weapons before I let this country fall," she said. "I won't let the Variants destroy us again, but I'm not ready to make that call. I want an Option B, C, D, E, and so on before nukes."

The room went silent.

The fact she had even considered nukes caught everyone off guard, including herself. She took in a breath, realizing her words equated to a knee jerk reaction.

"If we use nukes, then we are no better than Cornelius," Lemke said. "I will not be party to that, I'm sorry Madam President. I won't nuke our soil. There has to be a better way."

"I don't know," Barnes chimed in. "I think it might be time to consider making it option A."

"I agree," Festa said. "Especially after what we heard from that collaborator about the Variants being everywhere."

"They can't possibly be everywhere," Lemke said.

"No, but maybe there are more than we thought," Nelson said. "If they've all been tunneling and hiding underground, our counts could be wildly inaccurate. Perhaps it's time to call in help from Europe."

"They're in no position to help," Lemke said. "Half of the continent doesn't even have lights."

The conversation grew more heated, her staff arguing. Even Cortez was red in her freckled face, clearly wanting to interject her opinion.

But there was one opinion Ringgold respected more than any. She looked to Beckham who stood in the back of the room, his prosthetic hand at his side.

"Silence everyone," Ringgold said firmly. "I want to hear what Captain Beckham has to say."

The sudden summoning might have caught him off guard, but he didn't hesitate stepping up to the table.

"I don't know exactly what's going on, but I don't think we should jump to any conclusions yet," Beckham said. "Let Team Ghost and the other teams do their jobs before we make any rash decisions."

Cortez and Lemke both nodded in agreement.

"What we do know is that red webbing may be part of a biological communication network," Beckham continued. "We have to figure out a way to disrupt it before the next phase. Before they use it for something worse."

"Like what?" Barnes asked.

"I think the Variants are preparing a full out invasion. Those maps had other outposts marked. Every single safe zone was documented in there. They even mapped out routes into our strongholds. To me, that reeks of a plan of attack. Something we couldn't have fathomed. And if that's the case, then nukes won't stop them."

A red phone rang next to Barnes. He picked it up and held up a finger.

"Okay," he said. "Thank you, General."

Barnes hung up the phone, his eyes going straight to Ringgold.

"Madam President we just got word from Team

Ghost, they discovered something at the University of Minnesota," he said. "Some sort of mastermind creature."

Nelson looked at his computer screen. "I've got the footage here."

"Me too," Soprano said.

"Bring it up on the main screen," Ringgold said, turning around.

Horn and Beckham both stood for a better look but, before it came online, Barnes added something he had left out earlier.

"Master Sergeant Fitzpatrick said they found something else out there, Madam President."

She narrowed her brows at the General.

"What?" Lemke asked.

Barnes swallowed before responding. "Juvenile Variants."

***

The video footage from Team Ghost had Kate wondering if she was living in a nightmare. It certainly took her mind off Beckham and whether he had returned safely from his mission.

But it wasn't just the beast on the monitor, it was the report that the creatures were breeding again. How, she wasn't sure, but she knew Team Ghost wouldn't lie.

She took a step closer to the monitor to study the creature they had discovered. Carr and a couple of the lab techs huddled around her, just as transfixed as she was.

"You were right," Carr said. "There was something else sending signals to the Alphas and Variants across the webbing network."

Kate could only imagine what General Souza and

President Ringgold were thinking. She was surprised she hadn't gotten a call from them yet.

"We have two problems," Kate said. "Now that we know the Variants are breeding and digging tunnels in select locations, there's no telling how many of them are underground."

Carr nodded, still looking sick as the video continued playing over the monitor. Variants climbed around the huge beast connected to all the webbing tendrils.

"Let's focus on this new monster first and what we know," Kate said. "We know that the webbing relays signals much like the nerves in a human's body. Those signals can be passed directly into the Alpha's with their spindles. And the Alpha's can, in turn, coordinate with the lesser Variants."

"It's a complicated hierarchical system," Carr said. "Just like how a human body functions. The nerves send signals to muscle cells, which then react in kind, propagating signals to other cells and tissues but, in this situation, it's in the Variant network."

Kate tapped on the computer monitor. "It's like one monstrous brain. The puppeteer behind all the Variant and collaborator attacks."

Carr nodded. "A mastermind."

"Even the pink folds across the body are reminiscent of a human cortex."

"Those would dramatically increase the surface area of the monster if it was in fact some kind of central processing node. Maybe this specimen is like an enormous living computer."

"A monster coordinating attacks across the country with Variants and collaborators would definitely need a huge amount of processing power."

"If that's the case, then destroying it will disrupt the entire nervous system," Carr said.

Kate nodded. "We need to talk to President Ringgold immediately."

She shed her white coat as she headed toward the exit of the lab, hoping to also get word about her husband. Carr tailed her out the door with the techs looking on. They took the stairwell to the command center for the troops stationed on the island.

Sergeant Ruckley sat with a group of enlisted men and women around a bank of radio equipment.

"Doctor Lovato," Ruckley said, turning on her heels.

"I need to get ahold of President Ringgold immediately," Kate said.

Ruckley's brow furrowed. "I can patch you into someone else at the Greenbrier, but Ringgold's likely—"

"Ringgold. It has to be Ringgold."

The Sergeant looked ready to protest again, but she must have recognized the fire in Kate's eyes.

"You heard the doctor," Ruckley said "Call the emergency line."

The sergeant handed Kate a handset.

"Talk to me, Doctor," Ringgold said. "Preferably with some good news."

"Madam President, I'm afraid I don't have any good news. I think this creature is a brain, for lack of a better term, and it's coordinating the attacks across the country."

"I had the same thought, and I'm afraid they are planning something even bigger, especially with the discovery of juveniles," Ringgold said, pausing before she added, "I take it you haven't spoken to your husband?"

Now Kate was thrown off. "No, why? Is he okay?"

"Yes, he's fine, but what I'm about to tell you goes no further than this conversation, okay?"

"Of course," Kate replied.

"Operation Renegade uncovered intel that leads me to believe the Variants may be launching a larger offensive. Bigger than anything so far. Possibly an all-out invasion, and I have a feeling this monster is going to coordinate it and send out the juvenile hordes."

Kate's stomach dropped. Her thoughts flew to Javier and Donna and Bo and Timothy and Tasha and Jenny. All the people that had just endured hell only to realize that it might not be long before the world was upended again.

"Operation Renegade also confirms your theory about the webbing functioning like a communication network," Ringgold said.

"After this footage from Team Ghost, I'm even more certain that's the case," Kate paused to think, but had no doubt she was relaying accurate information.

"A few weeks ago, I wouldn't have believed any of this, but…"

Kate felt the eyes of the men and women in the command center on her, but she kept her focus on the radio equipment, and tried to still her breathing.

"The studies Carr and I have run are pretty conclusive," Kate said. "We're dealing with nerve and muscle cells that replicate at rates exceeding the most malignant of cancers."

"So that's how the webbing grew so fast?"

"Yes, and we also know from our cellular studies, the growth of the webbing consumes energy at an alarming rate. It requires an enormous amount of food matter to fuel the expansion of the network."

"How much are we talking?"

"I'm not sure, but Team Ghost reported that most of the Variants they encountered in Minneapolis appeared to be starving, despite the number of civilians that they'd kidnapped," Kate said. "To be able to keep Variants from fresh prey requires a vast amount of control. The webbing and the mastermind must have more power than we could have imagined."

"In your opinion, if we kill this brain, will it shut down the entire network?" Ringgold asked.

The president was a smart woman, leaping to a theory that Kate had just formed herself. But she hesitated, considering her response, knowing what she said next could cause or save countless lives.

She thought back to the images of the webbing at the stadium in Minneapolis and elsewhere in the country. She had seen so many horrific pictures of humans and animals strung up within the webbing. Many of which were still alive.

"Unfortunately, without biological samples from this mastermind and some live Variants to test, I'm not sure. If our theory is correct, destroying the mastermind will be like destroying the head of the snake," Kate said. "Cut it off and the Variants will lose all coordination and everything attached to the webbing will die."

"But will it stop the invasion from happening?"

"I believe so," Kate said.

There was no hesitation from Ringgold. "Then that's what we must do, Doctor. I know this is a longshot, but do you have any recommendations on how to destroy something composed of the tissues you've studied?"

"Again, it's hard for me to say, but burning that *thing* to the ground is a surefire way of destroying the tissue,"

Kate said. "I wouldn't delay, either. We have no idea if it can move or if it has detected Team Ghost's activity in Minneapolis. It may very well be able to use the tunnels to travel."

"Understood," Ringgold said. "We'll need a confirmed kill. In that case, it looks like we've got only one good option."

"Team Ghost," Kate said.

"That's right. We'll have bombers on standby, but if this thing is half as powerful as you're telling me, I want hard evidence that we've killed it before we can call this mission a success."

"And what about the juveniles?" Kate asked. "Team Ghost reported they could be living in the stadium where they discovered hundreds of human prisoners."

There was a pause on the other end.

"My gut says blow it to hell but, I haven't decided yet, I need to talk to my generals and staff first, and perhaps your husband."

"Okay," Kate said. "I'm sorry I don't have better news."

"Me too, Doctor, but this is the reality of our situation and we must face it head on and not give an inch. Good luck with your research."

"Good luck as well, Madam President."

With that, the call ended and Kate was left holding the handset while Carr and the others watched her.

She prayed that she was right about this creature and what would happen if Team Ghost destroyed it. But just like the past, thousands of innocent lives hung on her scientific judgment.

— 23 —

Fitz surveyed the dirt- and grime-covered faces of Team Ghost. The group had taken refuge in a building a block away from the Northrop Performing Arts Center.

Not more than a decade ago, the place had been one of culture and learning. Humans had evolved far enough to appreciate things in life beyond simple survival, valuing things like the arts and the sciences.

Ways to explore and explain life.

The Variants had evolved in their own way to destroy those things, but Team Ghost had another chance to turn the tables on the monsters.

"Ghost 1, you are to destroy the target and confirm it is destroyed," came the voice of General Souza.

"Copy that," Fitz replied. "We'll get it done."

His heart climbed to his throat as realization set in.

There would be no bombers raining hell down on the Northrop Performing Arts Center. Command wanted Team Ghost to take this beast out and then confirm it was dead.

"I can't believe this shit." Lincoln said. "Why the fuck we got to do it?"

"We're the guarantee," Rico said.

"It's a suicide mission if you ask me," Ace grumbled.

Dohi didn't make his opinion known, but Fitz could tell he didn't like it either. Hell, Fitz didn't like the orders, but he understood why Team Ghost had to bring the beast down.

They couldn't risk the strange monstrosity relocating and sprouting new roots. If they waited on a bombing run, the thing might simply disappear into the tunnels. It was like a cancerous tumor that they had to stop before it became malignant and spread further.

"Get your heads on straight," Fitz said. "This is our chance to bring down the network and stop an all-out invasion that could destroy the country and everything we have worked to rebuild. We *can't* let that monster live or escape."

"You know I'm with you, Fitzie," Rico said, forcing a pretty smile.

"Me too," Mendez said.

The others nodded.

"How much ammo do you all have?" Fitz inventoried the few magazines and then distributed them evenly. Everyone would get two for their primary weapon. It wasn't much, but this mission was supposed to be for recon—not to fight full-fledged battles.

Fitz had learned long ago that improvisation was the best tool for a soldier.

Tonight, improvisation came in the form of grenades. The team had six total among them. Fitz took two, and Mendez and Lincoln took the others.

"Take in some nutrition and water," Fitz said. "I'll go over the plan and then we move out."

Rico brushed a strand of pink hair back under her helmet as she sipped from her bottle. Ace bit off the end of a power bar. Dohi closed his eyes to meditate. Mendez crossed himself, praying, and Lincoln chewed noisily.

"So what's the plan, boss?" Lincoln said with his mouth open.

"Plan's simple. Mendez, Lincoln, and I will blow this thing back to hell with grenades while the rest of you keep the Variants off our hides from the catwalk over that stage. Clean, fast, and no mistakes. We're all going home. Got it?"

"Hold up," Dohi said. "I'm not sure the grenades are going to do the trick. We might need something else."

"C4 would be nice," Ace said.

"What you thinking, Dohi?" Rico asked.

"Those semi-trucks we saw at the loading docks. I could try and siphon out the diesel fuel. Even degraded diesel is combustible. Once a diesel fire gets going, it's pretty fierce and lasts a long time."

Lincoln shook his helmet. "So we can all burn in that place? *Hell* no."

"And siphon it with what, and into what?" Mendez asked.

Dohi used a knife to cut the straw off his camelback. "I just need something to dump it into."

Fitz liked the idea. "I think we can find something."

Lincoln grunted and turned away.

"Let's do it then," Mendez said.

Everyone but Lincoln nodded back, but he finally came around. Together, Team Ghost set off for the same entrance they had used to get into the building the first time.

On the way they found several plastic jugs in a pile of trash Fitz had spotted earlier. Dohi picked them up and moved over to the tankers while the rest of the team stood guard.

A single Variant spotted them while he filled the jugs. Lincoln threw a knife that hit the beast in the head before it could sound the alarm with a shriek. It crumpled against a curb and Mendez helped him drag it away.

"I'll carry those, you take point," Ace said. He picked up the full jugs of fuel.

Getting inside was easy with Dohi leading them safely back to the dressing room they had first taken refuge in. Fitz took a moment to get his bearings and to listen for hostiles. Then he directed the team toward the auditorium.

The sounds of clicking joints and squawks traveled down the webbing-covered passages along the way. Variants rushed in and out of the shadows, but the team used the jumbles of bodies hanging from the red vines and rotted furniture for cover, advancing slowly.

After fifteen minutes of creeping and even crawling, they reached the stairs. Fitz flashed hand signals. They split up toward the entrances to the auditorium. Rico, Ace, and Dohi continued up the stairs.

Once again Fitz watched Rico venturing away from him.

Keep yourself safe, he thought.

She looked back before she went out of sight, offering him a slight wave. Just enough to let him know she was thinking of him, too.

Once she was gone, Fitz entered the back of the theater to await their signal. He crouched on his blades and gestured for Mendez and Lincoln to spread out.

Then he reached toward his helmet to make sure the cam mounted there was positioned correctly. He wanted to capture every single second of what was about to happen.

Pale beams of moonlight bled through the decayed holes in the roof, bathing the whole chamber in soft illumination. A group of ten Variants lurked on the stage, some of them lying down, others perched like birds.

The giant beast they guarded remained in the same spot, webbed tentacles of tissue sprouting from its gargantuan body and stretching across the auditorium. Several Variants used the strands to climb like freakish children on a nightmarish jungle gym.

Another pack entered from the back stage and clambered up to the bulbous abomination with chunks of rotting corpses. They transported meat in a single file line, each of them dropping scraps into the beast's gullet before departing to find more food.

Dohi was going to dump a bucket of diesel down the same hole and then Fitz was going to lob a grenade inside. He glanced up at the stage using his night vision goggles, seeing the infrared tags from the other three members of Ghost perched on the catwalk.

He flashed his IR tag on his NVGs at them, and then grabbed one of his grenades.

The show was about to begin.

Another Variant climbed down the red tendrils overhead, and Fitz ducked down. Bones protruded from the monster's sickly, wart-covered flesh. The Variant dropped to the stage with a chewed-up human arm and jammed it into the abomination's mouth.

The crunch echoed through the auditorium.

Ace and Dohi both stood on the catwalk and dumped the diesel as the last of the Variants finished the feeding. The fluid rolled down the sides of the pink tissue and pooled around the monster.

Immediately, two Variants holding sentry craned their necks upward, eyes glaring around wildly.

They homed in on a match glowing in Rico's fingers.

One of the Variants shrieked in alarm.

"Eat this, fuck wad," she said, tossing the match down.

The abomination also looked up as the match hit the pink folds of its body, igniting upon impact. The flames cast the whole place in a ghoulish orange glow. Nerve tendrils recoiled and broke, crisped by the fire as Dohi and Ace finished dumping their jugs.

An ear-shattering roar exploded from the beast.

Fitz nearly drew back from the overwhelming sound.

"Now," he said to Mendez and Lincoln.

"Fire in the hole!" Fitz shouted.

They tossed their grenades onto the stage while Dohi, Rico, and Ace moved away on the catwalk.

The three men all ducked as the explosions rocked the stage, shrapnel lancing across the auditorium. Fitz got up with another grenade, but had to switch to his rifle as Variants bounded up the stairs toward his location.

Suppressed gunfire came from above. Rico, Ace, and Dohi firing to keep the beasts back and give the men a chance to lob their grenades.

Fitz fired a burst and glimpsed the burning monster behind the curtain of smoke. It had pulled back one of its flayed arms, snapping more of the spindly growths. For an enormous, bulbous creature, it seemed fairly agile, smacking at the blaze with its huge, deformed hand.

The space filled with the stink of barbecued flesh, and the enormous monster roared again. Variants flooded inside the auditorium, scaling the walls and webbing toward the end of the catwalk.

Dohi, Rico, and Ace held their ground, firing calculated single shots.

The fire spread across the stage to the seats, choking the air with smoke. They were running out of time, and the beast still wasn't dead.

Fitz sighted up the first Variant ready to pounce from the wall to the catwalk. A round punched into its flesh, knocking the monster down. Flames from the burning seats swallowed its corpse.

Dohi and Ace followed up with a volley of cover fire, picking off the advancing beasts. Another grenade sailed away from Mendez. This one smacked against the side of the creature's head. Its huge claw slapped it away, and the blast blew several Variants to pieces.

Burning flesh sizzled and popped on the stage.

The abomination pushed itself up on its feet. Fitz's initial impression that this was some lazy queen that relied on its workers to keep it alive disintegrated at the sight of the standing beast.

Another grenade arced through the air from Lincoln.

The beast swatted it away with a burning hand. The grenade sailed right for the seats in front of Mendez and Lincoln.

"Back!" Fitz yelled.

They dove to the ground, and Fitz took cover behind a pillar. The explosion rushed past him, the noise so loud his ears seemed like they were going to burst. He staggered around the pillar, bringing up his rifle in shaking hands to fire at monsters loping up the stairs.

Everything seemed to freeze as Fitz coughed on smoke.

Mendez and Lincoln were both on the ground, hardly moving, their bodies likely torn up from shrapnel. Chunks of steel catwalk fell to the stage and cables snapped from the ceiling.

The rest of the platform tilted. Dohi slipped, sliding down. The monster reached up at his boots with a burning hand.

Fitz grabbed the final grenade, but he couldn't throw it with Dohi right there. Instead, he brought up his rifle to fire at two beasts making a run for Mendez and Lincoln.

He scored two headshots and then aimed for the abomination on the stage still reaching for Dohi. Adjusting his aim, he lined up the crosshairs and fired at one of the creature's large eyeballs.

The beast let out a vicious roar and stumbled backward, groping at its face. Dozens of Variants had surrounded their leader, using their bodies to absorb rounds from Rico and Ace.

Even more creatures poured into the burning auditorium, now racing in from behind the stage and dropping from the holes in the ceiling. One of them used the writhing leader as a ladder to climb up toward where Dohi was dangling.

Rico inched out, the catwalk sagging slightly under her weight.

The Variant looked ready to pounce on the two of them. A three-round burst to the center of the Variant's back dropped the beast, and Fitz moved to another target. He pulled the trigger but the weapon had run dry.

Rico stretched out a hand, grabbing Dohi's and pulling him to safety. Ace fired to hold back the monsters climbing the walls, but it wouldn't be long before they were overwhelmed.

Team Ghost simply didn't have enough rounds, and in a few minutes the fire and the smoke would be too intense to escape. They had to get out now.

"Mendez, Lincoln, get up!" Fitz yelled. He coughed and ran over to them. Mendez had pushed himself up and managed to raise his rifle but Lincoln was limp on the ground.

The mastermind held one paw over its bleeding eye socket. As it struggled, more of the nerves pulled taut, then broke away.

"Mendez shoot it!" Fitz yelled.

The beast roared in pain, opening its maw wildly as gunfire painted the bulbous flesh. Fitz used the opportunity to lob his final grenade like a baseball into the black hole of its mouth.

"Down!" Fitz yelled. He shielded Lincoln's body with his own as the explosion boomed on the stage. Ears ringing and lungs choked with smoke, Fitz pushed himself up to confirm the beast was dead.

The rest of the auditorium was a hellscape, the conflagration enveloping the rotten curtains on the stage and the neglected auditorium seats. It took Fitz several scorching blinks to find the headless monster burning on the floorboards.

Tendrils of webbing popped around it, melted and charred by the flames. The creature seemed to deflate as the fire consumed the folds of its flesh.

Fitz made sure his helmet cam was broadcasting the entire thing. He wanted command to see this thing was dead. After holding the view for a moment, he helped Mendez pick up Lincoln.

As soon as Fitz picked him up, he felt blood soaking into his gloves.

"Get to the evac point!" Fitz yelled into the channel.

Dohi, Rico, and Ace disappeared from the catwalks, but Fitz could hear the suppressed gunfire as they escaped back down the stairs.

Part of the ceiling dumped into the auditorium,

feeding the crackling fire. Sparks flew upward as a column collapsed, one of the balconies crumbling over the body of the mastermind.

Variants shrieked as they were caught in the flames.

Fitz and Mendez carried Lincoln into the lobby where Ace and the others were waiting.

"Birds on the way," Rico confirmed. "I called it in."

Fitz nodded just as fire burst out of the theater doors. A burning Variant skidded across the carpet, writhing in pain.

"Go, go, go!" Fitz yelled as more burning Variants burst through the flames.

Dohi and Ace led them out of the front doors to an overgrown lawn bulwarked by brick-faced buildings. Holes littered the area from Variant tunnels.

Team Ghost didn't have far to go, but they might as well have been trekking halfway around the world. The holes vomited up more of the bastards in front of the team and even more came from the inside of the buildings, surrounding Team Ghost.

The Black Hawk scheduled to pick them up was supposed to meet them in the middle of this grassy field. He strained his injured ears to listen for the telltale thrum of the rotors, but he couldn't hear shit besides the monsters pursuing them.

Fitz loaded his final magazine and began picking off beasts on the lawn. Rico and Mendez were down to their sidearms, firing at the beasts coming from the performing arts center.

Ace and Dohi fired their final rounds at Variants flooding away from adjacent buildings. Several threw themselves through windows, glass shards flying. Others parted through overgrown grass on all fours like sharks surging through the surf.

Fitz worked his way from one target to the next until his bolt locked back. He let the rifle sag over his chest and drew his Beretta M9.

Flames from the performing arts center spread to another neighboring building. Fitz looked past the columns of smoke choking the sky for the chopper, but it still wasn't in view.

"Where is it?" Fitz yelled to Rico.

"I don't know!" she shouted. "They said fifteen minutes!"

The ground tremored violently beneath his boots, and he went back to firing his pistol. Pillars on the front of one building crumbled. Bricks fell next, crushing a handful of Variants.

"What's happening?" Rico shouted.

Part of the lawn caved in. Other canyons formed, trailing alongside the older holes.

"The tunnels are collapsing!" Fitz yelled back. He changed the magazine of his pistol, his heart leaping as Variants closed in all around them.

Lincoln continued to bleed out on the ground, both of his pant legs saturated with blood.

"Shit, shit, shit," Fitz said. The team crowded around Lincoln, forming a circle to protect their fallen comrade.

"Our six!" Dohi yelled.

"Three o'clock!" Rico shouted back.

The beasts were coming from all directions.

"I'm out!" Ace said. He switched to his shotgun, blasting a beast that leapt through the air at them. The corpse landed on the ground in front of Fitz, sliding to rest just in front of his blades.

Flashes suddenly lanced from the heavens. Fitz heard

the unmistakable bark of an M240. The sounds of gunfire had never seemed more beautiful.

A Black Hawk lowered out of the darkness, a crew chief sweeping the door-mounted weapon at the Variants leaping over corpses to get to Team Ghost.

"Let's go!" Fitz commanded.

The team formed a cordon around Lincoln as Ace and Dohi carried the downed operator to the chopper. They piled in with the help of a second crew chief and gently put Lincoln's limp body on the deck.

Fitz was afraid to check his pulse.

"Get us out of here!" Dohi yelled.

The chopper lifted as another building succumbed to the quaking earth. Fitz bent down next to Lincoln and pushed his finger against his neck.

The beat was weak, but it was there.

Rico was already digging through her medical pack, and Dohi had wrapped a tourniquet over a wound on Lincoln's thigh that was dark from arterial blood. She handed Dohi a pair of scissors to cut away his pants.

"What are those Variants doing?" yelled a crew chief.

Fitz looked down at the field below. The beasts had all stopped moving below. They appeared to tilt their heads like they were looking or listening for something.

The chopper continued to pull into the sky, but Fitz could still see the ground as the Variants suddenly funneled toward the holes in a mass exodus.

"Where are they all going?" said the crew chief. "It's like they just got an order to retreat. I've never seen anything like it."

Fitz focused back on Lincoln, trying not to worry about what was happening on the ground. Team Ghost had come close to the brink on Operation Shadow and had barely made it out of the city alive.

The bird curved through the sky.

"He's lost a lot of blood," Rico said. "We need to get him to a field hospital, ASAP."

"We'll take him to the closest outpost," said one of the pilots.

Fitz gripped Lincoln's gloved hand, wet with blood while Dohi finished cutting off the pants and exposing the wounds. He bent down with the rest of them to start working on Lincoln.

"Hang in there, brother," Fitz said.

Even with the tourniquet in place, Lincoln had already lost so much blood. The fluid pooled across the deck.

Mendez swallowed hard and looked up at Fitz.

"Something isn't right," shouted one of the pilots. "I don't see a single Variant on the streets below."

Fitz kept his focus on Lincoln.

Tonight's mission was supposed to have killed the queen bee of this Variant hive, disrupting the whole colony and causing them to scatter. But that wasn't happening, and he suddenly couldn't shake the feeling that all Team Ghost had done was disturb the nest.

"Fitz," Rico said.

He looked up to see her eyes glazing. She had a finger against Lincoln's neck.

"I don't feel a pulse," she said.

"How far do these damn things go?" Chase mumbled, gesturing down the blackness of the web-covered tunnel.

"Let's rest a few minutes," Fischer said.

The team halted, taking in water and the protein bars from their packs. Fischer had experienced fighters with him, from his personal security team and the hired trackers to Sergeant Sharp. Yet these tunnels still sent shivers through his flesh.

He used the stolen moments to study the webbing in the green hue of his night vision goggles. Two horns protruded out of the mass. He stepped closer to the wall and examined what was left of one of his bulls. Red vines webbed across the rest of the severed head, pushing out from its empty orbital cavities and roping out of the beast's nostrils.

"Son of a bitch," he whispered.

You have to get out of here, whispered a voice.

Fischer didn't turn to look for the source. No one else reacted.

This voice wasn't real. It was the same voice he kept hearing as they advanced deeper into the humid darkness. A voice he hadn't heard since before the Great War of Extinction.

The voice of his dead wife.

He ignored it. This place was making him crazy, and the exhaustion didn't help.

Fischer pulled down the bandana to take a breath of sultry air. He stifled a gag at the unobstructed odor. Then he forced down a gulp of water. Sweat dripped down his forehead, carrying with it a mix of black grime and dirt. He used the back of his hand to wipe it away.

They had been searching the tunnels for hours, plunging deeper and deeper into the vast network that stretched beneath his oil fields. He hadn't anticipated these Variant-made cavern systems to be so massive. And all this time they had spent down here, they still hadn't spotted an Alpha or any other Variant for that matter.

The only creatures they had discovered were more of his poor livestock massacred and dismembered by the ravenous beasts.

President Ringgold's administration had left him, his men, and his animals to die out here at the hands of the hordes. When he got back to his ranch, he was going to call up President Ringgold and tell her she had lost more than his vote.

If you get out of here.

That damn voice again.

"Let's keep moving," Galinsky said quietly.

"Hey, look at that," Chase said pointing up at a small hole at the top of the tunnel ahead, looking barely large enough for a Variant to slip through.

The hole let in a beam of waning sunlight. Seemed like the sun was setting.

He shuddered at the thought of being down here at night.

"Sir, we need to move," Tran whispered.

Fischer nodded and set off with the team.

Welling took point with Galinsky right behind him. The two hired trackers moved slowly down the tunnel, their rifles up. Tran and Chase kept on Fischer's flanks while Sergeant Sharp held rearguard. The rest of the men, led by the sergeant's surviving two soldiers, had veered off a few hours earlier to search another network of underground passages.

Their reports were no more helpful than what Fischer had seen—dead animals and zero signs of the Alphas.

The group pushed on for another ten minutes, not stopping until Sharp's radio crackled. He turned down the volume and then whispered a response.

"The other team find something?" Fischer asked in a whisper.

Sharp looked up and shook his head. "I think it's command, but I can't make out the transmission."

They pushed forward, ignoring the radio. Fischer had a feeling it was just more bad news from the outside. The only thing that mattered now was what was happening at Fischer Fields, not where the current administration and brass was watching safely from their bunkers and warships.

He was really starting to hate President Ringgold and all of the elites back east. She had spent the first few months of the war underground in a bunker like he had. And here they were again, both underground.

But this time the circumstances were far different. Only one of them was putting their life on the line to kill the Variants. Ringgold was safely protected in a bunker and surrounded by men and women armed to the teeth with all the country had at its disposal. Fischer was risking his rear to wipe out the beasts ravaging his fields.

Galinsky halted and gestured for Sharp. The sergeant squeezed past Fischer and his two guards. Being near the end of the line gave him the creeps.

The tunnels weren't just dark and hot—they stank of rotting flesh that his bandana couldn't mask. On top of that, the fatigue was starting to get to him, and hearing the voice of his dead wife wasn't helping matters.

You have to get out of here, she repeated.

Another voice sounded, but this one was real.

Sharp spoke quietly to Galinsky and Welling before making his way back to Fischer and his guards.

"Well?" Tran asked.

"There's some sort of chamber ahead, and they think they saw one of my men," Sharp reported. "There are two confirmed Variants."

"Alphas?" Fischer asked.

"Maybe. Galinsky is going to go check it out," Sharp said. "I'm going with. You guys stay here with Welling."

Fischer thought about arguing but decided to let the best hunters do the hunting. Especially if he was going crazy. The smartest man knew his limits, and the strongest wasn't afraid to admit them.

He brought up his rifle and waited while the men crept down the passage toward an intersection. Galinsky turned around the corner, and Sharp followed at a hunch. They vanished around the bend.

"I don't like this," Tran said quietly.

Chase also seemed nervous. He kept turning around to check the tunnel behind them. When he twisted back, Chase staggered slightly.

Looks like I'm not the only one exhausted, Fischer thought.

"Fuck, I need fresh air," Chase muttered.

"Hopefully we'll be out of here soon," Tran said.

Movement flashed at the end of the passage. Fischer raised his rifle but quickly lowered the barrel when he realized it was Sharp and Galinsky dragging an injured soldier.

As Fischer hurried over to help, he could tell right away the man was barely hanging on. Gashes crossed his face, oozing pus. His left leg was definitely broken, a bone protruding from his pants.

"I've got to get him topside," Sharp said. "I'll use that passage a few turns back, but I'm going to need some help."

Fischer looked at Chase. "You go with Sergeant Sharp."

Chase hesitated at first. "No, sir…"

"You need some fresh air, son," Fischer said.

"Yeah, but so do you, sir."

"I'm good." Fischer patted Chase on the shoulder and then nodded at Sharp.

The team split up again. Fischer and Tran followed the two trackers around the next corner where they had cut the soldier from the webbing.

Leave, came his wife's voice. *Leave now!*

Fischer ignored her, salty sweat stinging his eyes. The chamber came into view around the bend. The wide bowl was covered in red webbing and strung up animals. A Variant across the open space chewed on what looked like a…

Oh hell no, Fischer thought.

There wasn't much left of the carcass, but he could tell it had been one of his calves. The beast pulled a string of flesh off a leg.

Another creature buried its face into the open belly of the dead animal, pulling out intestines like spaghetti and slurping them through its gruesome lips. It bent over for another bite, exposing a back of hardened flesh.

Both the Variants were barely bigger than the dead calf.

Holy shit, those are children, Fischer realized.

He hadn't seen juveniles in years.

Welling raised a suppressed rifle, but Fischer put his hand on the barrel.

"I've got this one," Fischer whispered. He crept toward the entrance to the chamber. Just shy of the opening, he shouldered the rifle and aimed for the back of one of the heads. Past experience had taught him juvenile Variant armor was thick, but it wouldn't stop a bullet from this range.

He pulled the trigger and fired a shot into the head of the beast chewing on the leg. The whistle sounded, followed by an echoing from the crack of a bullet through skull. He took out the second beast with another burst to the head.

It slumped onto the carcass with a wet slap.

Fischer looked for other targets, and seeing none, he moved into the chamber to look at the dead Variants with grim satisfaction. Welling followed close behind.

The satisfaction was short lived.

An explosion of dirt came from the earthen walls behind him. Bursting from the webbing came a hulking figure with taloned claws the length of buck knives. This wasn't an Alpha like Fischer had seen before.

The ape-like face had huge nostrils and large, bat-like ears hanging from the side of its pointed features.

Fischer swung his rifle toward the beast as it lunged across the chamber and grabbed Welling by an arm. It pulled the limb from the socket. Welling screeched in agony. Then the monster ripped his arm clean off and threw it at Galinsky who was already firing at the bastard.

The shots boomed in the enclosed space, rounds punching into the monster's barreled chest. Fischer switched to automatic and opened fire. He had no time for shooting discipline with this monstrosity rampaging around the tunnel.

Blood squirted out of Welling's arm socket as he fell to his knees. He looked at Fischer just as the Alpha grabbed his head and popped it off like a cork. A geyser of blood splattered the dirt ceiling.

The whole chamber began to vibrate. Dirt rained from the ceiling.

Another Alpha bounded through the tunnel they had used to enter the space. Tran turned to fire, scoring a blast directly into its face. A hunk of the Alpha's pointed jaw blew off in a spray of red mist. The twisted remains of the jawbone hung off by a few strands of gristle.

The beast smacked him in the chest, sending Tran tumbling past Fischer. His rifle flew in the opposite direction.

The other Alpha that had killed Welling was on the ground now, bleeding out from multiple rounds while Galinsky approached, rifle blazing.

"You like that, motherfucker!?" he yelled.

It groaned and swiped at him from the dirt, bullets tearing through its flesh.

Fischer retreated toward Tran, still firing at the creature missing half a jaw. Several hits to the chest sent it staggering.

The creature on the ground swiped again at Galinsky's boots while he fired several bursts into the flaps of flesh over its back. The creature finally went limp, letting out a long moan.

Fischer bent down to Tran.

"You okay?" he asked.

Tran nodded, and Fischer helped him to his feet. He fired a series of bursts to keep the beast across the chamber at bay. It gripped the loose flap of jaw on its face and hunched down, screeching so loud Fischer winced in pain.

Drawing his pistol, Tran fired.

Fischer grabbed a fresh magazine from his vest and slammed it home.

Galinsky nudged the other beast in the head with his barrel while Fischer aimed at the deformed face of the one across the chamber. He emptied most of the magazine into the Alpha by holding the trigger down. The hail of gunfire sent it stumbling into a wall of webbing.

A human scream sounded in between the gunshots.

You have to get out of here! came the voice of his wife.

Not until I kill these bastards, he thought.

The second Alpha that Galinsky had thought was dead bit off his leg under the knee. He crashed to the ground, screaming in pain and gripping the gushing wound.

The monster grabbed his other leg as he turned and tried to crawl away. It yanked him backward and crunched down on his ankle with a maw-full of jagged teeth.

Another guttural scream sounded from the tracker. Fischer turned his aim on the creature but couldn't get a shot. With a sickening snap, the tracker managed to jam his buck knife into the skull of the monster. The monster collapsed again, blood pouring from its twitching jaw.

Fischer finished off his magazine into the beast against the wall and then drew his .357. He strode across the chamber toward the Alpha. Blood drooled from dozens of wounds, but it was still alive, and managed to reach out. He fired a bullet through the palm.

The hand fell away, and he fired shots into the cavities where a normal creature's eyes would be.

That did the trick.

The monster thumped to the dirt. He put another bullet into the skull, blowing a hole in one of the bat-like ears to be sure and then hurried over to Galinsky.

By the time he got there, the tracker was dead, a lake of blood pooling around him and the Alpha. Despite having a knife in its skull, the creature's back rapidly rose and fell in shallow breaths, its limbs shaking.

Tran limped over and aimed his pistol. He and Fischer fired their remaining bullets into the Alpha's ugly face.

Fischer lowered the smoking barrel of the *Monster Killer*. His stomach rolled at the gory sight of the dismembered bodies of the men he had hired to find these beasts. If they had families, he would find them and give them the money he owed them for today's job.

"I'm sorry," Fischer said, bending down. He closed Galinsky's eyes and then plucked the extra magazines from his torn vest.

Tran changed the magazine in his pistol and limped over to his dropped rifle.

"You good?" Fischer asked.

Tran winced, but nodded.

They set off across the chamber and out into the passage they had entered through. The webbing on the walls seemed to pulsate the farther they walked. Halfway back to the exit Sharp had taken to get topside, the ground and walls trembled again.

"Another Alpha?" Tran said.

This felt different. Fischer shook his head. It reminded him of something from when he was a boy and, for a second, he struggled to put his finger on it. The trembling grew worse.

Then realization hit him like a cold rain. When he was a boy, he'd been out on the ranch far past sunset. The cattle had been off in the distance, and he'd fallen asleep, passed out under the stars.

But the ground had shaken him awake. The cattle had been in a panic, running straight toward him. Spooked by a group of coyotes. Thousands of hooves slamming against the ground rolled over him like never ending thunder.

"Stampede!" he bellowed. "Run!"

They hurried toward the dying rays of sunlight streaming in through the opening in the tunnel. When they got there the rumbling ground grew into a full-on quake. Hunks of dirt broke from the ceiling, and webbing whipped loose from the walls. The entire tunnel system was coming apart.

Fischer helped Tran climb up into the opening and pushed him out. As soon as his boots were up, Fischer pushed his night vision goggles away from his eyes, grabbed the webbing, and started climbing.

He froze halfway up when something exploded into his periphery. From both sides of the tunnel, Variants flooded like a tidal wave of white flesh.

"Good Lord in Heaven," he said.

Fischer kicked out of the hole and onto a weed-covered field. Only a sliver of blood-red sun peaked over the horizon.

He heard what sounded like a helicopter over the screams of the Variants.

"Over here!"

Fischer searched for the voice. Sergeant Sharp and

Chase were waving next to the body of the injured soldier near a fort of trees.

Tran limped toward the men and Fischer followed. He looked over his shoulder as the chopping sound grew louder. A trio of helicopters descended toward their position, rotor wash bending dried grass and pushing up billowing clouds of dust. Instead of the normal Allied States insignia painted on the choppers, Fischer spotted blue circles with Orca Whales on them.

He wondered for a moment if they were real or if this was a figment of his imagination like his wife's voice.

Fischer blinked hard several times, but the birds were still there. He slowed as he approached Sharp who had run over, panting.

"Where are Galinsky and Welling?"

Fischer shook his head.

"What the hell happened?" Chase asked.

"The Alphas...," Tran began.

"Are dead," Fischer added. He looked toward the choppers.

Fischer and his team hadn't been the only ones to notice the choppers' entrance. Variants began to pop out of holes around the field.

"Form a line!" Sharp yelled.

The men raised their rifles to hold their ground. But instead of running toward them, the creatures scattered, spreading out like a swarm of locusts. That didn't make a hell of a lot of sense to Fischer, but he wouldn't question their luck if they escaped tonight.

"So President Ringgold finally sent us help. I guess it's better late than never."

"Those aren't Ringgold's soldiers!" Sharp yelled over the noise.

Two of the birds curved away, the mounted machine guns blazing. The third chopper continued forward and lowered toward Fischer and his men.

The soldiers that jumped out wore blue armbands with the same Orca insignia painted on the side of the birds.

"That radio transmission I got below ground was from a platoon under the command of General Cornelius!" Sharp yelled over the noise. "These are his troops!"

Fischer watched the birds spewing rounds over his fields, slaughtering the monsters before they could escape. Now this was what his tax dollars and donations were supposed to be used for. He wanted to revel in the sight, but could hardly find anything worth gloating about now.

Fischer Fields had survived, but just by a hair.

"Guess that makes it easy on who I'm voting for in the presidential election," Fischer said.

"Sir, after what I just heard, I doubt there's even going to be an election," Sharp replied.

— 25 —

The table in the PEOC was packed full with military officers, cabinet members, staffers, and the President and Vice President, all of them reacting to the news from Team Ghost. Beckham bowed his head, his heart aching at the report.

Specialist Will Lincoln had passed on the flight from Minneapolis to Scott AFB.

Another member of Team Ghost, lost in the line of duty.

Beckham could sympathize well with how Fitz must have been feeling. He had been there many times as the former lead of Team Ghost.

"I'm sorry about Lincoln, but his sacrifice could very well end this new Variant threat," said Brigadier General Barnes.

"He was a good man," Horn said. "One of the best soldiers to fight on Team Ghost."

Lincoln's death wasn't the only one.

Casualty reports flooded in from FOBs across the country.

Flashbacks to Operation Liberty and the other major operations during the Great War of Extinction played in Beckham's mind.

Operation Shadow was supposed to be different.

Team Ghost had destroyed the beast that Kate and Carr believed was controlling the Variant communication network. He had seen the footage of the grenade that blew the mastermind to pieces.

Now it was a waiting game on whether this would *really* end the threat of invasion. If it didn't, the military was preparing to face the beasts again.

In a matter of twenty-four hours, command had redistributed resources to protect outposts as well as distributed twelve thousand troops to the ninety-eight outposts. But with sixty thousand plus Variants out there and an unknown number of juveniles, Beckham was sweating missiles.

"Even without a mastermind coordinating them, we need to stay on alert for a full-fledged attack," Beckham said. "The Variants and collaborators are still out there, and we have no idea how many juveniles there are."

"We're ready, Captain," Barnes said confidently.

Beckham hoped Barnes was right about that and about Lincoln's sacrifice disrupting the invasion.

"I've just got confirmation that the final troops have arrived at their destinations," Barnes continued. "These additional forces combined with the existing fortifications at these outposts should withstand anything the Variants throw at us, especially since we're ready for their tunnels."

Side conversations continued as staff and officers went back to their jobs of monitoring the missions. Beckham sat listening to reports. From what he had gathered, Team Ghost was the only team that had made it out of the target cities so far.

Two of the six teams were confirmed KIA, and two of the remaining three were radio silent. SEAL Team 5 in Chicago had broken radio silence and Beckham was anxious to see the footage from their helmet cams.

Even though they had been retired for eight years,

Beckham and Horn were used to being in the fight. It never got easier sitting by while other men and women did the dirty and dangerous work.

Worse, Beckham hated that he was waiting *here* without his family. He tried to reassure himself that Peaks Island was well guarded.

But none of that helped his frayed nerves.

The voice of General Souza at SOCOM came over the conference phone in the center of the table.

"Surveillance aircraft are moving in on the following targets for observation," he said. "Minneapolis, Minnesota; Chicago, Illinois; Lincoln, Nebraska; Kansas City, Missouri; Indianapolis, Indiana; and Columbus, Ohio."

President Ringgold got up and paced while they waited for live footage, fidgeting with her collar. Beckham hadn't seen her this anxious in a long time. But he knew part of this had to do with the decision she was going to have to make about the US Bank Stadium in Minneapolis.

She still hadn't given the order to bomb it and destroy the Variants there, and if she did, she would end the lives of hundreds of human prisoners, if not more.

Maybe it's giving them mercy. Beckham thought back to the footage from Dohi and Rico. There was almost zero chance the military could save those people now, and they were all suffering unimaginable hell.

Beads of sweat dripped down Beckham's forehead. He wiped them away with a sleeve.

"Madam President," Barnes said. "I just received confirmation on the extraction of SEAL Team 5 from Chicago. We should have that footage soon."

Beckham exchanged a glance with Horn. The big guy was nervous, too, his right leg rocking under the table.

Lemke stood from his chair and joined Ringgold while Barnes spoke on his headset. The brigadier general's face suddenly turned white.

"What's wrong?" Ringgold said.

Barnes cleared his throat and pointed at the wall-mounted screen.

"We just received SEAL Team 5's footage."

Beckham strained for a better look at the images that came online, but it only took a moment to recognize the ugly beast as one of the brains.

"There's another one?" Horn said, eyes widening.

"If there are two, there could be more," Barnes said.

Lemke cursed and brushed his hair back. "I don't believe this."

Beckham couldn't believe it either. Their mistake could doom the country unless they located every one of the abominations and eliminated them before the creatures could coordinate a massive attack with their Variant and collaborator hordes.

The thought chilled Beckham to his marrow. He resisted the urge to get up and board a bird right back to Peaks Island and Outpost Portland.

They're well protected, he reminded himself. *They're fine.*

"I think it's time to consider taking drastic measures," Barnes said. "I can have all six of these targets destroyed in fifteen minutes, Madam President."

"There has to be another way," Beckham said. "Nuking the cities will mean our country *never* recovers. Plus, we just sent troops to outposts around those targets and, the fallout, even from low-yield nukes, will cause severe radiation poisoning."

"What other options do I have?" Ringgold asked.

Beckham hadn't been privy to all of the strategic

planning at command but he had a feeling Barnes wanted to test the limits of the damage they could inflict.

He was right.

"MOABs then," Barnes said.

Mother-of-all-bombs, Beckham thought. One of the most powerful non-nuclear options they had at their disposal.

"Drop MOABs on every site and send those monsters back to hell," Barnes said. "Starting with US Bank Stadium. It's not as much a guarantee as nukes, but it might do the trick."

"We could also send in troops to clear the cities afterward, but that would pull them away from the outposts," Lemke said.

"General Souza, are you listening?" Ringgold asked.

The voice of the SOCOM Commander crackled from the speaker in the center of the table. "Yes, Madam President, I'm listening."

"What do you propose we do in light of these new developments?"

"Problem is we don't really know where the other masterminds are and, from the footage Team Ghost sent, they clearly have the ability to move. If we did know their location, then I would say drop MOABs, but if we don't know, then we're just wasting ordnance."

"Good point," Lemke said. "Even if we wanted to, we don't have enough MOABs to level every potential nest for these masterminds. I think we're going to have to send teams back in to track them."

Barnes grunted. "How many Special Op teams do we have available?"

A knock came on the door and a Secret Service agent stepped in.

"We have a problem."

Beckham gripped the table, preparing to stand.

"Something's tripped the sensors about three miles from the perimeter," he said. "We sent out a team of Marines to check it out. Probably nothing, but I wanted you to know."

Ringgold looked to Lemke.

"We're safe here," he said. "Don't worry."

Beckham had a feeling she was thinking the same thing as he was about the fate of the Vice President's predecessor. George Johnson had died in this very room at the hands of Variants.

"Sound the alarm," Beckham said.

Barnes didn't seem to like that idea. "All due respect, but that could…"

"Save lives if there is something out there," Ringgold said. "Go ahead and do it."

The agent nodded and closed the door. As soon as he left, the debate over what to do next continued.

"I'm going to check this out," Horn said quietly.

Beckham shifted uneasily in his chair as Horn ducked out. His gut told him something was happening out there that no one understood, not even his wife.

"Madam President," Beckham said, interrupting the conversation.

All eyes were on him.

"Yes, Captain?"

"I'd like to propose something."

Lemke studied Beckham as he stood in front of the table.

"Go ahead," Ringgold said.

Before he could say anything the voice of General Souza came from the speaker.

"Madam President, our surveillance aircrafts are

sending back some disturbing footage."

Barnes turned on the wall-mounted screen with a remote. The screen divided into sections, each with the view from one of the aircrafts in the target cities.

"We're too late…" Lemke said.

"Variants are pouring out of the tunnels in these areas," Souza said. "We've scrambled bomber squadrons, but I need your authorization."

"There are so many," Barnes' face drained of color. "How is this possible?"

"They have been breeding," Beckham said. "They've been so far out of surveillance this whole time. Underground. In those tunnels. We underestimated their numbers."

"Do it," Ringgold said firmly. "Drop bombs on the hordes, and take out US Bank Stadium. Reduce it to ashes. I don't want any chance of anything surviving."

"Understood," Souza said.

Beckham swallowed hard and blinked from sweat stinging his eyes. He said a prayer for the people that were about to die, but knew the president was making the right choice.

The door to the room suddenly swung open, and Horn burst inside, his eyes wide.

"We've got hostiles moving toward our location." That Marine team was just ambushed by a pack of Variants."

Barnes shot up. "You heard him! Let's move, people!"

The room quickly emptied, everyone joining officers, staff, and soldiers in the open space of the PEOC command area.

Beckham went to look at the monitors. It wasn't just Variants out there. Several trucks had broken through the outer perimeter.

"Collaborators," Horn grumbled. "We got to get everyone the hell out of here, boss."

"It's safer down here," said Barnes.

"You sure about that?" Beckham asked.

On screen, hundreds of Variants stormed the machine gun nests and guard towers along the perimeter. The hordes stormed through the hail of fire, tearing apart soldiers on the front lines.

Barnes went quiet. Reality seemed to be sinking in. He snapped out of it a moment later and began barking orders.

Ringgold stood next to Beckham, her jaw clenched and face pallid.

"How did this happen?" she asked in a low voice.

"All this time we thought they'd been living like animals outside our safe zones, barely scraping by," Beckham said. "But they must've been preparing for this. Growing their numbers and keeping their children away from our drones, underground."

"My God, how do we stop them?"

Beckham didn't have an easy answer.

"We fight," Horn said in a gruff voice.

Barnes hurried over to them. "Air evac is ready. Madam President, things are beginning to look uncertain here. We need to get you to the USS *George Johnson.*"

"Horn, Beckham, I want you to join me," Ringgold said.

"All the way out there?" Horn asked. "Something else going on we don't know about?"

"We're getting reports of Variants attacking most every outpost," Barnes said. "At this point, the safest place from these tunneling bastards is at sea."

"What about Outpost Portland?" Beckham said.

A vein bulged in Horn's neck as he waited for a response.

"No report of an attack yet," came a voice from an officer monitoring the radios.

"I don't know about you, boss," Horn said, "but I'm not running off to some ship while our families are out there."

"Madam President," Beckham began, "I'm sorry, but I can't abandon my family."

Secret Service agents huddled around the group, waiting to evacuate the president and vice president.

"We'll stop at Peaks Island and Outpost Portland first," Ringgold said.

Barnes looked ready to protest.

"We need to get Doctor Lovato and Doctor Carr to safety if we have any hope of winning this fight," Ringgold said.

"I agree," replied Lemke said. "I'll inform General Souza and have him send some extra birds to extract the doctors and their staff and equipment."

"What about civilians?" Horn demanded.

"Evacuation will have to be on a case by case basis, but we will make sure your families are safe," Ringgold said.

Horn jogged to one of the weapon racks at the back of the PEOC and grabbed his M249. Then he grabbed Beckham's M4 and tossed it to him. They surged through the crowd as officers rushed to organize the chaotic defense and evacuation efforts.

Ringgold was waiting with one departing group in front of the elevator. Beckham and Horn met up with them.

"I'll hold this position, Madam President," Barnes called out. "Good luck!"

"You too, General," she said. "Give these bastards everything you've got."

"You can count on that." Barnes turned back to the screens.

The elevator doors opened, and Beckham squeezed in with the others. By the time they unloaded and got to the front entrance, the Variants and the collaborators had broken through the first line of defenses.

Muzzle flashes lit up the darkness like fireflies.

A LAW rocket streaked through the night, exploding against a guard tower.

"Holy shit!" shouted Horn.

A team of Marines and Secret Service agents led them through the gardens of the Greenbrier and headed for Marine One and Marine Two.

The rotors were already churning when Beckham saw the choppers. Several Marines formed a perimeter around the area.

Floodlights flicked on, illuminating the grounds around the White House. One of the Marines opened fire into the forest beyond the gardens.

Beckham couldn't see anything through the fence of trees and kept running, but Horn suddenly stopped and brought up his M249.

"Six o'clock!" he yelled.

He fired at what looked like ghosts moving into the floodlights. Beckham aimed at the camouflaged Variants and squeezed the trigger. Blood sprayed from wounds that sent the monsters tumbling.

An explosion boomed behind them, but Beckham kept firing at the flanking beasts. Ringgold and Lemke ran with their staff, protected by a dozen Marines and Secret Service agents. The group fired as they advanced, taking out creatures bounding out of the forest on all fours.

Beckham jammed in a new magazine and snuck a glance over his shoulder at the side entrance to the White House. A burning pickup truck had slammed into a pillar of stones, and two collaborators smoldered on the pavement. More soldiers spread out to secure the grounds.

"Boss, behind us!" Horn yelled.

Beckham squeezed off two bursts to take down a pair of monsters that had made it onto the lawn. Horn killed their comrades and then took off running with Beckham.

They had fallen behind the others. Lemke and half of the staff had already boarded Marine 2 while Ringgold and the other half piled into Marine 1.

Beasts flooded toward the grounded choppers. Horn stopped to lay down covering fire. Beckham did the same, scoring a headshot that took off the top of a creature's skull.

"Come on!" shouted Ringgold. She waved from the open door of the chopper before two guards pulled her back.

Beckham patted Horn on the shoulder and they took off running toward Marine 1. When they were fifty feet from the troop hold, a group of armored Variants burst from the bushes.

The choppers started to lift from the ground.

Horn fired at the pack of juveniles.

"Big Horn, let's go!" Beckham shouted. He grabbed him and pulled him toward the bird. One of the young beasts made it past the hail of rounds, losing half an armored limb in the process, but charging the two men anyway.

A shot to the head from the chopper took it down. Lemke was watching out from the open door, directing his agents to cover Beckham and Horn.

They reached to help Beckham and Horn into the chopper as it hovered just a few feet off the lawn. They crawled in just as a pack of Variants filled the open field.

Gunfire cracked all around. The Marines and Secret Service agents fired at the armored beasts reaching up with clawed hands as the chopper pulled away.

Panting, Beckham rose up on his knees.

"Thanks," he said to Lemke.

Horn lay on his back, his chest heaving. "Man, that was too close."

"Way too close," Beckham said.

This must have been it. The start of the invasion. If the attack on the White House was any indication, the Variants and their collaborators weren't pulling any punches.

A Marine shut the door and Beckham stood with the others to look out the windows.

All hell had broken loose across the former Greenbrier resort. Muzzle flashes cut through the night like miniature lightning strikes, and orange blasts bloomed from explosions.

"Barnes will hold them," Lemke said. "We won't lose the White House again."

Beckham had faith in the men and women down there, but it was going to be a tough and bloody fight. He didn't like abandoning them, but his family came first.

"Where are we headed?" yelled one of the pilots.

"Peaks Island!" Ringgold shouted back.

"Thank you," Beckham said.

"Yes, thanks," Horn added.

Beckham took a seat, trying to catch his breath and calm his thumping heart. Horn sat next to him, his big arms brushing up against Beckham.

"Everything's going to be okay, boss," he said. "We'll get through this."

Beckham wanted to believe that, but an update from one of the pilots shattered his hope.

"I'm hearing a ton of radio chatter," said one of the pilots. "Sounds like the Variants are pounding the outposts."

The reports continued to stream in over the seven-hour long flight to the island. By the time they were narrowing in on the location, outposts around the target cities were drowning in the masses of Variants descending on them.

"Change of plans," said one of the pilots. "The science team and families have been evacuated from Peaks Island and are meeting us at Outpost Portland. So far the Variants are still being held back further west."

Horn's leg went back to rocking and Beckham closed his eyes, in an attempt to focus his mind and keep calm.

When they touched down, a group had gathered in the landing zone. Daylight had flooded over the outpost. Dozens of people waited outside, many of them children. Even more were trying to get through a wall of Marines that held them back.

Beckham could tell they weren't going to be able to extract all of these people. Beckham and Horn jumped out into the cool morning air, navigating the thronging people as they hurried toward Sergeant Ruckley and a team of Marines surrounding the medical staff.

Army soldiers unloaded crates and boxes from several trucks. They carried them into the troop holds of other choppers that General Souza had sent. Several Black Hawks and even an Osprey had touched down.

"Javier! Kate!" Beckham yelled.

"Tasha! Jenny!" Horn shouted.

"Dad!" the girls called out, slipping between people.

Ginger and Spark barked and ran to Horn, their tails beating the air, oblivious to the threats closing in.

Beckham saw Javier next. His boy ran and wrapped his arms around him. Kate was talking to a Marine and pointing at the crates. When she finished giving orders, she hurried over and embraced Beckham and Javier.

Civilians began boarding the other birds, but combined with the equipment from Kate's lab, they were already filling up. Marines fanned out to help hold back the growing crowd pressing against those already holding onto the perimeter.

Beckham looked for Timothy, Bo, and Donna. He spotted them in a group on the other side of the Marines.

"Take Javier to the chopper," Beckham said. "I'll be right back."

"Where are you going?" Kate asked.

She followed his gaze to the crowd.

"I'll see if I can get them on one of the choppers," Beckham said.

Kate nodded and pulled Javier away while Beckham ran to the Marines running security. The crowd was shouting now, pushing at the Marines even more fervently.

In the background, he heard another shout. A glance over his shoulder confirmed it was Horn arguing with a Marine about allowing Ginger and Spark on the bird.

"They are coming with!" Horn yelled. He picked up Ginger under one arm and Spark under the other. "We'll hold them to save space!"

The dogs barked, clearly distraught. They weren't the only ones. Tasha and Jenny both cried even as the Marine gestured them all into the belly of the chopper.

Beckham continued to the gathering group of civilians the soldiers and Marines were fighting to keep at bay.

"Timothy, Bo, Donna!" he shouted.

They squeezed their way over to the other side of the crowd.

"They won't let us through!" Donna said.

"Get back!" yelled a Marine.

"Let them through," Beckham said. "They're with me!"

Two of the Marines looked back at him, but they shook their heads.

"Sorry, Captain," one said. "We have strict orders."

An engine fired behind him, and rotors beat the air. He had just seconds to get on the bird himself. Donna stared at him, fear in her gaze.

"Please, Reed!" she cried. "We need to get out of here!"

"It's going to be okay. This outpost is safe..." his words trailed off because he knew that was a lie.

No outpost was safe anymore.

"There will be another chopper," Beckham said. "I'm so sorry."

His heart kicked as he back peddled away, Donna, Bo, and Timothy all staring at him as he retreated.

"I'll be back for you, I promise!" he shouted.

The guilt burned deep in his chest. He felt like he was abandoning them and running to hide like a coward as he turned to run toward the chopper.

The rotor wash whipped against his body. He looked over his shoulder one last time at the growing crowd of screaming civilians. Then he climbed inside and the crew chief shut the door, blocking the view of the friends he was leaving behind.

Beckham found his wife and son, and Horn and his girls. The dogs were squirming in their grips, but putting them down wasn't an option in the tightly packed chopper.

"Timothy," Tasha cried. "We can't leave him!"

She grabbed Horn's sleeve. "Dad, we can't go without Timothy and the others."

"Why can't the others come?" Javier asked.

"There isn't room in this load," Beckham said.

Tasha wiped a tear from her eyes and turned away to get a view out the windows.

"We'll go back for them, I promise," Beckham said.

"Are they going to be okay, Dad?" Javier asked.

"Yes, sweetie," Kate said. She looked at Beckham, but he couldn't hold her gaze and he didn't know what to say to his son. Instead of responding, he turned to the window as the chopper moved over the ocean and into the morning sky.

While they flew to safety, the country was collapsing. He could almost see the flames of burning outposts in the distance.

The monsters had emerged from the shadows in the Allied States with their new ranks, overwhelming and destroying what humanity had worked so hard to rebuild.

Spreading like an inferno.

This time, Beckham feared the human race wouldn't be able to stop them. That they had only delayed the inevitable eight years ago.

One thing was for certain—humanity had entered another dark age of extinction.

End of Book 1

Extinction Cycle Dark Age Book 2:
Extinction Inferno, coming very soon!

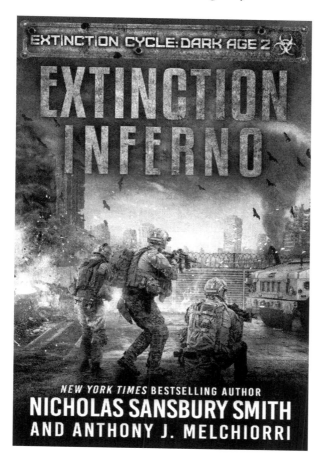

About the Authors

Nicholas Sansbury Smith is the New York Times and USA Today bestselling author of the Hell Divers series. His other work includes the Extinction Cycle series, the Trackers series, and the Orbs series. He worked for Iowa Homeland Security and Emergency Management in disaster planning and mitigation before switching careers to focus on his one true passion—writing. When he isn't writing or daydreaming about the apocalypse, he enjoys running, biking, spending time with his family, and traveling the world. He is an Ironman triathlete and lives in Iowa with his wife, their dogs, and a house full of books.

Anthony J Melchiorri is a scientist with a PhD in bioengineering. Originally from the Midwest, he now lives in Texas. By day, he develops cellular therapies and 3D-printable artificial organs. By night, he writes apocalyptic, medical, and science-fiction thrillers that blend real-world research with other-worldly possibility, including works like *The Tide* and *Eternal Frontier*. When he isn't in the lab or at the keyboard, he spends his time running, reading, hiking, and traveling in search of new story ideas.

Join Nicholas on social media:

Facebook Fan Club:
facebook.com/groups/NSSFanclub

Facebook Author Page:
facebook.com/pages/Nicholas-Sansbury-Smith/124009881117534

Twitter: @greatwaveink

Website: NicholasSansburySmith.com

Instagram: instagram.com/author_sansbury

Email: Greatwaveink@gmail.com

Sign up for Nicholas's spam-free newsletter and receive special offers and info on his latest new releases.

Join Anthony on social media:

Facebook: facebook.com/anthonyjmelchiorri

Email: ajm@anthonyjmelchiorri.com

Website: anthonyjmelchiorri.com

Did we mention Anthony also has a newsletter?
http://bit.ly/ajmlist

Printed in Great Britain
by Amazon